MW00613031

BONE PENDANT GIRLS
SIGNED BY
TERRY S. FRIEDMAN

Twisted Retreat
exclusive signed
edition

BONE PENDANT GIRLS

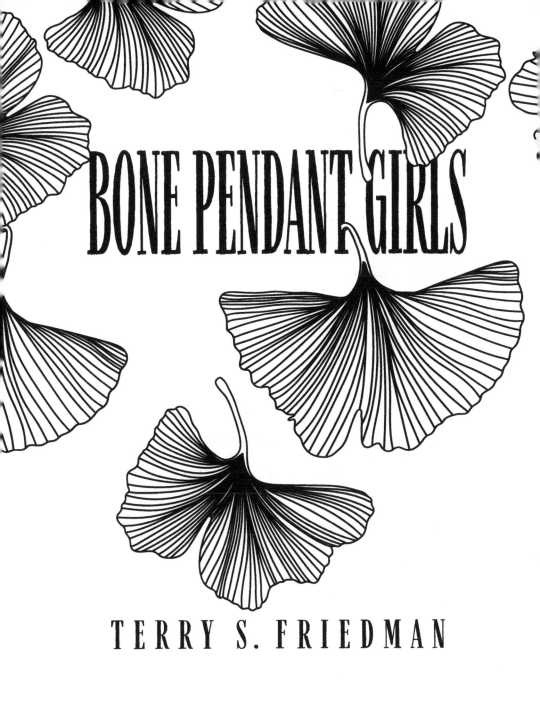

BONE PENDANT GIRLS

TERRY S. FRIEDMAN

CamCat Books

CamCat Publishing, LLC
Fort Collins, Colorado 80524
camcatpublishing.com

This is a work of fiction. Names, characters, places, and incidents are either products of the author's imagination or are used fictitiously.

Hardcover ISBN 9780744307924
Paperback ISBN 9780744307931
Large-Print Paperback ISBN 9780744307962
eBook ISBN 9780744307948
Audiobook ISBN 9780744307979

Library of Congress Control Number: 2023943113

Book and cover design by Maryann Appel

Artwork by David Goh, Enjoynz, George Peters, Vabadov, Val Iva, Yulia Plokhaya, Yuliia Khvyshchuk

5 3 1 2 4

*For my mom, who gifted me a love of words and
to my father, who showed me his humor.*

*For Jessica and Chelie,
who taught me everything I know about mothers and daughters.*

*For the faithful companions at my side during
this writing journey:
Ollie, Babyface, Tiggy, and Fiona.*

CHAPTER ONE

ANDI

November 5, 2022

GINKGO LEAVES DRIFTED DOWN like butterfly wings outside the gem show. They made a yellow carpet on the walkway to the boarding school's gymnasium. Within the swirling leaves, Andi heard a voice. Hollow metallic vowels rustled like leaves in gutters. Consonants scratched and thumped like animals trapped in heating ducts. When the frantic skittering of syllables merged into words, a ghostly plea slipped into her consciousness. *Trapped . . . help.*

"You'll find your way to the Other Side," Andi whispered.

Some days, the spirits refused to leave her in peace. Turning off their voices was like trying to keep a snake in a bird cage. The Shadows had been with her since she was four. Her mother had sent those spirits to watch over her.

But the voice she heard today was not the Shadows. They rarely spoke.

Please . . . help.

Andi opened the door. "I'm not the one to help you," she told the young voice. "I attract bad men."

The ticket ladies took her money and stamped her hand. She scanned the gymnasium from one end to the other. So many vendors. Where to start? Left, past the fossils, to a station called P and S Lapidary. They always had unique pieces.

Please . . . ma'am. The whisper had a faint Southern lilt.

"Aw, come on. Hijack someone else's head. Go talk to my ex-husband. Convince him to give me all his money." Andi looked left and right to make sure no one had heard. No need to worry. Odds were good that at least one other person in the crowd talked to herself.

Andi made her way past thirty stations. Past bargain-bound women rummaging in bins of clearance beads, vendors taking orders to set stones, miles of bead strands. She searched for the perfect, happy, shiny piece. Twice around the gym, and that whispering voice drilled its way into her conscience again.

Please . . . buy . . . me.

Cripes! The urgency of that sweet, young voice. She heaved a sigh. "Hope you're not expensive. Where are you?" Her feet ached and the place was stifling. "Where?"

Over here!

She couldn't see a damn thing through the shoppers lined up two deep at the stations. Up on her toes, down, from foot to foot, sideways. A tiring, annoying dance. Andi shivered despite the stuffy atmosphere.

Here!

Easing her way through the shoppers, she peered into a glass display case. Malachite beads, a red coral branch necklace, two strands of ringed freshwater pearls, and one pendant with a cameo-style face etched in bone.

The vendor with a bolo tie looked like her ninth-grade geography teacher. "Let me open that for you. The face pendants are going fast. Only two left." He lifted the hinged glass cover.

Me! A loud whisper from the carved pendant with a girl's face.

Andi looked intently at it. Like most cameos, the face was a side profile. Tendrils of the girl's curly hair escaped an upswept hairdo, framing her face. At first she appeared to be asleep. Then the girl's face turned and studied her too, eyes blinking as if she'd just awakened.

Andi shivered. In the spirit world she'd inherited from her mother, voices whispered. Images in jewelry didn't move.

What now? Andi communicated silently. Subconscious to subconscious.

Hurry, ma'am! Buy . . .

A woman who reeked of Chanel No. 5 snatched the face pendant from the case.

"Excuse me," Andi said. "I came here to buy that piece. It called to me." There now, she'd admitted she was crazy. She gave a lopsided grin and a shrug. "Please, could I have it?"

"Sorry, hon. I got here first." A condescending glance at Andi, and the lady wrapped her bratwurst fingers around the pendant.

"Not to worry, ladies," the seller told them. "I have another like this." He pushed the tablecloth aside, reached under the table, and pulled out a second pendant. "It's stunning, with Namibian Pietersite accents. I could let you have it for the same price."

No . . . me. An adamant voice.

"I don't want the other pendant," Andi said. "I came here for the one in her hand." At the next booth, a woman holding a jade jar stopped talking and stared at her. Andi blushed, knowing she sounded like a petulant child.

Suddenly the woman gasped. "Ouch! Awful thing cut me. It has sharp edges." A thin line of blood welled on Chanel Lady's finger, and she dropped the pendant as if it had bitten her.

Andi caught it before it hit the floor. The silver bezel felt ice cold. Slowly, the face turned, and a young girl's eyes gazed up at her and blinked. *Thanks, ma'am.*

She stared at the pendant. Her mother had warned about spirits attaching to people. If spirits attached, she'd said, terrible things could happen.

Chanel Lady cradled the darker pendant. Not a word was uttered from it. Maybe the tea-stained piece believed in being seen and not heard. Its bone face was younger. Pietersite in the top bezel had chatoyancy, a luminous quality. Thin wavy splotches of browns, blacks, reds, and yellows swirled through dark stone like tiny ice crystals in a frozen latte.

"Yes, I like this one better. Excellent quality Pietersite," Chanel Lady said.

"If you don't mind, I'll take her payment first." The seller gave Andi a conspiratorial wink, probably hoping to send the woman to another station before she started a fight with his customers.

"No problem. Is this ivory?" Andi asked. Whether vendors called it mammoth bone or not, elephants didn't deserve to be slaughtered for jewelry.

"Absolutely not. Wouldn't sell it if it was. Cow bone," he assured her.

With a triumphant smirk aimed at Andi, Chanel Lady turned and made her way through the crowd. Subduing an impulse to give her the middle finger, Andi turned back to the pendant. She studied the heart-shaped face, turned it over, and winced at the tiny price sticker. Was she insane? Andi couldn't afford that; she'd lost her teaching job.

"I'll need your address and email." The seller handed her a clipboard.

She'd fought over it and won—no changing her mind now. While he charged her credit card, Andi filled out the form for his mailing list. Then she weaved through shoppers to find a quiet corner by the concessions stand.

What the hell.

The pendant was a dose of credit card therapy. Unzipping the plastic sleeve, she lifted the piece by the bail. Two bezels set in silver. One disk held labradorite, a luminous blue stone with black veins, and in the second bezel, a face carved in bone. She shifted it in her palm, studying the details.

Had light played with the image, making it look like the girl moved? That sweet, innocent face seemed at peace now. It would warm at the touch of her skin.

Once more around the gym, and she left the show, slogging through the field toward her car, wondering how a whispering girl had convinced her to buy a pricey pendant. Yet, she had a sense that something other than her credit card bill had changed.

An arctic gust tried to snatch her cap. One hand on her hat, the other holding a bag with her purchase, Andi shook off a chill. She remembered the invisible friend who had first spoken to her when she was four and stayed her best friend until middle school.

"You can't go around talking to yourself," her father had scolded. A teacher later suggested Andi might be autistic. Infuriated, her father took her to a psychologist. The tests had shown nothing worse than a high IQ. On the way home from the doctor's office, her mother admitted: "Hearing beyond is sometimes more a nuisance than a gift, really." Her father gave her a disapproving look.

Andi brushed back an unruly strand of caramel brown ringlets and tugged her cap down over her ears.

After crunching through dead grass, she tossed her handbag and the pendant onto the passenger seat and cranked up the CD player. "Come Away With Me," Norah Jones crooned.

... to ... park, ma'am.

She glanced sideways at the small bag. Sleep deprivation, her father would say, but he'd never been invited to tea parties with ghosts. That was a secret she'd shared with her mother. "The voices will always be there," she'd told Andi. "You must learn when to turn them off." Over the years, Andi had discovered stress and lack of sleep made the "off switch" harder to control.

Cheer up, she told herself. Maybe hallucinations would come next, and some cartoon character would show up at the Wawa and buy her a cup of coffee.

Please . . . park, the plaintive voice whispered.

"It's winter in Pennsylvania. You are obviously not—why am I talking to a bag?" But the girl was so polite, and Andi was curious about why the pendant had chosen her. Okay, it might not be so cold in the park. Yeah, and maybe gas prices would plummet to a dollar fifty-nine overnight. Not likely, but fresh air might clear her head. She bought decaf at a convenience store, glad that she didn't see any cartoon characters, and drove to Franklin Township Park.

Finding a parking space was no problem. Andi shared the lot with a white plastic bag that blew from empty space to space like a kite loose from its owner, spiraling, tumbling down, then lifting again. Like a wisp of memory, nagging, then burying itself for a while.

"Talking pendants," she muttered, staring out the windshield. Frost had washed the green from the grass, turning the blades to bristly stubbles like a blond buzz cut. Sepia November. Fifteen days to her thirty-fifth birthday. Crusty brown mud puddles. Empty asphalt paths. Purple-gray trees with branches like bony arms reaching for the clouds. Not even a die-hard runner around. Here was a great place for answers to mysteries of the universe. One foot out of the warm car, and she wondered if her sanity had flown south for the winter. She slammed the door and stuffed the small brown parcel into her pocket. "A nice Southern girl with manners wouldn't bring me out here to freeze to death."

No voices now. Maybe Southern spirits had a freezing point.

Andi found a bench under some pine trees and sipped steaming coffee, warming her hands on the cup. Two playground swings squeaked out a seesawing harmony on their metal chains. It reminded her of winter in a beach town and metal store signs tossed by the wind, of a foghorn wailing in the night, of Lewes, Delaware, her hometown. She hadn't been home in years. Guilt and blame had festered like a wound that wouldn't heal between her mother and father. If only she hadn't been so eager to get into a stranger's car.

All this damn solitude must have turned her brain to scrapple. Andi stamped the numbness from her feet. "We're at the park like you wanted. So, why'd you choose me?"

Wind rattled the treetops. A single gingko leaf landed on the toe of her sneaker. No ginkgo trees in sight. This time of the year, she'd know if a gingko tree was nearby because the fruit smelled like vomit.

"Why the silent treatment?" she asked.

No answer. Angry gray clouds slid across the sun.

"Okay, I give up." She got up, pitched the cup into a trash bin, and started back to her car. When she slipped the pendant from its protective sleeve, a raindrop fell on it. Then another drop. And another. The rain tapped out a slow rhythm on the concrete trail, at first like the cadence of drums in a funeral march, later like fingernails slowly drumming on a table, increasing the tempo as if they were impatient. Over the pattering rain, Andi heard whispering, and the pendant girl's lips moved. *Please ... help.*

CHAPTER TWO

ANDI

ANDI WOKE WITH A START, chest heaving, hair pasted to her neck. Tiny ticking noises against the glass. Sleet mixed with wind. The numbers on her alarm clock glowed big and red: two fifteen. She exhaled.

The nightmare had begun with the slow, rhythmic scrape of a saw.

Back and forth. Back and forth. So real it seemed to be in her room.

"No, please don't hurt me!" a young girl's voice pleaded.

Two girls in a place with no furniture, probably a parlor once, grand at one time, she imagined, but dilapidated now with warped wood floors and peeling wallpaper. Embers in an old marble fireplace burned red and smoked, casting eerie shadows. Aluminum foil, candle, lighter, straw, rolling papers, and cigarettes next to a ragged sleeping bag. A girl of no more than fourteen lay on it, twitching. One girl, a junkie. The other held her hand. Her eyes made a circuit between a man with hair that sprouted like weeds and the junkie in withdrawal. Heart still drumming in her ears, Andi rubbed her eyes. Damn, she hated nightmares. Her father had said she'd outgrow them. When? she wondered as she plodded downstairs toward the kitchen.

The house felt so empty. Of course, Lance hadn't filled it much when he was there. He'd either been golfing or cheating with some young chick who thought he'd give her a lifetime of happy memories. She'd been that naive girl once, his trophy wife. The happiness drained out of the marriage about as fast as his Jack Daniels bottles emptied. Lance plus Jack equaled a bully. Andi had a lifetime of memories all right, but they weren't happy ones.

Whispering.

She rubbed her temples. Just a holly branch scratching against the window. In the kitchen, she banged through the pots until she found a kettle. Then she dug the remote from under a sofa cushion and tuned in to QVC for company. The host was selling cameos, faces in shell, a helluva lot more expensive than the one she'd bought.

Run away.

Andi eyed the pendant on the table. The girl's spirit seemed attached to her. Her mother never told her what to do if that happened.

The teakettle whistled and she jumped. What the hell was wrong with her? Being alone in the house had never bothered her before. She'd go back to the gem show first thing tomorrow morning and find out where the pendant came from. Maybe then she could turn off the voice or figure out how to help the girl cross over.

CHAPTER THREE

ANDI

"WE'RE GOING FOR A ride," Andi said as she stuffed the pendant into her purse. "Back to the gem show. Cripes. Stop talking to jewelry, or you'll end up in a psych ward." If that smelly Chanel Lady showed up again, Andi would give her a swift kick with her hiking boots. A glance at the thermometer, and she grabbed a down jacket and headed for the car. Her ten-year-old Pathfinder powered up, trailing happy clouds of exhaust: fossil fuel glory.

Traffic was light for a Sunday morning. People had either gone to church or they were sleeping in. The white Gem Show sign came up on the right. She turned and drove past the building. Boys in neon safety jackets waved her into the parking lot. Her tires bumped over the field, past orange pylons and into a space next to cattails.

After last night's hard frost, the grass reminded her of a stale Krispy Kreme doughnut. It crunched under her boots. She took a shortcut across a small stream. A lace of ice covered the rocks, but Andi managed to get across without slipping. When the doors opened, she found the vendor with the bolo tie at his station.

Big smile. Apparently he liked repeat business.

"Interested in that darker pendant from yesterday? Lady returned it. Said it gave her a headache." He laughed. "First time anyone returned my jewelry for that reason. More likely, it was that perfume of hers that triggered the migraine."

"She did leave a trail of Chanel." Andi wrinkled her nose. "Is that the only face pendant you have?"

"Sold two the first day. This is the last one," he said. "You like turquoise?" He took a concha necklace from the case and handed it to her. "Sleeping Beauty turquoise. That mine's closed now."

"Pretty, but I'll take the face pendant." The quiet one, she thought, but didn't add. Andi returned the concha and handed him her credit card. Now the cost would equal her car insurance bill. "Do you have the artist's business card? I'd like to commission some pieces," she lied.

He passed the credit card reader over the counter. "Wish I did. I could sell a lot more of these. Bought it from a fellow who sells his pieces on E-market.com. Site doesn't allow any sharing of personal information about sellers or buyers."

"Was the E-market person selling other things?" Andi asked. "What's his online name?"

"itemstogo.net," he said, handing her the package. "Hate to give away my trade secrets, but I find some pretty unique pieces online. Mostly, I buy from the Tucson show."

"Someday, maybe I'll make it to the Tucson Show. Thanks." She hurried toward the door, past the man in a red jacket who took tickets, the ladies with the cash box at the front tables, then outside. Andi hopped from stone to stone across the stream and back on to the field.

If an artist crafted beautiful jewelry that took hours to carve, he'd make damn sure people knew where to buy it. Something wasn't right.

Andi started the car and sped down Route 30, eyes peeled for cops. Recently, she'd gotten a three-point moving violation for running a light that went from yellow to red entirely too fast. Her best friend, Fiona, called it an orange light. Fortunately, no sign of a police officer today. No sign of terrible things happening except for her next credit card bill. The new pendant was quiet.

Next stop, the Warehouse Club, for Fiona's favorite—Hostess cupcakes. An hour later, cart full of paper towels, cupcakes, and frozen foods, Andi passed the checkout and wheeled through the first set of doors. Pinned to a bulletin board were missing persons posters. Mostly young girls. Jennifer, Kristen, Mariah. She pushed the cart closer and squinted. Mariah looked familiar. A former student? Maybe. Andi had taught English for five years before enrollment at the private school dropped and she was laid off. Outside, she unloaded her goods and returned the cart. Where had she seen that girl? Brain churning like a computer stuck on a command, she slid into the driver's seat, started the engine, and backed out.

Our mamas . . . sad, the Southern voice whispered.

"My mother is—holy shit! The pendant!" She pulled forward and parked. Fishing out her membership card, she headed for the bulletin board inside the building. Andi held the pendant next to Mariah's photo. Hell of a coincidence, that resemblance. A bitter wind roared like a train through the doors. Andi shivered and wrapped her fingers protectively around the carved bone face.

If anybody could find the truth about the girl, Fiona would. She was the diva of internet diving. Andi hurried back to the car and put her cell on speakerphone. When Fiona answered, she explained about the pendants and their resemblance to the missing persons posters and asked her to find out what she could about a Mariah Culverton.

"Of all the people in the world," Fiona mumbled, "somehow I got a friend who hears dead people. Why is that?"

Andi made her voice sound sultry. "Because you and I are beautiful and desirable women and other women don't like us."

Fiona laughed. "Yeah, right. We're crazy, is more like it."

"You might be crazy, but I'm not."

"I'm too tired to argue." She yawned to make her point. "Look, my boyfriend, Doug, has this friend who graduated from the FBI Academy. He's a private eye now. If I set something up between you two, will you let me sleep?"

"Okay, but no matchmaking," Andi added.

"Good. Now you and your whispering pendant drive home and stay away from orange lights." She disconnected, and Andi tapped the red icon.

How nerdy could a former FBI agent be? She grunted, remembering Fiona's last match for her, a classical guitarist. If he'd been a house—and he was six-foot-nine—the man would've been listed as a fixer-upper. She never did figure out how anyone who wore glasses that thick could see tiny notes on a music sheet.

She pulled into her driveway and gasped. Computer components, clothes, and jewelry littered the front lawn like a flea market on Black Friday. "Son of a bitch!" Andi slid out of the car and looked around. The upstairs bedroom window was wide open, with the curtain flapping in the wind. "What the hell?" Several cloth bags of groceries in one hand, she rushed toward the house and turned the key in the lock. "Lance?" she called.

No answer. She listened intently for movement. No sign of an intruder. Andi set her handbag and the grocery bags down in the office and was ready to get the rest of the groceries from her car when she heard something moving in the house. Grabbing her field-hockey stick from the closet, she hid behind the office door.

CHAPTER FOUR

ANDI

S OFT, SLOW FOOTSTEPS IN the foyer. Heart pounding in her ears, Andi propped the hockey stick against the office wall and dug through her purse for the sharpened credit card her mother had taught her how to use. No, that would require close contact. Maybe keys to his eyes. Still too close if he had a gun. All she had was a stupid can of mace that had probably dried up two years ago, and she'd left her phone in the car. A break-in during daylight hours. What kind of brazen nutjob would do that? She grabbed the hockey stick and held her breath, waiting.

A tentative female voice called, "Andi? Everything all right?"

"I'm in the office." Andi exhaled, recognizing the South Philly accent of her nosy neighbor. She stuffed the mace in her pocket and propped the hockey stick against a bookcase. "Gladys! You scared the crap out of me!" Andi shouted.

The fiftysomething woman wasn't competing for super model in her puffer coat, baggy Flyers jersey, frayed Keds, and capris that might have fit twenty pounds ago. She glanced from the hockey stick to Andi. Eyes recording like a video camera, Gladys was probably cataloging items for her next gossip. "I was just concerned, hon, because computers and clothes and even your jewelry case came flying out the window. I would've called the police, except I thought it might be Lance, maybe a little drunk."

"Was it Lance?" Andi asked.

"Didn't see his car, didn't really see anyone," Gladys said. "Couldn't find my glasses."

God Almighty, give me patience with this woman, Andi thought.

"Call the cops if anything looks suspicious!" It didn't hurt to have a neighbor keeping an eye on her house even if she was mining for fresh gossip. "Ah, divorce." Andi raised her hands in a gesture of despair. "It makes people stupid. You really scared me. Will you help bring my stuff inside?"

"Well." She licked her lips. Gladys's pointed nose twitched like a dog on a good scent. Finally, she nodded. "Of course. A woman needs female company at a time like this. Right, hon?" They walked outside together.

Gladys headed straight for the jewelry armoire. When Andi caught up with her, she closed the armoire door. Mouth gaping, the gossip snatched Andi's engagement ring off the lawn and was giving it an appraisal.

"VVSI. Platinum. Point eight seven of a carat." Andi filled in for her.

Gladys looked up. "Cheap son of a gun couldn't go for a full carat." She sniffed.

Andi picked up one end of the armoire. Gladys lifted the other. Panting, they lugged it inside, then tramped from the yard to the house, stacking Andi's looted possessions in a pitiful pile in the living room.

With each new trip, Andi was more annoyed. Now she understood what people meant when they said a break-in made them feel violated. Anything small enough to fit through her window had been on display in her front yard.

On the third trip, Gladys put a hand on her hip. "Take Lance to the cleaners, hon. You let me know if he gives you any more trouble. I got a twenty-two that'll set him straight."

Andi grinned. "By the time I'm finished with him, he'll be living on a steam vent under a cardboard box."

"That's the spirit." Gladys's slap on the back nearly toppled her.

She talked Gladys into helping her get the rest of the groceries from her car, and they headed inside. Now Gladys could add Andi's breakfast choices to her gossip. In return for a cup of coffee and fodder for juicy gossip, her neighbor vowed she'd keep an eye on the house.

"Sorry I didn't see anybody. Musta parked his car around the corner like Lance used to do when he had another woman in the car." Gladys clasped a hand over her mouth. "Sorry, you didn't need to hear that."

Her neighbor probably kept an eye on many homes and her fingers on a cell phone keypad in case a good scandal arose. No doubt Andi had provided a scandal a few times. When Gladys finally decided to go home and check her roast, Andi escorted her to the front door and frowned at the pile of belongings.

She returned to the office and dug a tablet out of her handbag. The NamUs website had just come up when she heard a car stop outside. Seconds later, the doorbell rang. An older man on her porch was wearing a white shirt, black tie, shiny loafers, and a squeaky-clean smile.

Just what she needed—someone who wanted to save her soul. Andi gritted her teeth, mentally fortified herself against an evangelical pitch, and cracked open the door.

"Look. I'm druid. We worship trees. Don't plan to convert me unless you grow leaves and sway with the wind. Have a nice day."

Then she noticed the telltale bulge of a gun holster under his jacket. Since when did missionaries start packing guns and smelling like cigars? Cripes. If you didn't repent, they'd shoot hellfire and brimstone into you?

"I'm closing the door now. Bye."

He'd wedged a foot against the doorjamb. "Mrs. Wyndham, your husband owes me money, and he ain't answering the phone." He looked over her shoulder into the house. "Is he home?"

Her phone played the *Jurassic Park* theme. She held up a finger and answered it. "Hey, Andi. You need to come on over. Got a surprise for you. Wear something decent, woman. No. Forget that. Wear something your mama wouldn't approve of."

"Fiona!" she protested, but she'd disconnected, which left Andi to deal with the man at her door.

The squeaky-clean smile was gone. He stood in her doorway, patient as a turkey buzzard waiting to land on roadkill. She studied him sideways.

"I'm on my way." She hung up. "Gotta go. Best friend needs me. She's ready to deliver the twins."

"Mrs. Wyndham, your husband owes me *a lot* of money," he said. "Where is he?"

"He doesn't live here anymore." Anything to get rid of the guy. Andi recited a number where she said Lance could be reached, and he doggedly jotted it down on a crumpled receipt from his jacket pocket. "And you are?"

"Joe Clark. You tell Lance if I don't get my money, somebody's gonna get hurt."

Andi narrowed her eyes and put all the steel she could into her voice. "I'm not responsible for Lance's debts. Get off my property." She slammed the door and watched behind a curtain until he'd pulled away in his black Taurus. Andi was a lot of things, but not stupid enough to invite some pistol-packing old fart into her house.

Eyes glued to the street, she keyed in the police number and reported Joe Clark.

Up the stairs and toward her closet she went. Wear something your mother wouldn't approve of. If she showed up in a little black dress, Andi would look like a complete idiot. Or a slut. No, maybe a low-cut sweater. To show off what? Why didn't her heart stop pounding? The prospect of some blind date at Fiona's? Not likely.

Wait! Dammit! A stranger had threatened her, said somebody was gonna get hurt. What if she'd pissed him off and he came back? What if he broke in tonight and—the hell with dress to impress whomever Fiona had dug up. She grabbed her car keys, went outside, and locked the house. Fiona had guns at her place.

Andi climbed into her SUV. She'd blown off that man successfully, learned to be single just fine. And she didn't need Fiona to arrange a mercy date.

Two streets from Fiona's house, a back tire started thumping, and the car listed. Cursing, she got out, glared at the tire, then kicked it. Mastered single life, yes. Changing tires, no. Andi checked her reflection in the side mirror. Long, caramel brown ringlets of hair, disheveled. She finger-combed the coils so she didn't look like a Portuguese water dog. Blue eyes, bluer than usual due to the polarized mirror. Andi looked down at the paint-stained jeans underneath her coat. Oh, who the hell cared? She ran the rest of the way to Fiona's place.

CHAPTER FIVE

ANDI

OUT OF BREATH, ANDI slowed at her friend's driveway. A clay pot of withered brown stalks decorated the front porch. *Whispering.* She touched the new pendant in her pocket, and a seedling of doubt grew about that sweet Southern voice and bad things happening.

Andi hurried down the sidewalk and up to the screen door Fiona's cat had shredded. Her friend was no Martha Stewart. The front lawn was a dead ringer for a compost pile. Most houses in the neighborhood were vintage forties Cape Cods. Fiona's was vintage garage sale, inside and out. Andi forced the warped front door open with a small kick to the door's bottom, entered the house, and called "Hello?" She put her coat on the arm of the sofa, where Honky would claim it as her new bed and leave cat hair all over it.

Fiona had attended Juilliard on a piano scholarship. She designed websites for musicians. The laptop was a third arm to her. Long blond hair in her eyes, she barely glanced up from the computer. "Well now, that's a sexy outfit if you're into the grunge look."

"Matchmaking again?"

"Never." Fiona grinned.

After tossing her purse on a kitchen chair stacked ten inches high in newspapers, Andi sat across from her friend. She moved a tower of junk mail to one edge of the table and scraped a chunk of dried cat food off the Formica so she had a place to rest an elbow.

Cell phone in hand, one very fine-looking man threaded his way around Fiona's boxes on the dining room floor. He pocketed his Samsung, slid out the chair beside Fiona, and shook the seat cushion until crumbs fell out.

Then he sat.

The man had to be married with children. All the good ones were taken. Too bad. She could wake up next to him every morning. Then she remembered her theory about fine-looking men. All ego. They'd rather pump iron than lift a finger to help their women. And sometimes they took their frustrations out on their wives. Nope. Not happening, Fiona.

He pushed a bakery box of blueberry muffins across the table toward Andi. "Have some. They're from my favorite bakery. Name's Eli Lake. Private investigator." He extended his hand. "Her man Doug," he said, pointing at Fiona, "sent me to check out your pendants, the ones that look like the missing persons posters."

Andi clasped his hand, determined his smile wouldn't melt away her distrust of him.

Whoever said the eyes were windows to the soul was wrong; a firm handshake usually told her all she needed to know. Labor had roughened Eli's hands. Maybe he was raised on a farm or a vineyard, or maybe he'd been in construction work.

Be very careful with this one, she decided. He passed the handshake test, but given his occupation, he lied for a living.

"You remind me of that famous hairdresser on TV," she said, "with a gun."

"Why would a hairdresser need a gun?" Eli's crow's-feet crinkled into a smile.

"To keep women from molesting him." Fiona walked to the counter, set out some cups, and poured coffee. Obviously pleased with her matchmaking, she placed the cups on the table.

"No background in hairdressing. I was a cop, then law school, then worked in the fugitive squad at the Philadelphia FBI field office. Too many constraints. I never liked 'staying inside the lines.'" He used air quotes. "I consult for the police, and women hire me to find runaway children and cheating husbands who don't pay child support."

She couldn't guess his background. Italian? Or Native American? Tanned skin, dark brown eyes, cheekbones, over six feet, long black ponytail. Handsome meant nothing to her, she reminded herself.

Andi's cup paused midair. Her phone was pinging messages like ticker tape. She turned to Fiona. "Apparently my phone is your personal playground."

Head down, her friend muttered, "I did put a few new apps on your phone yesterday."

"Thanks." Dating websites, Andi guessed. Probably every pervert on the East Coast was responding. She muted the phone and pulled a pendant from her pocket. "This is the new one."

Two voices whispering . . . *doesn't know . . . ma'am does . . . doesn't.*

Know what? Flip a coin. Argue somewhere else, she told the voices silently. God, she had the shivers. The hair on the back of her neck felt like cold, raking bristles. Her scalp tingled.

Fiona stared at Andi. "You're shaking."

"Just a chill," Andi assured her.

"She does look cold." Eli took his jacket off and handed it to her. She draped it over her shoulders. Woodsmoke clung to the leather. Andi liked the smell of woodsmoke on a man. Turn the romance off, woman, she told herself. He's a one-night-stand kind of guy. Besides, telling him about the whispering girls would be the death knell of any relationship.

What the hell was she thinking? She needed a relationship about as much as a flat tire.

Andi took a longer look at Eli. The edge of an ankle holster showed at the cuff of his pants. That made this a two-gun day. Two men, two guns. One who threatened to hurt somebody. The other offering blueberry muffins.

Eli followed her gaze to his cuff. "Keeps my leg warm. Sometimes I don't even have to wear a sock. Can I have a look at the pendant?"

Andi handed it to him. "Haven't checked the NamUs site yet on this one."

"Doug probably already told you this, but police don't search for runaways," Eli explained. "Missing persons and kidnappings aren't FBI business either, unless they're high profile or criminals. I fill the missing and runaway gaps, and believe me, there are a lot of gaps, about three-hundred-forty-thousand juveniles a year." Narrowing his eyes, he held the pendant closer. "Name etched in the silver. 'Bernadette.'"

Andi watched Eli turn the pendant over in his hand. Neatly printed letters wrapped around the bottom edge of the bezel.

"I thought it might be the artist's signature," Andi offered.

"Or it could be another missing girl named Bernadette," Fiona said under her breath.

"Maybe some weirdo's getting off on using missing person's pictures, or some artist thinks he's making a social statement." Eli absently clicked a ballpoint pen.

Fiona's fingers were poised over the computer keys. The laptop made little grunting noises like a dog digging up a buried bone. She scanned the screen, shook her head, and typed in something else.

"Bernadette," she muttered as she waited for the download. After four tries, she shouted, "Hot damn!" and turned the laptop so Andi and Eli could see it. "NamUs website. Bernadette Johnston, missing from Columbia, South Carolina. Looks like the pendant."

"It does." Eli set the pendant down and reached into his pocket. He pulled out a business card and began writing on it. "Was Bernadette the name you saw on the missing person's poster?" he asked.

"No, it was Mariah Culverton."

Fiona clacked away on her laptop, then stopped. "Mariah was last seen in Columbia too." She looked at Eli.

"I don't like coincidences," he said, still writing.

In the silence, Andi remembered Joe Clark and her small victory over the creep. "Hey, Fiona. Some guy came to my door looking for Lance."

"You need to move out of that house, and don't answer the door. Ever," Fiona told her.

Eli stopped writing and looked up. "I'm assuming Lance is your ex."

Andi nodded. "Guy with a gun wedged his foot in the door and said Lance owed him a lot of money."

"What exactly did the man say?" Eli sipped some coffee.

"That somebody was gonna get hurt if Lance didn't pay up. I offered him a number where he could reach Lance, then gave him the local police number." Andi grinned.

"Good response." Eli was writing again. "A gun is enough to intimidate most people." He looked up at Andi. "Describe him."

"Older guy, tall, bald, nose like a beak, squeaky-clean-smile, dressed like one of those religious pamphlet people."

"Did he give you a name?" His brow furrowed. "How about a license plate number?"

"Joe Clark," Andi said. "He was driving a black Taurus."

Fiona turned back to the computer again. "He's either a bookie or a loan shark. Her ex bets on losing horses."

Eli slid his business card across the table to her. "Did you report him?"

"Yeah."

"If you see him again, call me immediately." Eli set the pendant on the table and snapped a picture of it with his phone. "Fiona's right. You shouldn't answer the door if it's somebody you don't know, especially if he has a gun."

"Never trust any guy who packs a gun." Fiona pointed an accusing finger at Eli's ankle.

"I'm licensed to carry in several states," Eli mumbled as he turned the pendant over to photograph the other side. He tapped the bone with one finger and cocked an ear.

"The seller assured me it's cow bone, not ivory." Andi took a sip of coffee that had gone cold. "He didn't have the artist's information, said he bought it online."

"What about the other pendant?" Eli held out his hand. "Let me see it."

Andi searched her handbag. "I know I put it in here." She reached to the bottom.

When she started taking things out of the bag, Eli glanced at his watch. "Gotta go. Email me a picture of it, and find the vendor's receipt. I'll make some calls to the local police where they were last seen and let you know what I learn." He handed her another business card and told her to print her name, address, and phone number on the back. "For me," he said.

She gave him a deadpan stare. "How do I know you're really a private investigator? You could be Jack the Ripper or Ted Bundy. Anybody can have business cards made."

He tilted his head toward her friend.

"She'll vouch for me."

"No, I won't." Fiona laughed. "I don't trust you as far as I can throw you. You or Doug."

"Oh, don't worry about it." Andi wrote her address and phone number.

Fiona snatched his jacket off Andi, thanked Eli, and followed him to the door. When she returned, she gave Andi a thumbs-up. "I think he likes the shit out of you." She put their coffee cups in the sink, where they'd be growing mold three days from now.

Andi glanced at the NamUs site on Fiona's laptop. She didn't like coincidences either. In her opinion, anyone who believed in them was naïve as hell. But the girls weren't runaways or missing. They were ghosts. To explain that, she'd have to admit she heard voices.

CHAPTER SIX

MARIAH
May 2022

I WAS MARIAH THE STRAY long before I met Bennie. Teaming up with her kept me alive for a while. Wool cap pulled down to just above her eyes, mahogany skin, torn jeans, Bennie sang gospel music better than any fourteen-year-old I'd ever heard. She didn't belong inside a church though, and neither did I. Last May, I celebrated my seventeenth birthday on the streets of Columbia. There was nothing happy about my day as I walked those dark Carolina streets.

Boarded up windows, dark alleys, cats scrounging through trash cans. Strays, like me, Mariah the reject, a disgrace to my parents. Two cats screeched into combat, their fury ripping through the night.

My haven, an abandoned house with a broken window, was about ten city blocks away. Bennie had warned me about the muggings the day before, warned me not to walk this way at night. That girl would know. She'd survived the streets for over a year, no parents to call curfew on her, nobody to please but herself.

Three days free of my parents, and a chilly Southern night welcomed me to the streets. Damn wind. It tossed trash up and down the block. A trash can barreled down the sidewalk, slammed into a light post, and bounced off.

Maybe I should've stayed home. Hell, I could be all snuggled up in bed. My parents had hoped I'd amount to something, dreamed I'd become a doctor like Daddy. I'd trashed those dreams. Tugging on the hood of my windbreaker, I shoved AirPods into my ears as if they were tiny pacifiers.

Like a dog, I raised my nose and inhaled the Carolina night. Tea olives. I love that old cemetery on Sumter and Gervais with tea olive bushes, but its wrought-iron fence bared its teeth in the dark, like a vampire's canines in a dumb teenage movie. I hummed an old folk song my mother used to sing to me. "And they call the wind Maria..." Then I stopped. No sense letting anyone know I was out here.

Concentrate on the beats, on the slap and squish of shoes on the sidewalk, I told myself.

Two extra beats. What the hell? I slowed.

The footsteps behind me slowed too. I couldn't bring myself to turn around, so I sped up.

Like a cat stalking prey, the footsteps behind me came softer but faster.

Six blocks to go. Rain like tiny needles splattered off my hood. Not a soul on the street, except whoever was following me. All kinds of places where people could jump out and grab me. Stopping to tie my shoelace, I glanced over my shoulder. Nothing but shadows. Throat tight, I listened. Silence. I heaved a sigh of relief and started walking.

I passed Trinity Cathedral and the building with columns at the intersection of Greene Street and the Student Union building and walked another five blocks. Light shone from a second-floor window on the next block, a beacon in a burned-out neighborhood of brick storefronts. I speed-walked across an intersection. Halfway down the block, the sound came again. Footsteps. Then silence. Bastard wouldn't get me. I could outrun him. The best damn cross-country runner my school ever had, I'd already been scouted for a track scholarship at Carolina, but I'd ruined it. I took one long leap, like coming off the starter's block.

A hand clasped my shoulder, strong fingers digging in like cat's claws. I screamed.

"It's okay, young lady. I've been keeping an eye on you." A gravelly voice, like he had a cold.

I whirled to face the voice and looked into the eyes of an old guy with hair that grew in thick gray thatches. He wore a brown hooded robe like a monk. "Get your hands off me." I shrugged one arm out of my backpack and drew it back, ready to swing.

The old man smiled but tightened his grip. "You shouldn't be out here alone, child."

"My boyfriend's meeting me," I lied. "Plays halfback for Carolina." I lied really well when scared shitless; mastered that art early in life. I could also be contrite as hell.

"What kind of guy would meet his girl in a neighborhood like this, Mariah?"

I flinched. "How do you know my name?"

"Told you I've been keeping an eye on you. I have a shelter for runaways." One savage yank, and he snatched the backpack off my shoulder. "Come back to the rectory, child, where it's warm and dry. I'll take care of you."

My shoulder hurt so bad it felt dislocated. My neck stung where the straps had scraped. He'd about ripped my arm off stealing my backpack, and he was going to take care of me? One wistful look at the only possessions I had left, and I sprinted away.

Footsteps echoed behind me. Ragged breaths cut through the rhythm of my sneakers like a serrated knife. Maybe he'd have a heart attack. I hoped so, but he ran fast for an old guy. I raced across an intersection, oblivious to traffic. Faster. Faster. If I couldn't outrun an old man like him, I wouldn't last long on the streets. My lungs burned. Sweat dripped down my face, salty and bitter. I gasped for air.

Faster. Faster. Half a block later, a voice called to me, one I recognized. "Over here! In the alley!" A wooden gate swung open. I raced into the narrow passage and slid down a wet brick wall, ripping my jeans. Bennie bolted the gate behind us. She stooped beside me and put a finger to her lips. Clouds of our breath merged in the air like silent oaths, like silent prayers.

Footsteps stumbled by, and I held my breath. Bennie crouched, ready to defend us, a switchblade raised, its metal edge a silver ray in the darkness. When the footsteps faded down the block, she poked me. "Don't you ever go with him. You hear? Stay away from him."

"Scared the shit out of me." I sniffed.

"He get your backpack?"

Like some brokenhearted ten-year-old, I nodded. "Yeah, now I have nothing but freedom to carry around. And it's my birthday," I sobbed.

Bennie handed me a dirty bandanna, and I wiped my face with the oily red cloth.

"Well, don't expect no cake and candles at my hotel. I run the e-conomy Holiday Inn. Want towels, you steal 'em off some college kid in the laundromat. Want heat, you swipe somebody's woodpile. Want food, well, you'll figure that out. Now, let's go," she said, and the birthday present she gave me that night was my safety.

CHAPTER SEVEN

ANDI

MONDAY'S MELTED SNOW TURNED to black ice overnight. Impossible to see until it was too late. Andi's car had skidded off the road, down a snowy embankment, and here she sat, wearing the latte she'd been drinking. Twelve inches farther, and she would've hit a stone springhouse. Her breathing slowed, and she cursed PennDOT and the latte. One ring, two annoying rings— after three, Andi put her phone on speakerphone. "What's up?"

"Eli Lake. Can we meet Wednesday night at O'Brien's in West Chester? Dinner's on me."

"Sure. I love their boxty. Any news about the pendants?"

"I'm waiting for a call from the sheriff in Columbia. I'll have more information then."

Andi searched for a napkin or tissue to clean up the latte mess. "I hope PennDot salts the hell out of the roads and gets this black ice cleared by then."

"They will. Bring both pendants and the sales receipts. Did you find the other one?"

A man in a ski jacket knocked on the window. "You all right?"

"I'm okay," Andi assured him.

The Good Samaritan motioned toward her fender. "Busted headlight. You want me to rock your car out of that snowbank?"

"I can do it. Thank you," she said.

"What's going on?"

"I'm stuck in the snow. Yes, I found the other pendant inside the lining of my handbag. When I get home, I'll text you a photo of the Mariah pendant and the receipts. My schedule is clear for Wednesday."

"Good. O'Brien's at eight thirty. Seen that guy who came looking for Lance again?" Eli asked.

"No."

"Okay. You be careful," he said and hung up.

The whispering began again.

Not who . . . if . . . happens . . . she next.

Who's next? Me? Speak in sentences, Andi wanted to shout as she rocked the car out of the drift. A couple pushes from the Good Samaritan, and the SUV clawed its way onto the road.

"I'm next for what?" she repeated out loud, but the girls were silent.

At Fiona's, Andi got out of the car and surveyed the damage. "Note to self," she said. "You suck at drinking lattes and driving." Disgusted that one hot drink could cost her car repairs and dry cleaning, she kicked the edge of Fiona's front door to dislodge it and entered the house.

"Don't take it out on my door," Fiona said. "Hey, do you still have that six-shooter your ex gave you? Jackass that he was."

"Don't start. I'm not in the mood."

"Should've used it on him the day you got it, then celebrated your birthday that year by burying him in the basement. But then, he did have your place outfitted like a National Guard Armory."

Fiona glanced at Andi, and her mouth dropped open. "What happened to your coat?"

"I spilled a latte." Andi peeled it off and studied her burned hands. "Should've been wearing gloves. Any idea where I can get a busted headlight fixed?"

"You had an accident?" Fiona stood and gave Andi a quick checkup. "Are you okay?"

"Yeah." Andi walked toward the ancient Frigidaire and peered into the freezer. Damn.

Metal ice cube trays. After bending the aluminum lever back and forth, she whacked it on the counter. Two cubes shot out. More wiggling, bending, and whacking, and one cube yielded. "Why can't you have an ice maker like everybody else?"

"Old fridges last twenty years. New ones, you're lucky if you get two years." Fiona took the tray from her, turned it upside down and ran cold water over the bottom. All but one of the cubes thunked into the sink. She put them in a sandwich bag and handed it to Andi. "You okay?"

Andi trudged into the living room and sank into a recliner. She gently placed the ice bag on her hand. "Yeah. My SUV did donuts all over the Pike and almost took out a springhouse."

Fiona went to the window and checked Andi's car. "I'll ask Irv if he can fix it. He can fix anything, unlike Bailey who hires people to replace lightbulbs. Never understood how three so dissimilar kids could spring from the same parents." Fiona's expression softened. She obviously loved her brothers.

"Thanks. When I spun out, I swear Mariah and Bernadette were talking in my car." Andi waited for Fiona to tell her she'd lost her mind. "As if they knew each other."

"What did the girls say?" Fiona grabbed diet sodas from the fridge, popped the top off one, and held one out to Andi.

"'She next.'" Andi took the can and opened it.

"I believe in that other dimension, but damn. You're next?"

Andi shifted the ice bag and shrugged. "My father taught me to ignore the voices. He didn't want me to become a freak. This from a man who ran my life like a drill sergeant. A tyrant who had no idea how to raise a little girl."

"My life was one endless exercise in what he considered perfect behavior, except when he had his martinis and felt sorry for himself because my mother had logged more war time than he ever did." The cheap glass clock that Fiona kept on an end table chimed the hour. Andi checked her watch. It was ahead of real time by three hours.

Loud ticking punctuated the silence.

"Usually, I can turn the ghost voices off. But I have no control over the Shadows. When they show up, I'm either in trouble or trouble is coming. Mom sent them to keep me company when I was scared and she wasn't home to soothe me. They're dark gray beings with yellow eyes, and they smell like Mom's perfume. When I was little, I'd have tea parties with them. You want to hear what my father said about the Shadows?"

"No." Fiona spoke softly. "Your father's wrong. You're not a freak. Eli will solve the pendant girls' cases. They'll move on, and you'll reinvent yourself as a happy person."

"Yeah, and Lance's buddy who threatened me had a squirt gun in his holster."

"Maybe you'll get lucky, and he'll find Lance and either get his money or get even."

"I just want Lance to go somewhere else, far, far away."

"Come on, your ex pointed a gun at you not too long ago. Karma needs to bite that reptile in the ass." Fiona locked eyes with her. "Pissed off his dinner wasn't ready? You should've added a few hemlock berries to his arugula."

"I only married him to get away from my father," Andi admitted.

"Well, here's my advice on men. And this is from somebody who's still looking. Do the Goldilocks thing. Keep trying them out until you find one that's just right. Eli's a good start." Fiona leaned back in the chair. "He's gonna solve all your problems and make you feel like a woman again. You'll see."

CHAPTER EIGHT

ANDI

S HE WAS LEAVING FOR her divorce lawyer's office the next day when Eli called with news. Some good, some not so good. South Carolina Sheriff Hollister had hired Eli to consult on Mariah's case. Six months and Mariah's case was going nowhere, which is where Hollister's career was going too. The bad news was that the pendants had to be examined at a crime lab. Without the pendants, Andi wouldn't hear the girls talk. They'd be gone forever.

Damn. Her divorce lawyer put her in a worse mood. He wanted three thousand dollars up front. The weasel had complimented the carving in her pendant while he carved a huge hole in her financial security. On the way home, Andi needed to decompress. She pulled into a Wawa for coffee and a celebratory candy bar. When she returned to her car, she cranked up the heater. "Here's to being single forever." She raised her cup.

. . . two . . . ma'am.

"Two what?" Andi asked. "Is it *too* as in buy a candy bar for you too? Or maybe where are we going *to*? Help me out."

No answer, and Andi felt guilty. The girl was dead, for crying out loud. Poor kid wasn't great at communicating, but then Andi wasn't brilliant at figuring things out.

...more...

"Oh cripes." Andi set her coffee in the holder. "Two more what?"

A ginkgo leaf blew onto her windshield. She looked around. People buying cigarettes and coffee. A screaming toddler. No ginkgo trees nearby. "Why can't you speak in sentences?"

Learning, ma'am ... the park.

She took a long sip of coffee and turned the key in the ignition. "Okay, but here's the deal. I'm not driving to the park any more unless you promise to talk to me when I get there." Andi drove past an old, green mansion on the corner of the Pike. It looked dark and spooky; she'd never seen a living soul there.

Past the pharmaceutical research facility, and she didn't want to know what went on inside there. A few houses, then the park. She pulled into the entrance.

The same sepia scene in the park. If only all choices were black and white, life would answer all her questions, and she had a lot of them. "Two more girls dead?"

Not yet ... Stalking.

"Good. You're learning. Now, tell me which girls and where." Andi stepped outside and sucked air. Damn, it was cold. Two swings moved as if ghostly legs were pumping. She walked toward them.

A bearded man wearing a tattered baseball cap and a stained hoodie staggered out of the woods, carrying a paper bag with what looked like a bottle in it. He made his way toward Andi. "Aw shit!" She raced for her car, slammed the door, and clicked the door locks. The stagger changed to a slow lumbering trot. Andi pulled out before he got to her window.

She checked the rearview mirror as she sped toward the entrance. Rooted to the parking lot, the man stared at her retreating car. Drunk or drugged, she decided. And look at that. Those swings jiggled like someone had just slid off them.

At the park entrance, two ginkgo leaves lifted off her windshield and took flight, at first dancing in the wind, then, like two children chasing each other, they disappeared. Her brain shuffled what she knew about ginkgo trees on the way home. Healing. Memory enhancing. The only tree that had survived Hiroshima. Moth-shaped leaves. Nothing healing about two leaves that blew away. What she needed was a strong dose of Fiona to justify spending money she didn't have on a friggin' divorce lawyer.

She found Fiona hunched over a laptop in her living room. "Is the lawyer a hunk?"

"No, you'd think three grand might buy you the world's sexiest man alive. No such luck. He looks eight months pregnant and acts like he has some better place to be. Maybe he was in a hurry to chase an ambulance for the big money."

Her phone rang. "Unknown caller."

"Maybe it's Lance's friend," Fiona mumbled.

"He doesn't have my number." Andi swiped the screen to answer it.

"Mrs. Wyndham, this is Peter Rockford."

Southern accent. Andi glared at the phone. "Whatever you're selling, I don't want it."

"Actually, ma'am, there's something you have that I'd like to buy."

"Sorry. Wrong number." Her thumb crept toward the END icon.

"Did you recently buy two pendants with the faces of young ladies engraved on them?"

Now he had her attention. "How'd you get my number?" The whispering was one thing, but strangers calling her about the pendants? She didn't like that at all. "Hold on a second." She muted the phone and poked Fiona. "Guy wants to buy my pendants."

Fiona's head shot up from the laptop. "Ask for five times what you paid. If he won't pay, tell him no deal and hang up."

Andi considered that for a moment, but she wanted to hear what he'd say. "Yes."

"You do have the pendants. Good. They've been in my family for years. The faces on them, that's my great-grandma and my Nana. Someone stole them and sold Nana's things on E-market. Been searching ever since. I'll pay—"

"I didn't buy the pendants from E-market, and they're not for sale." She hung up.

Her friend glared at her. "Just once, could you take my advice?"

"That nice grandfatherly vendor gave my number to a stranger. I might as well rent a billboard on I-95 and post my profile! I'm not selling the pendants. Those girls need me."

"They're dead, Andi."

"I know that, but I need to find out what happened. Give them peace. Help them move on. Whatever. And I need Eli to help me."

Fiona gave her a sly smile. "Now you're making sense. Partner up with Eli. He'll satisfy all your needs."

Andi rolled her eyes, then grabbed a pillow from the couch and threw it at her friend. But in truth, her mood improved just thinking about meeting Eli on Wednesday.

CHAPTER NINE

FISHERMAN

D AMMIT ALL! FISHERMAN HAD etched all the pleasure his girls gave him into those pendants. That Wyndham woman had hung up on him, acted like they belonged to her just because she paid for them. He threw a shovel as hard as he could. It hit the side of the house and bounced into two metal garbage cans, setting off a clatter that sent a flock of crows into the sky.

Anger never solves anything, Nana would've said. He picked up the shovel and propped it against the side of his house. There is anger and there is vengeance, Nana had taught him. Vengeance is an act of justice. That was the answer his anger wanted. Vengeance.

Fisherman stepped over the cracked walkway to his house. He kept his yard the way God intended His land to be. Natural. Weeds, rodents, and snakes only offended neighbors who didn't understand the divine will.

Fisherman had inherited his two-story house from Nana. Two big pines kept anyone from peering into his front windows. Leaves had smothered his front lawn a long time ago, but those leaves danced and made sweet rustling sounds like girls' prom dresses in a hotel ballroom.

He didn't like visitors, never invited anyone to Nana's inner sanctum. Anyone who ventured onto his property, probably on a dare, got the devil scared out of him when Fisherman barged out the door with a shotgun. Why couldn't people leave him alone? Even his neighbors judged him the wrong way, as if he was some kind of Boo Radley stabbing people with scissors. In truth, Fisherman just didn't like people touching his things. A person had a right to privacy.

Damn those thieves! Two weeks ago, burglars had stolen his pendants and sullied his workplace. He'd crawled across their bloody footprints on the workroom floor, hoping they'd left one pendant. All those hours of carving and not one pendant was left. If it was kids who'd done this, they'd tell somebody about the bones and the drain full of blood. But kids wouldn't steal things like a Stryker autopsy saw. What would adult criminals do? Nothing, he wagered, because sinners weren't likely to confess unless caught, and thieves, by nature, were liars.

Fisherman heaved a sigh. So many empty spaces where Nana's treasures had been. When he lowered himself to the kitchen chair, it creaked, reminding him that he needed to start running again. He'd put on a few pounds from a beer or two but still had a solid body for a forty-year-old. His hairline had receded a little, but he'd kept most of his tightly curled red hair, and his green eyes still shone bright with the light of God. Not a fine-looking man, but not ugly either. Now, his big sister Dee, she'd been a beauty: corkscrew coils of flame-red hair, big green eyes, white, smooth skin like their mother's. The mother who'd dumped them at Nana's.

Dee hadn't liked Nana's rules or her willow switch. Truth was, his grandma didn't want her to grow up to be a whore, but Dee slipped out one night. A week later, she'd met him behind the school dumpster and brought him candy and baseball cards. Dee had new clothes, a tight sweater and a short skirt Nana wouldn't approve of. She put an arm around him and kissed the top of his head. "How about I buy you some Rocky Road ice cream? Your favorite."

He frowned and shrugged off her arm. "Where'd you get the money?"

"Earned it delivering things," she'd said. "I can't take Nana's crap no more. She won't let me date, makes me wear those god-awful dresses she sews. Chores all the time. Got no life."

"Nana just wants you to grow up to be good. That's all."

Suddenly, Dee grabbed his arm and turned it over to look at the thin welts on the soft underside. "When did she do that?"

Fisherman shrugged. "Didn't finish my chores. Said I was dawdling. Didn't hurt much."

Two weeks later, police came to Nana's door. They told her to bring Dee's burial clothes to the morgue. Dee had overdosed in a crack house. God knows he'd loved his sister. Sometimes in the middle of the night when he ached for Mama, Dee had sung to him. She'd been more like a mother than their own. The day they buried Dee, he swore on her grave he'd become a priest whose mission was to keep girls like Dee off the streets and their souls untarnished.

He stood outside his small workroom with silver insulation covering the walls. It was just big enough for a sink, a cot, his carving tools, a meat grinder, his saw, a workbench, and fryers for removing meat from bone. His pappy had used the workroom to make venison sausage.

But Fisherman was an artist. Da Vinci had hired grave robbers for his artwork. Fisherman didn't need to do that. The Columbia streets gave him models for his carvings, and they were free. He could preserve their innocence in bone. If the cops ever found Mariah's grave, they'd discover a surprise he'd left for them. A bonus for all their hard work.

Nana's clock struck the hour, reminding him it was time to bring home that runaway, the pretty blond, before somebody else got to her. Or maybe the brunette. As long as he had bone to carve, he was happy.

CHAPTER TEN

MARIAH

Ghosts are eavesdroppers and spies. We have nothing else to do. Listening to Andi's conversation with Fisherman, we knew he'd want revenge. He'd never let her keep our pendants. But Bennie and I knew a little about revenge too.

The e-conomy Holiday Inn is no longer our home away from home, but we still visit to see who might've taken our place. Damn! The girl Fisherman had been stalking had staked her claim next to the fireplace. Blond, wavy hair, an expensive highlighting job. Big blue eyes with long lashes. She wore Dolce and Gabbana jeans and expensive Italian boots. She was pretty enough to be a model.

"You think she stole those jeans and boots?" Bennie asked me.

"Jeans maybe, but not the boots. They look custom, like Luccheses. I'm surprised nobody's stolen them yet," I said. "Look at that, she has the newest iPhone too, and a power bank. If we drain that, we'll have plenty of energy for a while.

There's a learning curve to being a ghost. In the beginning, it took us months to realize what we could do if we had the energy.

We discovered that if we walked into a store that sold batteries, we could drain 'em and do all kinds of neat things, like moving price signs, setting off squeakers on dog toys, and—most fun—setting all the animated plush toys in motion.

We drained Blondie's power bank. *Call your mom before your phone runs out of battery*, Bennie told her. *Or better yet, go home.*

Blondie had a mummy-style sleeping bag, a plaid travel pillow, and a full backpack. "Why the hell would she want to live on the streets?" I asked.

"Same reason you did," Bennie reminded me. "You had some crazy idea about freedom."

I grunted, remembering those first few weeks and all the mistakes I'd made. Not happy memories. "Wonder what's in the backpack." I moved closer to check it out. "Marshmallows, chocolate, and graham crackers, like she thinks this is a picnic." I shook my head. "She thinks this is Girl Scout camp."

"She's in big trouble," Bennie said. "We need to scare her out of here and hope nobody kills her for those boots."

Our Holiday Inn was an old Victorian house built sometime in the 1800s. Rock solid but falling apart daily. No power. No water. The owner's ghost routinely spooked potential investors. It had been a roof over our heads, but street people did wander in and out.

Hey Blondie, Bennie said. *The neighborhood drug dealer, Melvin, he's gonna sell you some weed and get you hooked on cocaine or crack. Then one day when you need a fix, Fisherman will have himself a new pendant girl. That's how he got me.*

I wished she could hear us, like Andi.

The blond removed metal skewers and marshmallows from her bag. She hummed as she threaded the marshmallows onto the skewers like she didn't have a care in the world. I wondered how long she'd been on the streets. I also wondered why we bothered talking to her when we knew she couldn't hear us. Maybe we just wanted to connect to a living person our age. Being between worlds depressed the hell out of me. I wanted my old life back. I wanted to have sleepovers, to go to parties and concerts, to roast marshmallows with my friends.

"If Fisherman is anywhere nearby, he'll see smoke in the chimney and come here. We need to make her leave," I said. When the blond had her back turned to me, I snatched some water from an open bottle and sprinkled it over the fire. It hissed like a snake, and white smoke rose in plumes. *No light. No warmth. Go home, girl, before you wind up dead, like us.*

She did a 360, probably to see if she was the only one in the room. I could swear this girl sensed us somehow.

"Damn!" Blondie shouted when she realized the fire had gone out, and she whipped out a big purple Maglite. After shoving the wet wood aside with a skewer, she gathered the wood from beside the fireplace and built a new fire that looked like a log cabin with tinder in the middle.

"Must've been a Girl Scout," Bennie muttered, trying to blow out the flames, but that gave the fire more air. "Okay, we really need to freak her out." Bennie started turning pages of the magazine next to her and ruffling her hair. Blondie's hand went to her scalp, searching for whatever was there. In this place it could be a rat making a nest.

I knocked her water bottle over so it spilled onto her sleeping bag.

"No! How'd I do that?" she shouted. "Wait a minute. Somebody's messing with me. Are there ghosts in this house?" She looked around frantically, stared right at us for a moment but didn't see us. "Well, ghosts, find somebody else to pester."

"This girl has nerves of steel, like you," I told Bennie.

When the door opened and Fisherman came through, Bennie and I froze.

"Go away, old man!" Blondie shouted. "I'm not going to your stupid shelter."

He smiled like a kindly uncle coming to rescue her. "Rachel, my child, it's cold here, unsanitary, and you're not safe from the street criminals. They'll rob you blind and leave you to die."

"Been robbed. Been left to die. Ain't as bad as what he's gonna do to you," Bennie said.

Fisherman reached for her arm, but she slapped his hand away. "Don't touch me!"

"Oh Lord! Now she's pissed him off," I said.

Fisherman reached into his pocket and pulled out an ancient revolver. Whoa! I remembered that thing. Sucker had to be a foot long. He kicked her bag out of reach.

I shoved the bag back to her, and a phone fell out. *Call 9-1-1!* I screamed at her.

Blondie reeled with a burning marshmallow on a skewer and held it like a sword. It touched Fisherman's shirt, smoked, and caught fire. He dropped the revolver, patting furiously at the flame on his shirt.

Bennie shouted, *Get his gun. Shoot the bastard! Do the world a favor!*

The sounds coming from him were horrible. That marshmallow had burned a hole right through to his skin.

With a look of horror on her face, Blondie grabbed her phone and raced for the door. Fisherman snatched the gun off the floor and pulled the hammer back. I bumped his hand.

The sound of the shot reminded me of a door slamming shut. Thank God he'd missed.

Cursing, vowing revenge, Fisherman raced out of there.

Bennie shook her head. "He starts hunting for her with Melvin, and they'll find her before the cops get to her."

CHAPTER ELEVEN

ANDI

ANDI SPENT MOST OF Tuesday dealing with a broken water heater, a wet basement, and contractors who didn't show up. After the plumbers left, Andi and Fiona decided they should celebrate with margaritas at a local bar. Slightly buzzed and armed with a wet vacuum, Fiona came back with Andi to make sure the basement was dry. Andi unlocked her front door, flicked on the lights, and froze.

"Holy shit!" Fiona hissed.

Slashed sofa cushions, lumps of stuffing everywhere, chairs upended, their bottoms slit open, greeted them. The hope chest gaped, spewing her wedding dress. Jewelry she'd collected off the lawn was scattered. Andi keyed in 9-1-1 on her cell for the second time in three days.

Fiona grabbed Andi's arm and walked her outside. "You need to get out of this house. Put it on the market, sell it, and move in with me. Stay here any longer, and you'll wind up bankrupt or drowned in the basement."

"You want me to pack up my life in boxes and put them in storage? Well, I'm sorry. I can't do that. I love this house. And I need my own place." Oh God. She'd taken it out on Fiona. "I'm sorry." She hugged her friend.

"You'll get through this," Fiona assured her. "This is not the biggest crisis you've survived. Think about it."

Andi ripped out a vinca plant growing along the foundation of the house. "They were looking for something," she said.

"Sure looks that way." Fiona put up her hood against the sleet.

When the police arrived, Andi watched a burly, middle-aged officer trample her azaleas, checking for broken windows. The second officer rounded the corner past holly trees, then trudged back. "Broke a window in the back door," he told his partner. He turned to Andi. "That sign says you have a security system, ma'am. You didn't get a call?"

She pursed her lips. "When I didn't pay, they cut me off. I thought the signs would be a deterrent."

"We'll check inside," the burly one said. "You ladies wait here."

Once they were out of earshot, Fiona poked her in the shoulder. "You could've asked me for some help. I'll pay your bill tomorrow."

Sleet pelted the bushes. Four-foot-tall dead cleomes shifted in the wind, seed pods empty, stalks rippling like centipedes. She would've pulled them out long ago except for their wicked thorns. Apparently, there were a lot of thorny things she should've done. Trauma and stress had a way of making her procrastinate. And ignore things.

She and denial had history. Her father had encouraged it. Ignore the voices. Ignore the nightmares.

The police checked the house and yard. "Until that window gets fixed, I suggest you spend the night elsewhere, ma'am," said the beefy one.

"She'll be staying with me, Officer," Fiona assured him.

"Any idea who might have done this? Haven't had any reports of vandalism in this area lately," the officer said.

Andi took a deep breath. "Officer, somebody pitched my things out the window yesterday. I thought it might be my ex-husband then, but I'm not sure anymore." Not daring a glance in Fiona's direction because she should've filed a police report, Andi winced. "My ex drinks a little sometimes. Well, actually he drinks a lot most of the time."

Fiona tapped her foot in annoyance. "He's an alcoholic, Officer, who bets on losing horses, owes people money, and beats on her. He's trouble."

The cop flipped open his notebook. "The ex-husband would be?" He waited for her to fill in the name.

"Lance Wyndham," Andi said.

"Did anyone see him throwing things out the window yesterday?" he asked.

"No, my neighbor thinks the vandal came in from the back." Andi glanced across the street and saw a dark silhouette in the front window. Gladys, probably taking notes.

She pulled out more vinca growing out of a crack in the sidewalk. Darn stuff was invasive.

His two-way radio belched static, then went quiet. The burly one asked, "Was anything missing yesterday?"

"A few pieces of jewelry, but I might have hidden them someplace I can't remember." Andi massaged her temples and added, for Fiona's benefit. "Technically, it's still Lance's house until our divorce is final. He does have a key, but my restraining order should keep him away from me."

"Ma'am, whoever broke in today didn't have a key, or he wouldn't need to break a window," the cop told her. "If you'd filed a report, we would've been sending a patrol car through periodically."

"I assumed it was my ex, drunk and pissed off."

Fiona was tapping her foot again. "I told her eighteen times to change the locks. Does she listen? No."

"Changing the locks wouldn't have helped today," the beefy one said. "Someone may have found an unlocked window yesterday or picked the back door lock. Always make sure all your windows are locked, and use dead bolts." The big police officer shoved his notepad into a coat pocket and turned to Andi. "Best if you stay with your friend. Don't ever hesitate to call us if you feel threatened. If anything was stolen, you'll need to file a report. Meanwhile, you ladies be careful." He nodded a goodbye and then joined his partner at the cruiser.

Fiona pushed the front door open and made her way through the lower level, turning on lights as she went. "What's with that stuff by the door?"

"That's what somebody threw out the window." Andi tossed cushions onto the sofa and started picking up clumps of stuffing. Fiona eyed Andi's wedding dress. She ran a finger over the lace, then dropped it. "Happily ever after, my ass," she muttered.

The armoire Gladys had helped Andi lug inside lay in a corner of the living room. The lock had been pried open, one leg snapped off. Diamond tennis bracelet gone, two sapphire rings, plus the cameo her great-great grandfather had commissioned before he fought in the Civil War.

She rummaged through the pieces strewn on the carpet. "Jewelry missing. Should've put them in a safe-deposit box. More money I didn't have," she muttered.

Fiona came up the basement stairs.

"Dry down there now. Plumber fixed it right." She headed for the office, a woman on a mission. Seconds later, computer keys were clacking furiously. Somehow, she'd resurrected the laptop. "You okay?" she asked.

"Fine," Andi lied.

Then she remembered Gladys picking jewelry off the lawn. Maybe the missing pieces were there. If she didn't find them now, they might get buried in snow tonight.

"I need to check something outside. Be right back."

"It's dark out there. Take Ignatius."

"Your gun?"

"Yup. What's so important out there anyway?"

"My great-great grandmother's cameo." Andi snatched some waterproof boots and gloves from the foyer closet and slipped them on. She opened the door. "Ignatius wants to stay where it's warm. I have a Maglite that could double as a club."

"Fine. If you're not back in sixty seconds, I'm coming to get you."

Key in lock, rattling, rattling.

That was a new voice, a child's voice. *Are you talking about the burglar? What are you trying to tell me?* Andi asked.

No answer.

CHAPTER TWELVE

MARIAH

W E'D SCARED RACHEL AND Fisherman away. A small victory for us, so we decided to celebrate by going to the Riverbanks Zoo. No normal human being would ever visit the zoo after sundown, but we loved it. Bennie and I watched the monkeys, and I believe they knew we were there. One monkey would climb a tree on their little island that faced us and start jabbering. Another monkey would come over to see, and pretty soon, they were all jabbering excitedly.

Bennie and I were sitting on a bench, enjoying the show, when we heard this electric crackle, like a utility pole where the transformer had been struck by lightning. Human reflexes don't die with you, ghost or not. We jumped to our feet. Two life-size spirits floated around us, spewing sulfur from their mouths.

"Who are they, and why are they circling us like buzzards?" I asked, fanning the air in front of my face. "God, they smell."

"No idea." Bennie kept whirling, trying not to turn her back on either of them.

The monkeys were screaming now, which agitated the other animals. A lion roared. Tigers growled. Koalas were screeching too. The noise from them scared the hell out of us. They sounded angry, and angry animals sometimes find a way to escape. The crackling grew louder. Like the cracking of a thousand whips.

I could feel the heat from the spirits as they came closer. "Bennie? You okay?"

"Uh-huh."

Not a very convincing answer. "Bennie, what are we supposed to do?"

A roar. Two roars, and they didn't come from the zoo animals.

We grabbed each other and held on.

"What do you want?" Bennie asked.

They circled faster, coming closer, their heat and sulfur breath nearly suffocating us.

"Who are you?" How Bennie kept the fear out of her voice, I don't know, but the streets had taught her how to act tough.

"Who-Are-We?" they thundered at us. "Who-Are-We?"

Shrieking laughter. High-pitched sounds, right out of a haunted house of horror. We couldn't move. They had us penned in like the zoo animals.

"We are the Punishers." Two spirits spoke in one voice, a hollow sound, like an echo in a cave. "We have been sentenced to walk the earth and maintain law and order among the spirits. But justice for mortals must come from other mortals. Spirits must never interfere before mortal judgment has been passed."

"Who sentenced you?" I asked.

Electric crackles for what seemed like a minute. Bennie and I clung to each other.

"You do not ask questions. And you do not interfere. If you interfere again, we will sentence you to stay between the worlds forever. Do you understand?" the voices thundered and echoed.

"But we didn't interfere. We only tried to help the girl," Bennie argued.

I poked her in the ribs with my elbow, trying to make her shut up.

Again the crackling, the roaring, the shrieking. Now an elephant trumpeted. Every animal in the zoo was freaking out.

"You are impertinent. The question was, 'Do you understand?'"

The ground where we stood was a circle of scorched grass. The animals screamed, screeched, and bellowed.

I looked at Bennie and we both nodded. The Punishers disappeared amid more thunder bolts and electric crackles.

"Does that mean we can't give Rachel's name to Andi?" I asked Bennie.

Bennie did one of her head-bobbling gestures. "They didn't say we couldn't."

"Well, they did say we can't interfere," I argued. "Andi might be able to save that girl."

"Ain't nobody gonna save that girl if Fisherman wants her."

CHAPTER THIRTEEN

ANDI

DAMN. A METAL DETECTOR might be the only way Andi would find any jewelry on her front lawn tonight. A quarter inch of sleet coated the snow like granulated sugar. It crunched and grabbed at Andi's boots. Over that, a thin layer of dry snow. This was crazy, but she needed to find that cameo. Cripes, the burglar could be watching her from behind the neighbor's bushes. Her heart beat faster.

Yellow eyes peered from the holly trees. Dark gray shapes danced, ebbing and flowing, against the pink brick. The Shadows.

Wandering around in the dark was a stupid idea, but she wanted her cameo. If the snow melted enough for it to glitter, anybody driving down the street could steal it.

Something in the azalea bushes moved. A flash of white. Maybe a rabbit. She scanned with the flashlight. Nothing but wind rattling scraggly heads of sedum in the garden. She heard whispering near a rhododendron and moved toward the shrub. Whispering, muffled by wind and creaking branches. Andi strained to hear.

. . . not who you think.

Who is? I wish you'd give me complete sentences so I could under-stand.

A gust of wind blew snow into her eyes. She clenched her lids shut against the stinging flakes. When she opened them, the flash-light picked up a patch of blue. A blue hydrangea blossom. What the hell? A real hydrangea in November. She stooped and picked it up. Clusters of petals, two leaves, a green stem, not frostbitten. Even the leaves showed no sign of wilting.

Her heart was racing now.

She aimed the flashlight in lines across the lawn searching for anything else. About a foot away, she saw the family heirloom. Her great-great grandmother's eyes in a strong, determined face. Andi brushed the snow off the ornate silver bezel.

"Sorry, Grandma," she said. Through all her money troubles, she'd never sold the heirloom.

Something moved. Something rope-like, maybe a slice of old newspaper chewed up by the lawn mower. No, it had hard ridges, a silver clasp. She reached down. It moved as if jerked on a string.

"Come on, Shadows. I don't want to play. Cut it out." She reached again. It slithered through the snow like a phantom snake. Large bumpy beads attached to some yellowed, waxy kind of string. It reminded her of the strings in a dream catcher. Sinew or imitation sinew. The necklace ended in a hook and ring clasp.

"Dammit! Come here!" Andi lunged and it wriggled through her fingers.

Footsteps raced around an overgrown holly bush toward her. Oh damn! What a stupid idea this was! What if it was the burglar? She ducked behind a rhododendron and turned off the flashlight. Andi held her breath. Slow, cautious footsteps. The steely outline of a gun barrel. Maglite vs. gun. She'd lose.

"Don't shoot!" Hands raised, Andi emerged.

Fiona turned in a complete circle. "Jesus H. Christ!" Hand over her heart, she exhaled. "Why'd you say, 'Come here'? There's nobody here, for crying out loud."

Andi punched the button on her flashlight and aimed it at the necklace. "Look at that." She pointed a finger.

"Shee-it. Assault by a deadly necklace. Hope to hell it doesn't bite." Fiona lowered Ignatius and picked up the beads. "Another *Little Shop of Horrors* special."

Heart slowing, Andi said, "I've never seen this necklace. Every time I tried to pick it up, the damn thing jumped, like that practical joke with the dollar bill on a string."

"Probably your flashlight battery dying. Let's go in. No kidding, you didn't buy this?" Fiona handed it to her.

Andi shook her head slowly and took the necklace. The beads felt warm, as if someone had just been wearing them. "What are you trying to tell me?"

No answer from the girls. Andi and Fiona rounded the corner and stepped into the foyer. The furnace hummed loudly. Fiona had left the front door wide open. Andi took off her coat and gloves and held the necklace and the hydrangea in her hand.

"Where'd you get that hydrangea?" Fiona stamped snow off her shoes and left them lying in a puddle on the foyer tiles.

Andi moved the shoes to the doormat. "Found it next to my family heirloom." She kicked off her boots and set them beside Fiona's. "And those beads moved. I swear they're trying to tell me something."

"They?"

"The girls in the pendants."

"Why can't they just tell you outright what happened to them?"

"I think they're newly dead and don't have all their skills mastered," Andi explained. "It doesn't help that I'm a novice too. Tea parties with ghost girls were easy. This is a lot more complicated."

"Why can't the Shadows tell you?"

"They don't talk, although I do hear an occasional giggle from them. I only remember them talking once when I was lost in the woods. Sometimes, they help me find things."

"Hmph." Fiona headed for the office, plunked down into a chair, and pointed at the computer screen. "You're one lucky lady. This computer must have landed somewhere soft when it went airborne yesterday. Good news. Your ex's new business is bankrupt. Couldn't happen to a nicer guy."

Fiona glanced at Andi's sapphire rings and a tennis bracelet next to the computer and tilted her head. "They weren't there a minute ago."

"It's the Shadows," Andi explained. "They show up when trouble is about to find me."

"Well, they were a little late today," Fiona told her. "But I have something that the Shadows don't have."

Andi groaned when Fiona held up the shiny revolver with a wood grip. "Stop waving that thing around. You're making me nervous."

Fiona gave her an exasperated look and stuffed the gun into her bag. "Ignatius and I have been together for twenty years. Helluva guy, never complains, doesn't snore, doesn't fart, no expectations whatsoever. Load him up, pull the trigger, and he goes exactly where I tell him."

"Cripes, Fiona, you make a handgun sound like the perfect husband." At the moment, Andi had no use for a man or a revolver.

"Typical Yankee mentality. I grew up with rifles. Daddy took me hunting. Hell, Ignatius is a peashooter compared to the artillery in my old man's house. I'm a damn good shot, by the way. As long as you're with me, you're safe. Come on. Grab what you need, and we'll go to my place. You're not leaving my side until Eli solves the pendant-girl mystery and we know who wants to see you in hell."

CHAPTER FOURTEEN

ANDI

I N THE CAR, A HORRIBLE thought surfaced suddenly. "They never found my kidnapper. What if he broke in, looking for me?" Andi asked. She traced the dove tattoo on her hand. PTSD had clouded over all she remembered about her kidnapping except a big black car, a puppy, and the dove tattoo. But she'd never forget the pain from her parents' futile attempts to remove the tattoo.

"What? Why would your kidnapper from decades ago come after you?" Fiona drove like it was eighty degrees in her home state, sunny South Carolina, while Andi held on to the bar above the door, her eyes darting from the rearview to the side mirror.

"I think about him every time I see my hand," Andi explained. "And there's this little kid's voice. A new voice, saying, 'Key in lock, rattling, rattling,' as if she's being held hostage somewhere. Makes me wonder if she's been kidnapped and wants my help too." Andi shrugged. "As if I could help anybody," she added. Andi rubbed her face with her hands. "Damn, I'll never understand ghosts. Some answer sometimes. Others don't answer at all."

"Your kidnapper is probably in jail by now," Fiona told her.

"Maybe I'm the only one who ever got away, and it's eating away at his demented ego. Maybe he wants to finish what he began. What if he's still snatching girls?"

"You're not a girl anymore." Fiona grinned. "You'll be thirty-five and on your way to over the hill in twelve short days."

"Thanks for reminding me."

Snow drifted down in bread-crumb-size flakes. Hopefully, the one who broke into her house would slither back to whatever rock he'd been living under. But she had a feeling he wasn't finished with her yet.

"Tell me again why you had to buy that pendant." Fiona glanced sideways.

"It called to me."

"You better hope a box of Cocoa Krispies doesn't call to you in the grocery store. You'll end up with a year's supply."

"Very funny. I have my ghosts, you have your . . . Ignatius. But I don't have an arsenal of guns in my handbag. Jesus, you even named one of them. Wait. Do all your guns have names?" She clenched her teeth to keep them from chattering.

"No. Just Ignatius. That's to commemorate who I took it from." Fiona turned up the heat, and it blasted cold air at them. "Kid named Ignatius used to beat up my little brother Irv after school. Dumbass carried a gun in his backpack. One day, Bailey and I jumped good old Ignatius. Bailey, ever the older brother calling the shots, told me to beat the shit out of him. He assumed the little pissant would never tell anyone he got his stuffing ripped out by a girl. So I did. Meanwhile, he lifted the kid's gun. I left that little shit bawling in the marsh, praying to God a water moccasin would get him. No such luck, but he never bothered Irv again. Bailey said I'd earned the gun, and since then, Ignatius has never failed me."

Andi rolled her eyes. "What a guy."

Stubby brown roadside grass glittered as snow showers evolved to flakes flashing down from two directions like opposing forces. Slushy roads were on the verge of freezing, but Fiona drove on like a race car driver. That watched feeling again. She checked the side mirror and the backseat. Paranoia had set in like a giant tentacle wrapping itself around her.

CHAPTER FIFTEEN

MARIAH

ENNIE AND I SAT on the steps of our Holiday Inn, thinking about Rachel's fate and ours. Not much we could do for her, according to the Punishers. That blond had no idea what kind of pain Fisherman could inflict. A stray cat jumped out of a garbage can and scared the shit out of us. Then it came over and stared at the space where we should've been.

"Fisherman showed up at the Holiday Inn and said I had to come because you asked for me," I told Bennie.

"Ain't never ask for you," Bennie said. "I was dead long before he got you."

"Missed you so much it hurt, and I wanted to believe you might still be alive, so I went with him."

I picked up a couple bird feathers from the sidewalk and stroked them. Stray cat must've killed it. Funny, that old stray that hung around our Holiday Inn had lasted longer than I had.

"When I promised never to be on the streets again," I continued, "and not to tell a soul about him, he called me a liar. Took a long time, but I got the ropes off and escaped while he was sleeping. After he caught me the second time, I swore my daddy would pay a ransom. That pissed him off more. Told me he was doing God's work. Then he told me the story about his sister."

"Told me that story too," Bennie said. "Made me go through withdrawal in his attic, said he was purifying my soul."

Here I was, stuck between two worlds with a view of the world that only went backward to a place where I'd made my fatal mistake. Bennie and I had our anchors to the past. She kept a seraphinite stone in her pocket. Her angel rock, she called it. My anchor was a pocketful of ginkgo leaves. Moving forward didn't give us much hope. We had no real future. After all, we were dead.

The easy solution would have been for Bennie and me to murder our killer. Only we couldn't. Ghosts can watch, and if we have enough energy, we can move things, talk, and scare people, but we're like wisps of memories. Can a memory kill you? Metaphorically, maybe, but it can't damage a body. Dead people can't murder live people, no matter what all those dumb teenage horror movies say. Ghosts can't kill, because that would interfere with human justice, and that is forbidden. But we weren't clear about the line between interfering with justice and trying to save people. Not when it came to Rachel.

"I ain't worried about crossing over," Bennie muttered and disappeared.

When she just vanishes, it makes me feel so alone, and then I feel guilty for running away and leaving heartache in my wake. That's when I visit Mama. She probably expected me to breeze through my teenage years because school had always been easy for me, but I was determined not to become a nerd like Daddy. Anytime my father had free time—when people weren't accidentally cutting off their fingers and he'd have to sew them back on—he'd nag the hell out of Mama and me. He wanted me to attend an Ivy League school, just like him. Back then, I'd felt like a rag doll pulled in a direction I didn't want to go. Now, all I have is memories. Memories of belonging someplace.

I arrived home in time to see Mama drop the *State* newspaper onto the kitchen table and rub her eyes. The front page had a glamour shot of a pretty girl: ginger hair, straight teeth, happy smile. She'd disappeared. I could imagine the stuff going through my mother's head: predator on the loose, and my daughter's still missing. Too late, Mama.

She didn't need to worry about my body showing up on some hiking trail or in a ditch on the side of a road, but she had no way of knowing that. My mother folded the newspaper so the girl's face wasn't looking back at her. When the phone rang, Mama jumped, and the orange juice she was drinking splashed everywhere. Cursing, she blotted it up with a kitchen towel I'd bought for her at the school's Christmas Shop. I guess she remembered because she clutched it to her chest like a treasure, a cheap piece of cloth I'd embroidered with angels. The phone rang five times before she answered.

"Hello." She listened for a few minutes, squeezing her eyes shut. "Thank you for calling, Mrs. Sneed." Her voice was husky from holding back grief.

Sneed was the high school nurse. She was like everybody's mother: middle aged, overweight, gray-streaked brown hair. Nice, but you couldn't fake being sick with her.

Mama sighed. "We haven't heard anything yet." She swallowed hard. "No. Please don't mail her school records to me. That would be like saying she's not coming back. I can't . . . I can't erase Mariah that way." Her face all twisted, Mama listened for a moment. "No, I'll . . . please keep the records active."

Ah, so that's what they did when you disappeared? After some magic period—six months apparently—they begin to erase any trace of you. Damn. The refrigerator hummed. The dishwasher clicked into its next cycle. Seemed like the school was moving on, but like me, Mama was stuck in time. "The police have no leads. It's been six months without hearing anything." Mama broke down and started sobbing.

The nurse must have felt awful for calling. I felt like shit for running away.

Then my mother unloaded on poor Mrs. Sneed. About what it was like after miscarriages to try again and again for two years, how she'd spent the last months of the pregnancy flat on her back, how proud she is of me, that I'm so smart and have such a bright future. How she misses me, how empty the house is now. Mama looked like she'd aged ten years in those months.

She just kept crying inconsolably. That made me think of the times she'd comforted me. Scraped knees, lost contests, boys who didn't love me, two-faced girlfriends. She'd done her best. My father was never around much to help. He kept telling her I needed to stand on my own two feet. Well, I did. And now I was dead. Too late to tell Mama I was sorry. I couldn't tell her everything will be all right because I couldn't lie to her. And if they ever found me, Mama's world would come crashing down on her. I glanced outside at the rose trellis. Propped up against it, my bicycle gathered rust. Mama was a hell of a lot better off not knowing how my killer had carved patterns into my skin to make me do things. Besides, there wouldn't be much left of me by the time my body was found.

Gabby rubbed against her leg and made one of those cat noises, *thirrp*. She was probably missing me too. Before I left, Gabby had slept with me every night.

Mama picked up the cat and pressed her cheek to the soft, gray-striped fur. Her tears made little dark furrows, and Gabby purred like crazy.

Poor thing probably wasn't getting much attention.

I'd broken Mama's heart. I never knew closing that door would shut me out of her life forever.

She finally pulled herself together and grabbed a napkin to blot her face. "I truly believe she'll come home for Thanksgiving. I just hate to think about an empty chair." Her voice trailed off into a sob.

I wished I could spare her another disappointment. Mama thanked the nurse and hung up. Then she trudged upstairs to my room. My calendar was turned to the right month, but it showed blank spaces where reminders for concerts and parties should have been. Edward Bear lay on my pillow, right where I'd left him. He'd gone with me into tonsils surgery at Children's Hospital. Mama picked him up, hugged him, and cried harder. "Mariah's gone. She's been gone for so long. Please, God, make her come home. Whatever I did, help her forgive me, forgive her father. All she ever wanted was music."

Daddy had grounded me, so I took off. I'd gotten myself killed over a D in trigonometry. Now, I was trapped between death and the Other Side. Oh, I could go wherever I wanted, but suddenly, there wasn't a damn place I wanted to go but home for Thanksgiving dinner with my family.

Wind screamed around the corner of the house and rattled my window. Gently, Mama propped Edward Bear back on my pillow and walked downstairs.

Your conscience lives on long after your heart stops beating, and nothing, not even the needle Bennie and I had shared once, helps dead people forget. We only have the past.

CHAPTER SIXTEEN

FISHERMAN

GOD MIGHT FORGIVE ANDREA Wyndham, but Fisherman wasn't about to show any sympathy for that thieving Jezebel. It had taken him two days to find *his* pendants, and that woman wasn't selling them. He'd traced them from itemstogo.net to E-market. After he bid and lost on all four pendants, Fisherman had messaged the E-market seller and melted his heart with a sad story of stolen family heirlooms. Ten minutes of appealing to the man's sense of family, and the soft-hearted seller had given him the phone number of the lapidary company that won the four pendants.

He'd learned something at the seminary about persuasion before they'd labeled him mentally unfit for the priesthood. What did those sanctimonious fools know?

Fisherman used the same story on the lapidary man. "My Nana's house was robbed. Broke her heart. I'd do anything to get her pendants back. Nana's getting on now. She'll be ninety-four in a week. I bid on those pendants but lost the bids because my computer's slow as molasses in January."

But it was too late. The man had sold all four pendants at a gem show in Pennsylvania. Two were paid for in cash. The others were credit card purchases to Andrea Wyndham.

For a small fee, he intended to learn more about Andrea online. Already he'd found a phone number, email, and address that Andi had listed for the vendor's mailing list. He'd also discovered a phone number and address for her friend. Fiona had posted a promotional ad on Andi's Facebook newsfeed, which led him to her information. Really, these ladies should be more careful about their Facebook privacy settings.

"My, my. Look at this," he said pointing a finger at the computer screen. "Jezebel has filed for divorce. How convenient it will be to blame the ex-husband for whatever troubles befall her." He chuckled with delight. "DUI records. Even better."

Andrea's father lived in Australia. Good to know, since fathers tended to protect their daughters fiercely. Good fathers did. His father had never lifted a finger to protect Dee or his mother. No one would ever find that man. His bones had long ago vanished because Fisherman had used lye. Nana never knew what lay buried in her garden. She did comment, though, about it being a bad year for growing okra.

He peered into Jezebel's life, much like a surgeon, incising the body and laying open all the weak or diseased organs. Her loser husband owned a number of bankrupt companies. If something terrible were to happen to Andrea, Lance might receive a sizeable insurance settlement, which gave Lance a motive to kill Andrea.

The possibilities with this woman and her gambling and drinking husband were endless. Oh, how he'd make her suffer! That would satisfy him until Rachel became his next pendant.

CHAPTER SEVENTEEN

ANDI

ANDI GRITTED HER TEETH as she answered the phone.

"What the hell are you doing, filing a restraining order on me?" Lance yelled into her ear. "You bitch! Who do you think you are?"

"Did you throw my stuff out the window?"

"You got a restraining order because I threw a few things out the window? It's my fucking house! And you told the cops I broke in yesterday? What the hell are you talking about? I was in Jersey yesterday! You lying bitch!"

"You'd better put on your damn glasses and read the restraining order very carefully, because you just violated it!" Andi hit the red END icon, grabbed her coat, and drove to O'Brien's. She'd report his phone call later, and that should end his reign of terror forever. Maybe they'd lock up his ass.

Andi angled the car into a parking space on Gay Street in West Chester and walked down the cobblestone sidewalk toward O'Brien's. There it was again, that prickly feeling of being watched.

Think of something else, she decided. The borough had been a stop on the Underground Railroad during the Civil War. No parking problems in those days.

"You've got to learn how to be single again," Fiona had said. Lesson one: get to the restaurant without being hustled by panhandlers popping out of storefronts. A few people hurried down the sidewalk, an elderly couple, a man speaking Spanish on his phone, a coed. Hardly terrifying night stalkers. Since sundown, the temperature had dropped fifteen degrees. Bundled against the cold, a small group of twentysomethings loitered outside O'Brien's. Andi stepped over a pile of snow and jaywalked across the street. She peered into parked cars, studied the group outside the restaurant, and didn't notice anything suspicious.

O'Brien's advertised imported Irish antiques, a mahogany bar sent in pieces from County Cork and reassembled here, and of course, Guinness on tap. She looked forward to a good Irish meal. After entering through the carved wood door, she searched beyond the bar for Eli.

He'd found a table next to a gas fireplace. "Roads okay?" he asked, helping her out of her coat.

"Pretty dry," she said. "Where'd you come from? I mean, do you live around here?" She stunk at small talk.

"I live in Media. An old house that borders Ridley Creek State Park."

"Lots of deer meat for hunters there." Damn. She traced the cut glass of the table candle with a finger, trying to find meaningful topics. Nothing came to her.

"Yeah, they're so inbred, albinos are common. Park needs a tribe to weed the herd." He sipped something light yellow, probably a light beer.

A skinny, long-legged waitress in a little black dress appeared. She gave Eli a once-over and a flirty smile.

"Are you—you're not Adam Beach, are you?"

He laughed. "No, just a common Ojibwe from Minnesota. Adam's from Canada."

"Oh." The waitress blushed. "Can I get you something to drink?"

Andi ordered a glass of Riesling, and Eli asked for a ginger-ale refill.

"We have Guinness on tap," the waitress suggested. "The stout is a favorite."

"Sorry, alcohol's not on my diet." He patted his midsection. Could be a six-pack there if the way his shoulders filled the sweater was any indication.

"I'll get that right out." Miss Legs nodded and headed toward the bar.

Somehow, Andi had scored the best-looking guy in the room. Crewneck sweater, leather jacket, jeans, and cowboy boots. Eli's dark, shiny hair hung past his shoulders. No ponytail tonight.

"You're on a diet?" Andi asked.

"Not really, but it's a good excuse. Haven't had a drop of alcohol since my best friend died in a car crash. Drunk driver. I get my highs other ways, like sitting by the fire in an Irish restaurant, talking to a beautiful woman."

"And I'm sure you do that as often as possible," she said, wishing for a wittier reply. She wondered what Eli would dub her. Probably Dora the Explorer, in her baby blue ankle boots and a low-cut sweater with no cleavage to brag about.

"Downtime's a rare thing. Too many people disappear. Enough that I often have to choose between cases. Your pendants have given me a challenge, and I like a good mystery. Thanks for meeting me," Eli said.

"So, is this business or pleasure?"

He swirled the ice in his glass. "Both. I've verified that the pendant you're wearing is engraved with the face of a missing person.

The other one too. Thanks for the photos of the pendants and your copy of the sales receipt, by the way. Both girls were last seen in Columbia, South Carolina. A new Amber Alert about another missing girl their age was posted yesterday. And several other cold cases are labeled runaways in the Columbia area. People down there aren't happy about girls disappearing in a college town."

"What happens now?"

"Bernadette and Mariah's cases are still open," he said. "Limited leads on Mariah's case, almost nothing on Bernadette. I'll get a forensic work-up on the pendants."

"Is this really necessary? It could destroy the pendants. It'll feel like violating them—" She stopped herself before adding *all over again*, because that would suggest that she knew more than she'd told him, and then she'd have to explain that she could communicate with ghosts, and then he'd think she was crazy.

"Most people would give the pendants to the police and forget about it. Those necklaces must have hit an emotional chord with you."

She opened her menu and scanned the entrées. "Somebody named Peter Rockford called to buy the pendants."

Her deflection tactic worked. Eli looked up. "And according to Fiona, you said they weren't for sale. You have caller ID? Has he called again?"

"Only once. ID read 'Unknown.' Southern accent. He said the pendants were stolen from his grandmother and then sold on E-market. The vendor did tell me he got them there."

Eli grunted and held up his menu. "E-market's a dead end. I checked. I've talked to the sheriff in Columbia. We may have to get a search warrant for your phone records."

"It may not be worth the trouble. He only called once."

He looked over the top of the menu. "Those girls disappeared without a trace, and yet someone connected the pendants to you?

That's suspicious. Maybe the girls were abducted. If you were kidnapped, wouldn't you want—"

"Stop right there, Eli. You obviously did your homework on me."

His menu came down. "That break-in yesterday was suspicious, too."

Andi shot him an annoyed look. "What else has Fiona told you?"

"Only what I need to know to understand the context of the case. And she's made it very clear that if anything happens to you, she's gonna fire a round into me where the sun don't shine."

"She'd threaten the devil. What about the missing girls?"

He went back to his menu. "Mariah, age seventeen, missing six months, daughter of a prominent hand surgeon. Argument with her father made her run away."

Except for the argument part, Andi already knew that. "Had to be more than an argument with her father," she said. Their drinks arrived, they ordered, and Miss Legs talked them into Colcannon soup and goat-cheese salads.

"Anything else I can get for you?" she asked, tilting her pelvis in Eli's direction.

Nice touch, Andi thought. Probably improved tips. "Water would be nice. Very, very cold water," she told her. The waitress took off like a golden retriever to fetch.

Eli choked on his ginger ale and coughed into a napkin. "Didn't know cold showers worked with women. You're very funny."

"The cold water's not for me," she said. "That little black dress of hers doesn't leave much to the imagination."

He held up his hands. "I'm not going there. More than enough entertainment sitting across from me."

She liked a man who understood subtle sexual humor. Intuitive men made great lovers, she'd heard. Lance had no intuition. He'd been hit-and-run in bed.

The waitress returned with a tall glass of water. "I put lots of ice in it," she assured them. "Oh, I love the dove tat on your hand. With that faded wing, makes it look like he's flying."

"The faded part is where I tried to remove it." Andi decided Miss Legs had become a pain and was glad when she left to check on their dinner.

"Your kidnapper marked you. That's common in sex trafficking."

"Fiona really needs to keep her mouth shut."

"I'm glad she told me. What happened?"

Andi squeezed lemon into her water and stirred. "When I was four, I followed a man who said he'd give me a free puppy. Snatched me right out of my own backyard while my mom was on deadline for a news story."

Eli buttered a piece of bread and popped it into his mouth, eyes on her, waiting to hear more.

"Somehow I escaped. I don't remember much. I was unconscious when they found me."

She was rambling down a back road, avoiding any turns toward the day that had changed her family forever. "I never bare my soul before the entrée." Her best attempt at being witty to cover being evasive. Pretty weak. "So, you're pretty good at data diving. What would I find if I googled you?"

"Nothing," he said, too quickly. He reached across the table and took her hand. "Sorry, occupational hazard, the questions. Wow. Your hand's cold."

His hand was big, warm, and gentle. She removed hers to stab a piece of lettuce and drag it through some dressing. In the back of her mind, the idea of Eli's snooping flopped around like a dying fish on a pier. No eye contact, she decided, and stared into the blue flames.

He motioned with his spoon toward his bowl. "Try the soup. It's good."

Suddenly, he was very busy, stirring hot soup. Typical man, more interested in his stomach. Warm dinner, warm body, warm hand, a warm pair of socks. That's how her mind worked from warm body to warm socks. Sex versus socks. Three days ago, the socks would've won. She picked up her spoon. A woman had to keep some things a mystery, like a dysfunctional family and whispering girls.

"So, who are you really? Guardian angel, spirit guide, ghost of Christmas past?" She shot him her best imitation of a flirty grin. "On second thought, let's not talk about spirits."

He gave her a quizzical look. "Nothing spiritual about me." He shook his head. "I don't buy into that supernatural baloney."

In the kitchen a tray crashed to the floor. Silence descended over the restaurant.

"Hope that wasn't our dinner," Andi said. She tasted the soup. Earthy, thick, a bit salty. "I have this feeling I'm supposed to advocate for the girls. Do you think someone could've taken them as hostages?"

"No ransom note, and Mariah's family is wealthy. I take it you believe in spirits?"

Spoon poised midair, she nodded. "When you find people, are they always alive?"

"Not always. The ones I track into the woods are the saddest. I can't even imagine the terror of dying alone, too cold, too hot, drowned, with only the trees as witnesses. Suicides are tough too. The despair that brought them to that decision." He shook his head.

"Do they ever come back to thank you for finding them?"

"Not when they're dead." He gave a short laugh. "Haven't seen or heard from any lost souls lately."

A second later, his glass tipped, and water poured into his lap. His arm was nowhere near it. Nor hers, nor the waitress's. Girlish laughter came from the pendant around her neck. *Neat trick*, she told the girl silently.

Eli looked up from mopping water in his lap and motioned for a waitress to get more napkins. "Very cold water. Thanks a lot."

He gave her a lopsided smile, and they lapsed into laughter. A man who could laugh at himself and minimize an awkward situation—she liked that. Lance would have made a spectacle of himself by losing his temper.

When Eli moved to the dry chair next to him, she slid over a seat to face him. "No idea how I did that," he said.

"Maybe you didn't."

He frowned. "What do you mean?"

"Let's just say I attract accidents, and leave it at that." She handed him her napkin.

"It's been one of those nights," the waitress told them as she towel-dried the table. A waiter arrived with two plates cooling in his hands. When the table was ready, he set their entrées down. Miss Legs glanced at Eli's crotch, then looked up. "More water?"

"None for me," Eli said.

"He's already been baptized." Andi turned sideways and stifled a laugh.

Eli pointed at her. "It's not that funny."

She held a fresh napkin over her mouth, laughing harder than she had in a long time. If she didn't stop, she'd look like one of those LMAO emojis. "You're right. It won't be funny if you get frostbite. Oh God. I shouldn't have said that." She dabbed at her eyes. Eye makeup must be smeared to watercolors, her face a Monet, blue period. She straightened up. "That was rude. Sorry."

He stuffed a piece of salmon in his mouth. "Eat before somebody spills something."

"How did you get into this line of work?" she asked, cutting and arranging the boxty—a concoction of chicken, sauce, and mushrooms inside a rolled potato pancake—so it wouldn't dribble down her chin.

"In the fugitive squad, I discovered my talent for finding lost people. When I left the Philadelphia field office, I decided to stay in the area. Mainline people pay very well."

"Your family still lives on the reservation?"

He nodded. "Where are you from?"

"You didn't google that? Lewes, Delaware. Historic little seashore town."

"Family still there?"

Andi held up a finger until she'd swallowed. "So, you like living in Pennsylvania?"

His fork stopped short of his mouth. He gave a barely perceptible nod as if checking off a list of things she wouldn't tell him so he could find out later.

A muffled ringtone from her purse saved her from more questions. She dug for the cell and looked at the ID. "My alarm company." She touched the screen. "Hello."

A minute later, she jammed the phone into her bag. "There's a fire at my house. I have to go." Andi shoved her chair back and tossed the napkin on the table.

Eli was already on his feet. "We'll take my car. Get you there faster and safer." He flagged the waitress and stuffed a wad of bills into her hand. "Keep the change."

Andi's heart pounded. "Everything I own is in that house."

CHAPTER EIGHTEEN

ANDI

ELI LIT OUT OF THE parking garage and raced down Market Street toward Franklin Township with Andi giving directions.

"After the burglary last night, police told me not to stay there. I live in a quiet neighborhood, always felt safe there before. Been living alone for months with no problems. The middle-school kids must have grown up, because they're not blowing up mailboxes anymore." God, she was babbling like an idiot, anything to ward off rising panic. A break-in yesterday, today a fire.

The borough blurred by. A car with one headlight. Cars idling at the McDonald's drive-through. A kid in dark clothing with only the backs of his sneakers reflecting on the narrow shoulder.

"Had any electrical repairs lately?" Eli asked as he made a right turn.

"No."

"Maybe a pet knocked over a lamp."

"I don't have any pets. But I wouldn't mind a big dog that barks loudly and greets me when I come home instead of a husband threatening me with guns." Damn. She hadn't meant to tell him that. But then again, Fiona had probably already filled him in.

Eli slowed for a red light and drove through the intersection. "When Lance threatened you with a gun, you filed a police report, right?"

"Don't start," Andi told him. "I've already heard it all from Fiona. Change the locks and the alarm codes, get a security bank box. Don't let him get away with anything."

His silence spoke loudly. He sped past the shopping center with an Acme sign with an unlit *A*, then a marshy stream where geese and mallards nested in spring, past an antiques store, an industrial park. Andi waited for the lecture on safety and how she should report people who aimed guns at her.

"Besides the man at your door, any other visitors or phone calls that were unusual?"

"The guy who wanted my pendants and the jackass looking for my husband. I already reported that guy. Hell, my nosy neighbor Gladys probably bought a telescope to keep an eye on my house for me. Only problem is, if she doesn't know things, she either creates them or embellishes them. When I leave town and she collects my mail, I hear all kinds of wild tales."

She smelled the smoke from the Pike. God! The street was cordoned off, but her driver's license and his P.I. license got them past the police roadblock. When they climbed out of the car, her hand went to her mouth. Smoke poured from an upstairs window. She prayed it was only the bedroom, but if they were hosing it down, water might leak below, ruining her wood floors. From where she stood, it smelled like the inside of an old Band-Aid, plastic and chemical and sour.

The engines of the fire trucks revved and faded, cutting through the night air. Firefighters in heavy yellow suits lumbered across her yard, shouting to each other. A hose slithered across her lawn, a huge python, up the side of the house and into a broken window. Why just the bedroom? What did that mean? No signs of fire in the living room below. But the house would reek of smoke. The thought of some stranger setting a fire in her bedroom dropped like a rock into her stomach. Hell, if she'd been oblivious on a sleeping pill, the person who started the fire could've killed her and erased all evidence. She'd never bought a second-story safety ladder to use, so there would've been no escaping except jumping out the window and breaking her neck.

She bit her lip, struggling not to cry. "This wasn't an accident."

Eli scanned the scene. "Somebody's after something." He put an arm around her shoulder.

Andi looked up at him. "Somebody is not going to stop until he gets it. Is he?"

Before Eli could agree, nosy Gladys came racing toward them, her shiny face looking like she'd applied five coats of Oil of Olay. "Oh, honey, how awful! I'm so sorry this happened. Your Aunt Nancy came to visit you today. It's a shame you weren't home."

Andi stared at the woman. "If I ever had an Aunt Nancy, I never met her."

"Seemed like a nice lady, said she's a missionary and just came back from New Zealand. Said she hadn't seen you since you were a baby."

Eli spoke to Gladys. "Can you describe Aunt Nancy?"

"Oh sure, hon." Her eyes moved from Eli to Andi, and she winked at Andi. "Got yourself a better one this time."

"I'm a private investigator. So, what did Aunt Nancy look like?"

Gladys didn't miss the hint of impatience in his voice. She answered quickly. "Aunt Nancy had a beautiful full-length mink coat and a Louis Vuitton handbag. Really expensive-looking boots, although the poor woman had fat ankles—maybe diabetes—and I could swear her gray hair under the cute little red beret was a wig.

Glasses, green eyes, a ruddy complexion. I got a faint whiff of mothballs coming off that coat," Gladys said. "Otherwise, she smelled like she'd taken a bath in some gloriously expensive floral perfume."

"Thanks. Did you see anyone come in or out of the house?" Eli flashed her a smile.

Gladys pushed her glasses up on her nose. "Never saw 'em. Sneaky as all get-out. Must've gotten in from the back of the house. Called 9-1-1 soon as I saw smoke. I promise to keep an eye on the house. Right now, I'm freezing to death out here." Clutching her chenille bathrobe, the gossip took off.

"Eli, that woman has a screw loose. Gladys is not a reliable witness." She watched Gladys swing her front door open and disappear inside.

"Interesting comment about the mothball smell," Eli said. "Did that guy who threatened to hurt somebody smell like mothballs?"

"No. That guy smelled like cigars. Fiona thought he was either a loan shark or a bookie."

Oh God! Her beautiful house turned to a big black ice sculpture with a hole in the upstairs bedroom window. If she'd awakened to flames consuming the bedroom and a smoke-filled, dark hallway that ended in stairs, not one soul would've heard her screams when she tumbled down the steps. People closed their windows in the winter. Smoke inhalation might've killed her anyway.

She would not cry. Andi watched the last gasps of smoke belch from her bedroom window. "Anyone could've set the fire. Anyone. Even that guy." She pointed to a reporter taking notes on the other side of the road. "Hell, maybe my kidnapper came here to finish what he began?"

"That was a long time ago, Andi, so it's doubtful, but I'm not ruling anything out. If it was your kidnapper, I'll find him." Eli scanned the scene, then casually took out his cell phone and snapped pictures of the reporter.

A police officer approached them, and Andi gave him what he needed to file a report. She stared at her house, at the ladders to the upstairs window, the water freezing on the holly branches like candle drippings.

She loved that house. Tonight she'd be afraid to close her eyes. She'd pissed off somebody. Fear was strangling her like a rope, jerking her back into danger again and again. Somebody wanted her dead.

Eli touched Andi's shoulder. "Andi, you're not in a good place. How can I help?"

Bring back the dead, take back her stupid decision to push away her family, restore her house to the way it was. Not likely. He stood in the glare of lights, hair blowing into his face.

She squeezed his hand. "Nothing anyone can do," she said. "Some things in that room aren't replaceable."

He blinked hard as if blanking unpleasant memories of his own. "Maybe it's not as bad as you think. You're alive. That's what's important. If you'd been inside, Fiona might be looking for your dental records."

Firefighters reeled in hoses. Ladders cranked. The smell of wet, burned wood, scorched wires, and melted plastic lingered. Soot on the side of the house reminded her of the Shadows. Yellow eyes blinking—the Shadows were here! Why were they hovering around the reporter as if they were taking notes too?

"You're not safe here."

Andi glanced from her house to Eli. "But if I leave, I may have nothing to come back to." She would not cry.

A heavyset firefighter approached. Bags under his eyes and a slow gait suggested too many nights on late shift. He smelled of woodsmoke too, but she didn't like the scent on him. "You're Mrs. Wyndham?"

Andi nodded. She would not cry, would not show weakness.

"Rich Conway, Franklin Township Fire and Rescue. I'm a fire investigator." Then he glanced at Eli. "And you are?"

Eli showed his identification. "Is there evidence of arson?"

Conway didn't answer and instead turned to Andi. "Appears the damage is isolated to your bedroom. Someone wrote on your bathroom mirror. Red lipstick. 'Give back what is not rightfully yours.' Any idea who might do that or what it means?"

"Oh God." Acid churned in her stomach. She looked up at Eli. "It's the pendants."

The investigator scribbled a note on his pad.

She explained the call from Peter Rockford.

"You've contacted the police about that?" Conway wrote more notes.

"They know," Eli told him. "Unfortunately, I suspect Peter Rockford is an alias. No idea who he really is or where to find him. If there's no other information you need from Ms. Wyndham, I'll take her to a friend's house."

"Good idea." Then the firefighter turned back to Andi. "I'm really sorry, ma'am. Watch yourself, now. We'll let you know when you can pick up the NFIRS report. And by the way, we replaced the missing battery in the master bedroom's smoke alarm."

She felt like a frightened animal fleeing, desperately trying to outrun the flames, watching her life turn to ash. Maybe this will end if I find closure for the girls, she decided.

A final glance at the house, and Andi followed Eli to his car. Once they were inside, she unclasped the pendant's chain from her neck and took the other pendant from her purse. For a few seconds, she held them, wondering if she'd ever see them again, hoping they could just take the bone out of the bezel, get what evidence they needed and return them to her. *Goodbye, girls,* she told them silently and handed the pendants to him. "Take good care of them. If they could talk to you, they'd tell you a lot."

He put them into his pocket. "I'll do my best, Andi. Come on. Let's get your car at the restaurant, and I'll follow you to Fiona's."

When they drove away, the faint sobs of a young girl came from Eli's pocket.

CHAPTER NINETEEN

ANDI

A T FIONA'S PLACE, ELI got out of his car and held both of Andi's hands in his, a sympathetic expression on his face. "You gonna be all right?"

"Yeah. Thanks, Eli. Take good care of my pendants," Andi told him, and she wondered if the girls would talk to him. Probably not. "Let me know if anything odd happens."

"Like a burglary or a house fire or someone impersonating Aunt Nancy?" he asked. "Maybe the pendants are bad luck."

"No, they're not bad luck." Eli hadn't heard the whispering or seen the blinking eyes at the gem show.

She opted for a quick hug, and he drove off, promising to call the next day.

Fiona's little house welcomed her with heat humming, lights glowing, and the Siamese, sitting sphinx-style on the arm of the sofa. Honky Cat eyed her and blinked. Andi petted the silky gray head and rubbed her chest, hoping to coax a purr, but the cat hissed, swatted, and strutted out of the room.

"Wonder what's up with her." Fiona pressed the warped front door shut. "Isn't he the nicest man? Are you going to see him again?"

"Fiona, someone set my bedroom on fire." Andi plopped down at the table.

"Holy shit!" At the pantry, Fiona pulled out a box of Chardonnay and two plastic wine glasses with flamingos on the stems. "How bad was the fire?" she asked.

"It didn't burn to the ground. Isolated to the bedroom." That's where she kept the photo album her mother had made with all Andi's happy childhood memories, the ones when her mother had been home.

Newspaper clippings about her mother's accomplishments were in another album, also stored in the bedroom. The camera her mother had used for features that won her Pulitzers was in her closet. Her mother had given it to Andi as a birthday present, hoping Andi might become a journalist.

What a disappointment she'd been to her parents. But she would not cry, would not show weakness. Fiona performed the ice-cube-tray ritual.

Drown it, beat it into submission, gather the victims from the sink. Grudgingly, the tray surrendered the cubes. She plunked one into each glass, filled them, and handed one to Andi. Fiona raised hers in a salute.

"To firefighters."

Andi halfheartedly raised hers. "Somebody wrote, 'Give back what is not rightfully yours,' on my bathroom mirror."

Fiona stared. "It's those pendants."

"Yeah, but Eli has them now. Things have to get better for me tomorrow," she said. It sounded very Scarlet O'Hara.

Unfortunately, there was no Rhett Butler in her life, just a handsome private investigator and a feisty jazz piano player with a gun named Ignatius.

"Am I missing something?" Fiona propped a hand on one hip, waiting. "Why the hell are you so calm? You need to talk to that counselor again."

"I'm trying really hard to keep it together. Too damn much shit thrown at me. A burglary and a fire. Showing weakness is not going to make me stronger!"

"Says who?" Fiona stared at her across the table.

"Says my father, the drill sergeant. I've been bullied all my life. This is not new."

"Starting a fire in your bedroom is not bullying. Somebody tried to kill you! And besides, I don't think I like your father any better than I liked Lance."

"Well, that makes two of us. And don't you dare tell Eli those pendant girls talk to me. He doesn't believe in that stuff."

"Slow down, woman!" Fiona slapped the table and glasses jumped. "You're in denial."

"I am not. I'm in self-preservation mode. While you're at the computer, check on Eli. He says you won't find anything. I bet you will."

"Wish I could just bury things the way you do. You really don't want to talk?"

"No." Andi picked up a magazine and sank into a chair. She would not cry, would not show weakness. But she was damn close. "Sometimes, denial means survival. He could've set the fire while I was sleeping, and I'd be burned to an unrecognizable pile of protoplasm."

Fiona caught Andi sniffling and rushed over to hug her. "Andi, I'm so sorry."

"It's not fair," she blubbered out.

"No, it's not." Fiona patted her back. "Hey, what about the pendants? Did you lose them?"

"Eli's checking the pendants for DNA." She sniffed. "The lab will ruin the pendants, and I'll never see or hear from the girls again."

"Good Lord." Fiona gave her a hug. "Tell you what. I'll fit the girls' photos in my bootlegging great-aunt's locket so you can wear them both. Okay?"

Andi nodded. Sweet Fiona, always fixing things in her life.

"Peter Rockford is hellbent on getting those pendants. Makes me wonder why." Fiona leaned over the laptop and started typing. She hit the printer button and studied the menu for a few seconds.

A spider was heading for Andi's purse, with Honky in hot pursuit, when the cat suddenly lost interest. "Get that spider, Honky," Andi said. Once it crawled into her purse, she'd never find it until it bit her.

Instead, Honky snagged the string of beads from her purse and dragged it across the floor, growling. "Come on, Honky. Drop it." Andi bent over her, but a throaty rumble and a hiss convinced her to back off. "Make your cat drop that necklace, Fiona."

Before anyone could grab her, Honky pounced on the necklace and bit it. The fur on her tail tripled in size. She puffed up like a bird in a snowstorm and flew through the air as if an electric current had zapped her. Glaring at the beads, Honky shook the hurt out of her head.

"Poor Honky." Fiona picked her up. "Did you crack a tooth? Let Mama see." She lifted the cat and tried to pry her mouth open.

Honky struggled like she was going to explode until Fiona set her free. Then she hunkered back down, pale blue eyes fixed on the necklace, growling. "You're scared of a bunch of ugly old beads, you silly cat." Fiona frowned. "Hey, you think she's hurt?"

"Her skull's hard as a rock," Andi told her. "She could have a head-on with a freight train and survive. She's so mean she'd dent the locomotive."

"See," Fiona crooned, dangling the necklace in front of the cat. "It won't hurt you." Honky arched her back, hissed, and raced under the sofa.

Fiona bent down and peered under the sofa. "It's okay, Honky. You can come out. You know Mama would never let anything hurt you." She turned to Andi. "Something funny is going on with that necklace. Honky's never acted like this before. Maybe somebody died wearing it?"

Andi winced. "I hope not. It doesn't talk like the pendants, but it did slither through the snow as if somebody I couldn't see was controlling it." She held it up and studied it, then shrugged. "Got me," she said and buried it at the bottom of her handbag.

Fiona pulled the cat from under the sofa, and with Andi holding her, examined Honky's teeth. "Nothing broken," she said. Honky combined her wiggly act with claws and took off. Andi headed for the bathroom and some peroxide for the cat scratches.

Fiona watched the cat tear down the hall. "Sure doesn't seem hurt." Then she returned to the laptop. A half hour later and a dozen copies wasted, Fiona shouted, "Voilà!" and handed Andi an ornate silver locket with the girls' photos inside.

When Andi opened the locket, Mariah was crying.

Key in lock, rattling, rattling. Climb the golden tree.

The fairy-tale child's voice. Just what she needed.

What does that mean? Tell me! Andi hated sounding so grumpy.

No answer.

A voice she recognized spoke to her next. *He's hunting, ma'am,* Mariah whispered.

CHAPTER TWENTY

MARIAH

EVERYBODY ELSE NEEDED BADGES to get inside the crime lab. Not us. The morning after Andi's fire, Bennie and I camped out, waiting for experts to examine our pendants. Andi had suggested the reporter they saw last night at the fire was Fisherman. I know she wasn't serious, but it *was* him! According to the Punishers, we couldn't tell her, or it would be interfering with human justice. Wish there was some kind of user manual for spirits, so we'd know for sure when we were interfering. Eli took pictures, but they won't do any good. Fisherman can look like anybody he wants to. The man has all kinds of costumes and makeup too. Like a con artist. A deadly con artist.

Eli followed a man wearing a white coat through three rooms, swiping cards at each door until they reached the lab. "Dr. Arthur" was embroidered on his coat pocket.

Brick walls painted white, a couple of windows—the room where Dr. Arthur worked was boring except for the machines. This big cylinder thing that resembled an overweight telescope stood in one corner. A pistol lay on the counter next to it. Computers and laptops had screens with charts and graphs and information that might as well be in Greek. A shelf full of skulls stared down at Bennie and me. Well, at least somebody had found *their* heads. Two huge pieces of equipment that reminded me of copy machines sat on tables. Wires and tubes snaked from them to the wall where they were attached.

"Hey, Bennie," I said. "Imagine the instruction manual for these monsters. You probably need a special clearance to read it."

She wrinkled her nose. "I sure as hell couldn't work here. Hit the wrong button, and some machine blows up in my face." Bennie peered into a microscope and turned up her mouth. "I hated them science labs where you had to do stupid stuff like watch yeast grow."

Rows of bookshelves held red and green and black manuals. We found a copy of *Gray's Anatomy.* There was this basket thing that looked like a french fry cooker. I didn't want to think how they used it. Measuring tools and test tubes and big lamps on long bendable metal arms spread out on counters.

"Eli, haven't seen much of you around here lately," Dr. Arthur said. "Those rich Mainline ladies paying you enough to find husbands that skip out on child support?"

Eli handed him our pendants. "I'm consulting for a South Carolina sheriff," he said. "Sheriff's got a DA breathing down his neck and one pissed off hand surgeon who wants his missing daughter back. Only evidence the sheriff has comes from security cameras and a bunch of teenagers who swear they've seen her."

How dare he refer to my dad as a pissed off hand surgeon! I elbowed Eli's mug, and coffee spilled on his shirt. He cursed. I smiled as a big brown stain mushroomed on his white shirt.

"Rough night, huh." Arthur raised an eyebrow, watching Eli mop coffee with tissues. "Where'd you get these?" He turned each pendant over in his hand and studied the writing on the bezels.

"Got them from a beautiful woman recently separated. A friend of a friend of hers brought me into this. Either some jackass is using missing persons posters to sculpt faces, or we have some weird connection between MPs. Those etched images match missing girls from South Carolina."

"What? Recently separated, beautiful woman!" I shouted. "I don't trust Eli."

"I think he wants to hook up with Andi," Bennie told me, and she made her fingers into a gun and shot him. "I hate cops."

"Think the ex may have something to do with the missing girls?"

"Not likely." Eli crumpled the stained tissue and tossed it into the trash. "Actually, I think this lady's going to help me find those girls."

"So you expect to get lucky with the lady?" Arthur had a stupid smile on his face. "Figures, there's a woman involved," he mumbled and put the pendant under a microscope. Then he picked up a metal tool like my dentist used for scraping plaque and bent over the microscope, hand poised to pry out the bone.

Eli had been leaning against the door. He stepped closer to watch. "Any way you can keep from totally destroying the pieces? I told the lady I'd do my best to return them intact."

"You're kidding, right?" Arthur's voice was muffled as he hunched over the microscope, probing between bone carving and metal bezel.

"I'm not kidding. She was kidnapped at age four and feels connected to the missing girls."

"Uh-huh." Dr. Arthur was concentrating on what he saw under that microscope.

"When I contacted the hand surgeon, he offered me unlimited funds to find his daughter. Had to turn the job down. Conflict of interest. Six months with no answers, and the man is furious with the sheriff. Tell you one thing. His anger won't endear him to any P.I."

I must've looked sad because Bennie said, "At least your daddy's looking for you. I ain't remember mine. I was an infant. And Mama's new man . . . let's just say I left home because of what he wanted from me."

When I looked around the room, the horror sank in. Here I was, standing in the kind of lab that tries to connect dead people to living people. I felt pretty shitty about what my parents must be going through.

Arthur looked up. "Was the beautiful, recently separated woman's kidnapper ever found?"

"No, and it broke up her family. She's a nice lady, fairly fragile right now. I could see myself by her side in front of a fire." Eli looked around the room. He didn't seem comfortable there. Neither did we. I think he was trying not to breathe in too much. It smelled like formaldehyde, which reminded me of dissecting frogs in seventh grade. Not a happy memory.

Dr. Arthur gave a huffy little breath. "O-kay. White gloves treatment." He worked the tool under an edge. "She'll never know I touched it. My training included putting Humpty Dumpty back together again."

"I don't have that kind of training, but I can make a mean omelet." Eli found a paper towel, ran water on it and dabbed at the coffee stain.

"Morning-after omelets. I remember those, about two kids and five grandchildren ago." Arthur shifted the pendant under the fancy scope. "I've necropsied pets before. Agent Miller's cat killed himself over some grapes. Then there was an azalea-eating Bichon. Autopsy favors. But this is the first time I've examined a bone pendant."

Dr. Arthur couldn't fit his metal probe under the bezel. From his labored breathing, he was getting mad. The guy sounded like a heart-attack candidate. I hoped he didn't die before he figured out what he had under the microscope.

"Did the lady tell you what kind of bone this is?" Dr. Arthur asked.

"Vendor said cow bone."

"Hard to tell," Arthur said as he levered the probe between the bone and the bezel and gently rocked it. No luck. He picked up the pendant, turned it over and pushed on the bone. The guy must have thought a little force might weaken the glue and make the carving come loose. It didn't budge. "She's a pretty little thing."

"Maybe Arthur's okay." I grinned at Bennie. "He knows a pretty girl when he sees one."

"We were all pretty. Glue won't come loose," she said. "He uses Super Glue." We knew that for a fact from spying on him. Bennie and I had stood in the doorway of his workroom. Smiling, he'd sat hunched over a metal table. That's when we saw him fitting bone into the bezel. By the time he got around to gluing it, we were bawling. We watched him carefully inscribe our pendant sister's name on the silver, his own perverted monogram. I started sniffling, just remembering. Bennie put an arm around my shoulder and shushed me.

Eli gabbed away. "My friend Doug bet me it was yak bone."

"I don't believe this is yak bone."

"You've autopsied yaks too?" Eli had a deadpan expression.

Arthur gave him the side-eye. "When I was in Tibet, I did encounter jewelry made of yak bone. Where'd you say this came from?"

"Local gem show, but the seller purchased them from E-market. Somebody tried to buy them from Andi and fed her some bullshit line about how they were stolen from his family."

"Did you follow up?"

Eli nodded. "Guy gave the name Peter Rockford, had a Southern accent. Caller ID listed him as 'Unknown,' so I checked her phone records. He made the call from a burner phone."

"Prepaid cell phones, bane of our existence." Arthur shook his head and set the metal probe on the counter. "Polymer from hell." He removed the pendant from the microscope. "I'll need to dissolve the adhesive and pull this out. It appears to be dyed. Seems like there's layers of other material too. A chemist can track down the materials, but that will take some time."

Eli pursed his lips. "Andi was hoping to get them back tomorrow. Last thing she said was, if they could talk, they'd have a lot to say. So, tell me if they start talking to you." He flashed a lopsided smile.

That was it. *We were people*, I shouted at Eli. *We still are!*

Bennie kept trying to hug me, telling me it was okay, but it wasn't. Dr. Arthur had compared the pendants to necropsies of dogs and cats. Eli just wanted to hook up and make some money. Meanwhile, our killer stalked Rachel, and we were afraid to tell Andi because of the Punishers.

I pushed a beaker to the end of the shelf and it shattered.

"Damn," Dr. Arthur muttered. "Must be seismic activity."

"I didn't feel anything," Eli said.

Arthur found a manila folder and handed it to Eli. "Dustpan disappeared this week, borrowed and not returned." Then he looked thoughtful. "We have a new forensic anthropologist who specializes in identifying bones from different species. I'll call her. If we know what kind of bone, you might be able to track the sale."

Not dogs or cats. Dead people, I whispered. *We were people. Figure out who killed us. And you'd better hurry it up, because Rachel is next.*

CHAPTER TWENTY-ONE

MARIAH

B ENNIE AND I SAT side by side on a counter next to a big machine with a metal arm that looked like it belonged in a dentist's office. "A bone expert. That's cool." I felt much better after breaking that beaker. "As long as they don't send a priest who does exorcisms." I elbowed Bennie, and she giggled. We'd seen *The Exorcist*, and neither one of us wanted anything to do with the devil. It's the Punishers we need to worry about. They're like the Supreme Court in the spirit world. It's not like they put you in jail or something. If they sentence you, you might never be seen again, Bennie says. But nobody knows their rules for sure. Even when you're dead, you aren't safe.

"So that bone specialist works for NMS Labs?" Eli asked. He was scrubbing away at his shirt again.

Dr. Arthur nodded. "Yeah. She's board certified."

"Hey, that's what the TV series *Bones* was based on," I said, enjoying eavesdropping. "Heard that lady doctor worked at Ground Zero after 9/11."

I hopped off the counter and looked at my pendant through the microscope. Nothing much to see. Some lines and dots.

Both men were busy scooping up glass with manila folders. Eli was bent over. If I'd been alive, I would've given him a swift kick in the butt.

"This room is freezing." Eli blew on his hands and rubbed them together.

I was standing so close to Eli I could've grabbed a pair of scissors and cut off his precious braid. Bennie plopped into a computer chair and chewed her nails. "They can't do nothing 'cause they have no idea who killed us. We gotta work on that."

Lab coat billowing like sails, a woman walked in. "Morning, Dr. Arthur. What's up?" She had long jet-black hair and dark brown eyes. Bone expert, he'd called her. Why would anyone choose that career? What did she do when she was a kid, play with skeletons instead of Barbies?

Dr. Arthur introduced Sally Wang to Eli and pointed at the pendants. "We have two missing girls' faces on pendants. Can you tell us anything about the bone?"

Sally put my pendant, then Bennie's under the microscope. I didn't see how she could tell anything from that.

"How would you tell yak bone from dog bone or cow bone?" Eli asked. "Is there some kind of test?" He leaned against the counter.

She pulled her long hair away from her face and tucked it into a hairnet. "Yes, there is," she answered, peering into the microscope, adjusting it. "You can't tell a cow bone from a dog bone? Don't invite me to any barbecues at your house. Eli Lake, you disappoint me." Behind the scope, she had this big grin.

Dog bone. That was funny. I liked this lady.

"I'm a cat person, actually," Eli told her.

"It's not ivory. No Schreger lines. I'm seeing evidence of the Haversian system and pitting. Species, I'll have to work on." She removed the pendant from under the microscope and turned my pendant, then Bennie's, over in her hand. "Names inscribed into the silver. That's convenient. Handwriting looks the same, but we'll have an expert look at that." She picked up the metal probe and tried to nudge the bone out of the bezel. No luck for her either. Sally continued to poke and prod. "Where'd you get these?"

"Lady bought them at a gem show at the boys' boarding school on Route 30," Eli told her. "The faces belong to missing girls from South Carolina."

"A woman involved," Sally mumbled. "Figures."

Bennie gave a low whistle. "Man's got himself a reputation, don't he?"

Eli scowled. "You act like I'm some kind of Casanova."

Sally didn't look up. She'd wedged a scalpel between the bone and the silver and was working it around the edges.

"I have a friend who works in the Philly field office. Your nickname up there was Agent Abercrombie, and your omelets are world famous."

He raised his hands in mock surrender. "Cut me some slack. I'm not FBI anymore."

Sally's voice was muffled. "Definitely not resin. No marks from a cutting tool. Two missing girls." She looked thoughtful and put the pendant down. "I'll run some tests. And yes, Lake, there are methods to determine what kind of bone."

She went on about bone morphology and transition from cortical bone to spongy bone, something about amelogenins, gene analysis, and histological or DNA primers. Sounded like my father talking to the hospital on the phone.

All mumbo jumbo to me.

"It would be less complicated if it was one complete bone." Sally stared at the floor for a second and pointed to several slivers of glass. "Housekeeping's getting slack."

Arthur scooped up some glass. "Beaker fell. Guess we missed a few pieces." He dumped the glass into the trash and turned to Sally. "What do you think?"

She dropped the pendants into evidence bags. "I can't ID them based on the sample itself because there's not enough original bone. Nothing like I've ever seen, unique treatment, some chemicals used to make them. Could be some heat too. The glue and dye might make it easier to trace, maybe even the opaque gemstones in the silver bezels, although nowadays, because of the internet, gemstones from Zambia or Mozambique could show up in Norristown. It's probably been touched by many at the gem show, so fingerprints won't help." She paused, and her forehead wrinkled. "Missing girls' faces carved in bone, and the edges of the carvings have the same flourishes." She pointed to the leaves and butterflies around the border. "Similar style, similar handwriting. Likely the same artist. And if there are two, there may be more."

CHAPTER TWENTY-TWO

ANDI

A CHILDISH VOICE. *Key in lock, rattling, rattling. Climb the golden tree. Higher, higher.*

What does this mean? Tell me, Andi demanded, but the child fell silent.

Franklin Township Police wanted to know what Andi had that someone wanted. The arson investigator had filed a National Fire Incident Reporting System (NFIRS) report on Thursday, concluding the motive was revenge. A claims man told her he'd have paperwork by Monday. Andi's world was full of loose ends, dead ends, and ends without ends. She could deal with the spirit world, but the chaos and dirt in Fiona's house was driving her crazy. Her best therapy was clearing the clutter inside and the snow outside.

Andi was in the driveway shoveling snow when her cell rang again. "Checking on you after last night," Eli said. "Things settling down?"

She jammed her shovel into the snow, where it stood upright. "I'm fine. No fires or things tossed from my windows today." Andi shook the snow out of the overgrown junipers. Tufts of white scattered, catching the light briefly, shining like silver glitter and then vanishing.

A pause. "Somehow you've picked up some people who have no business in your business. I worry about that."

A gust blew snow off a branch and into her boots. She shook one foot, then the other.

"You said your husband threatened you," Eli was saying. "Tell me about that."

"Dinner was late. He was drunk. Lance pulled out his trusty sidearm and pointed it at me. I convinced him to leave." She left out the parts where he hit her and knocked holes in the walls with his fists. And the screaming, hers and his.

"How did you convince him to leave?"

"I whacked him with a hockey stick, and the drunken idiot dropped his gun. I kicked it under the sofa. When I set off the alarm on the security system, he took off."

"What happened to the gun?" Eli asked.

"I dropped it down a sewer in Center City."

"What kind of gun was it?"

"Why are you asking me all these questions?" Andi asked.

"Because I don't want the gun to show up with your prints and be used to commit a crime," Eli said. "You should've turned it over to the police with a domestic violence report. Was it registered to Lance?"

"I don't know," she admitted. "I wiped it clean. Nobody would've gone into that stinking Center City sewer for the gun. Believe me."

An exasperated sound on his end. "I hope you're right. That's how people go to jail for crimes they didn't commit."

Andi found more bushes to beat on. Pretending it was Lance's head made it even more fun. She liked that Eli was trying to protect her. "Ever been married?"

"Happily divorced," he answered. "My ex outgrew me. I wanted a career in law enforcement and kids; she wanted nothing to do with either."

"Maybe you outgrew her," Andi said. An icicle crashed off the gutter and shattered.

Marriages are like icicles, she decided, always hanging precariously until a sunny day came along and heated them up. Then the union melted into a dirty puddle you had to step over.

Damn temperature was twenty degrees. Shoulder to the phone, Andi headed into the house, where she pulled off her coat and wet gloves.

"My wife," Eli said, "found a building contractor with a normal schedule."

"Her loss." God, she was bad with chitchat. Tearing open a package of hot chocolate, she dumped the powder into a cup, ran water over it, then popped it into the microwave.

"When do I get my pendants?"

"A bone expert is working with Dr. Arthur. It'll be a while."

She rubbed her temple with two fingers. Circles. Around and round, no end in sight. If she told him the pendants talked, he'd never believe it.

"So, no news?"

"When they removed the bones from the bezels—" He hesitated.

"Keep going."

"You're not going to like this."

"Try me. Just say it."

"Fine. They found a lock of hair and some blood on each."

"I was wearing hair and blood around my neck?" She shuddered. "Oh my God! That's sick! Now what happens?"

"More tests. DNA matching takes sixty to ninety days. The sheriff is not happy about that delay. He wants answers so he can put this guy behind bars."

"Eli, what if this guy is still hunting girls?"

"What made you think that?" he asked.

Damn. Not a question she could answer truthfully. Think fast, Andi. "If somebody stole his two pendants, he might want to replace them with two more." Or he might want to kill the person who wouldn't give them back. Then she'd become a pendant.

"It's okay to be afraid. Be paranoid. That'll keep you alert. Right now, stay near Fiona. She has a permit to carry. Don't go anywhere alone. And Saturday, we'll go to the morgue together. I'll meet you at Fiona's. Meanwhile, call me if anything is suspicious."

"Can't say I'm looking forward to it, but if it will help the girls, I'll go." They hung up. Andi didn't like being paranoid, and she sure as hell didn't like being told not to go anywhere.

Andi opened the silver locket. *Not who you think he is.*

Well, who is? Her laugh held some bitterness.

And then she remembered her mother's warning.

If spirits attach, terrible things happen.

CHAPTER TWENTY-THREE

MARIAH

BENNIE MISSED THAT OLD stray cat at the Holiday Inn, and I missed my kitty too, so we decided to play with Fiona's cat. We wondered if Honky could see us like the monkeys in the zoo. When Fiona left, promising to bring Honky some kitty treats, we had the cat to ourselves, until a window shattered in the laundry room.

A leather-gloved hand snaked through the broken pane and unlocked the door. In walked this man dressed in a ski cap, black sweatshirt and pants, and black boots. Standard burglar stuff. He scared the shit out of us. "Hey, Bennie," I said, "Is that one of those Michael Myers *Halloween* masks?"

"Looks like the one in the *Halloween* movie. Damn. Enough beer to smell him in the next block," Bennie said.

Six feet tall, with broad shoulders and a beer gut. He swept through Fiona's kitchen swinging a baseball bat and smashing anything break-able within range. Glasses on the table, plates in the dish rack.

"Give back what's not rightfully yours!" he shouted.

Poor Honky Cat scrambled under the sofa the minute she'd heard the window shatter. He smashed the old RCA picture tube in the living room, grabbed the laptop off the kitchen table and heaved it against the refrigerator. Jagged plastic flew everywhere. Glass crunched like bones under his heels. I prayed he'd hit a live wire, get electrocuted, and light up like the Fourth of July. He slammed the bat into a flat-screen monitor on Fiona's desktop, then started toward the stairs.

A key clicked in the lock.

"We can't just watch. We need to do something!" I told Bennie.

"She's got a gun somewhere in that handbag. She's gonna send him to hell, where he belongs."

The front door opened.

"Honky," Fiona called. "Kitty Snax, your favorite." She stepped in backward, kicked the door shut and shook a small packet of treats. "Honky?" When Fiona flicked on the lights, her eyes went wide. Her jaw dropped. "No way in hell a cat did this," she muttered.

Honky wasn't coming out. Couldn't blame her.

Two green eyes and wiry black hair poking out of the ski cap, Fisherman stared at Fiona through that creepy mask. His feet were planted as if he'd grown out of the floor like an evil tree.

"Take what you want and get out." Fiona tossed her wallet at his feet. She rummaged through her purse. A compact hit the floor with a thud. Then lipstick, mascara, and eyeliner. Sunglasses dropped out with a metallic clatter.

Fisherman gripped the bat, ready to bring it down on her skull. "I don't want your wallet!" He took a step forward and swung.

Bennie caught the bat and gave it a twist.

He held on.

Bennie yanked on the bat.

Looking confused, Fisherman jerked the bat free and swung again.

Bennie twisted it violently, and I worried about how much more energy she had left. We hadn't siphoned much today.

Eyes glued to him, Fiona backed toward the front door, looking more annoyed than scared. I opened it. *Fiona! Run!* I shouted, then covered my eyes. I didn't want to hear bones crunching, didn't want Andi to come back and find her best friend lying in a pool of blood.

"Where's Andrea Wyndham?" Fisherman slurred the words but held the bat ready.

Fiona stared at the door, which had opened as if by magic. "What the—" She lunged for it, but he grabbed her arm. "Let go!" Fiona swung her handbag at him.

He glared at her. "That Jezebel stole from me. 'Whoso diggeth a pit shall fall therein: and he that rolleth a stone, it will return upon him.'" Spit flew from his lips.

"Asshole!" Fiona shouted back. "You break into my house and quote the Bible!"

Bennie had sunk to the floor, out of energy. I eyed a lava lamp with a purple lump. If I had enough energy, I could hit him with it. I ripped the lamp cord out of the wall and aimed the globe at his ankles. He lost his balance and released Fiona. Colored lumps exploded into tiny spheres, rolling across the floor like mercury.

Run like hell! I yelled at Fiona.

Fiona's hand dove inside her bag, pulled out a gun, and pointed it at him. Her gun hand shook a little, but her eyes were deadly calm.

"Where's Andrea?" he bellowed. "Give back what's not rightfully yours!"

She stood, feet braced, gun aimed. "Get out of my house!"

He gave a drunken laugh and wrapped the electric cord around his hands as if he was gonna strangle her. "I have God's protection."

"You fucking better!" She squeezed off a shot.

A clap like thunder burned my eardrums. She'd put a hole into the wall, just missed him.

Fisherman hauled ass for the back door. When he paused, I was afraid he'd come back.

Get him now, Fiona! I shouted.

Fiona fired another bullet at him and missed again. Damn! She could have ended it then.

Lowering the gun, she glared at the open door. "Bastard meant to kill me, and I can't put a bullet between his eyes." She stared into the darkness. "What the hell is wrong with me?"

Bennie turned to me. "How did he find Fiona's place?"

"Gladys. That woman has diarrhea of the mouth. I'm sure she knows who Fiona is and where she lives by now, or maybe he found her on Andi's Facebook."

Energy drained, Bennie struggled to get up. I helped her. "That was close," she said.

My breathing slowed down. It seems stupid to be afraid of the person who'd killed you, especially if you're already dead.

"Must've thought Andi was here alone," Bennie said.

"Thank God she wasn't."

We stood at the back door, listening to Fiona curse as our killer raced through the neighbors' bushes and disappeared. A distant car engine fired up. Somebody burned rubber. Figures. Cops are never around when you need them.

"Can't believe I missed," Fiona grumbled, stepping over the debris in the living room. She put the gun on the counter, fished her cell from her bag, and keyed in a number.

No answer there, we guessed, because she hung up after a while. Fiona dialed again.

"Eli, someone just broke into my house, looking for Andi. He said, 'Give back what's not rightfully yours.' Since—"

She listened, tapping her foot faster and faster. "No, she isn't here," she responded, her foot in overdrive. "*I'm* fine but—" Her foot came down with a thump. "Eli, there's a shitload of—stop interrupting! I don't know where she is. I know she's not supposed to be alone!"

Honky scurried out from under the sofa, meowing. She brushed Fiona's leg, then jumped on a kitchen chair.

"No, Doug's not here. We broke up. He didn't tell you?"

Apparently not. I wondered what else Eli had missed.

"Weapon? A metal bat," Fiona continued. "I kept it for a souvenir. You need to get here fast. I know robberies and vandalism are not on your P.I. menu, but it's about the pendants and Andi." Fiona chugged orange juice from the container and popped donut holes into her mouth. "Next time," she said, "I'll save everybody some trouble and just shoot him dead. Hell, you'd have body, prints, even the fingers. You'd get a big news story. Good for your business."

More foot tapping. "Hell yeah, I shot at him. And nobody better give me any legal bullshit about defending myself against being bludgeoned with a baseball bat . . . Yes, I'll keep the doors locked. And no, I won't touch anything. You phone Andi and yell at her for being alone. Meet her somewhere and convince her to stay away because this mess will freak her out."

Fiona disconnected and keyed in another number.

"I need you to come over right now," she said and listened for a few seconds. "Irv, I don't care if your favorite show's on. I need my brother here. Now."

Bennie checked out the pantry. "She has a brother named Irv. Poor guy. Bet kids picked on him in school. Hey, look. Hostess cupcakes. You know what I really miss? Peeling off the icing in one sheet, eating it, then poking a hole in the middle and scooping out the filling." She poked the cupcake. "Stale. Damn! I've missed eating junk food."

I went back to Fiona's phone conversation in the other room.

"No, I am not going to explain. All you need to know is I have Ignatius here with me," Fiona told Irv. "So hurry."

She hung up and dialed, just three numbers this time: 9-1-1. "There's been a break-in at my house." She gave the address. "Nobody's hurt. Intruder's gone; I shot at him, scared him away. He damaged my property and threatened me with a baseball bat."

"Cops can't get prints off the bat," Bennie said. "He wore gloves. Besides, our killer ain't got no record, so prints won't help. Melvin taught me that." Melvin, the neighborhood drug sleaze.

Fiona banged down the phone and walked to her bathroom. She sorted through bottles in the medicine cabinet, chose a green one labeled Xanax, shook out a pill and washed it down with some water.

Then she sighed and made her way back to the kitchen. "Don't touch anything," she muttered. "Like I didn't know that."

Honky hopped onto the kitchen table and hunkered down. Poor kitty. The cat's tail was three times its normal size, her blue eyes wild.

"Would've taken more than one Xanax if she knew what that man did to us," Bennie said.

Fiona paced from the front window to the kitchen until a car pulled up. Then she opened the door to a life-size Ken doll: blond hair, blue eyes, polo shirt under a bomber jacket, shoulders like a lifter. Had to be Irv.

Two steps inside, and he came to an abrupt stop. "Holy shit, Fiona! What the hell happened? Are you okay?" Irv looked her up and down and surveyed the room again.

"He ain't got no idea how close he came to losing his sister," Bennie said.

"Some asshole broke into my house." Fiona kicked the door shut behind him. It bounced open, and she kicked it again.

"God Almighty, Fiona." He hugged her. "Did you call the police?"

Fiona shook a strand of blond hair out of her eyes. "Jackass started swinging that baseball bat at me. So rip-roaring drunk, he kept missing."

"He kept missing because of me," Bennie said.

"And I nailed his ankles with a lava lamp." I wondered what she'd do if Fiona discovered two ghosts had saved her life.

"Somehow, I reached my purse, whipped out Ignatius, and scared him off." Fiona pointed to a hole in the wall. "I meant to kill him." Fiona looked puzzled. "Couldn't do it. I called the cops and Doug's friend, a P.I."

Irv looked around. "What do you have that somebody wants so badly?"

"Some pendants Andi bought. Jewelry with missing girls' faces on them."

Irv gave her a look of disbelief. "All this because of some pendants?"

"Bennie," I said, "maybe asking Andi to find our killer isn't such a good idea."

CHAPTER TWENTY-FOUR

ANDI

WHEN ANDI ARRIVED AT Fiona's, the street was buzzing with police cars. She parked across the street and raced toward the front door. A cop stopped her in the driveway.

"You can't go in there. It's a crime scene."

"I'm living here. Is my friend all right?" Andi peered around him, trying to see inside the house. "Fiona!"

The beefy officer stood there, stone-faced.

"Is my friend all right?" she repeated.

"No injuries, ma'am." He passed his flashlight over her and squinted. "Wasn't I at your house Tuesday for a break-in? Then you had a fire the next day. Last name's Wyndham, isn't it?"

"Yes! Please let me see my friend."

He spoke into his radio, and she heard Fiona in the background saying, "Let her in, for chrissakes."

Fiona's face was the color of a tin can when Andi rushed over to her. She glanced around the room and said, "Oh my God! Are you okay?"

"Shee-it. I'm fine," Fiona said. "Irv's here now. Eli didn't text you?"

"No." When Andi took out her cell, she realized he'd left several text messages. "Actually, yes, he did." She read the messages—*You shouldn't be alone! Stay away from Fiona's! Meet me at Starbucks!*—then greeted Irv with a quick hug.

"Somebody's not fine." Irv leaned over, examining the rug. "Fresh blood on the carpet."

Two cops moved in for a closer look. One police officer was tall and lanky; the older guy looked like he'd eaten his fair share of Philly cheesesteaks. They squatted on the carpet, staring at the dark stains.

Fiona broke loose from Andi and whacked Irv's shoulder. "That's barbecue sauce, you idiot," she said.

"You always put barbecue sauce on your rug?" Irv glared at her. "To what, clean it?"

Andi almost smiled, but then a sense of guilt crept in. She'd dragged Fiona into her troubles. And now poor Irv was in the middle of it too.

While Fiona pointed out the bullet hole in the wall and gave the police information for their report, Andi slumped on the sofa. The only way to end this was to find the guy. And deep down she knew she had to do it, but dealing with a cold-blooded killer scared the shit out of her.

Eli walked through the front door and stopped. He scanned the mess and gave a low whistle. "Somebody's pissed off," he said. Then he turned to Andi. "Why didn't you check your messages? I was worried!" When he saw the fear in her eyes, he sat next to her and draped his arm around her. "I'm going to find this guy and make things right."

He was a hell of a lot more confident than she was.

Not who you think he is, Mariah whispered.

"So what happened here, Fiona?" Eli asked.

When she finished talking, his expression changed like a stop-light switching from green to red. He put on his police-authority face and said, "You're not staying here tonight. Neither of you."

"They won't be alone." Irv stood, introduced himself and offered a hand to Eli. "I'll be on the sofa with my shotgun. Can't believe Fiona missed him. She's a helluva shooter."

"So I've heard." He shook Irv's hand. "Eli Lake. I'm a private investigator."

Fiona's clock chimed. His shoes scraping through broken glass, Irv walked over and fixed the hands. Fiona tilted her head toward the clock. "Don't bother. It's midnight somewhere. Guess I choked up. Daddy never taught us to shoot people."

A car pulled up outside, and Eli lifted the dusty curtain to look out. "Probably the ID guys. They'll need a facial profile of the intruder."

One of the crime-lab people carried the metal bat and some evidence bags outside. Fingerprint people were finishing when Eli let the ID man in. He called to Fiona, and they set up shop in the kitchen. She cleared a space on the table. Andi heard them back and forth. "Can't tell you much. He wore that creepy mask from the *Halloween* movie. I just know what he was wearing, and approximate height and body type."

Andi scratched her neck, shoulder, arm. *A manifestation of anxiety*, the counselor had said. There was sympathy in Eli's eyes as he massaged her shoulders.

On the arm of the sofa, Honky Cat sat sphinx-style, like a judge. When Andi tried to pet her, she flattened her ears and hissed. Too many strange people had invaded Honky's domain.

She knew that feeling well. Too many people with no business in her business. Eli concentrated on writing in his notebook. Dark circles under his eyes gave her the impression he hadn't slept much lately. She wanted to trust him; she needed for him to make things right. His phone rang, and he walked into the hallway to talk.

Minutes later, he returned.

"This afternoon, Lakeside Police went to Mariah's house to collect a hairbrush," he said. "Fortunately, her mother left the room exactly as it was before she disappeared. The lock of hair under the pendant bezel matched her color."

"Did the DNA match?" Andi looked hopeful.

"Too soon to know." Eli continued, "The hairbrush did have some hair with intact root bulbs, good DNA evidence." He drew a deep breath and exhaled. "'Give back what's not rightfully yours' sounds like Peter Rockford. Odd that he chose a biblical name."

"Peter Rockford?"

"Yeah, from my Catholic school days on the rez, I remember something about Peter being the rock upon which the church was built and being given the keys to heaven. Peter Rockford. Possibly this guy is religious."

"Well, he'd better say his prayers tonight," Fiona said, "because if he comes back, Irv and I are gonna make him look like Swiss cheese, and he'll be meeting Satan at the gates of hell."

"If he's smart, he's in the next state by now. You'll be here all night?" Eli asked Irv.

"Me and my shotgun." Irv nodded and followed him to the door. They stood outside talking for a few minutes, planning an Armageddon, Andi imagined. When he returned, Irv parked himself and his rifle by the front door.

Seconds later, she got a text message from Eli, reminding her that they'd be going to the morgue the next day.

Oh great. Just what she needed, more dead people talking to her.

Andi picked up a picture of Fiona with her brothers. Old oak tree with hanging moss in the background, the three of them smiling. At least Fiona had a brother who came when she needed him. Andi had no one.

She set the frame down and walked to the kitchen, thinking about leaving her own family, cutting them out of her life. About the mother who had died without her daughter by her side and the father she hadn't seen in years.

They'd been a happy family before she climbed into the kidnapper's car to get a free puppy. Then, years later, she'd run away with Lance, another bad man. Had they forgiven her for leaving those holes in their lives? Had they forgiven each other before her mother died?

"Bastard didn't touch my piano," Fiona told Andi. "Small consolation." She stared at the pile of metal and plastic that had been her laptop. "Thank God for the Cloud."

Andi put an arm around her friend. "I'm sorry. I have a knack for ruining people's lives."

Fiona pulled back and looked Andi in the eye. "Violence isn't always your fault, woman." She scooped up a dustpan full of glass. "You're the only one I'd tell this to, but when that man was swinging at me, I swear the front door opened itself. Guess it was the wind, but there is no wind. Then my lava lamp heaved itself at the guy. Gave me the creeps. It was them, wasn't it?"

Andi nodded. Good to know the girls intervened to help her friend. Andi stooped to pick up a thin brown scrap and turned it over in her hand: a perfect ginkgo leaf. "Any ginkgo trees in your backyard?"

"Hell no. When the fruit falls off, those things stink like a Philadelphia garbage strike in August." Fiona put a tie around a trash bag, stood, and rubbed her back.

Andi twirled the leaf stem between her fingers as a childish voice began singing, *Key in lock, rattling, rattling. Climb the golden tree. Higher, higher.*

What does that mean? Andi asked silently.

Why wouldn't the child answer? Was it a fairy tale Andi's mother had made up?

CHAPTER TWENTY-FIVE

ANDI

WITH A WHITE BRICK exterior and nondescript sign, the morgue seemed innocuous from the outside. But once Andi passed through the first keypad, it became a catacomb of rooms, each with its own lock. Cheerfully, Dr. Arthur pointed out the autopsy room and the special chamber for toxic autopsies with a high-tech ventilation system. Andi guessed it was his way of taming death. The more she looked at him, the more he resembled an undertaker. They, too, tried to make death part of life.

Dr. Arthur took her past places where they made Y-cuts into bodies. Rooms where tissue samples were saved in plastic jars with horrible brown juice. The stuff inside them reminded her of the package of innards stuffed into the turkey you bought for Thanksgiving.

Next stop, a place where they treated clothing in special machines so they could extract DNA samples. Big stainless-steel refrigerators that, despite the metal doors, reeked like Fiona's barbecue grease trap she never cleaned. The smell made her gag.

"There's room enough for seventy bodies here," Dr. Arthur boasted.

She hoped they'd never need interment for seventy dead people at a time. Andi smiled politely as he led her to a room with skulls on shelves.

"People who willed their bodies to science," he said, noticing her interest. "I use them with students to illustrate similarities and differences. Male, female, ethnic descent, age."

Focus on not losing your breakfast, Andi told herself. She had a ball growing in her chest that threatened to move north, and her mouth tasted like tin foil. Fighting the queasiness, she swallowed hard.

Eli put a hand lightly on her shoulder. "Let me know if you're going to keel over. Before the fact, okay?"

"Let's just get this over with," Andi said under her breath. "I'm more likely to barf."

To her relief, the tour ended in a room with typical business decor. A cheap speckled countertop with a phone, some cabinets, a copy machine, and an aluminum-and-particleboard table in the middle. She sank into a chrome chair, eyeing a fat manila envelope on the table and took a deep breath.

Dr. Arthur laid enlarged color shots of the pendants next to school pictures of the girls.

Yes, they had been real people, right down to the pink highlights in Mariah's dark hair and Bernadette's neat geometric cornrows and hair extensions. Sweet young faces to match the whispers. She would not cry, would not show weakness.

Pursing his lips, Eli studied the photos and shook his head. "Two girls go missing in the past six months, two pendants surface, and you found no new evidence."

"What we've found," Arthur said, "is a lot of ambiguous physical evidence. The glue can be bought in any hardware or craft shop. The dye is common tea. The metal bezel is standard at any jewelry supply store, and the opaque gemstone cabochons are available on eBay."

"So," Eli said, "you don't have any new evidence that will help me ID the guy."

Arthur gave Eli a stern look. He pulled out more prints. This set showed a tiny braid of hair and a dark spot that looked like dried blood inside the bezel. "We do have some DNA. It's going to take time."

Time. Her stomach ticked away like a bomb ready to explode.

The doctor turned to Andi. "I brought you here because there are things you and I and Eli know that only the murderer would be privy to. We've solved a lot of cases when the perp reveals himself by things he shouldn't know. We need your cooperation. The missing girls' case has drawn media attention in Mariah's hometown because her father is a well-known hand surgeon. Information must be held back. And we've just learned a federal judge's daughter is missing too."

"Gag order," Andi muttered. "That's easy for me. I don't know anything. I have more questions than answers."

"Don't go looking for answers either," Eli said. "I will. I get paid to find evidence even if the labs can't find anything."

Arthur cocked his head at Eli and narrowed his eyes. When he spoke, his voice was soft. "But we did find something, Eli. Hair and blood. We don't know yet for sure, but we think it's the girls'. We believe the person who made the pendants may have murdered them. In other words, these pendants could very well be the trophies of a serial killer."

His statement hung in the air, gathering horror like a corpse attracting flies.

CHAPTER TWENTY-SIX

FISHERMAN

ACE OF AN ANGEL, SOUL blacker than Satan's. He'd had about enough of his next pendant girl's foolishness. The Lord would judge her for setting his shirt on fire. His wounds looked infected, but a visit to a doctor would mean a lot of questions he didn't want to answer, plus he'd have to leave her alone. He didn't trust her for a second.

Fisherman unbuttoned his shirt, glanced down at the festering sores and grimaced. Lately he'd been sleeping on his back because they hurt so badly. Stupid girl. Kept threatening him—he, who was protecting her from the evil on the streets, keeping her pure—saying her daddy would make sure he'd rot in jail if one of the other inmates didn't kill him first.

Twice, Rachel had slipped away before he finally captured her. First, she'd burned him with a flaming marshmallow. Then the brat leaped from his car at a stoplight in the middle of Gervais Street, a busy intersection. Somehow, a car rounding the corner missed her. Worst part was the girl didn't learn from her mistakes. Her parents had probably never punished the girl. He followed Nana's example. In his house, there was punishment for not obeying.

One day, that little hellion even desecrated his Bible! Ripped out the pages, shredded them, then smiled when he saw what she'd done. And she didn't even stop after he punished her. Pushing my buttons, that's what Nana would've called it. Taking away food meant nothing to her; she could live on air. Punishment with the willow switch didn't work. The belt or his paddle had no effect either. He couldn't find the punishment that would make her learn a lesson. Bennie and Mariah had been good girls compared to this one. Of course, Melvin had helped back then, getting Bennie hooked on drugs. Too bad he was in jail.

Fisherman would get his favorite pendant girls back. Bargaining with any woman other than Nana was easy. He blocked caller ID and dialed. A click, and he said hello.

Damn that woman! She'd disconnected. He tried three more times before it went to her voice mail. He decided on a gruff voice, like some officious banker.

"Andrea, you stole two pendants from me. If you don't return them, I will replace them. One pendant will be replaced with a runaway, a beautiful blond. And the other . . . well, if you don't meet me at the State House in Columbia, South Carolina on Friday, November eighteenth, you will replace the second pendant. Show without the pendants, and the girl will die. Notify the police and the girl dies. Preparations are underway already. Need proof? Listen carefully."

He played the message they'd rehearsed, although he didn't like her ad libs at all. It was the best of many recordings he'd done.

"Help me!" The girl choked back sobs. "My name is Rachel. I wanna go home!" She sniffled, and her breath came in tiny gasps as if she'd been crying for a while. "I wanna . . . spend Thanksgiving with my family. He's crazy! He's gonna kill me! . . . Please . . . help me!"

CHAPTER TWENTY-SEVEN

ANDI

DETERMINED TO BLANK OUT the morgue, Andi started the car. Dusk was falling, turning the world to shadows and taillights and dirty snowbanks. In this section of road, the deer promoted car body shops. Just what she needed, another busted headlight. She turned on the radio for company, and the Bee Gees' "Staying Alive" came on.

"Yep, that's the plan and also not throwing up in my car."

All around her, people went on with their normal lives, driving down the road as if innocent girls didn't get murdered. As if best friends didn't almost get bludgeoned to death or bedrooms didn't get set on fire. As if no mother ever waited for a missing child to come home. As if no father ever blamed himself for not protecting his child. Acid churned in her stomach.

Losing a daughter had to be devastating. Andi hadn't given much thought to her parents' feelings after she left.

Her phone rang. "Unknown," the dashboard announced. She hit DECLINE three times, then let it go to voice mail.

Andi drove as far as a church parking lot across from the restaurant before her stomach threatened to erupt. Kicking the door open, she slid sideways across the driver's seat and hung her head outside the car, waiting. Nothing but dry heaves. She called Eli. "My stomach is not up for dinner."

An ultra calm voice from him. "Where are you?"

"Bible Baptist Church, across from the restaurant on Paoli Pike."

"I'm not far from you. Be there in a minute."

She would not show weakness, would not become a weak, blubbering dimwit.

Eli pulled in next to her car and invited her into his arms.

"The morgue was awful. The smell." Andi looked up at him. "Those girls are not just faces on a poster. They have mothers and fathers. They're too young to be gone." She broke down and cried, which made her feel so damn out of control.

He smoothed her hair. "I've seen tough cops lose it in a morgue."

"I'm not safe, not even at Fiona's, and she's not safe because of me. How do I resolve this?"

"We'll find whoever is behind those girls' murders." Eli held her tighter, as if together they could block out the horror and grief.

Cold was working its way up her legs. His coat smelled of new leather. She looked up. "Sorry I cried all over your coat."

"It's leather. Cows go out in the rain." Eli cleared a wispy curl out of her eyes. "Why don't you come home with me tonight?" He massaged her shoulders. "I have a spare room. At least, you can get a good night's sleep without worrying about intruders. You'll be safe. I promise. Even from me."

"But what about Fiona?"

"I'm sure Irv will be camping out with his shotgun again," he said. "Call her. Then you can follow me in your car. I have an old shirt you can wear and a spare toothbrush. I'll toss your clothes into the washer and dryer. I can be a very good mother."

She studied him. Was this a patented Eli Lake move, or was he just a nice guy? His enthusiasm made her nervous. Andi hadn't spent the night with another man since Lance, and she sure as hell wasn't in the mood for sex tonight.

He wiped away a tear with his thumb. "Think of it as a safe house. No obligations."

A safe house? Once she'd lived in a house she deemed safe—her own. But apparently the shelf life of safety in her marriage was pretty darn short: five years to be exact. But he was right, nobody in their right mind would threaten a former FBI agent.

She dug her cell from a pocket and tapped out Fiona's number. It rang twice before Irv answered. "You are such a good brother," Andi told him.

"Fiona's personal slave is more like it. I'll put my master on."

"Andi, you sound awful. Where are you?" Fiona asked.

"With Eli. He talked me into staying at his place."

"Good idea," Fiona said. "Tell him I'm getting calls and hang-ups. Caller ID says 'Unknown.' I'll stay at Irv's tonight, if you're at Eli's. And Andi, sleep with the guy, for God's sake. It will be good for you. Call it a rebound."

CHAPTER TWENTY-EIGHT

ANDI

A QUARTER MILE INTO THE woods, tires crunching on a gravel road covered by snow, Andi began doubting the sanity of her decision. Nothing around but tall, dark trees. Not one house, not one light anywhere, no one in shouting distance. What did she really know about Eli? He could stuff her body under a floorboard. Ridiculous—too Edgar Allen Poe. Oh hell, Fiona trusted him, and she knew more about men than Andi ever would.

Eli parked in a shed that reminded her of an Adirondack shelter, and Andi pulled in beside him. She slid out of her car, leaving the door open for light. Something crashed through the woods. Gasping, she ducked back into the car, ready to swing the door shut.

"Four-legged intruder, Andi. A deer," Eli said. "You're on the edge of the park. I like it back here. Reminds me of the rez. Not like the burbs."

"Guess you don't get many trick-or-treaters," she said, venturing one foot out of the car and then another, taking in the thick pines, a woodpile, brush everywhere. She'd always liked the outdoors, but his place felt heavy, like something dark had grown and wrapped around it.

A stone well looked intact. "You do have plumbing?"

"Of course. The house is eighteenth century," Eli told her. "Built for tenants from the original Ridley Mansion. It sat vacant until the sixties, when hippies moved in. After they left for the real world, it went vacant for twenty years. You should have seen it. Kudzu had tied it up like a tangled ball of yarn. The realtor said rumors are it's haunted, but I've never had any problems."

Andi froze, staring at him. She didn't need another ghost attaching.

"I promised to keep you safe. No evil spirits here." He unlocked the door. "My father and the woman who raised me smudged it."

"Not your mother." So, Eli had distanced himself from the reservation. "Smudged?"

"Purified. Smoked out the bad guys, like a priest or a rabbi blessing a house. Mom died when I was ten."

"Oh. I'm sorry. My place and Fiona's could use some smudging. Second thought, not Fiona's. It's a fire hazard. Maybe I should get smudged."

He laughed. "All it takes is a match, some sage, and an abalone shell."

The house had two sections. A huge fireplace dominated the older part, likely the kitchen from days when it was just one room. Pocked and scarred wood floors, two old wood-framed windows. It had a faint musty smell. In the newer section, wide pine-plank floors, a smaller stone fireplace, tiny kitchen, a living area, and a wood stairway to an open loft.

Not much privacy. That's what he called a spare room? One space partitioned off from the other bedroom by a folding screen? Andi was having serious second thoughts, but the drive back alone might be even more terrifying. "How many baths?"

"Two." He filled a kettle and put it on the stove. "I converted a closet upstairs."

She hadn't taken her coat off yet. Not much heat, maybe no furnace at all. Damn, what had she gotten herself into? Camping out in a haunted house in the middle of nowhere with a man she barely knew who had to smoke out the bad guys before he moved in.

"Drafty in here. I'll get you a jacket." He tromped across the creaky floor and returned with an Eagles sweatshirt four sizes too big. After putting her coat in a small closet, Eli crouched by the hearth. "I come from a long line of master fire builders," he said, stuffing newspaper under a store-bought log. Once it was lit, he added real logs.

Smiling, Andi sank into a lumpy sofa, rolled up the sleeves, then changed her mind and pulled her hands inside them.

"Woodstoves in the bedrooms. I'm burning corn pellets. Very efficient." Eli sat on the sofa and clasped her hand. "Warmer now? How's your stomach? Can I make you a sandwich?"

A log shifted. Sparks flew. Andi heaved a sigh. "I'm not hungry, but you should eat."

"I'll make a nice cup of herbal tea for you." He walked over to the kitchen and took pottery mugs down from a shelf. "Seventy percent of runaways return home after the first twenty-four hours. The pendant girls are unusual. There's a lot of sex trafficking out there, and they're the perfect age. Girls get arrested for prostitution. Their manager goes free, bails them out, and moves into a new neighborhood. Two sex offenders are registered in your township. One's living almost next door to the elementary school."

She watched as he tied two sacks of herbs in gauze, fastened them on the sides of the cups and poured hot water. "How can that be?"

"Criminals have constitutional rights too." He pursed his lips. "Here's what the Lakeside sheriff in Columbia believes." He grabbed a hoagie from the fridge. "Your girls ran away. Somebody on the streets may have offered them a modeling or acting opportunity, then forced them into prostitution or selling drugs. Young girls have romantic ideas that some kind soul will take care of them. Too often, drug dealers and sex traffickers fill those roles."

"Older girls have romantic ideas too. When I was twenty-nine, I married Lance and divorced my family. You'd think I was old enough to know better, but I left with my hero, Lance." She made air quotes around the word *hero*. "Thought I knew more than my parents about life and husbands, and I resented their judgment of him, so I made it clear that I didn't want to hear from them ever again. In my mind, I'm an adult runaway. A stupid decision that left me alienated from my family still today," she admitted. "I was the only child of a mother who spent most of her life winning Pulitzers, being a war correspondent, and then there was my father. Picture this," she said. "A little girl lost in a department store with her father searching. He finds her, scolds her for leaving his side, and takes her hand. Then he realizes it's the hand the kidnapper tattooed, so he changes sides as if that hand is poison."

"That's a terrible memory to be carrying around." He brought their tea and a Wawa hoagie to a coffee table made from an antique door topped with glass.

"You must have good childhood memories. When we first got here, you said it reminded you of the reservation."

"Yeah, I'll always love living in the woods. But the rez life wasn't for me. I left the rez after I found my little brother face down in a lake, dead from a drug deal. I was a cop then and should have seen it coming."

She pursed her lips. "After I lost five students in three years, I trained for the crisis intervention team. Drugs, alcohol, and suicides. Young people sometimes make poor decisions; I'm perfect proof of that. I'm sorry you lost your brother, Eli."

"I see it after the damage is done. You see it before it happens." He removed the herbs from the cups. "I'm not sure which is worse. Tea's ready." He placed a spoon near her cup and slid a jar toward her. "Here's some honey if you want it."

"What's in this?"

"Secret recipe." Police business face. "If I tell you, I'll have to kill you."

Andi shot him a look. "Okay, as long as it's not some kind of detox."

"It's clover, rose hips, and mint. What about your mom, the war correspondent?" Eli unwrapped his hoagie and took a bite.

She stirred in a little honey. "I was kidnapped while my mother was on deadline for a news story, and my father never let her forget she should've been watching me. Tore my family apart. Then the day after my twelfth birthday, a major TV network offered her an opportunity to do international investigative reporting. After that, she rarely came home, although she usually showed up for my birthdays. I still don't understand why my parents stayed married."

"Guess we both have skeletons in our closets." He crumpled the hoagie wrapper into a ball and got up to stir the fire. The place was warming up nicely. A muffled howling came from outside the back door, loud enough that she couldn't ignore it.

He must've heard it too. She followed him to the door, where he turned on the backyard light. Not that what was out there qualified as a backyard—trees and leaves and brush. In walked the biggest cat she'd ever seen. The fluffy caramel-and-black-striped beast could easily duke it out with anything smaller than a deer.

"Sig! What are you doing out there?" Eli asked. "It's too cold for cats tonight."

The cat wasted no time racing to an empty food bowl. He looked from Eli to the bowl.

"Damn," she said. "Your kitty is king of the jungle."

"Maine coon. Found him three houses ago out West. Somebody dumped a litter of kittens in the woods, hors d'oeuvres for predators. Nothing left of them but fur and some bones. Sig was the only one who made it. People assume kittens and puppies can naturally survive without their mothers. Cruel stupidity." Eli filled the bowl and watched the cat wolf it down. Then he led Andi to a spot in front of the fire, sat behind her on a braided rug, and massaged her shoulders.

"Feels good. Guess you like the strays." Andi leaned back, enjoying the warmth of the fire on her face, the warmth of his body against hers.

"You're a beautiful woman." He folded his arms around her waist. "Not a stray."

The cat finished licking the bowl and curled up on the hearth.

"I like it here." She turned sideways to face him. "It's peaceful."

He smiled. "Stay as long as you want."

"You're a nice man. Your wife should have kept you."

"I'm glad you didn't keep your husband."

Eli tipped her chin, and warm lips brushed hers. God, when was the last time she'd felt this way? The horrors of the past four days were washed away with a long, sweet kiss. Her chest felt heavy. Her heart pounded. She breathed him in, warmth growing inside her. He captured her lips a second time, and she wanted him to hold her forever.

A final gentle kiss, and Eli smiled down at her. "Hmm. Enough of that. I don't want you to think that's why I invited you."

"Oh damn. It's not?"

His crow's-feet wrinkled into a smile.

"So why *did* you invite me here?"

"To keep you away from the guy who left a message on your bathroom mirror and trashed Fiona's place. You should stay over this weekend. I don't fly to Columbia until Monday."

"I'm kind of old-fashioned about meeting a man and moving in right away."

Little smoke puffs sailed up the chimney, swirling, stopping, then drawing again. He got up and poked at the logs, added a new one. Flames scurried over it, found a dry spot, and caught fire. All she needed was a glass of wine to totally wind down and forget everything.

"Maybe I need to find the pendant killer before he finds me," Andi said.

"No, you don't." Eli shook his head resolutely. "Let the police do their job. And me. Don't play Nancy Drew, or *you'll* end up with your face on a pendant."

CHAPTER TWENTY-NINE

ANDI

A T 2:00 A.M., ANDI AND ELI climbed the stairs to the loft. Childhood memories, college life, and lousy marriages, all shared. She felt a bond with this man. He turned on an electric blanket and left a tribal blanket at the foot of the bed. Considering outside temperatures, the room was toasty. It would have been toastier if he'd shared her bed, but he was a gentleman, and she was a damn fool. Glowing embers in the corn-pellet heater lulled her to sleep.

The dream came a half hour later. Like the first time, the whirring of a saw, the whispering. *Runaway*. Now, she realized it was the girls' label for themselves. Maybe for her too.

A saw hacked through bone. Back and forth. Back and forth. A young girl's screams. Pain. The fuzzy edges of the dream sharpened and Andi became Mariah.

She fled from a dark silhouette. A man, she sensed that. Footsteps pounded behind her. Mothballs and the copper stench of blood. Andi dared not turn around; she was in a vacuum with flashes and images firing at her.

Mariah's voice, her voice. *Don't hurt me. I'll do whatever you want. Don't hurt me!*

A man held her arm under a carving tool that sounded like a dentist's drill. The high-pitched whir cut through the darkness.

No! She lay chained to a cot, twisting and clawing and screaming, *Stop! Stop!*

His eyes were crazed. *God gave you to me! I'm saving you from the streets! Be still!*

The carving tool bit into her skin, burning, burning. Andi could *feel* Mariah's pain. She flailed and freed herself. Now she was running, sobbing, breath coming in short gasps. A tree root like the claw of some ancient creature tripped her. She put a hand down on the cold earth to right herself. But she tumbled. Brambles bit into her flesh. She protected her head, rolling, writhing, her bare feet scraping jagged rocks.

The man caught her, forced her down.

No! she cried out.

He straddled her, a smile on his lips. His garlic breath gagged her. His eyes glowed, green orbs in the darkness, malice fueled by lust. *You are mine*, he said. *It's God's plan.*

Using her fingers like claws, she tried to rake his arms. Impossible! She felt no flesh, just a black space in the night air, an inky, greasy silhouette. Use teeth. Use knees. Use fists. Scream! Maybe someone will hear.

But her hands connected with nothing, clutched at air. Was he a man? A demon? A murdering ghost? He pressed his hands to her throat. She gasped for air and managed a shriek that he smothered before it reached her lips.

Arms reached through the darkness for her. Andi connected a fist with the solid thwack of skin against bone. Her knuckles throbbed. The pain was real. "Leave me alone!" Andi shouted. "Leave all of us alone!"

"Andi, it's me. Eli. Stop fighting me! It's a nightmare. You're safe."

A hurricane wind like a distant freight train echoed inside her head. Andi couldn't tell whether it was the dream or the wind outside, but she lay still, straining to hear a faint echoing voice. Not Mariah's. Must be Bernadette's voice.

Found . . . us . . . Holiday Inn, it whispered.

"Eli?"

He sat on the edge of the bed. "Want to talk about it?" His left eye was clenched shut.

"Oh God, what did I do?"

"I'll live." His fingertips probed the eye, and he flinched.

She clutched at reality, trying to erase the horror. Her breathing slowed. A dream, she wondered, or a subliminal message? Yellow eyes peered over his shoulder.

"I'm okay," she assured the Shadows.

"Come on," he said, nodding toward the steps. "We both could use some hot chocolate."

Woolen blanket around her shoulders, she trooped down behind him. He turned on a light in the kitchen and stood over the sink. His eye was watering and rapidly swelling. "Did that dream have anything to do with your kidnapping?"

"No. A psychiatrist couldn't dislodge that memory. It was about Mariah." She walked to the refrigerator, opened the freezer door, and handed him a package of frozen hash browns. "Put this on your eye." She winced. It hurt to look at him. "God, I'm sorry."

He grinned down at her. "I used to get beat up worse than this in kindergarten." Eli lit the gas jet under the kettle, opened and closed cabinets until he found some cocoa. Two heaping tablespoons into each cup, and he leaned on the countertop. "You scared me."

She took a deep breath, slowly exhaled, and sank into a kitchen chair. "I don't know how my mind conjures up this stuff," she lied. "In my dream, Mariah was tortured and strangled."

"Dreams are like that kettle spouting off. Healthy venting of the subconscious," Eli said.

When the kettle whistled, he poured steaming water into the cups. "Tortured how?"

"Guy carved her arm with some instrument." The man was greasy, black air instead of flesh. Nope, she'd leave that part out.

"I know detectives who swear they get clues from dreams. They claim the brain's working overtime, trying to solve a case. I pay attention to them, but sometimes they're just scary reminders that I'm not invincible." He picked up the hash browns and crunched the package until it was soft. When he applied it gently to his eye, he winced. "Must have been a helluva dream."

"I could feel every pain Mariah felt," Andi told him. "And there was this howling wind like nothing I've ever heard."

Sig hopped up on the counter. In one swift motion, Eli scooped him up and put him down. The big cat wound himself around Eli's ankles, an apology for his transgression.

He removed the frozen package and tossed it on the counter. Slowly, and with copious tears, he opened the eye. "Damn. How'd you learn to punch like that?"

"I was bullied in school. My father's a retired military officer. He taught me to box."

Eli picked something off the blanket and showed it to her. A leaf. "Where'd this come from? No gingko trees around here."

She wouldn't be explaining that either. "Maybe the blanket picked it up last time you had a picnic. What's your schedule in the morning?"

"I have to be out of here by seven. I'll cook one of my world-famous omelets, but no more Golden Gloves boxing practice tonight."

Standing on her tiptoes, she kissed his cheek. "I'm really sorry, Eli. One bad dream per night is my quota."

CHAPTER THIRTY

ANDI

A NDI OPENED ONE EYE to see Eli sitting on the end of her bed. "Omelet is on the stove," he said. She followed him downstairs, where her laundered jeans and shirt lay on a kitchen chair.

"Can you find your way out of here?"

She nodded and kissed him goodbye, a long, wistful kiss, and the door closed behind him. Yes, she could play house with Eli, could move right in. She dressed, cast one final look around his place, stepped outside, and made sure the door had locked.

Inside her car, she checked her phone for messages. Several missed calls and a voice mail from the same unknown number. She hit play. Oh damn! This was no telemarketer. That demented son of a bitch demanded that she hand over the pendants—or else. Andi played it again. Her mouth had gone dry, her stomach rumbled, her heart hammered. After the third time, she dialed Eli.

Eli answered, car noise in the background, and she read the message her phone had transcribed. "This bastard stalked Fiona and me, and now I have to meet him in Columbia to save another runaway, and I don't even have the pendants. Eli! I don't want my face on a pendant. I need to get out of Franklin Township today, but I sure as hell don't want to meet this guy in South Carolina."

"It gives us an excellent opportunity to catch him."

"Are you suggesting I become bait? Are you nuts? Last night you said yourself I shouldn't play Nancy Drew."

"Nancy Drew is a solo act. You'd have professional support. Look. I have a court case tomorrow, but I'll be there Monday evening, meeting with the sheriff. We'll set something up."

"Eli!"

"You and Fiona should fly to Columbia. Book yourself into a fancy hotel and stay alert."

"Fiona's brother lives just outside Columbia."

"What? I thought Irv lives here?"

"Not Irv. Bailey, her older brother; he's got some huge lake house."

"Great, so you won't be alone."

"Wait, I haven't even told Fiona about that message. I don't want to go to Columbia. This scares the shit out of me."

"I know. But I also know that your fear won't go away until we catch this guy. Playing along with his demands is our best chance at doing that."

She opened the locket, hoping for a sign. *Be careful . . . not who . . .* Great. Riddles.

So not helpful.

"What's your plan anyway?"

"I'll know when I get there."

"You don't even have a fucking plan?"

"Not yet. You just told me about his call, and I've never set foot in Columbia. We've got to take this opportunity, though. He's reached out to you again. We'll make contact."

"I don't want to make contact. Can't they use a decoy?"

"He knows what you look like. Just get yourself down there. We'll figure out the rest with the sheriff. And text me when you get there."

"Can't you come with us?"

"Honest, I'd drop everything and go with you, but I've been subpoenaed and can't get out of this. I'll catch an evening flight. We're gonna get this guy. I promise." When she didn't respond, he added, "See you soon."

Her hands shook. "Yeah, see you soon." She disconnected. "If I'm still alive."

It made no sense for the pendant killer to lure her to South Carolina when he'd spent so much time destroying her life in Pennsylvania. She'd assumed he lived here. But then again, the girls had all disappeared from South Carolina. Maybe Eli was right, and playing along was the only way to smoke him out.

It took a couple cranks to get her car going. Andi switched on the seat heater and set the thermostat for eighty-four, thinking about sunny South Carolina, what clothes to take, and meeting a murderer. Twenty-five minutes to Fiona's. No black ice, no deer laying down their lives for her, no traffic. Thank God. By the time she got to Fiona's, she'd convinced herself that the police would surely use a decoy.

CHAPTER THIRTY-ONE

MARIAH

I OWED IT TO ANDI to keep her safe. Fiona was on I-20 to Columbia, driving like a maniac. The car nearly went airborne when they hit a dip in the road. At first, Fiona had argued that they shouldn't go, said it was a suicide mission, but one call from Eli had changed her mind.

That man knew how to sweet-talk women, all right. Then Fiona had to sweet-talk her brother Bailey into letting them stay at his lake house, which was a pretty amazing feat, considering her house and Andi's had been trashed by a murderer. Neither woman had any luck booking a flight. The prices were ridiculous, so, they'd decided to drive. "Nothing like a road trip to get your mind off things," Fiona had told Andi. "Easy for you to be optimistic," Andi had grumbled.

"What the hell was that?" Andi shook off the sleep. "Speed limit's not eighty-five. What if the police stop us? Ever read about police officers who force women to have sex with them in lieu of a ticket?"

Fiona just laughed. "First, only fake cops do that. Second, people in South Carolina don't worry about stuff like that. This is the civilized world, with lizards and alligators and almost every type of poisonous snake known to mankind."

Andi groaned. "Great. I'll be safe here as long as I don't get bitten or eaten. Or killed by a serial killer."

Fiona laughed again. "Honey, compared to the lowlifes you've been attracting, gators would be a step up. Except for Eli, of course."

"She's wrong about that," Bennie told me.

I dropped a ginkgo leaf into her lap. "Well, I'll be damned," Andi said. She opened the locket, and I gave her a big smile.

"We're both damned." Fiona grinned. "It will be a race to see who gets to hell first. If you do, save me a bunk next to a hot devil."

"She wouldn't be joking about hell if she knew anything 'bout it," Bennie said.

"Fiona has some wisdom," I said.

Bennie gave a little huff. "About enough to fill a shoebox."

Fiona lifted a coffee cup and slurped. "Check your email. I sent what I found on Mariah." She concentrated on passing another eighteen-wheeler.

Andi scrolled through the attachment. I knew what it said. That I attended Spring Valley High School and took band: violin, percussion, and piano. That in April, I'd posted a blog with something called Emancipation Proclamation. Bitter stuff about how my father wanted me to go to med school, but I wanted to major in music education.

Now, Andi knew that I hated my father. Or that I thought I did. Until I realized, too late, that my rants resembled plots of hundreds of middle-school novels: my parents don't understand, they're trying to make me into something I'm not, why do I have to live by their rules. I'd give anything to live by Daddy's rules now.

Bailey had a place off Trenholm Road, back in the woods. Palmettos, scrub pines, and sumac. When they pulled in, a lanky six-footer came out to meet them.

"You didn't tell me he's handsome," Andi said.

"Don't get your hormones brewing. He's gay and he's married."

Bailey opened Fiona's door for her. "You were supposed to be here an hour ago." He gave his sister a hug and a kiss on the cheek. "I tried your cell, but—"

"Battery died at South of the Border, and this old Subie doesn't have USB ports. Couldn't find my power bank. Andi's bank was dead."

Fiona introduced Andi and they shook hands.

"I was worried," Bailey said. "Some coed got snatched at a local bar. Cops found her abandoned car on Trenholm Road. She's still missing." He grabbed two garbage bags from the backseat and hauled them toward the house. "You put bricks in these?"

We knew it wasn't our killer who had the coed. He liked young high school girls. Bennie eavesdropped while Andi carried Honky's carrier inside. The cat wasn't going to let them forget she'd been caged for ten hours.

She yowled like a demon.

"Irv told me what happened at your house," Bailey said. "That guy who came after you with a baseball bat, what'd he want?" Bailey pulled out a bulging garbage bag.

"Some pendants Andi bought," Fiona explained.

"All that destruction over jewelry?" Bailey dragged more things into the house, grunting and grumping every step.

"All that destruction over two dead girls," Bennie muttered.

On his third trip, Fiona touched Bailey's shoulder. "There's something I've been keeping to myself." She glanced around, making sure Andi wasn't around.

"Well?" Arms full, he looked down at his little sister.

She pursed her lips like she smelled something bad. "I can't find my new Glock. Used it last week at the shooting range. Somebody must've stolen it. I am so pissed."

"Irv's birthday present to you?" Bailey got wide-eyed. "You'd better hope it doesn't show up on the mean streets of Philadelphia. Did you register it?"

Fiona unlocked the trunk. "I got busy and forgot."

"For chrissakes, Fiona," he said. "You have to report it stolen. What about Ignatius?"

She patted her handbag. "Right here, where he belongs."

"Why would Fisherman want Fiona's gun?" I asked Bennie. "He's got that monster revolver."

"Most times," Bennie explained, "when somebody steals somebody else's gun, they're gonna use it so they don't get blamed."

The trunk lid made a screech that echoed in the night air. When something scurried through the bushes, Bennie grabbed me.

"You're such a city wimp," I told her. "Probably a squirrel."

"If I didn't have to be in Atlanta, I'd stay here with you," Bailey told Fiona.

"We'll be fine." She closed the trunk. "Your place will be like a vacation for us. Thanks."

CHAPTER THIRTY-TWO

ANDI

THE NIGHT AIR HAD a heavy stillness, like before a rainstorm, sticky-damp. Bailey turned the outdoor heater on and went inside for some wine. Beyond the deck lay a whole forest of fat old trees, where people or lake monsters or wood fairies could hide.

Andi plopped down in a padded, wooden Adirondack chair on Bailey's deck. Through the pine trees, she could see a slice of shimmering lake. "This feels a helluva lot better than the front seat of your car."

Fiona raised her middle finger. "Got you here, didn't I?"

"You did."

"Are we alone out here, or do we have company?" Fiona squinted at Andi.

"You, me, and the trees. I'm not vouching for Sasquatch, though, or murder hornets."

They giggled like drunken teenagers.

"What's so funny?" Bailey set a tray of sliced baguettes, salsa, and two bottles of Chardonnay on the table.

"Murder hornets." Fiona choked back a laugh.

He wound a corkscrew into a green bottle, twisted, and a small pop echoed through the woods. Yes, Andi thought, we've been corked all day, stuck in a bottle of a car, hurtling from state to state. Six hundred and eight miles, long overdue for decanting.

Her head felt like a cement footing, too heavy to lift, too dense to think.

Andi filled Bailey in on the pendants and morgue. Screw the police gag order. He wasn't the press; who was he going to tell anyway? Just in case, she made him swear to secrecy.

Bailey slathered salsa on a toasted baguette. "So, this psycho knows Andi bought the pendants, which are his trophies, according to the P.I."

Fiona nodded. "Long story short, yes. He tried to burn down Andi's house." She bit off a hangnail and spit it out. Andi wondered if Fiona should've left that part out.

Bailey stopped shoveling salsa and stared at her. A vein was pulsing in his neck when he went inside. When the sliders opened again, he set a pistol on the table. "You're sure it was arson?" he asked.

"Asshole left a message on Andi's bathroom wall." Fiona dipped her pinky into the sauce and tasted it. "You made this?"

Eyes bugged, Bailey towered over Fiona, using size to make a point. "Yes, it's fresh! Imported friggin' tomatoes!"

She turned up her nose. "Too much cilantro. Sit down."

"Jesus H. Christ, Fiona! You pissed off a murderer, and you're worried about cilantro?" He got only a shrug from his little sister, so he turned to Andi. "This is front-page news here. The press wants the sheriff's head on a platter. DA running for election has taken up the cause. Disappearing girls are bad for business in a university town," he told her. "Lakeside sheriff's followed up on a slew of false leads. They even sent dogs and a rescue boat out on the lake one day, thinking Mariah had drowned. And you come down here, ready to meddle in the case?"

"Look here, Bailey." Fiona sat up straighter. "We're working with a private investigator and the sheriff. Andi has new evidence in Mariah's case. They're gonna find the killer before he kills again."

"Well, let's hope he didn't follow you here." Bailey shook his head. "I really like my house."

Fiona put her hand on his knee and smiled at him. "We do too."

"You are such a brat." Although he wrinkled his brow, he didn't seem too upset. Andi could see the love between them. It stung. She didn't have family she felt close to.

"What about that other girl—Bernadette Jameson?" Bailey asked.

"Johnston," Andi told him. "Another teenage runaway."

Bailey's head reeled in her direction. "How would you know that? There hasn't been anything about that on the news. Only the Culverton girl."

"Cops don't pursue runaways, and Bernadette's disappearance wasn't publicized," Andi explained.

Bailey sank back into his chair and ran a hand through his blond hair. "Guy's still in Pennsylvania. No way he'd look for you here. But I'll call the police and tell them to keep an eye on you. Don't you worry. Nobody can find you here. Sounds like that guy likes young girls anyway."

Fiona shot Andi a look. Best not to mention that the pendant killer expected to meet Andi at the State House. "Thanks a lot, Bailey. You think that killer's not interested in old hags like us." Fiona smacked his forearm, then rubbed her fist. "Why do I have a brother with lead arms?"

Bailey ignored her. He turned to Andi and picked up the Beretta from the table. "Know how to use this?"

"I took the training," Andi told him.

He handed her the gun and closed her fingers around the grip. "Keep this on your nightstand. And don't turn off your phone for any reason."

If the price for staying here was keeping a Beretta beside her bed, she'd oblige. "Thanks." She stuffed it into her jacket pocket with the phone and realized she'd never charged it. Andi went inside to the kitchen and plugged it in.

They talked for another half hour, until Bailey excused himself, saying he had to catch an early flight to Atlanta. He reviewed the alarm, furnace, Wi-Fi password, and how to work the kitchen appliances with Fiona, told her to check in with him daily, and promised to see them soon. Fiona thanked him and waved as his Land Rover crunched down the driveway.

"Hey, I never gave you the tour. Come on." Fiona crooked a finger and they trudged inside.

"Why are you so cheerful this time of morning, you old hag?"

Fiona held up her middle finger. "Who are you calling a hag? I love this place. Come on." Honky tore through the house like she had demons in her head. "Cat loves those little green lizards. Eats 'em and leaves the wiggling tails," Fiona said.

Andi made a face. "Homeland Security, keeping the world safe from geckos."

Fiona led her down a hallway to a bedroom. With a sweeping gesture, she said, "This one's yours." Four-poster bed, Lafayette chair, claw-foot tables, dark green walls, and floor-to-ceiling windows facing a sliver of shimmering lake.

"Great view." Andi set her suitcases down, dying to test the bed.

"Wait till you see my room." Fiona dragged her across the hall. "When there's a moon, stars twinkle through the skylight." That room had floor-to-ceiling windows, and French doors opened to a landscaped courtyard with a small pond stocked with koi. Furniture made of roughhewn branches gave the illusion of sleeping outdoors.

"What do you think?" she asked.

"Definitely *Architectural Digest*." The hell with the tour; Andi wanted to sleep.

"Come on, I'll show you the rest."

Fiona did a great imitation of a *Lifestyles of the Rich and Famous* realtor. "This house boasts an office, stainless-steel kitchen appliances, spacious living room with a flat-screen TV, wet bar, and hot tub outside. Two and a half acres of privacy and a large carport where the owner keeps his collection of classic cars."

"Wonderful. Tour over." Andi anticipated pulling the covers to her chin and forgetting ten hours of back pain.

A piano riff echoed from her cell phone.

"Did you change my ringtone again?"

Fiona nodded.

Fifth ring, Andi answered. "Hello." Damn. It had gone to voice mail. She checked the messages. Three missed calls.

"Eli must be hot for you if he's calling at two thirty a.m." Fiona handed her a glass of wine.

"It's not Eli." Andi held up a finger. Balancing the phone, she tapped the screen as she walked to the bedroom, intending to collapse the second the call ended.

Guardian, 12:33 a.m. "Mrs. Wyndham, an alarm went off at twelve twenty-seven a.m. We couldn't reach your husband or you, so we sent the police. Call to let us know you're safe."

Guardian, 12:37 a.m. "Mrs. Wyndham, we couldn't reach anyone at the designated numbers. The police have entered your house. Call us immediately."

Oh damn. The next missed call was the police. "FTPD, twelve forty-two. Franklin Township Police calling. The security service called about twelve thirty a.m. We checked your house. The board over your broken window had been removed. We're concerned for your safety. Call us immediately."

"Aw shit!" Andi plopped down on the bed.

Fiona drained her wineglass and reached for Andi's. "You gonna drink that?"

"No, you can have it. Another break-in."

Her phone rang again, and she tapped the green button.

"Andi! Thank God you're all right." Eli's voice. "Why aren't you answering your phone?"

"I took the battery out to avoid being tracked," Andi explained. A long pause and a sigh. She couldn't tell whether he was annoyed or relieved.

"For your own safety, keep your phone charged and with you at all times," he said. "The police have an APB out on you."

"An APB? Why would—"

"Where are you?" He sounded annoyed.

"I texted you where we were going! Bailey's lake house. You could've called Fiona."

"I did, and it went straight to voice mail." Definitely annoyed.

She explained about the USB ports and the power banks. "How do you know about my alarm?"

"Your security company went down the list and couldn't find anyone. I gave the detective at the fire my card. He called me. Are you in Columbia now?" Eli asked.

"Yes, at Bailey's. It's off Trenholm Road. Why the APB?"

Another long pause. "Given the recent break-ins, police were concerned they'd either find your body or learn that someone had kidnapped you. Initially."

"What do you mean initially?" She sat up in bed.

"That was before they found an unregistered gun in your bushes. But there's more. A typewritten letter on your coffee table said Lance's body would never be found. Nor would yours."

"Oh my God!" Andi jumped off the bed and paced in front of the window. "Was it signed?"

"Yes, a pretty good forgery of your signature. Do you own an unregistered Glock?"

"Holy shit! No, I don't own any damned gun." She eyed the Beretta on her nightstand.

"What about a gun?" Fiona put her wineglass down.

Andi waved her off, so Fiona sat down on the bed.

Eli continued. "Any idea how a Glock ended up in your bushes?"

She squeezed her eyes shut, blanking out a needling suspicion. Fiona kept a Glock on the shelf by the back door. But she sure as hell wouldn't leave it in Andi's bushes. "So the police think I killed somebody and tossed a gun in my own bushes. That's ridiculous!"

"No evidence of murder. But if you shot your ex in self-defense, I'd vouch for you."

"Eli, I didn't shoot anybody! I don't own a gun, and I never wrote that damn letter." Call waiting pinged. The ID read FTPD. "Police calling. Gotta go." She thumbed off. If Eli thought she could kill her ex, she had a lot of explaining to do.

The FTPD call turned out to be from Officer Dale Petrucci. The first thing he asked was where she was. His second question was how long she'd be there, and Andi prayed they wouldn't make her come back to Pennsylvania.

She filled him in on when they left Franklin Township. That's when the scary questions began. Did she own the gun? No. Did she have an argument with her ex? The jerk admitted he threw her stuff out the window, and she'd reminded him about the restraining order. Did she know where he was? No, and she didn't care unless he was dead and she wouldn't have to pay the divorce lawyer anymore. Cripes, she shouldn't have said that. Too late now.

Officer Petrucci continued with more questions. How did an unregistered Glock end up in the bushes? She had no friggin' idea. What about the note? It sounded suicidal, like she was going to kill

Lance, then herself. Well, here she was, and killing Lance wasn't worth spending the rest of her life in prison. Her head was spinning after ten minutes. She finished by saying they'd probably find her ex with his new lover, Candy Taubenspeck, and by the way, he was a liar and a cheater, so they shouldn't believe anything he said. In fact, he may have been the one who planted the gun and the letter to get back at her for the restraining order.

Andi tossed the phone on the bed and stood at the window, peering into the darkness. Who would do this to her, and why? What if the police didn't believe her?

Fiona had passed out on the bed. Andi nudged her awake and told her about the note. "Somebody's trying to frame me for killing Lance." She scratched, neck, arm, head.

Her best friend yawned. "Hell, you don't even kill spiders."

She stared into Fiona's eyes and realized she might as well be talking to Honky. "Hope I have a good alibi if somebody did kill Lance. I'm going to bed." Andi pointed. "Yours is that way."

"I'll say you were with me." Fiona stumbled toward her room.

What about the Glock? Whose was it? "Fiona?"

Her friend leaned in the doorway, squinting. "Yeah."

Couldn't be hers. "Never mind."

CHAPTER THIRTY-THREE

ANDI

THE LAKE SHIMMERED LIKE a new penny in the moonlight. Andi fluffed her pillow and climbed into bed. The duvet smelled of cedar. Everything would be better in the morning.

Not likely. That bastard wanted her dead. She closed her eyes.

Eli's house had felt so safe. But now—did Eli really think she could kill her ex? He hadn't said so, but what if nobody believed her? What an idiot she was, telling the cop that she didn't care where Lance was unless he was dead. What was she thinking? She was not weak, but dammit, she'd cry anyway. Andi pounded her pillow as tears streamed down her cheeks.

She felt a slight depression at the end of the bed and expected Honky's blue eyes staring her down in the dark. Instead, a girl with a prom hairstyle and a long, flowing blue dress studied her. Dark hair, upturned nose, flowers in her hair. Andi startled, rubbed her eyes, and blinked.

"Oh my God! Mariah, is that you? Why can I see you?"

A metallic whisper from Mariah.

"Why can I see you?" Andi repeated.

We drained lots of batteries at South of the Border and at a movie theater too. It gives us energy.

"Drained batteries? What?" Andi was confused. "Never mind. Mariah, I'm so sorry about what's happened to you. Help me find the man who hurt you." She sat up and extended a hand. Mariah reached out a gossamer arm. The girl tried to wrap her fingers around Andi's, but the effort frustrated her. Andi couldn't imagine going through eternity without the touch of a human hand.

Here she was blubbering away about her troubles, and this poor girl, who was tortured and murdered by a serial killer, came to comfort her. "Why can I understand you better?"

I guess we both learned how to communicate. Please don't be sad about that call from the police. Eli will help you. Bennie and I think Eli likes you, really likes you. The girl smiled as if she were gossiping at a sleepover.

"Thanks for caring about me, Mariah. Why can't you tell me who did this and where to find him?"

Only mortals can bring justice to mortals. If spirits interfere, we can't cross over. Some things you can never get back. The image started to fade into streams of light like heat rising off pavement. *He captured Rachel when she was cold and hungry, and he's mad as hell at you. Be careful!*

Andi sat in silence for a long time, waiting for Mariah to return, then collapsed into the pillows. "Everything will be better in the morning. Not effing likely, Scarlett O'Hara." She closed her eyes and finally fell asleep.

The next morning, Andi wandered downstairs, following the scent of cinnamon rolls. Fiona had a cup of coffee ready for her. Andi cut a cinnamon roll into quarters, popped one piece into her mouth, and dabbed icing off her lips with a napkin. "I'm not so sure about Eli."

"What? Why?" Fiona raised an eyebrow.

Andi picked up another cinnamon bun. "His exact words were, 'If you shot Lance in self-defense, I'd vouch for you.' Add a forged signed confession to that and an unregistered Glock they found in my bushes. How could Eli even think I could kill anyone?"

Fiona's jaw dropped. "A Glock? Oh shit! Mine is missing, and I forgot to register it, but I sure as hell didn't leave it in your bushes. Your signed confession?"

"A note saying that no one will ever find Lance's body or mine, signed by yours truly. Apparently the signature looks real. I hope I straightened it out with the FTPD." Andi poured herself a glass of milk. "If they didn't believe me—"

"Holy shit!" Fiona set her coffee cup on the counter so hard, some of it spilled.

"If Lance ends up dead, both of us are SOL. Meanwhile, what are you going to do about the missing Glock?" Andi stared outside.

A redheaded woodpecker was keeping the deck bug-free, pecking away like a jackhammer. Fiona banged on the glass, and the bird flew off. "Don't worry about the Glock. I can do the paperwork online." She refilled her cup, snagged another cinnamon bun, and headed for Bailey's laptop.

"There's a fine for not registering it," Andi called to her.

"So, I'll pay the fine," she returned.

"When I couldn't sleep, I looked it up last night. It's five years in prison and up to ten thousand dollars in Pennsylvania."

Fiona stopped in her tracks. "Come to think about it, how am I gonna register a gun I don't have, and I don't know the serial number? Irv bought it, gave it to me for a present. Whoever framed you could get me in trouble too, if they ask about my Glock. Time to call Eli."

"He's probably in court."

"So send a message," Fiona told her. "Eli knows you couldn't kill anybody."

Andi wasn't going to jail because someone had tossed an un-registered gun in her bushes. She texted Eli, and he called her back almost immediately. "We're in trouble," she said.

"I'm aware. An arsonist set a fire at your house. A serial killer is after you. And someone is trying to frame you for killing your husband. If it's anything other than that, you gotta be more specific."

"You're funny." Andi unstuck a piece of bun from the plate.

"Not trying to be, believe me. So, what kind of trouble?"

"Fiona's missing her Glock, and it wasn't registered."

He heaved a sigh. "Does she know the serial number? Did she report it stolen?"

"Nope. And nope."

"Cripes. Put Fiona on speakerphone." When she came on, he continued, "Where was your Glock last time you saw it?"

"On the shelf by the back door."

"Did you have it before the break-in?"

"Yeah, took it to the firing range."

"And after the break-in?" Now, he sounded like a prosecutor instead of a cop.

"No, but I thought it was stolen from my car."

"Good grief. Keep your car locked. Listen to me," he said. "That gun means absolutely nothing unless it was used to commit a crime. It's not registered, but Pennsylvania allows unregistered guns in your house and at your business. You both should know that if you took the certification classes. Of course, if it's Fiona's, police will want to know how it walked over to Andi's. To my knowledge, there is no evidence the gun was used in a crime. Take a deep breath, both of you."

Fiona looked relieved but flummoxed. "So, what should I do?"

"Nothing, until I can check the serial numbers. Get Irv to text them to me. If the numbers match, you'll report it stolen during a break-in."

Fiona heaved a big sigh of relief and thanked him.

"I'll drop by both houses before I fly out tonight to make sure everything is secured. No more guns in either house?" he asked.

"None in mine." Andi chugged some milk.

Pursed lips from Fiona. "The rest are locked up in a space below the stairs."

"The rest?" Eli asked. "I hope they're all registered."

"They are," Fiona assured him, but Andi was pretty sure Ignatius wasn't.

"You can turn speakerphone off now. Andi, I'll pick you up tonight at eight," he said. "Text me your address. We're going to Cowboy Louie's Steakhouse on Gervais for dinner. Meanwhile, you stay put, and call me if anything's suspicious."

"But the pendant killer must be in Pennsylvania," Andi said. "How else could he stage all this?"

"He's hoping to meet you on Friday. That gives us four days to create a plan and find the resources to implement it. He's on his way for sure," Eli told her. "If he isn't there already."

CHAPTER THIRTY-FOUR

ANDI

AT EIGHT O'CLOCK, ELI pulled into Bailey's drive, and Andi went out to meet him. With a kiss on the cheek, Eli settled her into his rental car. Looking like a worried mother, Fiona stood in the yard.

Eli walked up to her, leaned in, and whispered something to her. She smiled, nodded, and went inside.

Then he came back to the car.

"What was that about?" Andi asked.

He gave her a sheepish grin. "Birthday party, Sunday."

"For me?"

"Yeah. It's supposed to be a surprise. Me, I hate surprises."

Now Fiona stood at the window, watching. If a serial killer hadn't threatened her best friend, she'd probably be patting herself on the back for successful matchmaking. Eli waved to her, and they pulled out of the drive.

"I predict you'll live to be ninety and become a very beautiful but ornery old lady."

"Ornery, huh? How's the eye?" Andi grimaced. His eye was at the purple-and-blue stage.

He raised two fingers to check the swelling. "Good thing I like you. I've taken flak from here to Jersey over this eye."

"How did you explain it?"

"A branch hit me in the eye while I was doing yard work."

Andi smiled. "I really am sorry."

She studied the cars around her. Three people on cell phones turning left, one guy biting his nails, a teenage girl putting on lipstick. "Eleanor Rigby" played on the radio, and she remembered Mariah talking about being caught between the worlds and how lonely it was.

"Did you fly on the airline that sends all luggage to Kalamazoo or the one that gets the runways wrong?" she asked.

He laughed. "Spirit Airlines. The flight ran on time. No airport hassles. *You* must have had one hell of a drive. How long did it take?"

"Fiona drove like a bat out of hell," she said. "Once you get past Occoquan on I-95, it's easy. We played cat and mouse with some truckers. Up the hill. Down the hill. You pass them. They pass you. It really pisses them off when two women get ahead."

"So, how long did it take?"

"Ten butt-numbing hours with a howling cat in the backseat."

The city of Columbia passed by, a church with a cemetery, the State House Park, the Supreme Court, then a succession of tall buildings, banks, and hotels, and a big arena complex. Cowboy Louie's Steakhouse was in the old warehouse district. Eli parked and they went inside. With longhorn heads, rusty horseshoes, old farm implements, lasso coils, and black-and-white photos of cowboys, it was more western than the Wild West itself.

They were guided to a dimly lit table toward the back, where the waiter lit their oil lamp and took drink orders. Her glass of Riesling and coffee for Eli arrived shortly after that. Sitting across from

Eli melted away some of Andi's anxiety. A buffalo head kept watch from above. Andi wondered about the buffalo's story, but she had no conduit to animals. Thank God. The waiter recited specials and they ordered. A flatiron steak for Eli. Andi decided on nachos.

"I talked to Sheriff Hollister today. He's worked out a plan." Eli studied her.

"I hope the plan involves a decoy for me."

Frowning, Eli shook his head. "Peter Rockford knows exactly what you look like. They've used this protocol before successfully."

"You've got to be kidding." She picked up the drink menu. Maybe she needed something stronger than Riesling. "Just what am I'm supposed to do?" Andi eyed the pomegranate margarita on the drink menu but decided against it. A headache threatened. She rubbed her temples. "I don't have the pendants. Dr. Arthur has them," she reminded him. "Why don't you guys just tie me to a railroad track and wait for a train to come?" She grunted.

He shook his head. "Andi—"

"I don't like hanging around murderers who torture and strangle girls."

Eli narrowed his eyes. "How do you know he tortures and strangles them?"

"Happened that way in the dream when I punched you."

"That was a dream. A really bad dream for both of us." Eli reached across the table and took her hand. "I'll be there. A team of professionals will have you under surveillance."

She raised her wineglass. "Here's to longevity and my good health."

The waiter came with their food. Once he was gone, Eli lowered his voice. "Do you have any idea how hard it was to get accepted by the FBI?" he asked. There was an edge in his voice. "All that training, not to mention breaking down cultural barriers. I'll be right there, protecting you." He cut into his steak and forked a piece into his mouth. Another man promising her safety. Maybe it was in the Y chromosome. He'd protect her. Bullshit.

"How could he know exactly what I look like?" Andi unstuck some nachos and stuffed one in her mouth.

"You're all over social media. LinkedIn photo from when you were looking for a job. Twitter, Facebook, Instagram, and there's even one photo that shows your tattoo. Trust me with your safety."

Andi hated that line worst of all.

Every time she heard "trust me," life took an ugly turn. "No offense, but the last guy I trusted beat the crap out of me and pointed a gun at me."

"Maybe we'd better talk about this somewhere else. Let's finish eating, and we'll take a drive." After they'd shared the last of the nachos, he got the waiter's attention and paid the bill. He pocketed the receipt and laced his arm through hers. "Let's get the hell out of Dodge, little missy," he said in a near-perfect imitation of John Wayne.

She followed him out the door. "But no matter what you say, this little missy ain't gonna lay down on that railroad track." Could she demand a decoy? If their plan failed, she'd die, and so would an innocent girl.

If it succeeded, Rockford might kill her to eliminate any evidence. A lose, lose.

They'd stopped at the end of the sidewalk under a lamppost when his phone beeped. Eli held up a finger. "Excuse me." He scrolled through messages and returned the cell to his pocket. "Nothing that can't wait," he said. "Anyway, a crime lab is assessing the bone. Unless the killer raises cows, there aren't many places to find bone suitable for carving. First time the forensic anthropologist saw it, she said it wasn't material typically used for jewelry. The bone resembled plastic because it was boiled and dyed. Hey, let's do a little sightseeing."

Andi stared at him. She suspected a ploy to sweet-talk her into the sheriff's plan. But being with him was better than staring out windows at Bailey's lake house, wondering if a killer was out there watching, waiting for the perfect opportunity.

Andi slid onto the passenger seat. "Did you talk to the man who sold the pendants?"

He started the car. "Peter Rockford fed the vendor the same bullshit he fed you. Pendants stolen, sentimental attachment, lost the bid on E-market. Unfortunately, the seller believed it. We have Rockford's IMEI, the cell phone's identity, where it was sold, and a log of calls, but the information listed when he registered the phone is bogus. With burners, you can trace the phone and the cell towers where it was used, but not its owner if they falsify the registration."

"Where were the cell towers?"

He winced. "The phone and cell towers were traced to South Carolina."

"How recently?" she asked.

He winced again.

"Oh shit!" A layer of condensation was building on Andi's window. She was tempted to write SOS on it. "He's here already, isn't he?"

Eli nodded. "Do you have a license to carry?"

The last of the nachos were rumbling in her stomach. "CWP in Pennsylvania. Bailey loaned me a Beretta."

"Don't tell the sheriff about the Beretta, and leave it in the car if you're with him. I use my Minnesota CWP here because there's no reciprocity with Pennsylvania." Eli stopped for a light, readjusted the rearview mirror, and fiddled with the side mirrors. "Andi, I don't want you ever alone down here. Keep Fiona with you. She probably has an arsenal in her handbag."

Andi gave him an incredulous look.

"Let me get this straight. You're scaring the shit out of me about being alone here, but you want me to meet a serial killer."

"In the presence of a well-trained team of law enforcement professionals."

Andi answered him with a huff and opened the locket. Mariah was frowning. Bennie mouthed, "No!" Apparently the girls didn't like the idea either. She snapped the locket closed.

Eli ignored her silence. "Serial killers have a pattern," he said. "Stress sets them off. A few murders, times of restraint, then murders closer and closer. I'll tell you what scares me."

"Right now, you're the one scaring me," she muttered.

"He lost his trophies." Eli glanced sideways, probably gauging her reaction. "That's a huge stressor. He set a fire and broke in at Fiona's. He's deviated from his regular mode of operation." Eli angled into a parking space at the State House. "And that forged note is an attempt at communication. He's taunting us." Eli shook his head. "We need to engage or else he's headed for a killing spree."

Andi focused on breathing slowly, afraid of what she knew Eli would say next. "You're the only one who can stop him."

CHAPTER THIRTY-FIVE

ANDI

ANDI AND ELI CLIMBED the State House steps and sat on the marble portico, looking down at the back of George Washington's statue and beyond that to some sword-wielding man on a bronze horse. "Homeland Security back then didn't do such a great job. Sherman leveled the State House," Andi told him. "And the battle rages on. All this undocumented immigrant talk on the news. Hell, my European ancestors were the first illegals. No green cards, no passports. Just a horse, a gun, and a bag of beans."

"You make me laugh, Andi Wyndham. It's been so long since . . . you know I'd never let anyone hurt you." He took her chin in his hand and kissed her, tasting her first, then leaning into her with a kiss that made her remember what passion tasted of.

He stopped abruptly, tipped her chin again, and kissed her lightly. "You're good medicine."

"Oh yeah? What do I taste like, wine?"

Over his left shoulder, she caught movement. A girl, dark hair upswept with pink side tendrils gently blowing in the breeze, long dress cascading, the twinkle of a rhinestone earring. Mariah stood on a marble section jutting from the side of the steps. Too bad old Wade Hampton couldn't rescue her. She'd figured out how to be seen. Maybe, Andi decided, ghosts can only be seen when you want to see them, a sort of mutual agreement.

Mariah eased down to the edge and sat. *He's not who you think he is.*

You keep saying that. You're not talking about Eli, are you?

No. Not him.

So who's not? Andi asked.

No answer from the girl.

For a few seconds, Mariah rested between the two lampposts with her legs dangling over the side, studying the world, maybe yearning to be alive again. A look of intense sadness in her transparent blue eyes, she turned back to Andi. *Find Fisherman* before *he kills Rachel. She's a pretty blond.*

Then Mariah evaporated into rainbow ripples like steam from rain on a hot summer day.

That's who killed you? A fisherman? I'll work on it, Andi answered, feeling guilty that she was currently working on hooking up with Eli.

"Andi? What are you looking at?"

She shook off the image. "Thinking about the missing girls. What about the pendant carver's saw?" That sounded like something her mother the reporter would say.

"It takes a special machine to cut bone," he said. "Should be easy to track down. A cutting instrument will have its own signature, like a knife or gun."

She mulled that over. "But you would need the original cutting machine for a comparison." Her eyes were glued to the marble wall, waiting for Mariah to reappear. Two college kids raced by on rollerblades, calling to each other, "Watch this!" Their voices were cheerful, carefree. Mariah had never made it to college. How the hell did that man lure her?

Want a free puppy, little girl? That's all it took with her. *Come with me. You can pick one out yourself.*

Stupid. She doubted that line would've worked on Mariah and Bernadette. Kids today were smarter.

"Andi?" Eli turned her head so that he could see her eyes. "Seems like you've slipped away to somewhere not so pleasant."

"Twenty-six years ago, a man promised me a puppy and I was kidnapped. I was naïve like the girls, but somehow, I escaped. Guess I owe something to those who didn't. A shrink might call that survivor's guilt." She took a deep breath. "Tell Hollister I'll do whatever it takes to save that girl. And myself," she added. "The one Peter Rockford is stalking now is a runaway named Rachel, and she's blond."

Eli nodded. "How would you know that?"

"A dream," she lied.

Eli stared at her. "I don't like being on the receiving end of your dreams." He pointed to his eye. "Hollister's not going to—"

"Unless there's a blond named Rachel who's been reported missing," she filled in.

"Do you have Rachel's last name?"

Andi shook her head. "No, just that she's blond."

Eli looked thoughtful. Then he took out his phone and sent a text.

The traffic light on the corner changed. A car horn honked, then another. Somebody wasn't paying attention. A bus rumbled by, leaving a sooty streak of exhaust. Across the street an NBSC sign flashed blue from a building.

"Hollister said he's limiting what he tells the parents until this investigation has more evidence. Tell you the truth, I'm not certain they need to know everything. Did I tell you a beaker slid itself to the end of the shelf in the morgue?"

Andi smiled. "Really. And here I thought you were not a spiritual guy."

He focused on the intersection. "My mother was a healer, what people today would call homeopathic. Men, women, and children came from all over the Midwest seeking cures. She died when I was ten, couldn't heal herself. That ended my spirituality."

The palmettos made silhouettes in the moonlight. Verdigris metal streetlights dotted the paths away from the capital building. Across the street, a gnarled tree with hanging moss graced the churchyard. Judging from the architecture, she'd bet the church was at least a hundred years old. A wrought-iron fence surrounded it. To the left of the building, a small graveyard. "Smell that?" she asked. "Tea olive bushes. I love tea olives. Come on." She took his hand, and they crossed the street.

Trinity Episcopal Cathedral, according to a small sign. A terrier sat inside the fence, wagging its tail. The little fellow dropped a red ball from his mouth and barked. She stopped and watched. He barked again and scooped it up, tail wagging furiously. Guess he wants me to see him too, she thought. "Let's go inside."

Eli gave her a quizzical look. "Why?"

"If anyone jumps out, you can shoot 'em." She poked him. "Humor me. I'm funny. Remember?" Like an invading army marching into battle, they crunched over tiny acorn shells. She dug through her purse, pulled out a penlight, clicked it and scanned the gravestones. "There." Andi aimed it at a small white marker. "Perlie the dog is buried in his family's plot."

"You've been here before?"

"No." A ball dropped at her feet.

Eli picked it up. "Where'd that come from? Balls grow on trees down here?"

"Throw it," she told him.

"Why? You gonna fetch?"

"Just throw," she said. "Don't hit any gravestones, or you might get haunted."

Clearly he thought she was pulling something over on him, but he tossed underhand. Seconds later, the ball dropped at his feet.

"What the heck?"

"Do you see the dog?" she asked.

He looked around, then reached for the ball. With a sideways glance at her, he tossed it again. It returned to his feet. "Holy shit," he muttered. "You see a ghost dog? You see ghosts?"

"Yes, Perlie's here. Guess this is as good a time as any to tell you. I can hear and see ghosts."

"Holy shit!" he hissed.

"You really shouldn't curse in a churchyard." She made a cross of her arms and grinned. "Remember the water that spilled in the restaurant? That was Mariah. Probably the beaker too. I don't think she likes cops, but don't take it personally."

He stared at her. "Are you serious? Hollister wants to meet you tomorrow. How am I going to convince him that Mariah talks to you?"

"The same way you just convinced me to lie down on those railroad tracks," she said.

CHAPTER THIRTY-SIX

ANDI

WHAT IF ELI'S KISSES were a down payment for risking her life?
Andi sat up in bed at the lake house. Of course they were.
Two Shadows watched from the ceiling, proving she hadn't
left her troubles in Pennsylvania. She slid out of bed and put on her
jacket and shoes. Too much chatter churning in her brain. Andi
needed some soothing night air.

Outside, pine tree limbs waved like giant fingers, pointing in
one direction, then changing their minds. In the moonlight, the lake
glistened like dark, rippled satin. Too damn quiet. No fire engines,
police cars, or trucks rumbling by. Maybe that's why she couldn't
sleep. Sliders were built into the wall of glass; Fiona had warned
her to keep them locked. She removed the pole wedged between the
doors and slid it open, pushing a screen aside. Then she sank into an
Adirondack chair.

About an hour ago, she'd been at the State House with Eli. Was
he thinking of her too? Probably not. She was the only idiot still
awake. Her thoughts bounced back and forth between Mariah and

Eli. The girl needed her. Eli needed her. She felt good about herself, cared for, connected. Cripes. Would she be alive this time next week?

Night sounds surrounded her. Pines danced with the breeze, a wind chime jangled solo notes. In the breaks between pines and oaks, stars twinkled like tiny lasers in a stage background. A twig snapped.

She leaned forward, straining to see. Just a raccoon with something in its mouth scurrying toward the lake. The air smelled of pine resin and mulch. Nature in balance. Yet her life was like a gyroscope, wobbling out of control, correcting, then wobbling again.

Find a fisherman, Mariah had said. Lakeside bordered several lakes. According to Fiona, in every one lay twenty sunken mailboxes and a couple of barbecue grills, a favorite extracurricular activity for high school kids. Hundreds of men around here must fish. And a runaway named Rachel? Without a last name, near impossible to find.

A squelching sound, a broken rubber seal, accompanied by glass gliding along on a track. Footsteps shuffled through the pine straw. With the moon nearly full, her friend's hair glowed white. She lowered herself into a lawn chair next to Andi and sang a couple lines from a song about having trouble sleeping.

"Number one cause of insomnia, woman. Love. Two truckloads of Ambien won't cure that ailment. So, is Eli worth it?"

"He must think I'm nuts." Andi kicked a pinecone off the patio.

"Why?"

"Ghost dog brought me a ball in Trinity graveyard. I told Eli to toss it. Ball came back."

"No shit. A ghost dog. What'd Eli do?"

"Threw it again. When it came back to him, he asked if I could see ghosts."

Fiona chuckled softly. "That's the only thing bothering you?"

Andi stared out into the woods. Wispy gray beings with yellow eyes stared back at her. The Shadows. She glanced over at Fiona, ever patient, waiting for an answer, but their friendship had survived silence before.

A short breath of wind skittered leaves across the patio. A twig with three ginkgo leaves landed in her lap. Andi smiled and twirled it between her fingers. Sisterhood of runaways: Mariah, Bernadette, Andi.

After clicking a barbecue lighter several times to make sure it worked, Fiona lit a citronella candle on the table between them. "A beacon, in case the lake monster's looking for us," she said. "Another ginkgo leaf?"

"It's become Mariah's trademark." Andi watched the candle flicker until the silence ate a hole in her conscience. Sharing your fears is healthy, she told herself, a sign of trust. "There's a new voice talking to me. A little kid repeating stuff."

"Repeating what?"

"A key rattling in a lock and climbing a golden tree. Other than that, she refuses to talk to me."

"Sounds like a fairy-tale rhyme. Hey, did I ever tell you about the Lake Murray Monster? Drunken fishermen fall overboard and drown, and a lake monster gets blamed. It never got Irv or Bailey though, and Lord knows, they used to drink like fish. Me? I don't fish or drink." Fiona gave her a conspiratorial wink.

Andi laughed. Her friend had an uncanny gift for tearing down melancholy firewalls. When they dropped back into silence, Andi knew everything she'd heard about Fiona's hunting skills was true. She could sit in a deer blind until the next century, waiting for a deer to show up so she could shoot it.

"Evening, ladies," a voice said.

Fiona came out of her seat, almost knocking the table over. "Jesus H. Christ!" Ignatius zigzagged through the darkness like a night-vision scope seeking its target. She squinted. "Where the fuck is he?"

Two Shadows dove in and out of the trees.

All Andi could see were pine trees, yellow cat eyes, and bushes. Maybe he was a neighbor. "Fiona, what if it's—"

"Get off my property before I shoot your trespassing ass," Fiona yelled. "Who the hell are you, and what do you want?"

"Was jus' do-doing a little night fissshing," the man said. "No harm meant. Lovely house you have."

Mariah had talked about a fisherman. The Shadows, agitated for some reason, circled a fat oak tree. Fiona fired a shot into the air. A branch cracked and thudded to the ground.

"Hey! Don't do that!" The man scuffled through the leaves.

Her friend fired again, and another branch crashed to the ground. "No harm meant," Fiona mocked him. "So just haul your fishing rod and your booze on out of here."

"Maybe we should call the police," Andi whispered, turning toward the sliders.

The scuffling sped up and faded toward the lake.

"Nah, old guy, probably drinking moonshine. Happens all the time around here." Fiona sank back into the chair. "So why can't you sleep?"

Damn. Southern justice simplified everything. Guy comes on your land, you shoot something. "Thinking about Mariah running away," Andi said.

"I took off for Myrtle Beach once," Fiona confessed. "Hitch-hiked. I could charm the socks off people in those days, fluttering my baby blues. Anyway, I blew off the last week of school, junior year. Worked at a corn-dog joint. Went back home though. Did you ever run away?"

"Yep, with Lance. You know that. Never looked back." She watched Fiona's face in the candlelight. For her, that must be the ultimate unforgiveable mistake. Family was Fiona's safety net. They'd grown up poor and earned their way into college. "I thought anything was better than home, even Lance. Totally dysfunctional family," she assured her. "Nothing like yours."

"You think mine wasn't dysfunctional?" Fiona laughed. "My daddy was an alcoholic. We liked him best when he was passed out or gone hunting. Mama cleaned houses. Ever read Pat Conroy's *Great Santini*? That was our daddy. All families are dysfunctional. Some more than others."

Andi twisted a curl around her finger.

"Somebody could do sociological case studies on my family. Mom always understood me better than my dad, and I think it pissed him off that we had a special bond because of our connection to the beyond. My parents used to go to war over me. Particularly after the kidnapping. Responding to the voices was their battle royale. Dad told me to ignore them or become a freak. It got ugly when Mom asked him why he'd married a freak. A question I still can't answer today."

"Opposites attract?" Fiona suggested.

"I think she was a rookie reporter with no money when she married him. Once the honeymoon was over and she had a stable career, my father's one-sided view of life probably drove her away. She traveled so much and couldn't take me with her. Her destinations were too dangerous for a kid. So I was stuck with my father. I hated them both for that. My mother for leaving me with him and my father for making home feel like a military base."

"I'm sure they both loved you in their own ways," Fiona assured her. "What about the Shadows protecting you? I mean, they didn't help when Lance was beating on you."

"They were terrified of Lance, like children of abusive men."

Fiona squinted. "Why did the Shadows attach themselves to your mom?"

"Ah, that would be Mom's first Pulitzer. It made *Time* magazine. A deranged dictator believed children were spying on him for his enemy, so he ordered soldiers to round them up and execute them in the street. Mom and her crew came upon the aftermath when soldiers tossed children's bodies into a mass grave and buried them. Later, I met some of those children at our tea parties."

"God, the things your mama must've seen." The candle flickered and went out. Fiona relit it. "What were those kids like at your tea parties?"

"Like normal children. Happy to be invited and delighted to have a living child they could talk to."

Andi smiled remembering.

"Holy shit. That gives a whole new meaning to invisible friends."

"Yep. Mom founded the war-lost children fund and an agency to help families locate their offspring. The end goal was to give them closure by marking graves with children's names and the dates they were born and died."

"Your mama had a good heart."

"She was very passionate about it. War-lost children who refused to cross over became the Shadows," Andi explained. "They rallied around Mom and showed their appreciation by caring for me when she couldn't be with me."

Fiona shook her head in astonishment. "You grew up with your feet in two different worlds."

"Yeah, sometimes they danced on the ceiling to cheer me up. Other times, they'd warn about trouble coming. When they showed up, it was as if my mom was there. That's the weird part. How would she know when I needed a mother?"

"Good moms sense when you need them," Fiona said. "Even if you're thousands of miles away. They must get some subliminal ping, or maybe their heart stops for a second to remind them of their connection to you. There's this invisible tie between a mother and a daughter. Nothing can sever it, not even if a daughter tries to pretend it's not there."

Andi had to acknowledge that even in death her mother hadn't abandoned her. The Shadows were proof of that.

"You think Mariah's mother knows in her heart she's dead?" Andi wondered.

"I bet she's holding out every ounce of hope her girl will come home. That's how she's staying sane."

As much as Andi wanted to give closure to Mariah, she dreaded the moment Mariah's mother would find out that all hope was lost.

CHAPTER THIRTY-SEVEN

ANDI

"Y OU'RE THE TALK OF the department," Sheriff Hollister said. "First big break in this case comes from a lady in Pennsylvania. Go figure." Hollister met Andi at the door of the conference room of the Lakeside Police station. The station was a small brick building on Trenholm Road with pink flowering bushes outside, nothing like Franklin Township's glass-walled, tax-dollars-wasting monstrosity.

Andi scanned the conference room. No different from the morgue lobby: aluminum-frame chairs, cheap pine table, institutional green walls. Eli sat across from the sheriff at an oblong table while Hollister took Andi's statement about the pendants. Hollister was a German shepherd of a man: sturdy, with black hair and a brown moustache and bushy brown eyebrows that didn't match his hair. Penetrating brown eyes studied her.

He handed her a business card. "If anything out of the ordinary should happen, call me."

She exchanged a smile with Eli. Hollister had no idea how often unusual things happened to her. "We did have a visitor last night, some drunk, old guy night fishing. Never actually saw the guy, just heard him," she said. "Fiona scared him off."

He tapped a cigarette on the table and made a note on a pad. "I assured Bailey we'll keep an eye on the lake house. Once you make that call to Peter Rockford to confirm the date and time, you'll have a twenty-four seven police escort."

Andi took a deep breath and mentally prepared herself for all the imagined scenarios that had kept her awake last night. It had taken Perlie, the ghost dog, to convince Eli. No way the sheriff would believe in otherworld beings without seeing them the way Eli did.

"We're using protocol from a 1985 investigation when two local girls were murdered." Hollister's chair squeaked when he leaned back. "A ten-year-old and a high school girl," he said. "Lexington County department worked on the case with SLED, the State Law Enforcement Division lab, and the FBI. A famous profiler wrote about it in his book."

A forty-year-old protocol? Oh good. After she was dead, maybe someone would make her a footnote. Andi imagined that freight train roaring down the track toward her.

"They used a victim's sister as bait," Hollister continued. "Can't thank you enough for helping us. I have every reason to believe we can arrest this man."

"You can't use a decoy for me?" Andi wanted to ask if they planned to take out a life insurance policy on her. Fiona could make some money that way, buy herself a wine cellar, a bigger house, definitely a new car.

"From what Eli's told us, he knows exactly what you look like, and Fiona too. If he thinks police are involved, he'll kill the girl he's holding hostage, and you'll never be safe again."

Andi could also die while they were trying to catch the pendant killer. This was all one big lose-lose proposition for her. The sheriff tapped the cigarette again and repositioned himself in the chair, a cheek-to-cheek shift. Maybe the man had hemorrhoids. Then he breathed out as if exhaling cigarette smoke.

"Eli seems to think you have some kind of . . . connection to the girls." Hollister cocked his head, solidifying his eerie resemblance to a German shepherd. She desperately wanted to trust him, wanted to believe he'd protect her.

The door of the conference room was open. In the hallway outside, coins jingled into a machine. A soda can banged into the slot, hit the floor, and rolled. Someone cursed, a woman's voice. Three phone conversations leaked into the room. One about who'd be picking up the kids. The other two, car accidents.

"I was kidnapped when I was four. It destroyed my family. This is how I pay it forward," she admitted. "A disembodied voice called to me at the gem show when I bought the first pendant, a young Southern girl, Mariah. I know it sounds weird, but she's one of the pendant girls."

Hollister scratched his chin, looking skeptical. In his line of work, chalk lines represented dead people. Bodies got zipped into plastic bags, and you never heard from them again. She understood that, but her life was different. Andi wished he'd just ask how it all worked but knew he wouldn't unless she made it easy for him.

"Mariah has talked to me since I bought the pendant. I've seen her too. She thinks a runaway named Rachel will be his next victim." She glanced at Eli, who was suddenly busy stirring coffee. "Mariah also told me to look for a fisherman. I know the girl is trying to help, but when she speaks, it's like listening to cell phone calls that break up intermittently. Honestly, I've spent most of my life ignoring ghosts' voices." Andi scratched her hair, neck, arm.

"Got Eli's text last night. Only Rachel missing is a girl from Charlotte, North Carolina. Not likely it's her. That's over a hundred miles from here and across state lines. Most runaways stay within fifty miles of their home," Hollister told her. "Did you get a last name or where she lives?"

"Sometimes the information I get is incomplete." Andi had a bad feeling about Rachel and a worse feeling about Hollister's plan. If something went wrong, someone would get hurt. Most likely, her. In TV cop shows, the bait always came away with holes in them. "Just wondering. What happened to the sister in that 1985 case?" She took several deep breaths, willing herself to be calm when she really wanted to bolt. Andi wanted to trust Hollister, but what did she know about his track record in policework? A 1985 case? That's the best they could do?

Eli reached for her hand. "Will you excuse us for a minute?" he said and walked her into the hallway. "The bait was well protected. What's wrong?"

A woman police officer, probably the person at the soda machine, gave Eli a head-to-toe appraisal.

"This feels all wrong, Eli. What do I know about police work? Not only do I not want to become the next face carved into a pendant, what if I end up being the reason he kills Rachel?" Andi asked. "Sometimes I'm not even sure if I understand Mariah's cryptic messages."

Eli took both her hands in his. "I *saw* that ball last night. Nothing like that has ever happened to me before. I'm staking my reputation as a consultant on you. The good old boys see me as a hotshot Yankee P.I. with a braid. A Native American. I can do things they can't, and I get paid a helluva lot better. There's room for resentment here. Hell, some of them may even mistake me for a hairdresser with a gun."

She smiled. Ten days ago, she'd said that, and he remembered. "You're a very funny man," she said, imitating his voice. A man she could fall in love with.

He draped an arm around her. "Come on. You're the first good break they've had in this case. Besides, the three of us are just doing some old-fashioned fieldwork today, nothing life threatening." They walked back to the room and sat down.

"This investigation was going nowhere fast," Hollister said, "and with these pendants you've given us excellent physical evidence. So if you're willing, I'm open to . . . working with you. Just please don't tell anybody. The press would have a field day. Papers have been on our case since Day One."

Eli spoke up. "She's a consultant. Like me. No other explanation needed."

"Okay," Hollister nodded. "We all want Rachel home for Thanksgiving so there's no empty seats at the table, and I'd love to have Mariah's case closed by then too. Meanwhile, one of our newest detectives did a little off-duty work. He talked to a con at the Francis Marion Detention Center and thinks we should interview him again. Why don't you come along? Maybe you'll have new questions for him."

"A con? What's his connection to the girls?" Andi asked. Cripes, she'd never met a con, never been to a prison.

"Melvin sold drugs to young people, in an area near where the girls lived," Hollister explained.

"You think the girls were buying drugs from him?"

"Yeah, I do. There's no evidence that Melvin killed those girls, but he might know who did." Hollister shoved his NASCAR coffee cup aside, fished through a drawer, and came up with a pack of gum. "You okay with some fieldwork today?"

She nodded, marveling at how easily Eli could convince her to do just about anything. Hollister let the dispatcher know where he was going, and they walked to his car. A new feeling of dread squeezed her stomach. Her master's in English hadn't included interviewing prisoners or baiting murderers. Either the police were desperate, or Eli had done a stellar sales job.

Maybe he'd sold her right into a body bag.

CHAPTER THIRTY-EIGHT

ANDI

"MELVIN DEALT DOWN BY the War Memorial. Next block from Trinity Cathedral." Hollister offered some background information on Bernadette's old supplier on their way to the prison. "We arrested him when a kid OD'd."

The sheriff had a cigarette in his hand, but he hadn't smoked it. By the time he got around to lighting up, the thing would be worn out, Andi thought. But that would save her from breathing in a car full of smoke.

"You trying to quit?" Eli asked.

"Got a baby on the way. My wife doesn't want secondhand smoke. Said it's either me or the cigarettes. I don't believe she'd throw me out, but she's right. It's not good for babies."

"It's not good for anyone," Andi muttered.

"Here, I'll be your smoking cessation counselor." Eli took the cigarette from the sheriff's hand and bent it in half. He opened the glove compartment and tossed it in. "Had a partner, a tribal cop. Helped him quit, cold turkey." Eli snapped his finger. "Just like that."

Hollister ran a hand over his chin. "He never went back?"

"Never. The man died of lung cancer two months later."

"Damn." Hollister banged the steering wheel and barked out a laugh. "Never met a P.I. anything like you. Who gave you that shiner?"

Eli shot Andi a look.

She smiled. "How *did* you get that black eye?"

"Rescuing a woman." His look spoke loudly—go there and you'll be sorry.

The sheriff glanced sideways at them. "Something tells me she knows all about it."

"He ran into a door," Andi told Hollister.

"Yeah, right." He changed the subject. "When's the first time you saw the girls?"

Take it slowly, she decided. Ease the lawmen into a world they'd have a hard time believing. "I bought the pendant and started having nightmares that night. Mariah didn't appear until I came down here."

Hollister and Eli said nothing. That's probably how these guys worked—drowning a suspect in silence and waiting for them to come up and spill their guts. She wasn't a suspect, and still, it worked.

"I had this dream one night about a girl, a junkie, and an old man who looked like an extra from *The Twilight Zone*. The junkie was sick, and the other girl was trying to convince the old man to help her. And there was this horrible noise, sounded like a grinding saw."

Eli glanced at her. "Did you get some sense of the place?"

"Big room, maybe an old parlor. It had been grand once, marble fireplace, warped wood floors. The girl said, 'Found us at the Holiday Inn.'" Andi caught herself scratching and stopped.

"The nearest Holiday Inn is a twenty-minute walk from the campus. That's assuming runaways live in hotels. They don't." Hollister shook his head.

"What evidence do *you* have?" Andi asked.

Hollister listened for a few seconds to his police scanner. "We know the date she left home, middle of the night. Turned the dang security system off and spent the night with a girlfriend who lived on campus. The coed admitted she picked her up one street over from Mariah's. One night there and she disappeared."

"Couldn't you track her phone?" Andi asked. "Most parents have GPS on their kids now."

Eli answered for Hollister. "She took the battery out. Not unusual for smart runaways."

"Campus cameras picked her up, and that girl loved the State House Park," Hollister continued. "We set up surveillance there and at places she'd been seen. We got all kinds of reports of sightings from teenage girls. Checked 'em all out, but didn't do any good."

"So, she was staying with friends?"

"Nah," Hollister told her. "Seems like Mariah cut all ties, like she wanted to stay lost forever."

"Forever is usually a short time for teenagers," Andi said. "What about a boyfriend? Maybe she met someone on campus."

"Nine-one-one received a call from a boy who said he'd killed her and put her body in the lake."

Andi nodded. "Bailey told us about that search."

"I authorized divers, boats, and cadaver dogs," Hollister told her. "Damn waste of taxpayer money. Boy's in jail now for that. Stupid. But your pendants are sending this investigation in a different direction now. We're gonna learn the truth. I can smell it." He reminded her of a German shepherd following a scent.

Fifteen minutes later, they sat across from Melvin in a visitor's room. Prison was a place she never wanted to visit again. Stone-faced guard at the door. Stale air reeking of cigarettes and disinfectant. Fluorescent light blinking on and off. Andi was sure the industrial brown ceiling fan over the table would maim somebody if it ever fell. Melvin wore blue scrubs with FMDC on the back. He was a beanpole with a scraggly goatee and fuzzy blond dreadlocks. He smoked, which likely drove Hollister crazy.

"I done already talked to that detective fella you sent 'round. I ain't sold nothing that killed a kid. Already tol' you and the detective that. Who's he?" He pointed his cigarette at Eli.

"P.I. and former Special Agent Eli Lake," the sheriff explained. "He's come all the way from Pennsylvania to investigate two missing girls."

"I ain't take no girls," Melvin assured them. "Sell a little weed on the street. Course I see things sometimes. This gonna cut my sentence?"

"It can't hurt." Hollister handed Melvin pictures of Bernadette and Mariah.

Andi opened her locket, and Mariah smiled at her. She averted her eyes from Hollister's photos. At the morgue, photos of the girls had set her emotions and her stomach roiling. That was the first time she'd seen images of the girls when they were alive.

"Hey, foxy lady." Melvin nodded toward Andi. "What she here for? Social worker or something? You wanna help me, sugar?" He wiggled his eyebrows.

Andi snapped the locket closed and shifted uncomfortably in her chair.

"The lady is a consultant." Eli narrowed his eyes. "Look at those pictures, and think really hard if you ever, maybe even once, saw either one of those girls."

"She too fine-looking to be a cop." Melvin blew her a kiss.

Eli's shoulders tensed. "Look at the photos," he growled.

A vein in Hollister's neck was pulsing. "Answer the man. You seen these girls or not?"

Melvin held the photos in his stick-like fingers, studying them. "That one," he said, pointing to Mariah's picture.

"You didn't know Bernadette?" Andi asked.

"Ain't know anyone named Bernadette," he said.

"Did you know a Mariah?" Eli asked.

"Yeah."

"Where'd you see her?" Hollister asked.

"She one of them rich kids run off to the streets. How much offa my sentence?"

Hollister asked the name of his lawyer and wrote it down. "Where'd you see her?"

"She lived in some empty house offa Greene Street down by Five Points. Couple kids lived there. Called it their Holiday Inn. Young 'uns, pretty girls. Probably doing it for money by now, got themselves a pimp or being managed. That's what the young 'uns do."

Eli and Hollister were writing furiously in their notebooks.

Andi's face lit up. "Are you saying that girl is alive?"

"Don't know, Blue Eyes. Them runaways come and they go. Hey, you ain't introduced me proper," Melvin whined to Hollister.

"My name is Andi. Did the girls hang around with a fisherman? Maybe he gave them free stuff or money." Andi caught herself scratching again.

He leered. "Lady, ain't no fishing holes on city streets. Just man-holes."

Melvin cocked his head this way and that, grinning. Hollister looked like he wanted to knock him off his chair.

"Do you remember a girl named Rachel?" the sheriff asked.

"Ain't know a Rachel. Been off them streets for a while. Must be a new one." Then Melvin acted like he'd remembered something important. "Oh yeah. This guy usta sell fish outta the back of his truck. Guess he went on down to Georgetown at night, iced 'em real good, and sold 'em in that empty parking lot on Barnwell."

Hollister wrote it all down.

"Was there a name painted on the truck?" Eli asked.

"No. You find him weekends, sittin' on a lawn chair with his *Wall Street Journal*. Old guy cain't hardly talk, let alone read. Probably illiterate. Got one of them Gullah accents or maybe he done had hisself a stroke. You call my lawyer tonight?" Melvin drummed his fingers on the table.

"Yes," Hollister answered patiently. "I'll call. You remember this guy's name?"

"Ain't got no name I know of. People just call him Fisherman."

Mariah whispered, *He's lying. Fisherman doesn't sell fish. He works for him.*

Andi scrambled to make sense of that. A fisherman who doesn't sell fish. Who works for whom?

Eli and Hollister grilled Melvin another five minutes and learned not one damn thing.

"He's lying," Andi said on the way out the door.

"Cons do that," Hollister told her.

CHAPTER THIRTY-NINE

MARIAH

F OR A FEW MINUTES, Bennie and I sat on the steps of the capitol where Andi and Eli had been the night before. The sky was winter gray. We looked out over the busy intersection of Gervais and Sumter, watched the cars go by, and viewed a world that had moved on without us. No families, no future, no hope. One big void we couldn't climb out of.

I stretched my legs and tried to loosen up my conscience too. "I thought it would get easier for my mama after all this time, but she still cries every night. A couple times, Mama's seen girls with hair like mine from the back and called my name. Sometimes the girl turns around and stares like Mama's a crazy woman. You ever feel guilty?"

"Hell, no. I just feel dead," Bennie said. "Mad I ain't alive no more."

"Well, I feel stupid and guilty. Mama might as well be dead herself. She's lost her job. Her friends don't visit anymore because she's depressed all the time. My daddy's not doing so great either.

Sometimes he drives to the high school at night and sits in the bleachers like I'm still marching at a game and he's watching me."

"You're depressing the hell outta me. I'm going to the zoo." Bennie hopped down the steps, then turned to me. "Wanna come?"

"No." A breeze rattled the palmetto fronds. Flag clips clanked against the metal pole. I had an eternity of time, stuck here unless I did something to get to the Other Side. I needed to figure out how to help Andi. The only solution I could come up with would be costly for everybody because The Punishers were clear that we could not interfere.

CHAPTER FORTY

ANDI

Andi hadn't slept more than three hours the night before. Nothing about the woods outside her window consoled her. Snapping twigs, creaking branches, and those squawking mallards set her mind on edge. If the police found this man, the killings might stop, but it wouldn't bring Mariah back. In fact, her mother would suffer more. No parent wants to know their child was tortured before death and her face etched on a pendant.

Around noon Andi's phone rang. It was Eli. Hollister had found the girls' Holiday Inn. He wanted them to meet there for what he called a walk-through. Andi figured he wanted to test her ability to communicate with the Other Side.

A little before three that afternoon, she and Eli arrived in the rundown neighborhood with trash blowing around the street, a dead cat on the sidewalk, and houses with broken windows that looked like the inside of a shark's jaws.

None of that bothered her.

It was the things she couldn't see but heard: more dead girls.

Eli leaned against the old wood-sided house while Hollister swept glass from the doorway with one shoe.

"The *State* newspaper ran an update of Mariah's story today," Hollister told them. "Our cold case has become very hot news. Media finds out I'm using you, I'll be in the *National Enquirer*." He ran a hand through his hair. "I can just see the headline: 'Stumped Southern Sheriff Hires Ghostbuster to Solve Case.'"

She took a deep breath and exhaled. "I'll do my best to help, but spirit talk is like a cell conversation in a train station. Drop-ins, drop-outs. All dependent on how long they've been dead and how much energy they've stored."

"Hmm. Sounds like my spotty cable service." Hollister unlocked the door. "I wrangled the key from a realtor. Can't be many folks making bids on this dump, although it was stately at one time. Money pit, you ask me."

Siding covered in algae. Gingerbread lattice around the gables like torn lace. Shutters dangling from rusty hinges. A grand old lady, left to fend for herself in rough times. Like Tara. The first stair sagged, then splintered, under Eli's boot.

"Watch your step," Hollister advised.

Inside wasn't much better.

Andi stood in the foyer, taking it all in. "What a shame. Old place like this left to rot." Inlaid oak floors warped, varnish worn to the color of ashes. Fireplace, soot stained, piled with beer cans. A shutter banged against the clapboards. Every thud made her flinch. It felt colder inside than outside. Not a good sign. Stepping over broken bottles, she walked to each corner of the room. Maybe a parlor once. The water-damaged ceiling sloped inward. Wallpaper hung in strips. Blue spray paint graffiti announced, "Welcome to the In."

"Somebody failed spelling." Eli steered her around what had been a glass transom. Syringes, wrinkled condoms, food wrappers with uneaten food rotting. It smelled like a garage stairwell in

Center City. Rancid. Hollister and Eli snapped on latex gloves and handed her a pair. She slipped them on and walked to the fireplace. Two ratty mattresses lay in the corner, stained and reeking of urine. Eli turned a mattress over with his boot.

Voices in her head, pleas for help, too many voices for any one voice to be distinguished. The cacophony reminded her of old sound clips from a psychiatric ward. Chills gripped her from head to toe. She closed her eyes, tried to tune in to one voice, to hear it clearly. There it was: *He's not who you think he is . . . he's not who you think he is.* The repetition picked up, faster and faster. Bernadette's metallic voice. *Not fish—girls. Soon there will be five of us.*

Rainbow vapor merged into the outline of a girl. Then the image filled in as if some unseen hand painted it. Mariah. Her dark, shoulder-length hair with soft pink highlights, curly like hanging moss. Prom dress, torn and bloodstained. Sobbing inconsolably.

Mariah, what is it?

Tell my mother I was stupid to run away.

Who killed you? Andi asked the girl silently. *We'll find him and end this.*

Tell her I loved her.

Mariah's sobs tore at Andi's conscience. Words she should have told her own mother. *Help us find you.*

Something cold brushed by her, heading for another room. She followed. *Did you both die here? Who is the fisherman?* Andi asked. Her heart pounded in her ears. A truck rumbled by and hit a manhole in the street, thumping.

Here . . . come here, ma'am.

I'm coming. Footsteps behind her. A thick layer of dust covered everything, yet in one long room, probably a dining room, it was disturbed. A mummy-style sleeping bag lay in front of the fireplace. Metal skewers like dropped pick-up sticks littered the hearth, and a backpack lay nearby.

Eli picked up the backpack and checked inside. "Marshmallows." He pulled out a bag. "Fairly fresh marshmallows." Eli checked the backpack's name plate. "Rachel." Frowning, he looked up at Andi. "No last name, no home address, no phone number, no email."

"Maybe somebody stole Rachel's backpack." Hollister eyed the water bottle on the side. "We could get DNA from that."

"What else is in there?" Andi asked.

Eli looked inside. "Graham crackers and chocolate bars."

"S'mores." Hollister made a disgusted face and took the bag from Eli.

Stooping, Eli picked up a wrinkled receipt. "Graham crackers, chocolate bars, marshmallows: 7-Eleven, dated a week ago. Do we have a description of Rachel?"

"We got nothing on a missing Rachel except the one from Charlotte, North Carolina," Hollister said.

Mariah had vanished, but the air was still thick. An icy draft blew behind her like a cold hand pushing her forward. Andi whirled to find Hollister's hand on his holster.

"What is it?" Eli stared at her.

Concentrate on the girls. *Help us,* Andi pleaded. Another icy nudge, gently shoving her toward a fireplace. In dust on the mantel, numbers appeared, traced by an invisible hand: 2-3-6-0-2.

"What the devil?" Hollister muttered. "You see that, Eli?"

He nodded.

Andi felt hands on her shoulders and jumped. A tentative touch, then a reassuring squeeze. "Eli?" But he wasn't near her.

The voices faded, then stopped. "Someone's humming now. 'Amazing Grace,'" she said.

"Andi?" Eli searched her face.

A car hit the manhole cover, and it thumped again. The sun shone through the overgrown shrubs outside a sooty window, casting shadows.

Floorboards creaked as Hollister stepped closer to the fireplace. Air in the room lightened. The girls had left.

Eli pointed at the neatly drawn numbers. "What does it mean?"

"No idea," Andi said. "But Mariah was here."

Hollister cursed at his phone when he couldn't take a picture of the numbers. "Dead battery. What just happened here?"

Go slowly, she reminded herself. Sometimes Andi couldn't believe what she saw and heard either.

"This is the place I dreamed about the night I bought the pendant. The same fireplace, wood floors, broken windows. A junkie, a young girl, and an old man."

"The old man was the fisherman?" Eli asked.

"Maybe," she said. "A young girl and an old man were arguing. I had a sense that she wanted him to help her sick friend. Maybe it was Mariah arguing with the man, wanting him to help Bernadette. At the time, I chalked it up to a dream." The accuracy of details from that dream startled her. "But this is the place from the dream." She listened for a few seconds to the house. Creaks, tiny clawed feet scurrying, and the wind trying to rip the shutters off.

"The numbers. What are the zip codes for Columbia?" Eli asked.

"That's not it." Hollister glared at his phone and cursed. "Eli, is your phone working?"

He fished it out of his pocket, turned it on then off. "Mine's dead too. Andi?"

Hers had half battery. She handed it to Eli, who punched in the numbers.

"Newport News, Virginia, is two-three-six-zero-two. Must be nice to have friends in high places, Andi," he grumbled. Eli carried her phone to the mantel and snapped a photo of the numbers.

Andi grimaced. "I don't think the fisherman fishes for fish. I think the pendant girls call him that because he fishes girls. Bernadette says there may be five of them soon."

"Five victims!" Hollister clenched his fists. "The sum bitch got another girl!"

"I told you. And I think her name is Rachel." Andi tried not to be impatient.

Eli kicked an empty orange-juice bottle. It slammed into a wall and spun like a compass. He kept his head down, maybe ashamed of his temper, maybe just pissed. "Did Bernadette say the next victim will be Rachel?"

"Not in those words, but yes."

"The worst damn part is we have no bodies," Hollister said. "What the hell does the bastard do with them?"

Eli stuffed both hands into his pockets. "Right now, we need to figure out what those numbers mean. Two-three-six-zero-two could be anything. Let's see what's upstairs. Might lower everyone's blood pressure."

They mounted the stairs. Hollister in front, then Andi, then Eli.

"Only thing gonna lower my blood pressure is locking up this sum bitch." Hollister glanced at Andi. "Sorry, ma'am. I keep forgetting my manners."

"Hey, my friend Fiona has the foulest mouth this side of the Mississippi. I'm used to it."

She followed him up the wide spiral stairway. The carpet was worn to bare floor in places. Like its inhabitants, the house was an architectural skeleton. Tara, she thought again. Carved woodwork, wide oak-plank floors, cracked marble fireplaces, tarnished brass and crystal chandeliers dangling with wires exposed. A few leaded-glass transoms had survived the onslaught by vagrants. They cast rainbows like ghosts on the walls.

Eli poked her arm. "Are they talking to you now?"

"It's quiet as a cemetery up here," she answered.

"No kidding." Eli shot her an exasperated look.

They walked from room to room.

Nothing but trash and empty cans. Dog food, tuna fish, soup, and beer cans. Syringes, a filthy blanket, used condoms.

"I don't think the old man who sells fish is the killer," she said.

"Neither do I." Eli draped an arm around her, and they came down the creaking staircase and back to the dining room, where the numbers were drawn. Gone! Two words replaced them.

"Sesqui Forest."

"Holy mother of Jesus!" Hollister shouted. "That's Mariah's house."

"The girl wants us to go to her home?" Eli asked Andi.

A slow tingle traveled from Andi's scalp to her spine. "Seems like it."

"Then that's exactly what we'll do." Hollister snatched the sleeping bag and Rachel's backpack on his way out the door.

CHAPTER FORTY-ONE

ANDI

"WE'LL STOP BY THE house, and I'll give the girl's mother an update. Don't know exactly how much I want to tell, though."

The sheriff and Eli plugged their phones into the charging ports of the car and were chatting away.

Between the smoke-saturated interior and the heat blasting through the vents, Andi was nauseous. She cracked the window and sucked in fresh, cool air.

"We never put the two girls together until you found the pendants," the sheriff told her. He folded a stick of gum into his mouth and chewed. Juicy Fruit. She could smell it. "We had zilch on the Johnston girl. With Mariah, every tip was a dead end."

"SLED ran a check on Mariah's laptop," he began.

"SLED?" Andi interrupted.

"State Law Enforcement Division. Anyway, they found multiple emails from a male who wanted to meet her. The last one named a place. Trenholm Plaza, a strip mall off Forest Drive. The emails came from an internet café in North Carolina. We were thinking sex trafficking, a groomer."

"What about the account's address?" Andi rolled up the window. She shook off a chill, but the queasiness clung to her.

"Account closed." Hollister made a turn. "Billing information went to a box from one of those mailing businesses, not the post office."

Her locket turned icy, and Andi opened it. Mariah was sobbing. She closed it. "Did they track the IP address?"

"Zilch," Hollister told her. "Most likely it was a teenage boy just leading her on."

"And you think the killer is selling fish at a vacant lot?" She wasn't buying that. "I just don't think that corner fisherman is sophisticated enough to pull all this off."

"He's a person of interest. That's all. A pervert could easily pretend to be an illiterate fishmonger. Selling fish gives him free time, access to people on the streets, no boss looking over his shoulder. It fits all nice and tidy. And there's a DA up for election who's panting down my neck. Dragon's breath. Let me tell you," Hollister said.

"It's protocol, Andi," Eli explained. "An informant fingered the man. Serial killer or not, the fisherman's a good person to question because of his proximity to the university. The proximity gives him opportunity." He stared out the windshield at a lady in an ancient Volvo poking along, doing thirty. Then a camper pulled in front of them with a right turn signal on and it slowed at every street, the driver looking for a street sign. Andi counted seventeen traffic lights before they reached Mariah's house. She could hear Mariah sobbing as they approached.

What is it? Andi asked silently.

I'll show you, she said.

CHAPTER FORTY-TWO

ANDI

FISHER OF GIRLS . . . *Fisherman . . . here . . . he's been here,*" Mariah chanted.

Andi looked out the window. Sesqui Forest, typical executive McMansion community, manmade lakes with wide boat docks. Saw palmettos and tall ornamental grass in licorice mulch around the foundations. Walks edged in monkey grass, azalea-wrapped pine trees. One day the young magnolias would be stately, but the brick houses couldn't be more than ten years old.

They pulled in front of a two-story colonial with a wraparound porch. Behind the house, a lake tossed lazy waves at the shore.

Fisherman's been here.

The hair on the back of her neck bristled. An icy hand tickled her scalp. Andi got out and slammed the door, and they headed toward the driveway. Something was wrong here—air was so thick she could barely breathe.

Very close. Mariah's voice.

"Who's very close?" she asked aloud.

Eli and Hollister turned to stare at her. Suddenly, an icy hand clamped down on her throat. Breathe, she told herself, it's not real. It's a panic attack. But the hand crushed her windpipe. She gasped for air, staggered. Eli rushed toward her and held her upright.

Andi clutched her neck, trying to pry off invisible hands. Her feet moved down the sidewalk, one foot in front of the other, like a child's game of blindman's buff. She was aware of Eli's touch, but her body seemed to be in two different places. Andi walked mechanically past a fire hydrant, past a pile of leaves, the sound of her rubber-soled boots padding softly on concrete. Her world was rippling, vision sharp for a few seconds, then dimming, then washing in and out. Breathe normally, she told herself. This is no time for a panic attack.

Here! Mariah's sobs ripped through Andi. She teetered, sucked in a short breath, and her legs gave way. Eli caught her. "Andi, talk to me."

"Better take her back to the car." Hollister's voice was so far away.

"Say something. Breathe. You're scaring the hell out of me," Eli said.

But she couldn't speak. A man stood over her with some kind of tool. Humming, he touched the metal tip to her skin. "No!" she screamed. The pain was intense, searing.

"Tell me what's happening. Talk to me, Andi." Eli gave her a little shake.

He was so far away. The scent of his leather jacket lingered, but the metal tool cut through the two dimensions. Loud humming. She covered her ears, squeezed her eyes shut. Now, Andi sped down a dark tunnel that smelled like something she recognized: the butcher's shop. Her heart raced. She ran, feet sloshing through something warm. Blood?

Leave this panic attack. Get away. Run away. She opened her eyes to an orange-gold sunset over the lake and exhaled.

"Good, keep breathing. I've got you. Keep breathing." Eli carried her toward the car. "What's going on?" he asked.

"I think . . . I think Mariah's sent me a terrible memory. Or maybe it's a panic attack."

"I'll put you in the car, where you can rest."

No! Here! Mariah shrieked. *Don't go! Here!*

Andi stiffened in his arms, and her vision swam through darkness and light again. She knew she was hyperventilating but couldn't stop herself.

"You're gonna be okay. Try to breathe normally," Eli told her.

Eyes tightly closed, she concentrated on breathing in and out, slow and steady. A burst of light flashed in her brain and showed a skeleton folded into a dark concrete hole. Dark curly hair, a pale blue prom gown. Fingers without flesh beckoned. Gasping, then filling her lungs with air, she shouted, "Stop!"

They were at the car now. Eli's brown eyes squinted down, his lips a determined line. He spoke softly. "God only knows how stressed you must be with all the crap that's happened to you recently. Everything's gonna be okay. I promise."

"No, nothing will be okay! She's here, Eli." Her voice came in weak bursts of air. Her throat felt like sandpaper, like she'd run a marathon during a Pennsylvania winter.

"Do you see her?" He glanced from the street to the lake, then back at Andi. "Where?"

"Her body is underground," Andi answered.

"Underground? Where?"

"Don't know. Inside concrete."

Eli nodded. "If she's here, we'll find her." He placed her in the backseat and told her to stay put, then closed the door. Face grim, he walked back to Hollister, who was standing near a sewer.

Propped on an elbow, Andi peered over the front seat. Hollister walked along one side of the street while Eli walked along the other. They met again at the sewer, talked, and returned to the car. Eli opened the door and glanced in. "You look better," he said. "But stay here, no matter what happens. Promise."

Andi nodded. She sat up, eyes wide, heart thudding in her ears. She looked out the back window. The car trunk opened, blocking her view. Things back there scraped and thudded until Hollister found something. A crowbar? The lid closed.

Slow, deep breaths. Her stomach was knotted, chest heavy.

"Please God, let me be wrong," she whispered.

CHAPTER FORTY-THREE

ANDI

HOLLISTER PRIED UP THE SEWER cover and set it down on the sidewalk. Both men peered down. "Please God, don't let it be Mariah," Andi whispered.

Head down, Eli took several steps away from the sewer. Then he returned and stared down it again. Eyes closed, Hollister pressed a fist against his forehead. Oh God! All those months and the girl lay right outside her own parents' home.

A woman came down the steps of Mariah's house. The sweater draped over her slender shoulders made wings in the wind. The resemblance to Mariah was unmistakable. Eyes wide, mouth gaping, she sped up. If she saw what was in the sewer . . . Eli approached the woman to block the view. She tried to move past, but he stopped her.

Don't let Mama see me! Mariah wailed.

I won't, she assured the girl as she slid out of the car. In six steps, she was beside Mariah's mother. Eli's eyes met Andi's. He nodded a solemn confirmation.

She introduced herself to the woman and walked her toward the house. Glaring at Andi, Mrs. Culverton stopped abruptly and pushed Andi's arms off. Her gaunt face was contorted in anger, in horror. "Why are you here?" Then she turned around. "What's in there, Sheriff Hollister?"

Hollister, phone to his ear, didn't answer. Eli glanced at Andi, motioned toward the house with his head, and thumbed numbers into his phone.

"Let's go inside." She forced a smile.

But the woman didn't move. "If this is about my daughter—"

Hollister intervened. "It's okay, Mrs. Culverton. Andi's working with us. Go on back to the house with her. I'll be there in a minute."

Don't let Mama see! Mariah wailed.

The metal in her locket was icy against her skin. *I'm trying, Mariah. Trying really hard.*

Grasping the woman's shoulders firmly, Andi managed to turn her toward the porch.

"What are they doing?"

Andi swallowed hard. What possible words of comfort could she offer a mother whose daughter's bones lay inside a sewer only steps from the family's home? That poor woman had to *feel* what lay inside that sewer.

"Come on." She guided the woman up the porch steps.

Help Mama! Mariah whispered.

As the sun slowly sank through dark red clouds, the pristine suburb churned into chaos.

The first police car arrived with flashing lights. A coroner, crime scene people, Columbia Water company officials. God only knew how many other people would be there shortly. The press would come too, like sharks sensing blood.

"What did they find?" Mrs. Culverton pushed the front door open.

"You have a beautiful house," Andi said, hating herself for such an inane comment. Why would Hollister and Eli entrust her with comforting a mother, when she'd missed her own mother's funeral? She grasped the woman's shoulders and gave a reassuring squeeze, steering her toward a large room overlooking the lake. "Can I get you something to drink?" Andi asked.

I'll take care of your mama, she told the girl.

"Not thirsty." The woman's shoulders sagged. Her breath came in little gasps. But even the things Mariah's mother might imagine couldn't be as horrific as what really happened.

Andi picked up a photo of Mariah, a recital picture. Careful to use only present tense, she said, "Mariah's a beautiful girl, looks so much like you. Is piano her favorite instrument?"

No reaction from her mother. She stared straight ahead, refusing to look at the photo.

Inconsolable sobbing from Mariah.

The front door opened, and two sets of footsteps treaded across the wood floor. Andi turned. Eli and Hollister had left the scene for the technical people and come to the house.

Mrs. Culverton walked toward them and collapsed. Andi reached out, couldn't catch her, and knelt by her side.

Mama! Mariah wailed.

Hollister and Eli rushed over, picked up the poor woman, and carried her to the sofa.

"What's her first name?" Andi asked Hollister. The sobbing inside her head faded and grew, a tide of sorrow unleashed.

"Faith." Hollister's voice was a hoarse whisper.

Andi looked down at the unconscious woman. "Sleep long and well, Faith," she said. "God help her when she wakes up." For Faith and Mariah, there was no future, only memories.

The sobbing grew in her head. Mariah grieving.

"Dr. Culverton's on the way." Hollister took Faith's pulse.

Eli went to the kitchen and brought back a wet rag, a Christmas towel with embroidered angels. He bent over Faith, wiping a single teardrop that dribbled down her cheek. The tenderness of this gesture tugged at Andi's heart. He must have seen a lot of heartbreak in his time, but his hands trembled.

"Bastard!" Hollister hissed. He clamped and unclamped his jaws, keeping his lower lip taut. For months, Mariah had lain inside a cold, dark sewer only steps from the safety of home.

Westminster chimes echoed in the silence, and Faith's eyes opened. She gave a start when she saw Eli. "What . . . what happened? Who are you?"

Stooping next to her, Eli's voice was soft, soothing. "You fainted. Your husband is on the way. I'm Eli Lake, a private investigator working with the sheriff. Is there anything we can get you, a drink, something to eat, your phone?"

Faith struggled to sit. A sob escaped. Six months of denial, and she gave a convulsive shudder. "You found my little girl. She's been there all along. Somebody put my baby in the sewer!" Faith's eyes were hollow, the light gone from them. Hope gone. Her only daughter lost forever.

Eli grasped her hand. "We don't know that. Nothing has been confirmed yet."

The sobbing in Andi's head ebbed, then rose to the wails of a panicked animal trapped by a predator. Andi closed her eyes. *Mariah, she gave birth to you. That umbilical cord, that invisible tie, can never be separated. You're not trapped by death*, she told the girl. *You're bound by love.*

"No!" Faith's scream pierced the silence. She grasped Eli's hand, dug her fingers into his shoulder. "No! It can't be Mariah!"

Eli glanced at Andi. Hope had left his eyes too. She could imagine what he was thinking. The bastard had dumped the girl outside her own home, mocking the police, defiling her parents' lives there forever.

Tell me what to say, Andi begged Mariah. Something brushed by, an icy air current. Then Mariah shimmered into view on the couch next to Faith. She wiped her mother's tears with one finger and nestled her head on her shoulder. Faith stopped sobbing, as if aware of her daughter's presence.

Tell her I was stupid, Mariah said. Then she took Faith's hands in slender transparent fingers. *Tell her I love her.*

"Your daughter loves you very much," Andi said.

Faith sniffed. "You know Mariah?"

Andi shook her head. "Only through this investigation." She hated herself for lying. "But I think that's what she'd want you to know."

Transparent blue eyes streaming, Mariah spoke again. *Tell Mama it wasn't her fault. I never should have run away.*

Andi weighed the girl's words. She didn't want to send this woman into deeper shock. "I think if she were here, she'd say it's not your fault she ran away. I'm sure she loved you and her dad."

Faith turned to Andi. "She's our only child. So pretty, so smart. Did commercials when she was little." She paused to blow her nose. "When we went places, people used to give my daughter things all the time because she was so cute. She has such a sunny disposition. Everyone loves my Mariah. Who would do this?" Faith's face fell into haggard lines again, and her cries rose and fell in waves. "She—I never even said goodbye."

The front door opened, and footsteps pounded toward them. Faith stood and wrapped her arms around a man with salt-and-pepper hair, cleft chin, and Mariah's clear blue eyes. Father and mother embraced, their grief melting each other.

Mariah joined their circle. *I love you. I'm so sorry, Daddy*, she said. *I was stupid.*

They stood very still. Andi was sure they somehow felt their daughter in their embrace to comfort them.

"She loved both of you," Andi said, choking back tears. Her own guilt clutched her heart. She'd never said goodbye to her mother either.

CHAPTER FORTY-FOUR

MARIAH

M Y PARENTS' HEARTS WERE broken. Yesterday for me was worse
than the day Fisherman killed me. Poor Mama just retreated
inside herself, like a turtle safely locked inside its shell. My
father had canceled all surgeries and appointments for the first time
I can remember.

We came to eavesdrop on Andi's call to Fisherman at the Lakeside Police Building. I had high hopes for Andi's bargaining skills.
Confidence in Hollister and Eli? Not so much.

"Fisherman ain't gonna answer," Bennie told me. "Why would
he?"

"Because he wants our pendants back," I told her.

One ring.

Silence.

Two rings, three.

"Good evening, Mrs. Wyndham," he said. The bastard always
checks caller ID before he picks up.

Andi flinched like she wanted to unload that last name fast.

"Call me Andrea," she said. "I want to confirm the time and place we'll meet tomorrow."

Flanked by a blinking wall of electronic stuff, Andi sat ramrod straight, probably scared shitless. Eli's eyes were glued to her. Hollister pulled a pack of Tums from his pocket, shook out two and sucked on them.

"Glad you understand that Rachel's life depends on you returning my pendants to me. Two for two. Rachel and your life for my pendants, and we're even."

"That doesn't sound like Fisherman," I said.

Bennie shushed me. "He's disguising his voice."

If it was Fisherman, I imagined him sitting on his ratty red velvet sofa in his living room, thinking about how stupid cops were.

He was right.

The media was going to chew Hollister a new one.

"I swear it doesn't sound like Fisherman."

Bennie gave me an irritated look. "Hush up and listen."

One of the techs put a finger to his lips to tell Andi to wait for Fisherman to speak. Long seconds ticked by. I'd seen that tracing stuff before in a movie. Triangulation—tracing the phone by cell towers. Andi scratched and fidgeted.

"Read about that fire at your place in the *Daily Local* newspaper online. Were the pendants damaged?" he asked.

Andi looked ready to pee herself.

Tell him they're fine. Then stay with the script, a barrel-shaped cop wrote on a pad.

"The pendants are fine," she said with a quiver in her voice. "Is Rachel okay? I'd like to talk to her."

"You want to hear her voice?" We heard a click and that same recording of Rachel begging for help played.

"That doesn't prove she's alive. Why didn't he put her on the phone?" I asked.

"'Cause he can't control what she'll say," Bennie said. "That girl's smart."

"I need proof that she's alive and well." Andi read from the script. "Text me a photo of her with today's newspaper. November seventeenth."

"You do what I say, and you'll see her in person. Otherwise, she's dead and so are you. Columbia, South Carolina State House tomorrow at nine thirty a.m."

"I need more time," she told him. "That's a long drive."

A click, and he was gone.

CHAPTER FORTY-FIVE

ANDI

ANDI LEANED AGAINST ELI'S car door at the police station, arms folded. "Dammit. What if he's already killed Rachel?"

Eli kicked a piece of gravel and watched it skitter across the parking lot. "Don't give up hope." He pulled Andi into an embrace.

She listened to his heartbeat and his steady, regular breathing. A streetlight above them hummed. "Let's go to my hotel room. We'll order takeout. It'll give you a chance to decompress."

Food wasn't what she had in mind. "I'll call Fiona. Otherwise she'll worry."

Eli nodded and they climbed into his car.

Andi keyed in Fiona's number and left a message as he pulled out onto the road. Slow, deep breaths. Maybe she could exhale the memories. Not likely. A long drive downtown left too much time to think about dead girls, grieving mothers, and an impending meeting with a serial killer.

She clutched the locket. *Who is this fisherman? Where does he live?* Andi asked silently.

No answer.

Help us find him.

Silence. Then Mariah's sobbing. *Wish you'd never found me. My poor mother.*

Andi could only imagine Faith's anguish. Fear might be worse than truth for parents of missing children, but not in Mariah's case. No parent finds peace knowing their child was discarded in a sewer.

Six damn months. Insects, rats scurrying over a child who had so much to live for. The image of that child folded into a sewer was stuck like a projector burning a hole through film. Metallic saliva pooled in her mouth. "I think I'm gonna be sick. Please stop."

Eli pulled over into a church parking lot, and she kicked the door open, hung out. Dry heaves again. She looked up and cleared the wet hair clinging to her cheeks.

Eli helped her out of the car and into his arms. "If you hadn't lost it soon, I would've been worried. You okay now?"

Clinging to him, she let his heartbeat wrap around her like a warm blanket. "God, why am I losing control like a weak idiot?"

"I've tracked people from plane crashes, people lost in woods who had to be identified by forensic anthropologists. Those cases didn't hit me this hard. You're anything but weak." He kissed the top of her head and offered a Tic Tac mint. "My shoulder is unconditionally yours, no obligations."

She popped the candy in her mouth, wiped her sweaty face, and kissed his cheek. Sympathy pulled their lips together in a testing-the-waters kiss. When it ended, Andi was certain they were ready to jump off the pier together—whether it was love, lust, or just one really bad day.

About twenty minutes later, Andi followed Eli into the hotel elevator, then to his room. She walked to the window and pushed the curtain aside. *Key rattling in lock. Open the window. Run!* That small child again.

Who are you? What do you want from me? she silently asked. Still no answer, but the child's voice seemed more and more familiar.

"Hope you didn't pay extra for the view." Andi looked out over a gravel-coated roof and big gray condenser units.

"Hollister made the reservation. It's a good location."

The décor was typical Americana, except for the four-poster bed and white down duvet. Sketches showed Columbia with trolleys, tall brick buildings, and horse-drawn carts. Exhausted, she sank into a mauve upholstered chair. The bed with its snowy white duvet beckoned.

To sleep perchance *not* to dream.

Eli slipped off his jacket and draped it over the desk chair. "Take off your coat. Stay awhile." He freed his dark shiny hair from the band and shook it loose. No one like him had ever taken an interest in her. Lately, bald men on crutches hit on her in bars. Fiona got the body builders.

"I know just what you need." He filled the coffeemaker with water and set the dials. That wasn't what she had in mind.

She hung her coat on the chair over his. In the mirror she saw a woman with tangled caramel ringlets and dark circles under her eyes. Perfect face for an Ambien ad. She ached for the man fussing over a coffee cup. He'd won her trust, and she'd introduced him to the Otherworld. "Call it a rebound," Fiona had said.

The coffeemaker groaned and started to chug.

Sitting on the edge of the bed, Eli leafed through a phone book. He checked his watch and returned to the listings. "How about Chinese?"

"Chinese is fine. Make it spicy." She just wanted to melt into his arms.

He turned a couple of pages. From where she sat, it looked like menus. "Spicy Chinese might not be a good idea. Is your stomach okay?"

"It's fine," she said. The coffee machine puffed louder, more insistently.

In each cup he put a tea bag made from gauze and kite string. The machine roared and exhaled. He poured water into two Styrofoam cups.

"How about pizza? Maybe a nice pepperoni or sausage?"

That was it.

She burst out laughing.

He turned almost spilling the tea. "What's so funny?"

"Eli, what I really want is you."

"Yeah?" A slow smile spread from crow's-foot to crow's-foot, and he set the cups down.

She stood and put her hands up his sweater. He hissed through clenched teeth. "Cold hands, warm heart. The hell with pizza."

Lips to hers, he became a man with a mission. The sweater came off; he tossed his shirt on the floor. She pressed against him, hard nipples to a warm chest. He kissed her neck. Warm breath in her ear. "Are you sure this is what you want?"

Standing on her toes, she pulled his head down until she could lick the tip of his ear. "There's something I have to tell you, Eli. I'm not a virgin."

His laughter began as a long exhale and picked up until his chest rippled. "God, you make me laugh." He carried her to bed. "It's okay. I'm not either."

Apparently he'd mastered Disrobing 101 with outstanding scores. He pulled her jeans off with ease and removed his. Eli looked pleased with her thong. She was pleased he wore no underwear.

Andi wiggled around until her cheek rested against his ear. "I need you now, but I'd prefer not to give birth to any junior detectives."

Eli broke away, rummaged through his bag, found a foil packet, and cast a glance at the mugs. "I think my tea has lost its steam."

"I can always reheat it." She motioned him back to bed.

"Will you respect me in the morning?"

"I'll think of you in an entirely different way," she said.

CHAPTER FORTY-SIX

ANDI

ELI'S PHONE WOKE THEM around 6:00 a.m. Ear pressed to it, he listened for a while. Andi yawned and snuggled closer while Eli answered some questions, then turned on the speakerphone.

Hollister's voice. "Hope you slept well. I need to brief you, and we're gonna prep Andi and wire her up. She must've turned her phone off. Got any idea where she is?"

"Yeah. Want to talk to her?" Eli asked.

She glared, clutching the sheet to her as if Hollister could see them.

"We met for breakfast," he explained with a grin and lay the cell down between them.

"Andi, we need to dress you in clothes that conceal equipment. What size are you?"

"Size eight. Kevlar head to toe works for me."

"Don't you worry about safety. A whole team of professional lawmen will protect you. Soon as you get here, we're gonna wire you and review the script."

"Can't wait," she said, and Eli disconnected. He cheered her up by sharing a shower.

When Eli strapped on his guns, she realized that today he might have to use them to protect her.

"Be careful," she told him. "I don't want to lose you."

He kissed her. "We Ojibwes were navigating the woods without GPS thousands of years before your ancestors got here. I have no intention of getting lost in a park."

"Smartass."

At the police station, they handed her a Kevlar vest and another script. This time she had to memorize it. Too bad she couldn't write it on her arm. Too bad the Kevlar wasn't head to toe. Hollister's people dressed, wired, and familiarized her with a map of the park.

"This is the plan," Hollister told her. "You wait at the meeting point for him to show. Take this." He handed her a small red gift bag. She hoped to God there was a gun inside, but instead, two jewelry-size wrapped boxes rested in the pink tissue.

"Don't I get a gun?" she asked.

Hollister shook his head. "Shouldn't be any shooting. The guy approaches, you follow the script. Give him the pendants. If he wants to see the pendants first, he'll have to unwrap them. While he's doing that, we'll arrest him."

"Gee, sounds like a no-brainer." She huffed a tendril of hair out of her eyes and glanced down at the bag. Easy as being tied to a railroad track with a freight train coming.

"Stick to the script," a skinny man with Woody Allen glasses told her.

"Like Moses' people stuck to the commandments," she said under her breath.

Eli gave her a shoulder hug while a techie tested the button video cam on her blouse. "It will be over after today, and you can sleep. I'll be right there with you."

Great. She had two boxes wrapped in pink paper to protect herself. Everybody else had guns. They didn't have to sit next to a serial killer with a bag full of nothing useful and negotiate for Rachel's life. And hers.

"If he threatens you, give him the bag. There's a homing device on it. Drop it and kick it away from you," the skinny man said.

Eli glared at the man, then turned back to her. "There won't be any threats. We'll be right there. Trust me."

"Don't say that!" She could hear the freight train of doom roaring down the tracks again, and the oh-shit song played at rock concert decibels inside her brain.

They had just put her in an unmarked car when a text showed on her phone. "What the hell? He's changed the time from nine thirty to ten o'clock at the War Memorial." She got out and showed her phone to Eli.

Peter Rockford texted time changes and locations twice more, forcing the police team to set up and break down surveillance at three different locations before the final call: ten forty-five at the Confederate Women's Monument.

Fifteen minutes early, Andi set out for the sculpture, hoping the three bronze angels would watch over her. She wondered if Peter Rockford had someone watching over him too.

Satan probably stood at the gates of hell, smiling at his servant.

CHAPTER FORTY-SEVEN

ANDI

HEART POUNDING, ANDI STUDIED the layout of the park. The
State House occupied a busy corner with the South Carolina
Supreme Court across the street, Trinity Cathedral, the cemetery, and some tall buildings. If there were snipers protecting her,
would she see them on tops of the buildings? Probably not. Maybe they didn't have snipers. If Peter Rockford got past the cops, he
could haul ass for Pendleton or Assembly Street and disappear. No,
don't think about that. Listen to the pigeons cooing and traffic whiz-
zing by. A horn blasted and she jumped.

What made her believe she could bring down a serial killer? She
glanced at Eli. His braid was tucked under a wig and a Penn State
cap. He had a camera like it was just another day in the park. What
if she tipped the serial killer that cops were in the park? What if she
royally screwed this up? Someone would die. Her first. Then Rachel.
She tripped over a crack in the sidewalk and struggled to regain
her balance. I'm going to end this now, she told herself and walked
faster. After today, Peter Rockford will be in jail. He'll stop stalking

Fiona and me. Either that, or I'll be a face on his next pendant. Dead and between the worlds, like Mariah and Bernadette.

A car backfired, and she ducked instinctively. She glanced around. Police hadn't cordoned off the park. Of course not, that would warn the damn bastard. If her heart would just beat normally and her stomach would settle down. She should've eaten something, but fear had killed her appetite. *Killed*, don't think about that word. Andi walked around the bronze sculpture of a lady sitting with two cherubs at her side and a life-size angel behind her. She read the inscription by William E. Gonzalez on the plaque. ". . . unfaltering faith in a righteous cause . . . they faced the future undismayed by problems and fearless of trials."

Well, Confederate ladies, if your spirits are out here, I could use some emotional fortitude, she thought. Andi sat on the wall near the statue.

Whispering behind her. The pendant girls! Eyes and ears like an owl, scanning the park, Andi only caught snatches of their conversation. Something about a kid sticking gum on the statue during a field trip, then Mariah asking if Andi was terrified.

"I'm okay," she said aloud. First lie she'd ever told the girls.

Eli gave her a quizzical look and clicked off pictures like a tourist while the sheriff fed the pigeons popcorn.

Five college guys on skateboards came rolling through the park. What the hell? Skateboarding was illegal here. *Chunk*, up a bench. *Chunk*, down a bench, wheels grating on sidewalk like marbles rolling off a long table. *Chunk*, around a corner. Clattering, one came off the board. The skateboard flipped. He caught it in midair. These guys were good. They skated in and out between statues. They scaled the railings and the last step of the portico. Hollister whistled at them like a gym coach and hitched a thumb toward the street. The skaters ignored him. How would they know the guy feeding pigeons was a sheriff?

A frumpy middle-aged lady was carrying a purple Vera Bradley bag with a thermos, a Kentucky Fried Chicken bucket, and a blanket. Damn. How are they gonna get rid of her? Andi wondered. And why was she eating fried chicken at ten forty-five in the morning?

Eli moved closer to the lady. He snapped a picture, didn't take his eyes off her.

"Great," Andi muttered, forgetting that she was wired. A serial killer wants to make me into a pendant, and Eli's worried about some bag lady on a picnic.

Eli talked to his cuff. A mike there, she guessed. He looked pissed. Andi figured he was bitching about people wandering in and out of the park. Meanwhile, Andi sat on the wall by the statue, scratching head, neck, arm. Waiting. Waiting to meet a ruthless killer.

The bag lady plopped down beside Andi. "Such lovely hair you have. Like those ladies on cameos," the woman said.

Andi gave her a sideways look and turned up one corner of her mouth. Go away, lady, she wanted to scream. Find someone else to talk to.

"Well, well, well. We've known each other for a long time, haven't we, my dear? And what a beautiful dove tattoo."

Cripes. She was waiting to meet a man who murdered young girls, and some lonely bag lady wanted to chat. "You must have me confused with someone else. I'm waiting for somebody. Go away. Please." Apparently the bag lady didn't hear the annoyance in Andi's voice. There she sat, smiling, checking for something inside her bag.

"Lovely day for a picnic," the lady said. "That's what your dear Aunt Nancy would say. You were just a baby when I last saw you."

"I don't have an Aunt Nancy." Holy shit! Peter Rockford was a woman? But the Aunt Nancy comment couldn't be a coincidence. Suddenly, Shadows circled the woman like a swarm of angry hornets.

The lady wore a long brown skirt and hooded pink sweater. A multicolored scarf circled her neck. Mighty big feet in those brown mid-calf boots. Chubby ankles too. Makeup had caked in the creases of her forehead. Frosted hair. Probably a wig.

Every muscle in her body begged her to bolt. Andi's eyes darted all over the park, searching for the fastest escape route. But she had to make this work.

The girls were whispering again.

. . . scar on his hand . . . left my mark, Bennie said.

She's not who you think she is. It's Fisherman! Mariah shouted.

She's not who you think she is, two voices chanted now.

Andi stared at the woman's hands and slid off that wall. Oh God, she couldn't do this. The person sitting next to her murdered girls. A bus sped by, belching diesel. She stuffed the bag into her coat pocket, wishing again police had put a gun there.

But *her* life and Rachel's depended on making this work. Andi willed her voice to be calm. "I have the pendants." She dug her hand into the pocket. "Is Rachel nearby?" Eli gave her a discreet nod behind his camera.

The blast shook the park. A statue exploded, sending bronze and marble into the air. Hollister collapsed on the sidewalk, bloody gash in his head, a big chunk of marble next to him. What the hell? Rockford had blown up a statue to distract the cops.

A triumphant smirk on his face, he stood and hooked an arm around Andi's neck. The killer jabbed a gun to her temple.

"Drop the gun!" Eli's command was deadly calm. His eyes were locked on the man's hands. Three cops came out of the bushes, service revolvers pointed.

"Let her go." Gun leveled at Peter Rockford's head, Eli acted a lot cooler than Andi felt.

Rockford let out a theater laugh, an evil sound that echoed through the park. "I want my pendants!"

"Hurt Andi and you'll get nothing," Eli warned him. "Where is Rachel?"

Andi felt like some object they were bartering over.

Peter Rockford hitched Andi's neck upward and sneered. "She'd make a lovely pendant. Don't you think? I said no police. Rachel will die today. Andi may not live to see tomorrow."

She struggled to break free, but he was too strong.

Two big Shadows circled him.

"I said let her go." Eli was closing in. Three other policemen moved closer too.

Cops miss seventy percent of the time. Read that online. Mariah's voice.

Not helpful, Mariah. She prayed the girl was wrong. They needed to take this killer down today.

Rockford tightened his grip until Andi wondered if he'd break her neck. "Hand over my pendants!" His voice thundered through the park like he was God.

"She can't give you anything unless you release her." Eli's gun hand was so steady.

He relaxed his grasp a little, but she wasn't free of him.

"Andi, give him the bag." Eli spoke like he was telling a toddler to put something down.

She reached into her pocket, dropped the bag, and kicked it away from her, exactly as they'd told her to do. Breathe, she told herself. In and out. Her windpipe felt crushed.

The serial killer released Andi and lunged for the pendants. Skateboarders' wheels cut in front of him, almost ran over the bag. Now there were more of them, coming from three different directions, rolling right through a crime scene. One look at men with guns, and those skateboarders rolled right out of there. Rockford raced into the middle of them.

"Hold your fire," Eli shouted.

The elusive bastard fled toward the Greshette Building with two cops trailing him and skateboarders scattering all over the park. A backward glance, and he fired three quick shots. The police officer closest to him collapsed on the sidewalk, holding his belly. The injured man just lay there while another cop bent over him, talking into the responder clipped to his shoulder.

Rockford threw open the glass door to Greshette and disappeared.

Andi picked up the bag with pendants and stuffed them into her pocket. "He'll change clothes and walk out like he's the custodian and he's been working. Probably has different clothes in his bag," she muttered.

Eli tried to hug her.

"Trust me!" she spat the words and shoved his arm off her. She stared at the wounded police officer. They were carrying him toward an ambulance.

"Get me the hell out of here!" she told Eli.

CHAPTER FORTY-EIGHT

ANDI

"H E COULD'VE KILLED YOU if he wanted to," Eli said, starting his car.

"That's comforting." Andi wasn't sure who was more pissed, Eli or her. "I shouldn't have freaked. Police work is not my forte." She dug the pendants from the bag and unwrapped them to be sure they hadn't broken.

Eli glanced at the paper and looked away quickly. Then his eyes were on the road.

Inside the boxes, the pendants were wrapped in napkins, then with miles of Scotch tape. Andi unwound and unwound until she saw the shiny edge of a bezel. She lifted it and gasped. "It's empty! The bezel's empty. Where's the bone?"

Silence.

"You sent me to meet a serial killer with this? They aren't even the original bezels!"

"We would have arrested him long before he opened them." Eli concentrated on the road.

"Where the hell is the bone? Did they ruin the carvings?"

He pulled over into a drugstore parking lot, cut the engine, and reached for her hands.

She folded them out of his reach, her mouth a tight, angry line.

"Andi, they had to slice them to get DNA. I'm sorry. Lab results came back human bone."

"Human bone! The girls' bones?" Her heart pounded.

"I'll get the remnants back to you. I promise. You're safe. That's what's important."

"When did you plan to tell me about the bone? *After* I'd met the sick bastard who uses his victims' bones to make jewelry?"

A sheepish look and Eli heaved a sigh. "I didn't want to scare you."

"You lied to me. How long have you known?"

"An omission, not a lie," he said softly. "When those pendants went to the lab, they became physical evidence. If we'd asked for them, the lab wouldn't have given them to us. They're keeping them for a trial. That's how it works, although if the families ask for them, I think they might be entitled to bury them." He continued in police mode. "I asked Dr. Arthur to handle them carefully, and I'm sure he did. At the morgue you saw how careful they are with chain of evidence. Once the bone was removed from the bezel they found hair and blood, evidence of the girls. But they needed DNA from the bone to prove the bone was theirs too." He reached for her hands again. "I'm sorry."

Eli looked so tired, so defeated. She clasped his hands and sighed. "I thought they could examine them without destroying them. With some fancy forensic equipment. I still don't like it, but I get it. My beautiful pendants are ruined."

He leaned over and kissed her cheek. "Yeah, but you just survived an encounter with a serial killer. I'm worried about you. Rockford can easily find out where Fiona's relatives live. I want you to stay with me. Fiona too." Eli steered back onto the street and stopped at a light.

Andi tossed the bezels into the bag. They'd desecrated the pendants for the sake of DNA, and the bastard had slipped right through their fingers. "I hoped this would be over today." She heard the anger and disappointment in her voice. "And what about Rachel? He's gonna kill her."

Eli looked sideways at her. "We're all worried about Rachel. I swear to you I'll make this right. I'll find this bastard if it takes me all night."

She listened to the sounds of the city. Car engines, sirens, squealing brakes. Her own heartbeat. Yes, she was alive, but how long before he found her again? And what about Rachel?

Eli was thinking out loud again. "He's good with makeup. Could have a background in theater. Homeland Security will get involved because of a shooting on the capitol grounds. That damn building should've been locked down. Operations go wrong sometimes. Nobody could've planned on skateboarders rolling through a crime scene or an explosive in a statue. They should have him planting it on security cameras," Eli rambled on. "No way in hell it's the corner fish seller. Unfortunately, he's still a loose end we have to tie up."

He paused for a young boy crossing at a light with a chocolate lab tugging the leash and turned to her. "Feeling any better?"

"No." She shook her head.

"I'm sorry," Eli repeated. "I thought we'd be driving back with Peter Rockford in custody. Now we're driving back with a police escort."

Andi watched the dog and the boy crossing the street. *Want a free puppy, little girl . . . Hurry or they'll all be gone. Key in lock, rattling, rattling.* Too bad she couldn't erase that damn memory. Why had the child attached to her? Did she have anything to do with Mariah and Bennie? And why didn't she respond when Andi talked to her?

Eli drove down Gervais toward the lake house. "Media's gonna tap dance on Hollister's liver. A serial killer blew up Strom Thurmond's statue. That's a capital offense."

She groaned. "I'm not in the mood for police humor." Andi opened the locket. *We screwed that up, but Eli swears he'll find the guy. Sorry, girls.* She snapped it shut, not wanting any feedback from them.

"I did my best to protect you. How's your neck?"

"I'll live." She thought about how many times in her life she'd said that, but today it meant something.

Eli pursed his lips. "I think meeting the fish seller will uncheck some boxes." He pulled into the lake house drive and parked.

"Yeah, I have a craving for a good piece of flounder." Andi slid off the seat and walked to the door. Eli tousled her tangled ringlets and tipped her chin.

"I can make everything go away. Stay with me tonight?" He did his best to convince her with a kiss.

To top off her marvelous day, a text pinged. She checked her phone. "Oh damn. I need to pick up Fiona. Her car died." Andi broke away from him. "She left me Bailey's car keys. I'll bring her back to the house, and then take his car to Barnwell Street to meet the fish seller. I'll have a police escort. Will that give you enough time to find Peter Rockford before he kills Rachel? Or me?" She couldn't help her sarcasm.

Eli gave her an exasperated look. "I can come back at three o'clock to pick you up."

"Thanks, but I'll find my way there. If I get lost, I'll ask the policeman behind me."

CHAPTER FORTY-NINE

ANDI

ANDI WAS STILL SWIMMING in adrenaline when she parked on Barnwell Street. She now had a twenty-four seven police escort, for all the peace of mind that gave her.

Noise from the tire business across from the fish seller was deafening. A jackhammer echoed off the cinderblock walls at irregular intervals. Workers shouted. Country music blared. Metal tools clanged on cement. Those workers would be deaf by middle age.

Looking haggard, Eli met her. At least this time, she was more likely to come away from their field work with a pound of fresh shrimp than a bullet hole or a broken neck.

Hollister approached them, wrinkled shirt, bandaged head, and a scowl.

"How's your head?" Eli asked.

"Five stitches and eighteen bullshit reports to file. Now a meeting with a man who sells fish. Look at him. He's shorter than the guy in the park," Hollister grumbled.

"No concussion, I hope," Eli said.

He grunted. "A dent in my head. Nothing compared to losing a good deputy. Guy could be paralyzed for life. If he even makes it."

"I'm sorry to hear that." Andi pursed her lips.

Across the street, their man of interest rearranged ice in bins and then sat, newspaper in lap, waiting for a customer. His old blue pickup looked sandblasted, and one side mirror was duct taped. He'd set up in an empty auto parts parking lot with a For Rent sign in the window.

The man rose from his chair to greet a young couple. "Hey," he called and spoke to them in an accent she'd never heard. Gullah, Hollister had explained. Charleston dialect. Originally West African. The fish vendor pulled out several fillets from an ice chest, they made their selections, and he wrapped it in white paper. Poor guy had no idea he was the target of a police stakeout. Looking pleased, he returned to his lawn chair with frayed white-and-green webbing and picked up a *Wall Street Journal.* Melvin had claimed the fisherman couldn't read. Andi found his facade sad rather than sinister.

This fisherman's shoes had seen many miles, his black cotton pants were worn shiny, and he wore a faded camo jacket. Nothing about him seemed evil enough to murder girls and carve jewelry from their bones.

"Let's do it, so I can finish my paperwork," Hollister said.

They made their way across the street toward the fish seller.

Eli glanced at Andi. "Just following leads, Andi. Wouldn't be the first time a prisoner lied. Sometimes they just like watching us make jackasses out of ourselves. Drug dealers make the best liars." He pointed out the police stationed on four corners in case the old man tried to flee.

Stupid. Senseless.

This wasn't the guy who'd nearly broken her neck. Suddenly, the air changed. She flinched at a car horn. A tingle crept down her scalp. Something nudged her toward the truck.

Andi hesitated. Then a second little shove.

Okay, I get it. She turned away from Hollister and Eli, toward the open tailgate.

"Haa una fa du?" the man greeted them.

"Doing fine," Hollister answered without hesitation. "Sheriff Hollister, Lakeside Police. This here's our consultant, Eli Lake. Got some questions."

"Ain't done nothing," the old man protested. "Got a license. Show it to you."

Andi gazed back at the fish seller. Could this be the girls' killer playing a low-country fisherman? The Shadows showed no interest in him.

Hollister pulled photos from his pocket and handed them to him. "You recognize these girls?"

He shuffled through them and gave them back. "Seen 'em oncst or twice but not lately."

Andi turned back to the truck. "Not buried under the fish, please," she muttered. The briny smell made her gag. Shrimp, flounder, grouper, mackerel, sea bass, all laid out with heads attached. Right off the boat. Labels on the cooler showed the careful scrawl of a schoolchild.

"Fish clean $2," a sign in red marker proclaimed. Silver scales glistened like spilled sequins in worn plastic bins. A fillet knife lay at the end of one bin.

Here, ma'am, Mariah whispered.

She wandered around to the cab and peered in. Please God, don't let there be a bloody saw. *What am I looking for, Mariah?* Silence. *What do you want me to see?* More silence. Somewhere nearby, a church bell chimed. Another church rang out, "How Great Thou Art."

"... last time I seen 'em ... they was going to the War Memorial. I worried 'bout 'em.

"Fella sells drugs there, hoped they got no bidness with him. Two real purty chillun, them girls. Ain't seen 'em since spring. Reckon that priest runs a shelter got 'em a safe place."

"What priest?" Hollister's voice.

The fish seller's front seat was littered with McDonald's wrappers, crumpled receipts, and a black-and-red backpack. "What am I looking for?" Andi repeated.

Mariah appeared, leaning on the front fender with Bernadette. The two moved toward her, their silvery rainbow images like a hologram.

"What's going on here?" Andi whispered.

He's not who you think he is. Mariah pointed in the fish seller's direction.

"I know that." Andi folded her arms. "What am I looking for?" She moved to the other side of the truck. The girls followed. "Who is the fisherman? Help me." Any police officers watching would surely think she'd lost her mind, whispering to a truck. Eli glanced over, cocked his head, then continued the interview.

You got something that belongs to me, Bernadette said.

"Please don't talk in riddles." Andi expected them to vanish at any moment. Avoidance came easy for spirits. Too bad she couldn't just disappear when she didn't want to answer questions. "Find another way to communicate with me."

A single ginkgo leaf fluttered down on the windshield of the truck. "That's the best you can do?" she asked. "A leaf."

Name's Bennie, not Bernadette, a voice said. *Fisherman got me too. This guy ain't who they think he is.*

Then the two vanished. Andi groaned and snatched the leaf. Like a giant moth's wing, fluttering close to a flame.

Key in lock, rattling, rattling . . . climb the golden tree. The child's voice again. Why did this stupid fairy tale keep nagging her? *Talk to me, child. Who are you? Why have you come to me?*

No answer.

The only connection between this fairy-tale child and the missing girls was the ginkgo tree that turned golden in the fall. Andi twirled the leaf between her fingers.

"Ginkgo has healing power," Eli told her.

Startled, she banged her elbow on the truck's side mirror.

"Sorry." He gave her a lopsided grin. "You hear ghosts, but I can sneak up on you?"

Andi rubbed her throbbing arm and gazed into the window. "Look." She pointed at a ginkgo leaf on the backpack. "It wasn't there a minute ago. Get permission to look inside."

Eli gazed from the leaf in her hand to the truck. He turned in a circle. "One inside. One outside, and no ginkgo tree around," he said, and walked back toward Hollister.

In five long strides, the sheriff stood beside the truck. The old man followed.

"Ain't nothing but a USC backpack. Dunno how it got there," he told them. "Ain't no law against having a Gamecock backpack. Is there?"

"Would you mind opening the door?" Hollister pointed.

"If you say so. Ain't got nothing to hide." The fish seller pulled the handle and a hinge screeched.

"Hand me the backpack, please," Hollister said.

Brushing the leaf onto the floor, the old man grasped the strap and gave it to Hollister. Snapping on gloves, the sheriff unzipped the bag and pulled out an iPod by the wire. A name was factory-etched into the chrome back.

"Mariah Culverton." Hollister shook his head. "Monogrammed."

Andi sucked air. "Oh shit."

The sheriff nodded and let the iPod slip through his fingers into the pack. Two plainclothes people handcuffed the old man.

"Ain't never seen that bag till just now!" the fish seller protested.

A detective read him his rights and walked him to a cruiser.

Head down, Andi plodded toward Bailey's car, thinking about what Bennie had said. *He's not who they think he is.* Hollister needed public opinion on his side to keep his sheriff's job. He needed a suspect. She heard footsteps behind her, and Eli caught up. "You and the sheriff are wrong," she said.

Eli narrowed his eyes. "He had the personal effects of a dead girl in his car."

"I was wearing two pendants made from their bones. Does that make me a killer?"

He touched her arm. "How did that bag get inside the truck?"

She stopped walking. "Bennie says, 'He's not who they think he is.'"

Eli closed his eyes and put a finger to the bridge of his nose as if he was getting a headache. "Did the girl say it wasn't the fish seller?"

"No."

"Come on." Eli took her hand. "I want you there when we check the backpack."

Andi puffed out her cheeks in scorn. Helluva coincidence the bag just happened to show up in the fish seller's truck. Everything inside could be coincidental too.

CHAPTER FIFTY

ANDI

"WHAT IF IT WAS planted?" Andi asked. They sat in Hollister's car while his radio squawked nonstop.

"It's a lead." Eli reached into the backpack. "Besides, it couldn't get worse after today."

Hollister clicked his tongue. "My mama taught me never to say things like that."

Snapping on gloves, Eli started removing things from the backpack. Photos of the girl's cat, Mariah's high school ID, the scratched iPod, a hairbrush. He put each one into a bag and passed it to Hollister, then Andi. "Her phone should be in there," Andi said.

Eli moved the bag around and searched. "It's not."

"That hairbrush should be easy to check against what we have," Hollister said.

Lip gloss, mascara, powder, tissues, worn leather journal, and a gel pen. Typical stuff for a teenage girl, except the journal. Eli opened the small, black, leather book with water-spotted gold-edged pages. "I'll be damned," he said, leafing through the pages. "Day Three on the Street," he began. "Today, I met this asshole named Fisherman. A priest who runs a shelter. I think he's a pervert. He smells like mothballs. Weird-ass hair comes out of his head like weeds."

Eli turned to Hollister. "That verifies what the fish seller said about the priest who runs a shelter. Is that a church outreach program?"

Hollister was thumbing in information on his phone. "Only three Catholic churches here. No priest runs a shelter that I know of, but I'm putting that out to the department. Detectives will check agencies and churches. Someone has to know about this guy." He finished his text and told Eli to continue reading.

"I'm coming back to Bennie's place, the Holiday Inn, and I get turned around in the dark and hear footsteps. Paranoid, I slow down. Well, he does too. When I speed up, he speeds up. When I bend to tie my shoelaces, this asshole comes after me. He knows my name.

"I thought I was going to die right then. He grabs my backpack. I decide he's crazy enough to kill me over the backpack, so I haul ass. Says he's a priest. Bullshit!"

Andi pursed her lips. "Mariah knew, poor kid. Should've gone home then."

When no one else spoke, Eli continued reading about how Mariah met Bennie and how Bennie knew Fisherman was stalking girls. Eli looked up. "Bernadette's nickname is Bennie. Mariah thinks the man they call Fisherman is old."

"Guy can be whatever he wants. He was a middle-aged woman today," Hollister said.

"To a seventeen-year-old, everybody's old. When do the entries stop?" Andi asked.

Eli scanned pages. "Looks like about fourteen days left."

"Maybe it isn't her journal," Andi suggested. "Why are there entries after the bag was stolen?"

"Her handwriting can be analyzed." Eli skimmed down. "She does say Fisherman is stalking her. Not *the* fisherman or the fish seller or fishmonger. It's just Fisherman," he said. "Listen to this: 'Our Holiday Inn. Can't sleep. Bennie's shooting up. Slaying the dragons, she calls it. Helps us ease our consciences and forget the life we gave up. We steal food when people aren't looking, swipe coeds' stuff and sell it. Occasionally, I can talk some naïve college guy into buying—'"

"Wait a minute." Hollister held up a hand. "Andi's right. After Day Three, the backpack was stolen. The journal must not have been in the bag when the priest took it."

Andi wrapped a thread around a loose button on her coat. "How would Fisherman know who she was?" She tested the coat button and it held.

Hollister nodded. "Must've been working with somebody else who *did* know her name."

"Melvin," Eli filled in. "He was selling Bennie drugs."

Andi remembered pretty Bennie, tall, long eyelashes. *You got something that belongs to me,* she'd said when they were looking at the backpack in the truck. Not anymore. A crime lab had what was left of the pendants. Nothing in Mariah's backpack belonged to Bennie either.

Eli set the book in his lap, marking the page with a matchbook from the cup holder. "What do you think?" he asked Andi.

If someone else wrote this journal, it couldn't be Melvin. She doubted he could put a sentence on paper. Was forgery in Fisherman's repertoire? Had he forged Andi's name on that supposed murder/suicide confession he'd left on her living-room table? "This journal seems like something a teenage girl would write," she said, "but I don't understand how it ended up in a backpack that the priest took from her on Day Three. It shouldn't be here."

Hollister took out a pad and jotted a note. "Keep reading."

"Maybe she kept the journal at their Holiday Inn." Eli picked up the book. "Day Seventeen on the Street. That guy who sells fish on the corner creeps me out. Talks like he knows me. Can't understand half of what he says. Yeah, I think he's messed up in the head. Too damned friendly. I'm afraid he's stalking girls too. I don't trust anyone.

"Fisherman often shows up when I'm coming back to the Holiday Inn at night. I hate that guy. Right now, I can't outrun him. With this cold, I can't breathe. Bennie said I should stay at the Inn till I get better. She's gone to steal some medicine. I just want some chicken soup and my own bed. I started praying at night for God to forgive me for all my stealing and lying. Maybe I should go home and take my chances."

"If only she had gone home," Andi said.

"What about this man who sells fish?" Hollister held an unlit cigarette.

"Oh, come on." She heaved an exasperated sigh. "He's an illiterate man who sells fish on a corner and talks to people, girls, boys, any warm body. A lonely old man."

"How'd the backpack end up on his front seat?" Eli snatched Hollister's cigarette, bent it, and handed it back. He gave the sheriff a big smile. "Just helping you break the habit."

"Thanks for nothing." Hollister stuffed it in his pocket. "Old fellow sure doesn't strike me as the type who steals backpacks from kids." He checked his phone for messages.

Andi focused on the journal. "Who put that backpack in his truck, and how did the journal end up inside the backpack? I'll find out," she offered.

She followed Eli to the police station, where they questioned the fish seller. The poor man sat there in handcuffs, begging for someone to pack his fish into the coolers in his truck. "How did the backpack get in your car? . . . Did you leave the truck for any length of time? . . . Do you live alone? . . . Ever hear of Melvin Robinson? . . . What about this priest who runs a shelter . . . where is the shelter? . . . Seen a young girl named Rachel?" Hollister and Eli took turns.

Hollister pulled photos from an envelope and spread them on the table. Mariah's bones in the sewer. His eyes didn't waver from the old man's face. "You know anything about this?"

He stared at the photos, horrified. "No! Who would do sucha thing? Evil. Take 'em away."

CHAPTER FIFTY-ONE

ANDI

A NDI EXCUSED HERSELF AND left Eli to his interrogation, sure this fisherman wasn't the one who killed girls, and she drove to the cemetery where Perlie the ghost dog was buried. She felt at home surrounded by the bumpy brick paths, stories on old headstones, and tea olive bushes at Trinity Cathedral. Andi wandered from grave to grave. Maybe it was the sense of family here that appealed to her. A shabby-looking pigeon perched on a gravestone, watching her. Dampness mixed with cobblestone and moss gave the place an earthy smell, like a freshly worked garden.

She patted her purse for Bailey's gun and checked for other visitors. Andi was alone; not even Perlie was here today. But a cop stood at the fence, watching as she walked down the cobblestone paths. A marble tomb with lichen growing like roads across the lid, roads that led to dead ends. Children dead of diphtheria, scarlet fever; twins who died within days of each other. Mothers whose milk came, a painful memory of what they had lost. A cemetery of people taken too soon.

Focus, she told herself, on a priest who calls himself Fisherman. Hollister had ordered his people to hit the streets and squeeze every source they had. Church agencies, children's youth services, runaway hotlines, teen shelters—they'd all get calls before business hours closed. He'd brought in the FBI too. The agents would probably replay the video from her button cam until it was worn out, and they'd check State House surveillance camera footage too. All useless because of his disguise. The bastard had counted on that, but tech people might find something.

Once a computer composite was released, news stations and newspapers would rally with a massive search for a man who changed his appearance at will. Dead end. Focus on the girls. "Did Melvin have something to do with the backpack in the truck?" she wondered aloud.

A leaf fluttered down like the wing of a fallen butterfly and landed on the toe of her shoe. No ginkgo tree nearby. She smiled. Sisterhood of the ginkgo leaves, sisters who'd never had a chance to say goodbye to their mothers.

"Did Melvin call Fisherman after we left the prison?"

Ginkgo leaf. She'd take that as another *yes*.

"Any connection between the killer and the corner fisherman?"

No gingko leaf. But was that a *no*?

One more and it had to be a yes-or-no question. Andi pondered for a few seconds. "Did Mariah have the journal inside her backpack when Fisherman captured her?"

No gingko leaf.

Good. She'd kept it somewhere else. Andi stooped and gathered the leaves. Remembering Eli's words about their healing power, she stuffed them into a coat pocket.

Very few people knew police would be investigating the fisherman at the corner, and all of them worked with law enforcement. Except Melvin.

"Help me out here. Why would Melvin lie for Fisherman? And why was the journal in the backpack?"

Bennie's image painted itself in, and she sat on the lid of a stone coffin. A skinny girl in a worn USC sweatshirt, torn jeans, cap pulled down almost covering her eyes, she could have passed for a scruffy freshman coed.

Snuck that journal into the backpack before Fisherman planted it, Bennie said. *Spying on him pays off. Fisherman planted it when the old guy was gettin' the fish in Georgetown.*

"Thanks, Bennie, and for the gingko leaf messages too," Andi whispered.

Mariah's got a thing for them. Her mama and her planted a ginkgo tree. Later, she gave her mama a gingko pendant dipped in gold.

Soft footsteps, and Eli was at her side. "Had a feeling I'd find you here."

He ain't who you think. And golden tree ain't no fairy tale, the girl added.

Andi silently thanked Bennie.

You're welcome, ma'am. Better tell Eli to find Rachel fast. Fisherman's getting the room ready and setting up his tools. Bennie vanished into streams of color like oil in a puddle after a summer rainstorm. Andi wondered if the form they took depended on their moods. Sometimes they were as clear as a hologram, other times a watercolor dot-matrix image. Possibly this was a game for the girls, a respite from boredom. Andi pulled a ginkgo leaf from her pocket and twirled it. A golden leaf. A ginkgo leaf. What was the fairy-tale child trying to tell her, and why didn't she respond to Andi? The voice was familiar, yet she couldn't identify it.

Eli plopped down on a tomb.

"Bennie says Fisherman is setting up to kill Rachel. Meanwhile, you and Hollister waste time interrogating an illiterate fish seller." She stared at him. "This doesn't make sense to me."

240

"Probable cause. He was in possession of the dead girl's backpack and journal. That's physical evidence. And we can't be sure he didn't kill Mariah," Eli told her.

"Fisherman knows way too much about me. And he's always a step ahead of us. Ever wonder if he might be a police officer?"

"I've considered that, but today wasn't anybody's fault. A bomb in a statue, skateboarders, a building not locked. Nobody could have guessed it would go down that way."

"I'm exhausted," Andi admitted. "I know I screwed up today, should've made the exchange work."

"He pulled a gun on you," Eli said. "In retrospect, that was a lousy location for an exchange, too damn many variables, but Fisherman was calling the shots, and we couldn't risk Rachel's life. We came friggin' close to losing you. Stay with me tonight, okay?"

She locked eyes with him. "Maybe I'm making things worse. Maybe it's time for me to bow out and let you find Fisherman. He's got Rachel."

"I think she's the girl from Charlotte. No proof though. Just a gut feeling."

"Look. I'm not cut out for this investigative work. I'm certainly not anything like my mother, who thrived on dangerous situations. I can't sleep, and during the day, I'm always waiting for somebody to jump out and grab me." She stood and looked at the gravestones. "I don't want to end up in a cemetery just yet. I need to sit here and think. Don't feel like you have to stay with me. You can go back to what you do best, finding people. Find Fisherman, please."

"I don't want to leave you here alone, Andi."

She motioned with her head. "I'm not alone. There's a policeman at the fence. His car is parked on the street."

Eli took a deep breath and exhaled. Finally he spoke. "Offer stands for you to stay with me tonight. Are we okay? What happens to us when this case is closed?"

"I don't know, Eli. I don't know anything."

He began to walk away but then turned back to her. "Andi, you're stronger than you think. Don't doubt yourself." He waited a few seconds for her to speak, and when she didn't, he left.

Andi listened to his feet crunching through the acorn shells. Once he was gone, she inhaled the solitude of that graveyard, trying to find peace. When clouds rolled in, she walked back to her car, realizing that she might have pushed Eli out of her life.

CHAPTER FIFTY-TWO

ANDI

Back at the lake house, Fiona and Andi sat by the fireplace, trying to relax over a glass of pre-dinner wine. "The story made WIS TV News," Fiona told her. "Scrolling headline read, 'Bomb in the park. Police fatality.'"

"I never should've agreed to this, and now a policeman is dead because he tried to help. Nothing will bring those girls back. Or the policeman." Cross legged, Andi sat on a fake zebra rug, staring into the flames, hoping they'd burn away her anger and disappointment, hoping they'd bring some peace. But Hollister's plans had literally gone up in smoke today, and she didn't feel a damn bit safer. Suddenly, her body shook with sobs. Damn! She needed to get her emotions under control.

Fiona spoke softly. "He did his job, Andi. It's not your fault. But you and Eli can bring them justice. And maybe even prevent further killings."

"I quit the case."

"You did?"

"Yeah." Andi stood, snatched a tissue from an end table, and blew her nose. She moved Honky from rocking chair to sofa, sat down, and leaned back in the chair, letting the movement calm her. One rocker bumped. The other creaked. The old black chair had its own percussion.

"I've never known you to quit anything once you'd dug yourself in. You told me once that the one good thing your mama passed on to you is perseverance." Fiona settled Honky in her lap on the sofa. She cocked her head. "What made you say you'd quit?"

Andi recounted the horrifying events during the meeting with Fisherman, why she considered questioning the fish seller useless, and ended with, "Eli wanted me to stay with him tonight, but I said no."

"Ah, now we get to the heart of it. You sure did back out of that relationship fast. The man cares about you, Andi."

God, she was tired. Andi pulled up her legs and wrapped her arms around them. Her mind slipped back and forth between the park and the man on the corner and Eli, like the rockers of the chair, bumping and creaking, going nowhere. "Lance said he cared too, and look where that got me. Eli's just doing his job and getting a little sex on the side."

Fiona let the silence stretch out. "At some point, you'll have to stop bringing Lance into your relationships and learn to trust again. You didn't tell Eli you quit on him too, did you?"

Andi shrugged. "Said I didn't know."

"Oh, for chrissakes, Andi. Give the guy a chance. After you dashed his hopes, he still wanted you to stay with him tonight? That man's a keeper. You need to make things right tomorrow."

Andi shot her a look, but Fiona was right. She shouldn't have pushed Eli away. He was the best thing that had happened to her in a while. "This is not about Eli. Or my distrust of men, Fiona. The girls, they ran away because they thought their home life was terrible. When they realized it wasn't, it was too late. They never had a chance to go back home and make things right. To ask for forgiveness. And give it."

The heat pump cycled on and off. A log popped. The fire cast shadows on the ceiling. Andi studied the flames for a few seconds. Flames like memories that burned bright, faded to glowing embers that flickered occasionally, then ceased to exist.

"I'm just like them. I ran away with Lance, eloped, made my own shitty life, and never looked back. I told myself that my parents had done everything wrong and it was right to cut them out of my life. The longer I stayed away, the harder it was to find my way back home. Many times, I considered calling my mother, and each time I didn't connect with her, the road to forgiveness lengthened." Andi inhaled, exhaled, and swallowed her shame.

"Independence has a nasty price tag." Fiona got up, jabbed at the logs, and settled Honky back into her lap.

"My father left messages on the answering machine. I deleted them without listening." She studied the flames for a few seconds. "One day, I let the messages play. The memorial service for my mother had been the day before." A single tear rolled down her cheek. She wiped it and another came.

Fiona handed her a tissue. "Helluva thing to live with, not saying goodbye. What happened between you and your mother?"

Andi crossed her arms and stared into the flames. "On my sixteenth birthday, my mother and I planned a big party at the country club. She'd won a Pulitzer that year, and I'd bragged that my friends could meet my famous mother. Mom didn't show up, nor did she answer her phone. My father and I worried she'd been killed or arrested on some bogus political charge. When Dad reached her that evening, Mom was on a yacht with some insanely rich prince of an obscure country. Hammered, he said. Drunk."

"Ouch."

"No matter how many times she apologized, I felt in my heart, she'd abandoned me for her career. My father and I saw less and less of her. Mom's last cameo appearance was to tell me that she'd researched Lance and he was a loser. That stung more than my father's disapproval."

Little sparks rose like fireflies up the chimney.

Fiona rubbed Honky under the neck. "Andi, I know you're committed to these ghost girls because you share their pain and you want to make things right somehow. But you'd better be careful: don't think you have to risk your life because you never said goodbye to your mother. I'm not sure that helping the girls move on will help you forgive yourself."

"They need closure. And so do I."

"I know. But enough of all that." Fiona stood and tugged on Andi's arm. "I stopped at Maurice's Piggy Park. And now I'm gonna teach you how to eat real Southern barbecue. Come on."

Vanna White-like, Fiona gestured toward the kitchen and Andi followed. "Ambrosia for the gods awaits." Fiona hunted through the cabinets, dug out paper plates, and then put Andi through a crash course on Southern barbecue.

CHAPTER FIFTY-THREE

MARIAH

BENNIE AND I WERE IN Eli's room when he called Fiona. I sat in a mauve upholstered chair, and Bennie balanced on one arm. We were furious because Fisherman got away, so I sent Eli a message. He'd chilled water bottles in a hotel ice bucket, and while he was sucking one down, I bumped his arm, and all twenty-two ounces spilled into his lap.

We only heard his side of the conversation. "Fiona, it's Eli. I'm worried about Andi."

Knowing Fiona, she'd come up with a line a whole lot better than, "Why the hell didn't you blast that guy to hell when you had a chance?"

Eli held the phone away from his ear.

"Give him hell," Bennie said, and we cheered Fiona on.

When the noise died down, he put the phone to his ear again. "Are you finished?"

Apparently not. More yelling.

Finally he interrupted. "I know our stakeout failed miserably. Fisherman should be in jail. But Andi's in danger and you are too." Eli held the phone away and looked like he wanted to shoot it. "Andi came away safe. I made sure of that. Now I've listened to you. For Andi's sake, hear me out. Hollister put men at Bailey's place, but I'd feel better if Andi and you stayed with me. Can you talk her into it?"

Not from what we heard.

Bennie chewed her nails. "What if one of Melvin's old drug buds followed Andi home? I didn't see nobody, but then I wasn't looking neither. I say we pay Melvin a visit and haunt the hell out of him in case he asked somebody to hurt Andi. Maybe we could get us some answers too. We'll stop off at a hardware store and drain some batteries."

"I'm in." This time, I looked forward to kicking a live person's butt.

Melvin was lying on a cot in his cell when we caught up with him. I spied the toilet paper. "Hey, let's do a little interior decorating," I said, and we started flinging lines of it through the air, winding it around the bars, shredding it like confetti. Damn, it had been a long time since I'd papered somebody's house. I'd forgotten how much fun it was.

Beady little eyes drawn together, Melvin sat up, muttering, "What the fuck?"

I emptied his Marlboros on the cot and broke each one in half.

Melvin snatched up the stubs. More WTF's. You would've thought I'd snapped off his fingers. Bennie laughed hysterically. "Too bad he cain't hear us," she said.

He kept cursing until Bennie tossed a Bible at him, hitting him square in the head.

That shut him up, and he held his head like his brains were going to leak out.

"Can we make him see us?" I asked.

"Not unless he wants to." But we'd figured out something new at the Holiday Inn. Bennie picked up a pad and pencil and wrote, *The girls you had murdered want some answers.*

Melvin stared wide-eyed as the pen flew over the paper. "Who's there?" He rubbed his eyes. "I ain't kill nobody," he whined, raising his skinny arms in surrender. "Jesus help me."

The guy in the cell across from him stared through the bars. "Shut the hell up, you retard. Waste that toilet paper, they ain't gonna give you no more."

Bennie was writing again. *Why'd you make them blame that old guy who sells fish on Barnwell Street? That man ain't do no harm.*

"Who's there?" Melvin demanded.

Bennie printed our names. Then we looked at each other, nodded, and pounced on Melvin, pummeling him. Of course he didn't feel it, but it made us feel better. We discovered that while our energy was draining, his fear was filling our reserves again.

"I ain't mean for you to get dead." He coughed. "Leave me alone! Go away!"

"Shut up. You going mental?" The inmate in the next cell was visibly annoyed. "Guards!"

Melvin managed a muffled scream. "It wasn't me. Bennie gave up Mariah for a fix! Fisherman got you 'cause when Bennie was high, she told him where you was."

My chin could've hit the floor. I'd seen Bennie pretty desperate for a fix, but that couldn't be true. Bennie had died before me.

"You lying sack of shit!" Bennie yelled. "You helped Fisherman find girls and got them hooked on drugs. I never gave up any girls."

A guard showed up and called for backup. Code something. Two prison guards pounded down the corridor toward Melvin, wrestled him into handcuffs, and dragged him off. He kicked and screamed like he'd lost his mind. "I ain't kill no girls! Lord God Almighty, why them girls after me? Devil musta sent those girls. Jesus help me!"

Bennie and I grinned, but we knew we might have to pay for this later. Who knows what Punishers do to ghosts that mess with the living despite the warnings? If we were in trouble with the Punishers, we'd find out soon.

CHAPTER FIFTY-FOUR

ANDI

DETERMINED TO DRINK OFF one horrendous day when a serial killer eluded the police after almost breaking her neck, Andi refilled her wineglass. The ambrosia for gods didn't help her forget. "Rain must have followed us up the coast," Andi said. According to WIS News, a late tropical storm was brewing. Pines ruffled like sails in the wind. Bony fingers of branches scratched the windows. The temperature had dropped twenty degrees.

Fiona checked the thermostat and plopped down in her favorite position, hunched over a laptop. "It was a dark and stormy night." She gave a wicked laugh. "Eli called and wanted us both with him tonight. Those hotel beds are never big enough, so I begged off. Hope that's okay."

Andi looked up from sewing a button on her coat. "You're hilarious." When the house phone rang, Andi jumped.

"Look at you. All brave." Fiona lifted the phone, said hello several times, then hung up. "Wrong number. Didn't even have the decency to apologize," she muttered.

Wrong number? Andi didn't buy that for a second. Somebody was checking to see if they were home. "You don't think that—"

"Just a wrong number. But I could call Eli back if you want."

"No. He says I'm strong. You said I have my mother's perseverance. And we have plenty of wine here. So this is where I'm going to park my paranoid self."

Andi tied off the thread and snipped the end. "I'll go see what our guardian angel is doing." She checked the driveway and then the window. Nothing moving out there. A couple scary trees. Nobody was in Bailey's little indoor garden but fat orange fish. Where was the detail sent to watch them twenty-four seven? She shook some fish food from a container left on the patio table and stood over the tiny pond. "Little guys first. Be polite. No hogging." An obese fantail with bulging eyes ignored her, scrapping for pellets, nipping tails. "Somebody's gonna get hurt," she scolded and closed the garden door behind her.

In the kitchen, Fiona was glued to the laptop, as always.

"Hey! No sign of a cop anywhere," Andi told her. "Should we—"

"If he's any good, you won't see him." Fiona jotted notes on an envelope and looked up. "You're not a quitter, Andi. Come on, let's do some investigating."

Andi nodded reluctantly. "The enemy of my enemy is my friend."

"Okay. Still nothing on Bennie, but I found Mariah's dad's web page with a bio. Check it out while I get the mail. Then I'll pull up Catholic shelters for runaways. Back in a minute."

Andi settled into Fiona's chair and checked on Dr. Culverton. Boy, did Mariah's father get good patient reviews. Solid five out of five.

The front door slammed open. Fiona raced down the hallway and dropped a pile of envelopes on the kitchen table. "You're right. There are no police officers out there!"

Andi's phone played the *Magnum P.I.* theme song, and she shot Fiona an annoyed look but clicked ACCEPT. "Hollister said we'd have protection. There's no cop here, Eli."

"Stay inside and lock the doors. We'll be there in a couple minutes," Eli promised.

CHAPTER FIFTY-FIVE

ANDI

ROOM TO ROOM, WINDOW TO WINDOW. Nothing two-legged out there except birds. Andi stared out the floor-to-ceiling windows, suddenly realizing anyone outside could see her too. "Fiona?"

"I'm here." Fiona came down the hallway with Ignatius, checked the chambers, and left the gun on the table next to a pepper grinder. "Plenty more where this came from." She disappeared and returned with a sawed-off shotgun. "I get the big sucker."

"Aren't those illegal?" Andi pushed the barrel away.

"If I have to use it, bastard won't live to report me."

"If you have to use it, I hope to God I'm not around," Andi said. "Two firearms double-parked on the kitchen table. Better get rid of them before Eli and Hollister show up. My license to carry doesn't mean shit here. Bailey's gun is in my purse, where they'd need a search warrant."

Fiona slid Ignatius into a pocket and hid the shotgun under a pile of magazines. "I can shoot a cottonmouth in the eye," she said, heading toward the front window. "Don't you worry."

Andi's thoughts turned to the girls. *He's not who you think he is.* Cripes! If Fisherman knocked at the front door, she wouldn't know him.

Of course, he probably wouldn't knock.

In the living room, Fiona peeked through the curtains. "Three deadly-looking squirrels." She pointed to a leafy nest in an oak tree. "If you squint a little, you can just make out the barrel of an AK-47."

Andi smacked her shoulder. "Fiona! This isn't funny."

"Some police protection," Fiona grumbled. "If I ever find our guardian angel, I'm gonna rip one of his wings off. Go around back. No wait," she said. "I have a question for you, and be honest with me now. An old high school friend who works at the recording studio here called and said they need somebody on keyboards for a documentary. The piano player they'd scheduled is in the hospital. I wrote the soundtrack for it, sent it to her weeks ago. So I said, sure, I'd help, but now I'm thinking maybe I shouldn't leave you alone tomorrow. If you don't want me to go, I won't."

"Go. It's a great opportunity to see your name on the screen. We can't allow this bastard to control our lives. I refuse to give him that much power over me."

Andi sounded braver than she felt.

"They're here," Fiona called.

Hollister's Crown Vic pulled into the driveway, and they got out.

"About time." Fiona welcomed them inside. "How about a cup of coffee?"

"No thanks," Hollister said. "If you don't mind, I'm gonna search the property. Miss Fiona, you can give me a tour." He turned to Eli. "You take care of business with Andi."

Fiona raised an eyebrow. "Okay. Tour starts outside. Don't slip on the duck poop."

Andi's stomach did a dive. Hollister had Eli delivering bad news. She was sure of it.

Eli slid onto one of the bar stools and glanced at the pile of magazines. "Haven't seen one of those in a while. That'll get the job done," he said, resting his arms on the countertop.

Something bad was coming. They'd better not ask her to be bait again.

Eli's voice was soft. "I'm worried about you. I do care." He took her hands in his. "Andi, I'm sorry." He shook his head, jaw clenched, and lips pressed together. "I didn't mean for it to happen this way."

"For what to happen which way?" she asked, pulling free. She would not be bait for a serial killer again.

"This started out as business, a challenging case for me. Consulting fees from Hollister. Beats the heck out of chasing deadbeat husbands and fathers. This case was a great opportunity, and your skills were an asset. Christ, Andi, I don't want you to think I deliberately put you in danger so that I could be some kind of hero. Our plan at the State House literally blew up today, and I'm sorry I put you through all that."

"Who would've guessed Fisherman would play it that way? No need to apologize." She clasped his hand and forced a smile.

He returned her smile. God, he looked tired. "Along the way, something happened between us. I don't want you to think I'm using you. You can bow out at any time."

"I'm not meeting Fisherman ever again." Andi studied him for some clue about the news he had. "And I'm still not happy that you didn't tell me my pendants were annihilated. Destroy the object that connects to spirits, and there's no way to communicate anymore." As soon as the words slipped out, she regretted them.

"What did you think would happen at the lab?" There was an edge to his voice she'd never heard before. "And besides, you're still communicating with them somehow."

Andi lifted the locket from her neck. "Photos of the girls inside."

He gave a frustrated little huff.

"Let's not argue. If you want to bow out, that's fine, but understand things go wrong sometimes in the police world. I worry that you've made me into someone I can't be. Deceit is part of my job, but not when I'm off duty. I do care about you."

She studied him. The man looked contrite. Maybe Fiona was right, and Andi was backing out of this relationship, looking for a reason not to trust Eli. "I'm sorry. I overreacted," Andi admitted. "But I'm scared, Eli. Where is that policeman who's supposed to be here? Did the guy go out for coffee and not come back?"

Eli shook his head. "The officer stopped at a 7-Eleven for coffee and caught a robbery in progress. He had to stay at the scene, so he called in and we came. There is a second officer here somewhere. His phone must not be getting a signal."

Andi felt stupid now. "Oh," she said.

He donned a veiled expression. "I do have news. Positive ID from the odontologist on Mariah's teeth. We're meeting her parents tomorrow at three thirty. If you'd rather not go, it's okay."

Andi walked to the window. Mariah was probably braver than Andi would ever be. She owed it to the girl and her family to help them find closure. "I'll go."

He put his hands on her shoulders and turned her around to face him. Eli took a deep breath. "I promise someone will keep an eye on you, but I'd feel a lot better if you and Fiona stayed with me tonight."

"We'll be fine. I just need some time to process all this. My emotions are bouncing all over. Bitchy one moment, paranoid the next." For the briefest of moments, she thought she saw hurt in his eyes. Then he headed for the door.

Fiona met Eli at the door, whispered something in his ear, and he nodded. Probably about her birthday party, a surprise that Eli had leaked.

"Eli?" Andi called, and he turned around. "Thanks for caring. Sorry I've been a bitch."

He came back and put his arms around her. "You've been through a lot," he said, kissing her. "Healing is a slow process. We're going to be all right."

CHAPTER FIFTY-SIX

ANDI

ANDI SAT IN THE backseat of the sheriff's car next to Eli. Yesterday a serial killer. Today she had to face Mariah's father, and the news wasn't good. A sense of dread had tied her stomach in knots. When she heaved a sigh, Eli reached for her hand and gave it a reassuring squeeze. "Cheer up. Tomorrow's your birthday."

"Yeah, I'll be celebrating another day that a serial killer didn't put my face on a pendant." She forced a smile and squeezed his hand.

The sheriff glanced in the rearview mirror. "We spoke to the officer who pulled double duty at Bailey's last night. When you were looking for him, he was questioning some old drunk in a bass boat a little ways down from Bailey's. We couldn't reach him because his equipment got wet and quit working, but he was there."

An old drunk fisherman in a bass boat? Probably the same guy Fiona had spooked.

Andi opened her purse to occupy herself, to distract herself from what would come next. Tucked in a corner under her cell phone were the beads she'd found in the snow, the ones Honky hated. She fingered them. Warm, as if someone had just worn them.

"Nothing unusual last night at your place. A couple deer, some noisy mallards, a family of opossums," Eli told her. "You ever fall asleep?"

He'd been there all night. He did care.

"Slept two hours. Couldn't stop wondering if Fisherman was watching me." She slipped the beads over her head and repositioned her hair around them. Good accent for the black sweater, highlighting raccoon eyes that concealer couldn't hide. Maybe she'd sleep tonight.

Maybe the federal deficit would disappear too.

"There are reports from street people about the priest, but no one seems to know where he lives," Hollister said. "Some describe him as a monk. Others say he's a priest with a white collar. The rest have the man either bald with a moustache or with a full head of dark hair and clean-shaven."

"In other words, nobody knows what the hell he looks like," Andi said.

"We'll find him," Hollister said. "SLED has good forensics people. We have an excellent composite artist who's comparing sketches to find common characteristics."

"Are sketches physical evidence?" Andi asked.

No answer from the sheriff or Eli.

"We're gonna find this sum bitch," Hollister assured her. "A community theater company said they had a guy working with them who'd been trained by that famous sci-fi makeup artist. The ID guy made a sketch based on what they remember about him. Of course, nobody knows where he lives."

"And Rachel?" Andi asked.

"Rachel's images are online, and the newspaper and TV stations will make her disappearance top priority," Hollister told her.

"Your department should have some time, because he tortures them first." As if that was a good thing.

"We'll find her before that." Eli clasped his hand around hers.

She gazed out the window. In Pennsylvania the first killer frost had occurred weeks ago and the first snow had fallen, melted, and frozen again. Columbia was still green. In November.

Cocking an ear, Hollister listened to chatter on his police band for a few seconds. "Wife found out we're having a girl," he announced.

Andi smiled. New life among all this death. "Congratulations. When's the due date?"

"April twenty-eighth. I have my own girl not even born yet, and already I'm worried. Changed how I think, being a daddy. All night long, I tried to find the right words. How do you tell parents their kid's been made into jewelry by a serial killer?"

Don't tell her about the pendants! a panicked voice inside Andi's head cried.

We won't, she promised the girl.

Hollister turned off the four-lane road into Mariah's development and wound his way through streets of showcase brick houses. Two-acre lots of sandy soil, raised gardens, pink flowering bushes in bloom. A safe, quiet neighborhood until yesterday. Andi caught herself scratching as Hollister pulled into Mariah's driveway. "I still wonder why she ran away," she said. "Had to be more than grades. The girl was obviously well cared for."

Hollister clicked out of his seat belt. "A McMansion doesn't make a home. Lots of kids are happy in low-country shacks with tin roofs and a soybean field out back."

From his tone, she'd bet Hollister had been one of those kids. They walked up the brick sidewalk and rang the doorbell. Mariah's father answered. Tom Culverton's blue eyes were drained of hope and the bags underneath them held months of worry. His gait was slow and mechanical as he showed them to a large room, a family room, overlooking the lake.

Andi positioned herself between Eli and the sheriff on a blue leather sofa. Beyond the window at the end of a boat ramp, a wave runner was sealed inside a blue watercraft cover for the winter. Three brightly colored kayaks hung from one side of the boathouse. Reminders of better times, of parents who'd provided their child with everything she needed. Everything tangible, except safety; but safety didn't come with a guarantee. A white ibis preened on the shore. Nature in balance, only steps from Fisherman's mockery of a grave surrounded by crime tape.

A glorious yellow ginkgo tree grew beside the boathouse. Andi stared at it.

Faith noticed her interest. "Mariah and I planted that tree on Arbor Day one year," she told her. "It's due to drop all the leaves any day now. They do that. All those beautiful yellow leaves drop in one day."

The golden tree. The fairy-tale child. She was the first spirit who spoke to Andi but didn't reply. Why was that? Andi struggled to connect the child to Mariah's ginkgo tree.

Ask Mama about her ginkgo-leaf necklace. Mariah appeared and sat next to her mother.

"Do you have a necklace made from a ginkgo leaf?" she asked Faith.

Mariah's mother stared. "How do you know about that? Mariah bought it at a craft fair. Begged her daddy for the money so she could give it to me for my birthday. Yes, I still have the necklace."

"I read about it in her journal," Andi lied. "Mariah's a very good writer."

Faith flashed a distant smile and nodded. "Yes. She's also a talented musician. Plays six instruments." Andi wondered if Dr. Culverton had prescribed an antidepressant. Eyes rimmed in red, her attempt at composure, legs crossed, chin up, was heroic. The button-down shirt she wore hung in folds, as if she'd lost weight. Andi noticed again the resemblance between mother and daughter: dark hair, turned-up nose, and flawless fair skin.

When she unbuttoned her coat, Andi's eyes met Eli's. He'd probably slept less than she had. "Thanks for keeping an eye on me," she said softly.

An older woman Andi assumed was their housekeeper brought a tray of coffee, pastries, and cups. Eli glanced from the coffee to Andi, and she knew what he was thinking. In Mariah's own house, he'd better not pick up anything liquid, or Mariah would make sure he'd spill it.

She poured a cup, took a sip, and glanced over at him. "It's good. You should try some."

A sideways look. His patented don't-go-there expression.

Suddenly, Mariah's father crossed the room toward her. "What in God's name do you have around your neck?" Eyes narrowed, he pointed at the necklace.

"I found it in the snow outside my house," Andi told him. "Is it Mariah's?"

CHAPTER FIFTY-SEVEN

ANDI

"**G**IVE IT TO ME." Mariah's father's face was flushed, his eyes two angry slits.

Andi slipped the necklace over her head and handed it to him. From the chill working its way down her spine, she had a good idea about the origin of those beads.

"Those big white beads. Do you know what they are?" A vein in the man's neck pulsed. He held it up to the light, touched the beads and shoved the necklace back at her. "They're knuckle bones. You're wearing somebody's fingers. Get that abomination out of my house."

Honky's crazy reaction to them suddenly made sense. For the first time, the beads felt ice cold. Andi clenched the necklace protectively. Please God, she prayed, don't let those bones be his own daughter's. *Are they yours, Mariah?*

They're Bennie's, Mariah said. *She had long, graceful fingers.*

Coffee threatened to erupt from her stomach. She sucked air to stay calm. Her mouth tasted like a copper mine. Slow, deep breaths.

Andi leaned toward Eli. "They're Bennie's," she whispered and stuffed the beads into his jacket pocket.

"I'll put them in the car." Eli's cowboy boots clicked on the inlaid floorboards and echoed through the beautiful house that seemed so empty. The front door opened and closed. Shadows hovered in one corner.

Andi forced herself to concentrate on something else. Outside the floor-to-ceiling windows: a rusting Schwinn propped against a rose trellis, a weathered tree house, a wooden jungle gym, all once part of a carefree world. On a sofa table, Faith had gathered treasured mementos. Framed pictures of Mariah playing violin and piano, her band hat, a teddy bear, and a baby blanket. She'd seen this before when one of her students died. The deceased child's possessions became enshrined before the memories faded. Then one day, parents finally released the associations and packed them in the attic. Mariah's father folded his arms. When he shifted, the leather chair creaked. Andi imagined him in that worn recliner, feeding his daughter a bottle, later watching the Disney Channel with her; still later, handing over car keys.

"I heard about yesterday." Dr. Culverton fixed Hollister with a cold glare. "How you met the killer and lost him." He set his cup on the table. A porcelain cup hit a saucer, a discordant sound.

Her father might as well have lobbed a chunk of marble at Hollister, judging from the sheriff's expression. "We're doing the best we can, Dr. Culverton. I lost a deputy. Almost lost our consultant, Andi, too." The sheriff pulled a bottle of Tums from his pocket, popped two into his mouth and crunched the tablets. "We've since found your daughter's backpack in a man's truck. He sold fish in the area where your daughter was frequently seen on surveillance cameras. Apparently, she loved the State House Park." He took a sip of his coffee, perhaps to make the Tums go down easier. Perhaps to delay the inevitable. "We're here about the dental report."

Dr. Culverton's expression didn't change. He just kept staring at the sheriff.

He's always like this, Mariah said, as if reading Andi's thoughts. *I think he loved me when I was little. But then it seemed like nothing I ever did was good enough. Actually, nothing anyone did was ever good enough. Maybe he wasn't comfortable being a father, or maybe he ran out of happy feelings after seeing so much pain in his office.*

Andi marveled at the child's wisdom. Did that insight come with death? The front door opened and then closed, and Eli returned to the sofa, a question in his eyes. Is the girl here? Damn, he could read her. She nodded.

Hollister poured more coffee, and Andi bet he was wishing for something stronger. He pulled an envelope from his pocket.

Mariah sat down next to Eli. He'd chanced a cup of coffee, probably craving caffeine to stay awake. When Eli set his cup down with both hands, Mariah rattled the rim until a little coffee sloshed out. Two Shadows sitting on the arm of the sofa next to Eli giggled.

Among the living, silence hung heavy in the room. Andi's senses were heightened. She noticed that every painting in the room hung a little crooked. A silvery cobweb clung to one corner of the curtains. Underneath an ornately carved Asian chest lay dust balls. Like its residents, the house seemed suspended in time, waiting for news that was inevitable.

The doorbell chimed, and footsteps padded toward it. A hinge squeaked.

Faith filled in the awkward silence. "You know, my last thought every night is a memory of my daughter. She's also my first thought each day. Mariah's my morning star. We love watching the stars together. Her daddy bought a first-class telescope, and now it's our Saturday-night pastime."

"Your daughter is extraordinary," Andi blurted out. "Sometimes I have—it's just a sense, a feeling that Mariah's speaking—"

"For God's sake, Hollister." Tom Culverton's coffee cup clattered again. "You brought some charlatan psychic into this case! What about odontology? The *scientific* evidence."

"I'm not a charlatan or a psychic."

You see why I had to run away? Mariah asked.

She did, all too clearly. *Despite the tough act, he loves you, Mariah. Parents make mistakes too.*

He bullies Mama too.

"Six instruments she can play, and her piano recitals, so gifted. She wants to be a music teacher," Faith gushed.

Andi noted her use of present tense. Denial.

The housekeeper took several tentative steps forward, then marched in, grimacing as if she expected to be chastised. "There's a priest at the door, Dr. Culverton. He insists on giving you something."

"Get rid of him." Tom waved a hand.

"No, wait!" Eli was on his feet with Hollister at his side, racing toward the door.

"What now? You'll arrest a priest for soliciting souls?" Mariah's father followed them.

He's not who you think he is . . . not who you think he is, Mariah's voice chanted, growing louder and louder. *Not who you think he is . . . not who you think he is.*

Andi rushed to the front door too. Hairs on her neck bristled. On the doorstep lay a Bible. Three ginkgo leaves fluttered on top. "Fisherman! It's him! He fishes souls."

"What is that psychic talking about?" Tom asked. He put a protective arm around Faith.

Eli scanned the area from the front porch. "No car. No sign of anyone." He turned to the housekeeper. "Describe the priest."

"Messy-looking gray hair, tall, green eyes. A priest, for heaven's sake," she said.

Hollister raced to the Crown Vic and brought back a pair of gloves and an evidence bag. He dropped the Bible into the bag. "Come with me," Hollister told Andi. "You search the shoreline, Eli. I'll take the streets."

Eli bent down to look at something in a narrow stretch of dirt— footprints? Then he turned back to Andi. "If I don't see you tomorrow, happy birthday." He sprinted toward the lake with two Shadow companions.

"You'd better see me tomorrow," Andi called after him.

Shoulder holding his cell, barking out commands to a dispatcher, Hollister ran to the car and motioned for Andi to get in. "We'll be back," he told the Culvertons as he ran around the car to the driver's side. "Bastard has the balls to show up when I'm here," the sheriff growled, shoving the key into the ignition. The engine roared to life. Cursing, the sheriff jerked the steering wheel and rolled onto the street. "See anybody who faintly resembles this guy, holler."

There wasn't a soul in sight. Upper-middle-class America. A dead girl inside a sewer, a killer on the streets. Hollister was in deep trouble. With properties stretched out like this, Fisherman could hide anywhere.

CHAPTER FIFTY-EIGHT

ANDI

POLICE SCANNER SQUAWKING NONSTOP, Hollister cruised through the neighborhood. A middle-aged man was collecting mail from a miniature lighthouse mailbox. The sheriff hit the brakes and rolled his window. "Seen anybody out here in the past fifteen minutes? A priest maybe?"

The man shook his head.

"Lock your doors. Let the police know if you see anyone who doesn't belong." Hollister pushed the window button and drove away.

More squawking from the scanner.

Hollister spoke into the radio. "I want every available officer here in Sesqui Forest. Deputy Mills coordinates. Knock on every door within five miles of the Culvertons' address. The other side of the lake too. I want every single vehicle checked, including cars in driveways, all parked vehicles. Neighbors should inventory water vehicles, jet skis, bicycles too. Any stolen vehicle, I want to know. Eli Lake is searching the woods. Twenty-four-hour surveillance on the

Culvertons. Meanwhile, I want a composite from the housekeeper. We're gonna put this guy's face on TV. Somebody's got to know him. You copy all that?"

Andi peered into the crimson sunset. Bastard had perfect timing. Another thirty minutes, and he could stand next to Hollister and thumb his nose without anyone seeing him. No streetlights here. Andi picked up the evidence bag from the console.

Hollister glanced sideways. "Don't handle that bag. Could smudge the prints."

"Maybe there's a marked passage," Andi said, "to send us in the wrong direction."

"Yeah, he'd do something like that, wouldn't he?" Hollister blew through a stop sign.

"He can't just vanish," Andi said. But he had. Fisherman came and went as he pleased and killed with impunity, like Satan himself. Once the sun set, there wouldn't be a hope in hell of finding him. Eli had grown up in the woods, had been a tribal cop, but even the academy couldn't prepare somebody for this psycho. "Will Eli's phone get service out there?"

Hollister patted her knee. "Don't you worry about Eli. Every police officer between here and Columbia will be camped out in this neighborhood soon enough."

An old car sitting at the end of a driveway caught Andi's eye. "Why would somebody leave a classic car like that in the open?" A big black car that reminded her of a fat black beetle. An old Hudson maybe?

Where's my puppy? You said . . .

Key in lock, rattling . . . climb the golden tree.

Who are you, child? Andi asked, certain by now that the fairy-tale child wouldn't answer, and she suspected she knew why. Once, she'd been trapped in a black beetle of an old car. Her four-year-old brain had built a cage around those memories. PTSD, the doctors had said. This old car had unlocked the cage. Chills, goose bumps. She rubbed her arms. What was happening to her? Was she sinking into insanity or sinking into her past?

"Andi? You warm enough?" Hollister asked.

"I'll be okay," she told him.

Room full of princess dresses and tiaras. *I don't like being dressed up like a princess. I don't wanna wear that other girl's clothes. They smell bad. I want my mommy.*

She shook off another chill as trapped memories came flooding back. The car. The golden ginkgo leaves. Her heart hammered away. But the memories weren't finished with her.

Key rattling in a lock, rattling, rattling. She struggled with the warped window. Finally it opened. She was free! Racing down a road with her hair flying, running as fast as her legs would carry her. The golden tree welcomed her, and she climbed into it. Higher. Higher. More memories awakened. A little girl with ringlets clinging to a branch. Her fingers had ached, and she'd wanted the bad man to leave her alone.

"You come down outta there!" the evil man had shouted.

He shook the tree violently. Now she'd made him angry. He'd warned her not to do that. Andi's leg slipped, but somehow she stayed on that branch.

"Come down here this instant!"

More shaking. Andi was terrified.

A runner stopped near the tree, and a woman's voice asked, "Hey, why are you shaking that tree. What's up there?"

The evil man ran away.

When Andi looked down at the woman, her hand slipped. She clung to the branch with only one hand. Maybe she shouldn't have climbed so high.

"Hold on. Try to hold on," the woman's voice called to her. "I'll get help."

Her little body had dangled until she couldn't hold on any longer.

The little girl who believed in fairy tales crashed down through the branches, understanding now that this tree couldn't save her. Andi couldn't catch hold of anything but a handful of golden leaves.

The next thing Andi remembered was a hospital room and strangers peering down at her.

Oh God! That's why the fairy-tale child never answered. She wasn't a ghost. The fairy-tale child's voice was her own! That's why the voice was familiar. Repressed memories of the kidnapping had been trickling into her consciousness. But who gave her those words, that fairy tale embedded so deeply into her brain? Who made her memorize those words? Her mother had sent the Shadows to help her escape.

Now the monster in her memories and nightmares was loose. She shivered uncontrollably. Come back, she told herself. Don't stay in the past. That's where the spirits live. You're a grown woman. Stay in the present. Mariah and Bennie need you. Eli needs you.

Hollister asked again if she was warm enough. She rubbed her arms and shook off the chill. A brief visit from her darkest past, and she was ready to confront her darkest future.

"Something about that old black car is wrong," Andi said, praying repressed memories and nightmares weren't coloring her sense of reality. But nightmares did mix a little truth with a heavy dose of fear to make them real.

CHAPTER FIFTY-NINE

ANDI

"STOP!" ANDI SHOUTED. "Go back to that old car!"

Hollister slammed on the brakes, and the seat belt bit into her shoulder. The sheriff jammed the gearshift into reverse and backed up until they were beside the car. "Been there for a while, got a pile of leaves on it," Hollister said. "That's odd. Nothing but pine trees around. You stay here." Hand on his gun, he angled out of the seat and approached the antique car with a Maglite. He peered into the car windows and came back. "It's an old Hudson. Nothing unusual except for those leaves, but I'll get the owner to open it."

He started down a long drive.

Andi got out and followed him.

"Thought I told you to stay in the car." He slowed. "Make sure you let me know *before* somebody shoots at me."

Andi gave him a thumbs-up. "I'll catch the bullets. The house is empty."

"How do *you* know that?"

"Because I bet Fisherman checked before he parked here," she said.

"You're pretty sure that's his car."

"Ginkgo leaves. There are no ginkgo trees here," Andi explained.

Hollister did a 360-degree turn, and she followed his gaze. Scrub pines and kudzu choking out anything else that might grow. Wisteria and poison ivy climbed the nearest tree.

"I'll be damned. You're right. The ghosts put them there?"

Andi nodded. "That's Mariah's signature."

Crimson sunset dimmed to gray as their shoes crunched along the gravel. She turned, scanning for movement behind the trees, listening for the snap of a twig or rustling leaves. What was the difference between luck and intuition? Fine line, she guessed. "I've always wondered how bad guys get away. Maybe a voice inside tells them when and where to disappear. Or they have help from the devil. Why is that?"

Hollister shot her a skeptical look. "I chalk it up to a twisted mind. That's all."

The house was dark. Not even a porch light. While Hollister knocked, Andi checked the yard. A girl of about seventeen stood beside a stately magnolia.

Mariah, what about the car?

"Andi! What are you doing down there?" Hollister pounded the knocker a third time.

"The car, Mariah. What do you know about the car?" Andi said aloud.

Belongs to Fisherman's dead pappy. She disappeared.

"Who are you talking to?" Hollister peered around the back of the tree.

"That's Fisherman's car," Andi told him.

"And you know that because—never mind. I got probable cause." He walked back to his Crown Vic and unlocked the trunk.

After rummaging around, he pulled out a crowbar and snapped on latex gloves. He tried the door. Unlocked. Not even a squeaky hinge. Someone had taken good care of it. No interior lights. Hollister shined a Maglite over the front seat. Spotless cloth seats, faded dark blue, light blue, and light gray stripes.

"Nothing but a pile of prayer cards." He picked one up. "I come from a long line of Baptists. What do Catholics do with these things?"

Andi's stomach went acid. "They're used at funerals." She stared at the one in his hand. Picture of St. Anne. "Andrea Wyndham, November twentieth, 1987, to November twentieth, 2022. That's tomorrow!" The bastard knew her birthday. The other cards had names on them too. Mariah Culverton. Bennie Johnston. Rachel Van Der Donack, Fiona McPherson.

"Fiona! Why'd that son of a bitch have to bring her into this?" Andi pulled out her phone, keyed in numbers, and listened to ringing. No answer.

"Rachel Van Der Donack!" the sheriff shouted. "God bless those prayer cards! Well, there it is in black and white. It is the girl from Charlotte. Lord, let that girl be alive, or her daddy's gonna—Hell, no. I don't like this one bit. More than probable cause." Hollister pried open the trunk. Neither spoke when they saw a bloody army blanket. The smell was something Andi would remember forever.

CHAPTER SIXTY

MARIAH

HOW FISHERMAN MANAGED TO escape unseen, I don't know, but I think the devil gives him tips on how to get away with murder. The bastard acts normal, blends in, and nobody suspects him. After he dropped off the Bible, he pedaled off on a bicycle, whistling "Dixie" while I screamed at Hollister, "He's there!" Too late. The sheriff and Andi were already in his car.

Hollister never saw Eli come back for my old Schwinn. Tires were low, and Eli expected a lot out of that rusty bike, but he raced down the road about a mile until it ended where a new housing development hadn't broken ground yet. Panting, Eli wore a disgusted expression, probably thinking Fisherman had taken a different street. "Over there!" I said, but of course, he couldn't hear me. He'd seen it though, a gravel utility road, with the bicycle Fisherman had ditched. He propped my Schwinn against a pine tree and headed into the woods.

Eli raced through the mud, deeper and deeper into the woods, occasionally stopping to listen, tracking my murderer by his footprints. Fisherman was about as quiet as an elephant in a peanut factory, scuffing through leaves like he owned the place. I had a feeling Eli could sneak up on a person, and you wouldn't know it until he tapped your shoulder.

It was raining now, a steady rain that turned any hollows in the ground into columns of mist that resembled spirits rising out of the ground. Fog drifted in as Eli moved from tree to tree, bush to bush until he was behind Fisherman. "Police! Hands on your head!" he shouted.

Gun in his hand, Fisherman wheeled around. Three shots rang out, and Eli collapsed, holding his leg. Eli fired more shots, but Fisherman disappeared into the fog. Grimacing, Eli ripped the material on his pants leg and checked. Two big, nasty holes, blood running out, made me sick to look at.

He unbuckled his belt, tied it around his leg and lay back, breathing hard. When he angled a phone out of his pocket, nothing lit up. The screen looked like a concave spider's web. Guess he fell on it. He tried several times, then heaved it against a tree. Glass and metal ricocheted everywhere.

He lay there breathing hard. Eli hadn't said anything since he got shot. Not even a curse. Slowly, he got up and moved forward, a kind of shuffle-and-stumble motion, until he fell and didn't get up again. His face was all twisted, his khaki pants leg soaked in blood. He'd been shot because of me, and I felt like shit.

Eli crawled to a ditch. It looked like kids had dug a foxhole, probably playing paintball games. He rolled into it and lay so still I thought he was dead. Bending over, I put a hand on his shoulder. He flinched. "Mariah?" he said, voice barely a whisper. Dirt and leaves had mixed with blood on his face. "Tell Andi I really do care."

Could he see me now? That didn't seem like a good thing. *Are you—?*

"Dead? Hell no. But get Andi."

He made rakes of his hands and pulled mounds of leaves and dirt over himself. Two Shadows helped bury him.

Maybe Eli covered himself in case Fisherman came back. Then he'd just rise out of those leaves and kill the bastard. Or maybe he was digging his own grave.

CHAPTER SIXTY-ONE

ANDI

HOLLISTER SHOUTED INTO HIS speaker microphone. "Whoever fired those shots, report in! People on the lake and in the woods, check in!"

A husky voice. "Shots came from the other side of the lake, sir. Nothing we can see, probably a ways back from the shoreline. We're on it."

Another voice. "Anybody heard from Eli Lake?"

No replies.

Hollister stared into the darkness. Running a hand through his disheveled hair, he punched in numbers on his cell. "Get me a K-9 unit. Somebody pick up a T-shirt from Eli Lake's room, Harrison Inn on Gervais. Give it to the K-9 unit. Hell no, I don't like this one bit."

Shots fired? Andi prayed Eli had fired them, and the man who owned this Hudson was dead. Breathe, Andi told herself. She stared at the dark stains on the matted carpet inside the trunk. Duct tape, rope, a bloody blanket. Butcher-shop smell. Yes, the man was a butcher. Whispering, whispering, too many voices to hear clearly. She imagined the girls pounding on the heavy steel, sobbing, pleading for their lives. Andi had to walk away.

Hollister called for a CSI unit. He keyed in the license-plate number and checked the glove box for a registration. No registration, but the license plate came up with the name Lloyd Mason. "Find Lloyd Mason!" Hollister shouted.

The answer came back minutes later. "Registered to a man who'd be a hundred fourteen years old. Address is a vacant lot."

"Son of a—!" Hollister said. "Sure would be easier if those dead girls told us who this sum bitch is and where he lives," Hollister said.

"It's like chasing mercury balls," Andi told him. "If they don't want to answer, they vanish. Only mortals can bring justice to mortals. It's up to us."

"Ain't that way in the movies," Hollister grumbled. "Ghosts want revenge. They get it." He stomped a clump of dirt off one shoe. "I need to secure this area. Go on back to the car. Storm's gonna intensify any minute."

Andi trudged toward the Crown Vic. Trees hung over the drive, creating a canopy so thick moonlight couldn't filter through on a clear night.

Scuff, scuff, scuff.

She stopped, listened. Nothing. Andi opened the door and dropped onto the passenger seat. Something hard poked her. An evidence bag with Bennie's knuckles. Leaning her head back on the seat, she closed her eyes and inhaled, exhaled. Slow, deep breaths. Something like a wrecking ball was growing in her chest. First the memories. Now the back of that trunk.

That bastard had crammed living girls into that ancient Hudson. When he'd finished with them, he'd probably used it to transport their bodies to wherever he buried them. Mariah and Bennie had taught her about the fragility of life, how one lousy decision could alter life forever. Yet most decisions were reversible. The only obstacle to reversing a decision was death itself. And maybe that wasn't really an obstacle, not if you could hear beyond.

Andi opened her eyes. Sirens, strobing lights, boots tromping through weeds and gravel. Pulling her coat tighter around her, she keyed in Fiona's number. Still no answer. Fiona was always camped out next to some device that could deliver a message. Had the bastard lured her friend into a trap? She texted, messaged, then called her again. No answer, but the text was delivered, so the cell was on.

White-tinged, puffy clouds moved past, revealing a hazy rainbow slice of moon. A break in the storm? Moments later, black clouds rolled an ominous curtain over it.

Lights were trained on the Hudson, where a forensics woman dusted a fender. Crime-scene investigators crouched in the driveway, making casts of tires and footprints. The yellow flashing lights of a tow truck cast eerie shadows. Odd that Fisherman would sacrifice a car. Maybe he'd planned to come back for it. Or he was nearby watching, waiting until she was alone. Andi glanced at the backseat. With all the police nearby, the man couldn't possibly be there. Or could he?

The tow-truck drivers stared at the car trunk. One of them yelled, "Look at this. Over here!" Cops came from all directions. She listened through the open car door.

Hollister squatted near the fender.

"Paint's scratched here." A man in a Def Leppard T-shirt said, "My wife made a scratch just like that when she put my son's bike in the van."

Hollister looked disgusted. "Sum bitch just rode away on a bike."

Clutching her coat around her, Andi reached for the door handle. The sky unleashed a torrent of rain as she slammed it. Cops and evidence people raced for cars. Sheeting rain roared off the roof, cascading down the windows, obscuring her view. Engine noise from the winch. Wire screeched around a drum, and chains clinked so loudly that she could hear them through the closed door. The tow-truck people must've connected the car and hauled it onto the flatbed of the truck.

Yellow lights whirling, the tow truck pulled out. Three police cars, bars no longer flashing, drove off. Hollister made one final scan of the scene, got into his car, and backed down the driveway. His wet coat smelled of mildew and sweat, his shoes of earth and pine straw.

Rain drummed on the roof with urgency, as if trying to remind Andi of too many unresolved crises. "Fiona's not answering her cell. Eli isn't either, and what about Rachel?" she asked the sheriff.

"Now that we know for sure who Rachel is, SLED can get evidence from the car and fingerprints off those prayer cards and maybe the necklace." Unlit cigarette in his hand, he listened to police chatter for a few seconds.

"But what about Rachel?" Andi repeated. "Mariah says Fisherman's set up his tools."

"Rachel's safe as long as Eli keeps Fisherman occupied in the woods. Knowing Eli, he'll stay in the woods till he has that lunatic in handcuffs . . . or sends him to hell, where he belongs. Meanwhile, I'm gonna take you to Tanner Dawson's. He was police chief before he retired." Hollister glanced across the seat, probably gauging how scared she was. "He'll keep you safe, so you can sleep tonight, and then I can concentrate on finding Rachel."

"I can't leave Fiona alone in that house," Andi argued. She opened the locket. Both girls were sobbing.

CHAPTER SIXTY-TWO

ANDI

HOLLISTER WAS ANNOYED. He didn't have time for an argument from her, Andi figured. His Crown Vic idled at the intersection of Two Notch Road while he popped Tums and she argued. Fiona shouldn't be alone during this storm. What if she'd already come back to an empty house? If Andi hadn't gotten her into this mess, she'd be safe.

The sheriff let out his breath like he was dealing with an ornery teenager. "Okay. I don't like it, but we got plenty of people around Bailey's, and Fisherman won't come around if he sees a police presence. Besides, he's probably still in the woods, trying to get away from Eli."

Perseverance had paid off. She'd worn him down. "Take me to Bailey's, and you can concentrate on finding Rachel."

They drove to the lake house in silence. Hollister checked inside and talked to the nearest police officer.

Andi thanked him and set the security system. She'd seen that holy card with Fiona's name. The date of death was tomorrow on hers and Fiona's. Andi tried to remember if one of the holy cards had Eli's name on it too.

The security system counted down the seconds to arm again. Andi checked Fiona's bedroom and throughout the house. No sign of her. She should be back from her recording session by now. Oh hell, she was probably waiting out the storm somewhere.

Bailey's wind chimes clashed like three-year-olds pounding xylophones. Just what she needed to soothe her battered nerves. Rain and wind and water cascaded off the roof. Thunder rumbled. She checked outside. Her police guardian, coat dripping, was huddled under the soffit of the house. Poor guy looked miserable. If Eli was still out there, he'd be soaked too.

Andi opened the window beside the guard. "Have you seen Fiona? She's not answering her phone."

He shook his head. "Pulled out this afternoon in a red classic T-Bird. Never came back. Bailey has one fine car collection."

"Thanks. Want some coffee?"

The cop held up a thermos. "No thanks."

She closed the window and tried Fiona's cell again. If there was such a thing as a soul storm, Andi was in it. She had a theory that life revolved around cycles in which negative energy attracted more negative energy. Misfortune would pile up like wood on a bonfire until it threatened to consume her. Then one day, the negative energy would just disappear. Andi had stumbled onto one hell of a bonfire.

Worry eating away at her, she sat in the bumpy rocking chair. Fiona had warned about a possible emotional toll, but Andi never imagined that toll might involve losing her best friend. She bit her lip. When it came to matters of the heart, Andi had a knack for losing everything.

Eli might solve all his cases, but she could lose him too. Had she made things right with him? Oh hell, she'd dragged them all into this mess. Thunder rumbled again, making her aware of the storm outside. Andi stopped rocking.

The house had no gutters. Steady dripping should have lulled her, but it made her edgy, like a clock that ticked too slowly. Andi glanced at the laptop on the kitchen table. It had timed out to an old screen saver with colorful marine life. Oblivious to terrifying thoughts swimming in her head, the fish swam in and out of coral, tiny rainbows moving in a calm blue sea. Andi tapped the space bar and sent them into cyberspace.

The front door slammed open. "Fiona, is that you?"

She took the gun from her purse. Adrenaline growing rocks in her stomach, Andi crept around the corner of the entry to the kitchen, gun in front of her. If it was Fisherman, she'd unload that Beretta into him. If it was the Shadows, she'd tell them to get lost. If it was Fiona, they might shoot each other.

"Fiona?" She peered around the open door.

Movement! Leaves rustled, a twig snapped, soft footsteps. The halo from a flashlight bobbed along toward the front door. She planted her feet, gun in front of her, ready.

The Maglite backed around a corner of the house. "Don't shoot! FBI Agent Lowell, ma'am. Looks like the door blew open. You okay?"

She lowered her gun. It wasn't the same guard she'd talked to earlier. They must've changed shifts. Hollister had brought in an FBI agent to guard the house? "Thanks for being out here in this mess."

He peered around the corner. "That's my job."

An army of palmetto bugs marched through the doorway, trying to find a dry place. "Get out!" she told them.

A Shadow blew orange-blossom breath at them, and they retreated.

Lowell gave a low whistle. "Wish I could command my teenagers that way. Lock that door. Good night."

Andi closed the door and turned the deadbolt. She dug her phone out, hoping she'd missed a voice mail from Fiona when her phone was muted. Nothing new. Just the message Eli had sent before they went to Mariah's. She read it again. *11:37 a.m. Andi, I care about you more than I've cared about anybody in a long time.* Okay, she could fall in love with this guy. Too damn bad she never told him that. Hindsight was her screwed-up operating system when it came to people she loved. She keyed in his number. It went to voice mail.

A branch bounced off the roof. Lights blinked, then flickered out. Andi glanced from a hurricane lamp to the kitchen drawers. Had to be matches in there. She foraged for them, then went from room to room, lighting candles and lamps.

Her phone glowed in the darkness.

She studied the flame in an antique glass hurricane lamp. A scrim of carbon coated the globe. Andi turned the rusty knob to lower the wick. Dark shapes moved across the ceiling like spirits awakened, and the kitchen was bathed in an orange glow. "Oh shit!" A puddle near the door. Rain had flooded over the tracks of the sliding doors and was trickling toward the Oriental carpet. Where did Bailey keep a mop and bucket? Where the hell was Fiona?

Her phone played the *Andy Griffith* theme song. Fiona must've programmed that ringtone for Hollister. "Fiona, if I ever see you again, I swear I'm gonna glue your fingers together." She hit ACCEPT.

"No word from Fiona?" Hollister shouted like she couldn't hear him through the storm.

"Nothing."

"I'll put an APB on her. Agent Lowell says you've lost power. Everything okay?"

Currently her bodyguard was outside sucking down a steaming cup of coffee from his thermos. Poor guy. She wondered who he'd ticked off to get that duty. "Power's out, but I have candles and hurricane lamps. I'm fine. Is Eli back?"

"No. Canine team's looking for him."

"Please let me know when you find him."

Hollister continued. "We're still looking for Rachel, and profilers are concerned that Fisherman could've made his way home to her. Just about anyone would pick up a guy who looked like a priest hitching a ride. Wish to hell we knew where he lived. We think he's more interested in killing Rachel than you at the moment."

"Well, it's good to know I'm not at the top of his bucket list."

Papers rustled in the background. Hollister must be in his office. More rattling papers. "Interesting development. We're missing part of Mariah's pelvic bone. And get this, bones from *three* hands were found."

"Bennie's knuckle beads may match the third hand. Maybe Fisherman tossed some of her bones into Mariah's crypt to throw the investigation off."

Andi pulled the sooty globe off the hurricane lamp and wiped the inside with a napkin.

"Lab said a match between the saw teeth and the finger-bead segments probably won't be found because the knucklebones have been boiled and filed down. Guy's real crafty."

She replaced the globe and watched carbon build on it again. "Was Mariah strangled?"

"What makes you think that?"

"At the Culvertons' house, I had a panic attack, and it felt like someone was choking me. Can bones show strangulation?"

"Yeah, hyoid bone if one was found." Hollister sighed. "We're dusting for prints on the car and Bible. When we get this guy, he won't last two nights in jail. Child killers are at the bottom of the cons' food chain." He paused, as if contemplating something. "Storm's taken out a lot of power lines. Fiona may be stuck on a back road. She'll turn up, and Eli too. Stay put. Keep your security system on. It should work fine on backup power. I know Bailey has guns. So much glass in that house, you might want to keep one on the nightstand, but don't shoot Agent Lowell."

Not comforting. How many people had he posted out there?

"Okay. If you hear from Eli, would you ask him to call me?"

"Will do. And you were right. Fisherman marked a passage in the Bible. It began, 'Vengeance, sayeth the Lord.' Call me if anything's not right, anything big or small, anytime. It's okay to be afraid," Hollister added. "Fear keeps you alert."

She didn't want to be alert. Unconscious sounded good. A long, deep sleep even better. "I just opened a bottle of wine. Plenty of candles and a fireplace. I plan to be asleep very soon." Andi hung up, feeling empty. She'd feel a lot better when Fiona got there. And Eli.

The banner on the security console flashed red. Armed. She called Eli again. "It's Andi. Please call so I know you're safe. And thanks for being my guardian angel last night. I owe you one." Searching for the right words, she paused. "I care about you too, and I don't want to lose you. Be careful."

Andi tried Fiona again. Still no answer.

For the next half hour, she mopped floors and peeled candle wax off Bailey's antiques. A fire, a bottle of wine, and Andi had a good buzz. When the laptop battery glowed red, she blew out the candles and headed for her room. Towels lined the glass doors like sandbags on a delta. She gathered the soggy towels and tossed them into the tub, then pulled dry ones from the linen closet.

Brain cells thoroughly marinated, she climbed into bed. "Dance away, Shadows. I need some entertainment tonight." No sign of them. Closing her eyes, she sank into the pillow-top mattress, pulled the down duvet to her chin, and prayed for blessed unconsciousness.

CHAPTER SIXTY-THREE

MARIAH

L AST TIME WE'D TRIED TO help Rachel, two giant Punishers tag-teamed us, circling us so we couldn't move, blowing sulfur fumes at us, setting the grass near us on fire. "Spirits do not interfere with justice!" they'd roared. Looking in on her wasn't interfering. In fact, Bennie and I went to Fisherman's hoping she might've escaped.

We came through his door and headed for the small room where he did his evil work. "Damn, I hate this place," Bennie said. "Smells like mold, boiled collard greens, and blood."

All those overgrown bushes and weeds. Seems like anybody who drove by should've realized the person who lives here is crazy. Four girls had died there so far, including us. And if Hollister didn't do something quick, Rachel would be next. Her beautiful blond hair looked like a rat's nest now. There she was with her dinner untouched on the floor next to her. Fish sticks and peas. Nobody would eat that crap. Poor thing looked like a wilted flower. Head down, legs folded under her, she lay curled up on the floor. Her legs were black and blue where he'd attached the leg irons. Hadn't taken Fisherman long to break her. Shoot, first time we saw her she was living like a princess. Now, her life was fish sticks and peas.

Bennie grimaced. "Ain't no fun having nothing to do all day but read the Bible and do crossword puzzles. Won't help if she's gonna try to starve herself. He'll beat her until she eats something. Or use his tattoo tool on her. He tried that once with me, and I left my mark on him. Then he used a paddle with holes in it to beat me half to death."

"How many times did you escape?" I asked.

"Never could. He kept me in the attic. You escaped?"

"Yeah, three times. That's when he rigged the leg irons on the cot." I knelt beside the girl, and she suddenly looked up. Could she sense us? If only we could talk to her like we could to Andi. "Eli will find you. He's a good cop," I told her. It probably wouldn't happen, but she couldn't hear me anyway. At least I didn't think she could.

Stooping down, Bennie peered under the sink. I asked what she was doing, and she pointed at a piece of metal. It had a circle on one end and a long stem on the other. Reminded me of the pin that kept a hand grenade from going off. The key to her leg irons! Bennie drew back her foot.

"You can't kick it toward her! That's interfering! Don't do it!" Nothing is worth us being stuck between worlds forever. "Don't do it," I repeated.

Bennie had a defiant look on her face.

That's when we heard a car pull into the driveway. I looked out the window. It wasn't Fisherman. On the side of a white SUV was a sign shaped like South Carolina in two colors of blue intersected by a tree with one leaf. Department of Health and Environmental Control, DHEC. Two old guys who looked like they should've retired twenty years ago got out with clipboards. They didn't look impressed with Fisherman's messy yard.

CHAPTER SIXTY-FOUR

ANDI

THE WIND WOKE ANDI at 3:00 a.m. She got up, walked to the bedroom window, and searched the darkness for movement. Something big streaked between the trees. There it was again. Every dendron in her body was at full alert when it turned and leaped off toward the lake. White tail and antlers. She could stand at the window and let the wildlife scare her or go back to bed and wake up rested in the morning. Andi locked her door and shuffled back to bed. "I see dead people. What the hell am I scared of?" she muttered and closed her eyes.

Wind howled through the trees like a ghost train.

She ignored it.

Something crashed on the roof.

Nothing she could do about fallen branches.

Thunder rattled the windows. Andi sank under the covers. According to Fisherman's holy cards, she was supposed to die today. Damn, there were no curtains to close, although the rain came off the roof like a waterfall.

Probably better that she couldn't see what lurked out there. Lightning slashed through the trees.

Her phone rang, and she lunged for it. Damn! "Unknown," but she answered anyway. Not Fiona or Eli. No one. The battery was low, so she plugged it into her battery bank and checked for a message from Fiona. Nothing. Would she know if Fiona was in danger? Would the girls tell her, or would the bond between friends send her some sign that Fiona was in danger? Cripes. Fiona was probably sitting out the storm in a bar somewhere with a dead cell phone.

And where was Eli?

Behind a bald cypress tree, yellow cat eyes blinked. Another Shadow joined the first, and then another. Yellow eyes like laser beams barreled in and out of the trees. Something had agitated them. But she didn't see anything suspicious. Maybe they were just playing a game of tag.

Andi got up and padded toward the kitchen for a glass of milk. The hurricane lamp still had plenty of kerosene. The flame burning much too high, it reminded her of hell. She'd promised to save a spot down there for Fiona next to a hot devil. Where was Fiona?

Climbing back into bed, she faced the wall opposite the window. A sniffle. Then another. No, she would not cry. Would not show weakness.

A deafening crash, and the window shattered, spewing glass everywhere. An Adirondack chair lay in the room. Andi stared at it as if it had flown in of its own accord. The alarm was deafening. A dark form stepped through the jagged opening. He knocked the phone out of her hand, grabbed her by the hair, and dragged her out of bed. A man in a dark jacket.

"Let me go!" She kicked at him but connected with the night table. Bailey's Tiffany lamp shattered on the floor. Where the hell was Lowell? Strong arms caught her under the armpits. She dropped her seat, trying to be dead weight, but his grip didn't lessen. He hit her with the butt of a gun. The dark room went white, then sickening orange, then inky black.

Seconds later, Andi felt her body bumping along the damp ground. She awoke and inhaled. Wet pine straw and freshly turned earth. Not a dream. These could be the last smells she ever sensed. Think. Lie. Fight.

She dug her heels in, dropped her butt. Twisted, jerked. Hands tightened on her wrists in a vise-like grip. Sharp rocks and downed branches ripped holes in her thin pajama bottoms. Hair and leaves and pine needles stuck to her face.

Mothballs. The bastard smelled like a frail old man—or woman—yet he'd easily hauled her through the broken window and across the patio. They were heading toward the lake. He would duct tape her hands and feet and throw her in.

Or he'd hold her head under until her lungs filled with water. She threw all her weight against his pull, twisted against his grip. That's when she noticed his FBI jacket.

He stopped and gave a smug smile. "I need to make you a saint so I can add your relic to my collection. This is God's mission."

"Let me go and I'll make sure you get the pendants."

How much time had passed? It took seconds before the alarm company called the house. The answering machine would pick up. No, it wouldn't. No electricity, and it was probably programmed for Bailey's cell anyway. With trees down and power out, police couldn't get there for at least ten minutes. The bastard had plenty of time to kill her.

Something lay on the ground in the woods. A tree. No, it was Agent Lowell. Oh God, don't let him die.

"I'll get your pendant girls back," she lied. "I know where they are."

Fisherman stopped but didn't loosen his grip. "Enjoying your last birthday?" He gave a short laugh.

Terry S. Friedman

"I swear to God, I'll get them," Andi said. Hell, she would have promised her firstborn child or any number of things she didn't have. "If you kill me, you won't get the pendants."

"If I kill you, I'll have a new pendant." Fisherman motioned with a revolver half the length of her arm. "Move, and if you run, I'll make the pain exquisite."

Shivering, she levered herself up off the muddy path, plotting an escape route. No way to outrun a bullet. Mud squeezed between her toes. Glass slivers stung as she limped along. If the alarm call had gone through, she'd need to waste more time. A stumble, and she screamed, holding her ankle. "Ow! Ow! I can't walk." Her voice echoed through the trees. With any luck, she'd make enough noise for someone to hear. Damn. Tonight, everybody had their windows closed against the pounding rain. No houses nearby anyway. God, her head hurt.

Fisherman hauled her up by one arm as if she were a naughty child. "Shut up and move!" He marched her toward an old car parked on the other side of the woodpile. It fit in well with Bailey's antique classics. A blue vintage Cadillac with fins.

She sank like a rock to the ground, tried jerking out of his grasp.

The bastard held on. At the car he opened the trunk. "Get in," he said.

Andi remembered another bloodstained trunk.

He poked her with the gun. "Get in or I'll shoot you!"

"You need those pendants for your relic collection." A hopeless glance around. Trees, a woodpile, old cars. Not a living thing in sight. If she climbed into that trunk, that might be the end for her. "You need those pendants for your collection," she repeated.

"I can start a new relic collection. Perhaps that's what God wants."

"God wants justice, not murder!" Andi swung an arm and knocked the keys from his hand. She lunged for them, but he tackled her to the ground. They rolled through leaves and muck and rocks, gasping and panting. Andi clawed him like a cat in mortal combat, tore at his skin, at his eyes, at his clothes, ripped loose a pants pocket. The bastard straddled her, slapped her face again and again. The stink of him, mothballs and sweat. She gagged and tore with fingers and nails. Finally, his wallet tumbled from the torn pocket. A dull thump in the leaves.

He stopped pummeling her, felt his pocket, groped through the mud and pine straw. She was free. Run! Flight instincts kicked in, but her head ached. It felt like a dream, when her mind told her one thing, but her body refused to move. Every muscle screamed.

Scrambling up, he grabbed her hair and dragged her back to the old Cadillac. "Now you've done it. Gone and lost my wallet and keys. I'm gonna enjoy making you writhe in pain, hearing your cries for mercy, witnessing that last shudder before you die."

"Bastard!" She beat at him, got loose, and ran a few steps. Her head reeled and she teetered. Sobbing, she seemed to watch helplessly from above, as if she were someone else. He duct-taped her mouth, hands, and feet, heaved her inside, and slammed the trunk lid. That horrible, finite sound of metal against metal cushioned by rubber seal, like a hermetic coffin lid. She drew her knees into the fetal position.

Footsteps. Something scraping through the leaves. Ha! Bastard couldn't find his keys. Now, he'd have to leave her there. Then she remembered the three kids who'd suffocated in the trunk of a car in Philadelphia because no one had ever thought to open it and look.

Yellow cat eyes peered through the darkness at her. A small Shadow tucked itself around her body. *Don't be afraid*, it whispered.

Why can I hear you? She spoke silently. *Shadows never talk.*

Because you're between life and death. Her yellow cat eyes blinked. *Don't you remember me?* The little Shadow looked puzzled. *I am Devika. We found you when that bad man kidnapped you. Don't you remember the key rattling? We kept him from opening the door. We showed you the window and helped you open it. You were such a good tree climber. You climbed right down that big tree outside the window. I told you what to do after that, repeated it over and over again like a fairy tale, and you repeated it too. That was the last time I spoke because the Punishers were angry. They told the Shadows that we must never communicate with mortals again.*

But—

Your mama gave us a job, taking care of you.

But aren't you scared of the Punishers?

The Punishers won't do us any harm, the Shadow answered. *Interfering with justice isn't bad if it helps someone. That's what our mamas taught us. We can't cross over, is all. But we don't really want to. We like it here, between the worlds.*

She needed to focus on escaping. Andi stretched her fingers, twisted her body, groping for anything sharp to rub the bindings on, to saw them loose. *Can you get the tape off me?* she asked.

I'll try, the Shadow said.

Icy fingers struggled with the bindings. *I can't do it.* The little Shadow started to cry. *I need scissors.*

God, her head hurt. She gagged. No! Vomit now and she'd choke on it. Blackness faded to orange, then white. She passed into unconsciousness.

CHAPTER SIXTY-FIVE

ANDI

A SIREN! MUFFLED, YET A distinctive wail. Andi sat up and banged her head against the trunk lid. Dammit! Then she remembered. She was locked inside an old car. Footsteps pounded away. Andi closed her eyes, desperately trying to put the pieces together.

Did Fisherman kidnap me?"

You need a friend. I'll stay with you, the Shadow told her. *But this man isn't the one with the puppies. Your mama says you were his first and the only one who ever got away. She also says he'll come back for you. But this is not the one.*

Why can you talk to my mother, but I can't?

Don't you remember? You told her not to contact you. Ever.

Oh God. What had she done all those years ago? The air grew heavy with moisture. An acrid smell lingered in the trunk. Earth or oil of some sort. Maybe blood. Her fingers touched a small, cold metal object, and she brushed her thumb over the ridges. A pendant! The bastard had killed again. How long before he killed her too? The Shadow rubbed her back in circles the way her mother had when she'd had nightmares. A kind gesture, but it didn't lessen her fear.

Hot, humid air closed in around her in that cramped space. She squeezed her eyes shut and screamed. A ball of fear grew in her chest, squeezing the air from her lungs.

Don't use up all the air. No one can hear you scream, the Shadow told her.

The sirens shut off. Footsteps, doors slamming, engines idling, the crackle of radio static. Muffled shouts.

"He busted the window and got her. Door was locked from the inside," shouted a man with a heavy Southern accent. "We'll check the rest of the house."

"FBI agent's got a pulse. Just knocked out." A younger voice.

"Cole, put him in your car and drive him to the hospital." Hollister's voice. "Somebody give that agent a coat before he goes into shock."

"Checked the lake. Nothing I could see there, sir."

"She ain't inside. Not Miss Fiona either."

Static on radios echoed through the woods. A dispatcher code for something on Forest Drive, a downed power line blocking a road, a car in a ditch. Hollister barked out orders, delegating until Andi wondered how many men were left out there.

Dammit! This was like listening to a radio play, like helplessly watching a plane spiral out of the sky. Andi screamed into the duct tape covering her mouth: "I'm here! Fisherman's wearing the agent's coat!" But the Shadow was right. Nobody would hear her. The Shadow snuggled closer.

"I found a wallet. Guy's a priest!" The Southern accent.

"Lemme see that," Hollister told him.

Fisherman's wearing Lowell's jacket! She willed them to hear her the way the girls did, but it didn't work that way. With her mouth taped, her voice was no more than a hum. All she could do was listen.

"Sheriff, I'm Special Agent Roy Blales, from Quantico," said a new voice. "I checked the owner's cars. Nothing. But a car's missing. Fresh tire marks."

Andi moaned. "There is no Agent Blales. It's Fisherman!" The missing car is probably the T-Bird Fiona is driving.

Hollister addressed his team. "We have four people to find." He named them. "Take a good look at the pictures I sent to your phones. As for the suspect, we don't have an ID on him. He could look like your Great-Aunt Hattie, for all we know. We figure he's an actor." The sheriff assigned who would look for whom and said, "Agent Blales and Kenny Parker, stay here a minute."

Andi struggled with the bindings. "No! It's Fisherman!"

"Address on this driver's license reads Irmo. Forty-Three Palmetto Drive. I want you to check out that address. Rachel may be there. Make sure you follow protocol. Her daddy's a judge. If Fisherman is there, we may need a SWAT team or a hostage negotiator. Report back."

"Kenny Parker, don't go with him! He's Fisherman!" Andi screamed into the duct tape.

I'll get Mariah, the Shadow said. *Don't be afraid.* Then she vanished.

Leaves swished.

Feet raced away.

The voices faded.

Car doors slammed.

"No!" They'd mistaken a killer for one of their own. She tried to rock the car with her body, to bang her feet against a taillight. "He's not an FBI agent! I'm here!"

Suddenly, the steamy interior turned to frost. Andi could see her breath.

Eli needs you, ma'am, or he's gonna bleed to death, Mariah told her.

Get me out of here! I tossed his car keys somewhere in the woods. Find them.

A moment of hesitation then, Mariah's voice. *Okay, ma'am. I'll do my best.*

The Shadow curled itself around her.

CHAPTER SIXTY-SIX

MARIAH

OUTSIDE THE LAKE HOUSE, I sifted through leaves with my sneakers and said a prayer, something I hadn't done in a long time. Without Andi, Eli would die in that ditch. I didn't envy him, slowly bleeding to death out there. Good thing darkness, cold, and rain don't affect the dead. Where we are, we feel nothing but sorrow for what we have lost and the need to find our way to the Other Side.

Fisherman had faked out the cops. He even had a cop chauffeur, Officer Parker. Wearing a stolen FBI jacket, driving around with flashing lights, no one would stop him. Bastard! Meanwhile, time for Eli and Andi was running out. I had to find the missing car keys.

Being alone in the woods with rain coming down in sheets and wind snapping off pine tree branches terrified me. But the good news is that ghosts are waterproof. Rain goes right through me.

Focus on the keys.

I had to find them. Damn. Too many boot prints. They could be ground under the mud by now, and I'd never find them.

Somebody touched my shoulder and I screamed.

"What are you doing out here?" Bennie asked.

"Looking for Fisherman's keys. Andi's in the trunk. Eli's bleeding to death on the other side of the lake. He tracked Fisherman for miles before Fisherman shot him. Help me." I bent and pushed something shiny with a stick. Old gum wrapper. "I hate litter bugs."

Bennie grunted. "Damn woods. Things living out here, and I can't see 'em. Biting, screeching, blood sucking, slimy things, crawling outta bushes."

"You're a wimp, city girl. Bugs don't bother ghosts. Besides, there's nothing here but leaves, dirt, and a lake." Just in case, I did a quick survey. Nothing living that I could see. In fact, somebody could get murdered out here, and a body wouldn't be found until spring when the boaters came.

"Hold up a minute." She poked me. "I can pick that lock. Come on. All we need is a screwdriver and a paper clip."

We took off for the house. Glass glittered like diamonds on the path. If Fisherman had dragged Andi out of bed, her feet must look like ground meat. She'd be wet and cold inside that awful trunk. That Shadow couldn't help. It was just as scared as she was. I'd been in that trunk once myself, but not while I was alive. Hell, the claustrophobia would've killed me.

Suddenly, three Shadows darted in and out, streamed over the treetops, their yellow cat eyes like fireflies in mating season.

"We can find things," one said.

"Whoever finds the keys gets a prize," another shouted.

"This ain't no game," Bennie told them.

We entered the house and traipsed down the hall toward the garage. That pegboard wall was a work of art, with shiny tools hanging in neat rows. I snatched a couple screwdrivers.

Outside, Shadows were jumping up and down with joy.

"Found them!" a child's voice shouted. A set of keys floated toward us, and we raced back to the car. I was starting to like those Shadows.

It took me some time to find the keyhole. When I lifted the trunk door, I saw Andi lying very still on the floor of the trunk with a Shadow hugging her. For the second time tonight, I whispered, *Are you dead?*

CHAPTER SIXTY-SEVEN

ANDI

"I'M NOT DEAD." Andi's voice sounded like a croak. One eye was open now. Such an effort. Andi swung her legs around until her feet dangled over the bumper. Synapses misfiring, muscles aching, one eye nearly swollen shut, she wouldn't be moving at lightning speed. She winced as Mariah peeled the duct tape from her mouth. Bennie unwrapped her feet. Then Mariah unwound the silver strips on her hands.

Eli ain't gonna make it unless we get him to a hospital, Mariah told them.

Andi stood slowly and took a couple deep, painful breaths. "Where is Eli?" She'd be lucky if she found him before passing out again.

On the other side of the lake, probably about five miles from my house, deep in the woods. Let's take your car, but you'd better put some shoes on, Mariah said.

Andi's head throbbed. Wet pajamas clung to her skin like plastic wrap and sealed in the clammy cold. She wondered if this was how lying in a body bag felt. Dampness worked its way up, much like the chill she got in the presence of the dead.

Andi stumbled over to a tree and leaned on it for a few seconds, telling herself to breathe normally. She should've parked Bailey's car in the garage, but it wasn't raining when she'd left it under the carport with his classic cars. Head down, she hobbled toward the house and found what she needed. Forcing one leg to move, then the other, Andi crunched through the glass toward Mariah with keys, phone, shoes, and a raincoat.

Past Fisherman's blue Cadillac, where rain poured in through the open trunk. Past a fat tree stump with stagnant water and across the driveway, toward Bailey's SUV. Sucking air, she hoisted herself into the Explorer, stared at the key, then lifted a limp hand and fired up the car. Andi knew she was in no condition to drive, but time for Eli might be running out. On this night of all nights, she would not be weak, would not cry, but dammit, she didn't want to lose Eli. Tires spinning through mud, she pulled out with Mariah in the front seat, giving directions, and two Shadows in the back.

Big tree down. She weaved around it into the other lane. Traffic lights out. Andi leaned closer to the front window to see through the blur of rain as the wipers pumped furiously.

"Good thing nobody's out tonight." Andi hit the defogger switch, and the fan blasted air. It was damn hard to see between the rain and the tears welling in her eyes. She swiped at her eyes and sniffed.

A gossamer arm reached out to touch her shoulder. *Don't cry, ma'am. We'll find him before it's—we probably should hurry a little.*

Wheels spun as the car shot forward. Andi fished a cell phone out of her pocket, plugged it into the USB port and touched the emergency icon.

It rang and rang. "Answer the damn phone." Andi put together several strings of obscenities and punched the numbers this time.

"Hello." *Click.* "Son of a bitch, they hung up."

She was getting a bad feeling about this. Why couldn't they hear her? Mariah directed her through a series of turns, shortcuts, until she arrived at a cul-de-sac across the lake from Bailey's house. Andi parked in a vacant lot and touched her face. Blood was trickling down her forehead, pine needles stuck to it. One eye was so swollen she couldn't see through it. Mariah led her into the woods. Feet squishing inside tennis shoes, face wet with rain, sweat, and blood, Andi trudged along in the dark with her phone lighting the way. "Don't leave me now, Eli," she whispered. "I got you into this, and I'll get you out of it." She hit the emergency icon again. This time she heard a voice.

"I need to speak to Sheriff Hollister now! Find him, wherever he is," she said. Her breath came in ragged gasps. "We need paramedics at the lake, behind the Culvertons' house. Eli Lake is bleeding to death in the woods. You got that?"

Dead air. No, they didn't get it. Maybe the cell towers were down.

She listened for a few seconds. "Damn. Dropped the call." Andi called again and waited for an answer. "Tell Hollister the wallet they found is—son of a bitch! They keep hanging up on me." Her body shook uncontrollably. Andi couldn't tell whether it was from cold or being bashed on the head.

Mariah walked her to a tree. She leaned on it, breathing hard. If the dispatcher hadn't heard Andi, maybe she wasn't alive. "Am I dead?" she asked suddenly.

I don't see that faint rainbow hue we have, Mariah told her.

Maybe I haven't been dead long enough, she suggested.

Doesn't matter. We need to find Eli. Come on. Mariah raced ahead, then stopped.

What's wrong? Andi asked.

I'm trying to remember landmarks. A tree with a crooked trunk. Pieces of broken phone. Damn! In the dark, nothing looks familiar.

Mariah walked back the way they'd come.

Andi stumbled along behind her. The girl kept turning to make sure she hadn't passed out. Phone glued to her ear, she barked out commands to a dispatcher who'd hang up on her. Perseverance, my ass. Andi stomped her foot and yelled, "Mariah! Where the hell is Eli?"

I thought I knew, ma'am.

Andi stared at her. *Ghosts can't see in the dark?*

Looks like the place, but he's not here. Everything looks the same. Trees, stumps, vines, leaves, Mariah said.

A blast of wind whipped at her raincoat. Andi turned to the wind and shouted, "Eli!"

Something crashed through the woods. Something big and brown flashed by. A dog, a deer, a coyote. Too much noise for human legs.

Mariah whirled around. Shadows huddled behind two trees. Branches snapped in the distance. Then silence. Whatever it was, the damn thing was alive.

Let's get out of here, ma'am.

CHAPTER SIXTY-EIGHT

FISHERMAN

FISHERMAN HATED LOOSE ENDS. Time to dispose of Officer Parker and Eli Lake. He had commandeered Parker's police SUV and his radio. A gun can be very convincing, especially when it unexpectedly knocks you out. Good thing Hollister hadn't paired him with a bigger man. Parker was in the trunk.

Taunting the police was one thing. Getting sloppy was to be avoided. Tonight he played an FBI agent. If he ran into Hollister's people, it would be a brief encounter that ended with last rites for them. But first, time to finish off Eli Lake. He'd drag Jezebel's boyfriend to the police SUV, put him in the trunk next to Officer Parker, find a good place on the riverbank, and push the car over. No sense leaving behind any evidence. The Lord could carry the car off to wherever it pleased him.

"Well, look at that. A white Explorer parked at the edge of the woods." He remembered that car with fancy hubcaps and the rainbow decal from Bailey's. Good Lord, what was all that ruckus? Sounded like a herd of wild boar scrambling through the woods.

Then he heard a woman's voice calling for Eli. Jezebel. How had she gotten out of that trunk? Did the police rescue her? No matter. Thank you, Lord, for delivering her to me yet again. She'll lead me to Eli. And this time neither would get away.

Raising his eyes toward the canopy of dripping trees, he prayed, "Please God, end this deluge soon. I have work to do." When the rain didn't cease immediately, he asked his nana in heaven to keep an eye on him and keep him safe. Tonight, he'd need all the help he could get.

Parker's police radio crackled. "At Bailey McPherson's property. Trunk open on one of the classic cars. We found used duct tape and ropes inside and a piece of jewelry with a name inscribed on the bezel."

So, it wasn't the police that rescued her? How in God's name had that woman escaped?

CHAPTER SIXTY-NINE

ANDI

A NDI TRAMPED THROUGH THE woods with the pendant girls at her side. Keep the water in sight, she told herself. Can't afford to get lost. Storm clouds slid aside, and for a brief second, a hazy sliver of moon appeared. Tendrils of fog rose from the ground like spirits. "Eli!" she called.

No answer.

"Please God, don't let him die." A sob escaped, and Andi told herself again: this is not a time to be weak. The two girls floated along beside her, as clear as photographs but with rain falling through, not on them. No prom gowns tonight, just the uniform of youth: jeans, hoodies, tennis shoes. Uniform of dead girls who wished they were alive.

You and Eli must be drifting in and out of death right now, Mariah said. *But he'll hang on as long as he believes you're still on this earth.*

Andi staggered through endless leaves, fallen pine boughs, a muddy deer track, and a tiny stream framed in green velvety moss. Her wet sneakers might as well be leg weights.

She wandered over to a live oak tree and rested her head against one gnarly branch. Here she was again, taking refuge in a tree. Once a ginkgo tree had hidden her, had kept her kidnapper from capturing her again. This time an angel oak tree, symbol of the South, might protect her. Hanging moss dangled on it like tinsel on a Christmas tree. When she came out from under it, she'd be wearing some of that gray tangle in her hair and whatever lived in the tree. Spiders, aphids, ticks, one happy little bug community. God, she was tired.

She called Eli's name, once, twice, and trudged off again. They probably hadn't gone far enough to find him.

Leaves rustled in the woods. She reeled around, searching the darkness. Wind carried a voice faintly. "An-deee," someone called, as if trying to awaken her. Or had she imagined it?

"Eli! I'm coming." Oh God. What if he had joined the others who whispered and called to her? What would it be like to hang on to the fragile thread that marked the end of life and the beginning of death? Maybe she already knew.

A scream ripped through the sky. Flapping wings signaled the culprit, a barn owl. Bennie sidled up. *This place creeps me out. Gimme the streets any day. Screaming birds, and there got to be snakes. Nothing human 'round here except you tramping 'round, loud enough to wake the dead.*

'Wake the dead.' That's funny, Bennie. God, her head was spinning. Synapses misfiring.

Bennie gave a short laugh. *Yeah, I'm a regular comedienne. Put me on TV.*

Andi tripped over a gnarled oak root. The little Shadow pointed ahead to another. Andi cleared it. *Thank you.*

A small army of Shadows now followed them. Silent but vigilant.

Those children can be very helpful, she told the girls.

Well, no offense, Bennie said, glancing sideways at the Shadows. *But children can be a real pain in the ass.*

Think little brothers or sisters, Bennie. Helpful sometimes, a nuisance other times, but you have to love them. Little Devika helped me escape from my kidnapper.

Then she heard it. Chanting *inside her head*, as soft and rhythmic as the beat of her heart. Native American chanting in a language she'd never heard before. Eli chanting. No, that meant—No! Maybe she *was* dead and Eli too. Fear rumbled through Andi like thunder. She let the chant drive her forward. Andi glided over rocks and roots and deadfall as if the woods had become her natural home.

"Andree-ah. Come out, Jezebel. I capture the big girls now," Fisherman called.

How does he know I got out of his trunk? Andi asked.

Probably saw Bailey's car, Bennie said.

"An-dree-ah." That mercury-smooth voice calling again. "Mariah ran away from me. Look what happened to her. You won't get far. God will help me find you."

The girls and the Shadows disappeared, but it didn't concern her, nor did she worry about facing a monster who made young girls into jewelry. Eli needed her.

Andi ducked behind a tree. Dammit. Her breathing was too loud. She tried to command Fisherman the way she did the girls. *Go away! Leave me alone.*

Suddenly, someone grabbed her hood, jerked her backward, and pulled her to the ground. "Don't be afraid, my dear. Nasty weather out here for a pretty young woman like you." Rain hat pulled low, FBI jacket keeping him dry, Fisherman looked down at her, smiling. "How'd you get loose? Well, it doesn't matter now, does it?" He pulled her upright.

Why didn't he just shoot her? Too quick, too easy. The man liked to play with his catch, to reel it in slowly, watch it squirm and suffocate. Besides, a shot might alert police.

"Help!" she screamed.

Footsteps padded through wet leaves. She scanned the dark trees and saw nothing, but the sounds came from behind them.

Gun pointed at something she couldn't see, Fisherman turned in a circle.

A voice inside her head told her to run. A Shadow's voice.

Rustling, twigs snapping. Fisherman reeled in that direction. He took several steps backward. Suddenly, a rock the size of a softball struck his shoulder. A second bounced off his hat. He howled, then crouched, arms wrapped around his head. Shadows hid behind trees, watching. More stones flew from all directions, striking him, the ground, the trees.

Protect yourself. Get out of the way. A Shadow's voice. Andi covered her head and rolled until she slammed into a hemlock. She peered through the dead bottom branches. Five girls pummeled Fisherman with rocks while he cowered like a dog. Was it now *five*? Rain fell through all the girls. Bennie, Mariah, and two other girls in prom dresses. The vendor had mentioned two other pendants, but the fifth? Please God, don't let it be Rachel. Andi smiled suddenly. The fifth ghost defending her was the invisible friend from her childhood.

She forced herself up. The ghost girls swirled and melted into each other until she couldn't identify faces. Fisherman absorbed the blows with low grunts like a dumb beast. He whirled in her direction and scurried sideways like a crab, toward her. The Shadows lobbed rocks, clumps of dirt, branches, pinecones, whatever they could find on the ground.

Move! A Shadow's voice. Someone pushed her from behind. *Don't look back!* Another shove propelled her forward until she stumbled into a ditch. Her head hit something hard, and white lights flashed behind her eyes. Pain, then blessed silence enveloped her. When she regained consciousness, a hand emerged, pulling dirt and leaves over her.

CHAPTER SEVENTY

ANDI

A NDI AWOKE TASTING DIRT, feeling the warmth of another body in that ditch. It curled around her as if they were nesting spoons. *The little Shadow?* No! A dirt-encrusted hand clasped hers.

"Eli?"

"Shhh." He pressed the cold metal shaft of a gun into her hand.

Footsteps shuffled through leaves at a slow, stealthy pace. Fisherman was still alive. Five angry ghosts and her Shadow friends hadn't deterred him. They'd only slowed him down.

"Eli?" she whispered, her voice tense with terror.

His hand squeezed her shoulder. "Shhh."

Scuffing feet nearby, the snap of a branch. Harsh breathing. Waiting to be discovered, she clutched the cold metal. If she was dead, could she still feel pain? Sweat and blood ran down her forehead, burning her eyes. But she could hold Eli, smell woodsmoke on his leather coat. Branches snapped. Bushes rustled. Fisherman made no attempt to hide his presence.

Eli squeezed her hand. "Be still."

A cautious step, a pause, then crashing through the woods away from them.

"God has a plan for you, Andrea," Fisherman called, racing in the direction of the noise. "You won't escape this time. And when I have you—oh my—you'll make such a beautiful pendant." Muffled by rain and wind, the words grew fainter. "The pain will be exquisite, Jezebel." Fisherman's voice, from farther away.

She clung to Eli, who had wrapped his arms protectively around her. Then Andi's flight instincts that had carried her to safety once before kicked in. She pushed herself up, but Eli grabbed her arm. "Not yet."

Slowly, Andi understood. The girls and the Shadows were keeping Fisherman occupied, creating a ruckus to lure him away. Head still spinning, blinking to focus, she listened. Nothing but wind in trees. "Let's get out of here, Eli. We'll find a boat launch and get you to a hospital."

He propped himself up on one elbow, then fell back. "Shit." He hissed.

"You can hear me?"

"Yes." His voice was hoarse. "Why wouldn't I?"

"Maybe we're both dead," she whispered.

He laughed grimly. "Then we've gone to hell."

Bending closer, squinting into the darkness, she examined his wound. Blood had soaked his pants leg, but Fisherman had missed the femoral artery. With all the mud and leaves, they both risked infection. She angled out of the ditch, using an elbow, then a knee, to hoist herself up. Andi touched the aching sticky spot in her scalp. Helluva lot of blood for a dead person. She had to be alive.

She hooked Eli under the shoulders and heaved. Stupid idea. A woman with a concussion couldn't move a large man. Clenching his teeth, Eli rolled sideways, trying to push himself up. Finally, he teetered at the edge of the ditch. "You fall back again, and we're both dead." She found a pine bough, stripped the branches, and handed it to him. "Lean on this and me."

"Dying in a ditch ain't my style, little missy." A very weak John Wayne imitation. "I plan to go out in a blaze of glory."

"Sunset's a hell of a long time away, cowboy."

He took one step, leaning against her. Then another and another. All eternity passed as they made their slow, painful way toward the shore. She searched up and down. "There!" she said. But it was so damn far away. "Rest. I'll drag the boat down here."

She wasn't moving very fast, and now she was in the open. It took what seemed like forever for her to reach the boat. No engine, just a plain aluminum fishing boat. Frantically, she searched around for oars. They were under it. Quiet. Quiet. Don't toss those oars into the boat. They'll make noise. Gently, she placed them inside the boat, grabbed the cement filled coffee can that anchored the boat and put it next to the oars. Adrenaline spurred her down the shore. The boat scraped over the muddy terrain, and she prayed the Shadows would keep Fisherman far away. Whispered curses, drags and drops, and stopping to clear her head—she managed to drag it to where Eli had been standing. Where was he? "Eli!" she whispered.

"I'm here." A noise under thick bushes. He hauled himself toward the boat, crawling like a paratrooper. She pulled the boat into the shallows, and after three tries, Eli managed to climb inside. Groaning, he lay at the bottom of the boat, face pale, contorted in pain. Andi fixed the oars into locks, climbed in, and pushed off.

Shadows helped Andi shove the boat into deeper water. They drifted onto the storm-choppy lake toward a boat launch and lights on the other side. Waves slapped the sides. Rain pocked the black surface. Summer camp was the last time she'd rowed. Every time she pulled, one oar flapped uselessly and splashed. Yet somehow, the boat moved in sideways zigs through the water.

CHAPTER SEVENTY-ONE

ANDI

"KEEP THOSE OARS QUIET," Eli whispered.

Mid-stroke, Andi turned to him. "You want to row? I think not. Are there alligators in this lake?"

Eli managed a soft chuckle. "No, but South Carolina has water moccasins. Let's not capsize. Besides, the lake is cold as hell."

"Hell's not cold, Eli." Her oar slapped the water, and the boat swung sideways. She aimed the bow toward a cove on the other side. Where were the lights she'd seen? The sprawling ranch-style home lit up? The boat launch? Damn this fog! She'd ended up somewhere else. Cattails over there, dense woods, and probably snakes, all poisonous. "Don't snakes hibernate?"

A sharp crack pierced the silence.

Her body jerked. Pain seared through one shoulder.

Andi pitched sideways and toppled over the gunwales and into a cold darkness that swallowed her. Murky water sealed over her head. She kicked sluggishly. Mouth full of water, Andi clawed back to the surface. Two more shots rang out as she spat water gritty with sediment, then ducked under again. Her legs, suddenly like iron, pulled her down. Her lungs were on fire.

Thirty-five lousy years old, and life was over, her grave the bottom of a South Carolina lake. Maybe that was Andi's punishment for deserting her family. She'd always wanted to be a mother. Now ghost girls and Shadows were the only children she'd ever have. Silently, she called to them, saying goodbye.

The ringing in her ears faded to a sweet, low voice. Floating freely, arms outstretched, she opened her eyes to the most complete blackness she'd ever known. It wrapped Andi in a cold, inky cloak, forced her heartbeat to slow down even more. Would death greet her kindly, gently?

A few feet away was a faint glow. Then a rainbow mass of light grew brighter in the murky depth. A woman who looked almost exactly like her coalesced, painted in Monet colors by an invisible artist. She clasped Andi's hands.

It's not time for you to join me, Andi.

Mom? You're here!

Of course I am. I'm always with you. Even if you don't want me.

But it's you who didn't want me. You chose a different life.

I didn't choose a different life over you. I am who I am, like all of us. And I am your mother with every fiber of my being.

You broke so many promises.

I broke only one. Two days before I was supposed to come home for your birthday, I found myself in a war-torn village. My crew had found corpses in the street, and I did my job, documenting the scene with photos. The dead talked to me, and I listened until snipers started firing at us. When my sound man was killed, the rest of us escaped on a prince's yacht. He owed me a favor. I'd rescued his reputation once. The State Department told me to hold back the story until the governments resolved the situation. They never did.

You didn't even tell your family?

Perhaps I should have. We all make mistakes.

What was the difference between missing a birthday and missing your mother's funeral? No clock or calendar dictated forgiveness. All those empty, stolen years flooded over Andi. She'd deprived her mother of an only child. How selfish she'd been.

Oh God, Mom. I'm sorry for doubting you. I should've known better. I miss you so much.

Andi, I'm proud of you. You've grown to be so strong. I almost lost you once, and here you are, fighting for your life again.

I don't want to fight anymore.

You must. Always.

The light shimmered and faded. *Happy birthday, Andi*, her mother said. *You're not ready for the Otherworld yet.*

The mass of light burst apart, then faded to darkness, leaving only the sound of drumming, steady and firm as the heartbeats of those who loved her.

Mom!

Finish what you started, Andi. You never were a quitter. We're alike that way, her mother whispered.

Andi twisted around, straining for another glimpse. *Mom! Don't leave!*

A gentle force propelled her upward.

I love you, Mom.

Andi surfaced, coughing up water. The boat drifted like an unlit funeral pyre. Arms and legs numb with cold, she flailed toward it. "Eli?" she whispered, coming up at the stern, staying low.

He leaned over the side and gripped her wrist. "Andi! I thought you'd drowned."

Treading water, she reached for the gunwale, gasping for air and coughing up water for a few seconds before she tried to speak. "Apparent . . . apparently I'm . . . I'm not allowed to d-die on my birthday."

"Jesus, Andi. Get in." He wobbled on one arm, lost his balance.

The boat rocked; she grasped the stern to steady it. "You think there are snakes in here?"

"No snakes, Andi. They go south for the winter, and the alligators are vegans. Will you get into the damn boat!"

She smiled, gazing up at him. "Eli, are we dead?"

He shrugged. "We will be soon unless you get in! Hurry!"

Three kicks, and she dragged herself over the gunwale. Eli wrapped an arm around her, and they lay huddled as the boat rocked. He checked the wound in her shoulder, then pulled her closer and kissed her. "You'll be okay," he said, but he didn't sound convinced.

"If I live through tonight, I might fall in love with you," she told him.

"Little missy, I could ride off into the sunset with you too."

Cold lips brushed hers, and she kissed him. They lay silent until Andi whispered, "My mom was under the water." He held her closer, and she laid her head against his chest, comforted by his heartbeat. When the keel scraped bottom, Andi raised her head to scan the shore.

"No," Eli whispered. "Let it drift."

"But he's still out there!"

Eli nodded. "Let him pull us in. Then shoot him."

CHAPTER SEVENTY-TWO

ANDI

ANDI PATTED HER POCKET for the gun. "It's gone," she whispered. They'd lodged in a stand of cattails. Brown tubes on pale slender stalks that reminded her of bones. Tangled swamp grass, green algae blanketing the water, a rancid smell. Their boat washed ashore sideways, bumped forward, then back, buffeted by waves. Not a house in sight. No lights, no sounds of traffic. But she'd seen lights. Where were they now? Patchy fog enveloped them.

"Use the gun on my leg. Unless he's reloaded, Fisherman only has three bullets left," Eli told her.

She detached the Glock 43 from his ankle. "But it's wet."

"It will work."

A light bobbed down a narrow path. "Hey there!" a man called. LPD jacket, red curly hair, green eyes, bushy eyebrows. "Hollister will be so glad to see you. Here, lemme help." He sloshed through the shallows. Hat pulled low, responder on his shoulder squawking, he looked like a cop, but she knew damn well he wasn't. She'd recognize that voice anywhere. Andi suspected he'd taken the LPD gear from Officer Kenny Parker, which meant he'd injured another police officer.

Yellow cat eyes watched from the shore.

Shadows, distract him for a minute.

Mud clods plopped into the water like big brown raindrops. Fisherman stared at them.

Andi slipped over the far side, into the cold, dark water, putting the boat between them. Waves slapped at the boat. A ripple of movement through the cattails. Maybe just the wind.

Fisherman fired once into the boat then turned the gun toward her.

"Eli!" she cried out. Hand shaking, heart pounding, Andi fired until the gun was empty, missing each time, as if the devil himself had redirected her shots.

Smug smile, Fisherman said, "You shoot like a girl." But when he fired, his hand jerked upward, once, twice. Bennie! The girl stood beside Fisherman, fierce determination in her eyes. Cattails bent and rippled. He whirled and the rustling stopped.

"Unless he reloaded" echoed in her brain. Bastard could still use the gun as a club. He slogged through the muddy water toward her.

Bennie stood, arms extending in front of her, holding a thick branch. She brought both arms down. His wrist cracked, and the gun plummeted into the water. He reached for it, one hand desperately fishing through the muddy shallows, the other one dangling uselessly.

Use your wits. You can do this! the little Shadow told her.

Andi yanked an oar from the lock, reached to the end of it with her left hand and swung. Dammit! She'd just clipped the top of his head, but he toppled sideways into the water. His hat fell off, and one bushy eyebrow was cockeyed. He rolled faceup, hair tossed by the waves. Suddenly, he spat water, propped himself on an elbow and glared at her. "Big girls deserve longer torture. You'll die ever so slowly," he said, rising from the water like a snake, like Satan himself.

Shit! She'd sliced her hand on the rusty oar pin. Blood dripped down her wrist.

The bastard rushed toward her.

Finish him! Bennie shouted. *You cain't go to hell for killing a devil.* Perched on the sides of the boat, the girls watched. *Justice for mortals must come from mortals*, Bennie said.

An army of Shadows marched along the shore.

You can do this. Trust your instincts, a Shadow child told her.

Andi bared her teeth and swung. The crack of wood against bone echoed across the lake. Fisherman's legs folded. He fell back into the lake with a loud splash. Still gripping the oar, she fought her way through mud that sucked at her shoes, through cattails, the slippery bank, a tangle of marsh grass. The bastard sat up! She'd smash his throat, stop his damned breathing.

Somewhere down the shore, a shot cracked, then another. Too far away. Dammit! By the time anyone reached her, she'd be dead. Cattails flattened under a gust of wind, rippling, bending, bowing, whispering as if possessed. Something was in that water with her, something stealthier than a human. Something that might be worse than Fisherman.

Look out! Bennie cried, and the girls vanished.

Ignoring searing pain in her hand, she jabbed the oar into his throat.

He clutched his neck, thrashed like a wounded animal, gasping. "Help me, Lord!"

She brought the tip of the oar down on his throat again. He coughed, sputtered, gasped.

Andi swung, this time aiming for his head. "Die, dammit!" she yelled, bashing at his skull again and again until he didn't move. Cattails waved their pale stems, bowed, undulated.

Keening from the reeds! She moaned, covered her ears, held her breath against fumes that reeked of rotting flesh. Like inside-out ghosts, they came, the Punishers. Black where they should be white. White where they should be black. Rattling the cattails like dry bones, racing like wisps of fog over the ripples Fisherman had left. Three, then more. Electric crackles, blurs of gape-mouthed howling spirits. Women, she marveled. Their long-matted hair swung wildly as they darted around Fisherman's body. Hot sulfur spewed from their mouths. They swarmed over him like vultures on a fresh kill. With one savage leap, the first one landed on his chest. She shook him, probably making sure he was dead, and gave a brief nod to Andi, perhaps to confirm Andi had brought him to justice. Then their work began. Andi heard the sickly snap of his neck. Another growled as she brutally tore off an arm. Bones crunched. The water churned into a pink froth. Gagging, clutching her bleeding wrist, Andi crouched in the shallows, afraid they'd take her along with Fisherman.

A freight-train wind roared past her as his body was dragged to the middle of the lake by unearthly hands. After The Punishers took what they wanted of him, Fisherman's body spun down, down into a funnel. The arms that had once carved girls' bones were first to disappear into that angry lake. Then the funnel spun faster until it had swallowed all of him.

A streak of lightning, and the droning faded. The stench drifted away. Water around the vortex rippled in concentric circles that grew larger, flattened, and disappeared. A breeze carried only the rustle of lake grass and the slap of waves against the boat. Andi climbed back into the boat. Rocked by the waves, it washed in and out. She bent over Eli, pressed an ear to his chest. Yes, soft, irregular beats. She kissed his cold lips. "Hang on, Eli. I need you."

He lifted a hand as if to touch her face, but it fell back. "You killed him?" he whispered.

She nodded. It was over.

CHAPTER SEVENTY-THREE

MARIAH

ENNIE AND I WATCHED fog swirl around those police officers
and the boat like it wanted to consume them and make the
whole nasty scene disappear.

"Look! Fiona must've run track. She's hauling ass toward Andi,"
Bennie said.

"Get that woman out of here!" Hollister shouted, pointing at
Fiona.

"I'll go." One young cop peeled off and chased her. Their feet
struck the shoreline in sharp splashes like whips cracking. The officer closed in on her with Hollister catching up.

"This is a crime scene. You can't be here. Where the hell have
you been? Don't make me arrest you," Hollister yelled.

"Heard the food's good in jail." Fiona vaulted over a branch on
the shore. "My best friend almost got sucked up by a damned waterspout. I'm not leaving." She raced into the water, but the young cop
grabbed her. Too late.

She saw inside the boat.

They lay silent, nestled together, Andi's hand bleeding in rivulets down Eli's jacket.

"No! Oh shit. Goddammit! Andi! Eli!" Fiona struggled to break free.

"Don't touch anything!" Hollister growled. He felt for Andi's pulse, then Eli's. "Go on back," he told a deputy. "Take Miss Fiona home."

"No!" Fiona cursed that guy up one side and down the other and she didn't move.

"Get 'em out! Christ, they lost a lot of blood. Somebody else try to get a pulse. Damned if I can find one," Hollister said.

Three cops raced toward Hollister. They did a fireman's carry, gently setting Andi and Eli on the muddy shore. Then they checked vital signs.

"Got a real faint heartbeat," one cop called.

"Me too, on Lake."

"Avery, you secure this area." Hollister laid his coat over Andi and heaved a sigh. Cops teamed up, keeping them dry, stopping bleeding, and checking their breathing and pulse.

Hollister whipped out his phone and punched in numbers. "Damn thing is dead again. Anybody got a phone that works?"

One by one, they took out their cell phones and tried that thing clipped to their uniforms. Dead. A couple cops had chargers. They were dead too. We'd drained them all, and now that Andi needed help, cops couldn't use them.

Then I remembered. Fiona wasn't there when we'd drained the batteries. *Fiona! Give Hollister your phone!* I screamed, wishing she could hear me the way Andi does.

"Miss Fiona, is your phone working?" the sheriff asked. He told the deputy to release her hands.

A great horned owl called and another owl answered. A sad sound, and I thought about how much those women depended upon each other. Fiona just stood there staring at Andi and Eli. She looked so lost.

"Your phone, Miss Fiona, is it working?" the sheriff repeated.

Mechanically, she reached into her pocket. "After what I paid for this phone today," she muttered, "it damn-well better work." Sure enough, it lit up. Fiona unlocked the screen, and handed it to Hollister. I never thought I'd see Fiona cry, but seeing her best friend and Eli unconscious and bleeding must've sent her over the edge. She was sobbing like a baby.

"Go on over there." The sheriff motioned with his head. "Talk to Miss Andi. Tell her help's gonna be here real soon."

Hollister began barking out orders on Fiona's phone. Ambulance, CID Commander Wilson. He needed lights, boats, a dry shelter, forensics people, a generator.

Poor Andi and Eli were lying so still on the shore, their blood pooling in small puddles with a cop standing by holding an AED just in case—no, I didn't want to think about that.

Fiona stooped next to Andi. "Please don't go. Don't make me feel guilty for the rest of my life that I showed up too late." She took Andi's hand, the one with the dove tattoo, and held it to her heart. "Feel this? It's my heart breaking into a million pieces. I should've been there for you."

A nightbird sang a mournful song. I wanted to cry too.

Fiona plopped down on the shore next to Andi, oblivious to the mud and sheeting rain. "I'm not gonna leave you this time, Andi. I promise." Between the sobs, I heard her say, "Never should've gone to that studio. Oh God, why'd I do that?"

Hollister was still making calls. He keyed in a number, described the scene, and said something about CID.

"Where the hell were the cops when Andi needed them?" I asked.

"Two coves away, seeing waterspouts." Bennie sneered.

"Waterspouts, my ass. Those Punishers were more like the National Organization of Dead Women," I said. "Wish we could've stopped Fisherman before he got to Andi."

"I tried." Bennie looked sad.

Water slapped the sand and weeds in angry waves. Cattails shifted and rippled as if armies of the dead were walking among them. Branches like skeletal arms with broken fingers floated in and out. I hoped to God I wasn't seeing parts of Fisherman washing up.

An inflatable boat with an outboard motor geared down and drifted in. Two cops with lime-green jackets and mammoth flashlights got out. "Found a hand floating out there, middle of the lake. Waterspout must've ripped him apart. It'll take divers days to find what's left."

"Never seen anything like it." Hollister took a cigarette from his pocket, stuck it into his mouth, and felt his pockets for matches. One of the boatmen lit it. "Thanks." He inhaled deeply, punched numbers on Fiona's phone, and reported the hand to CID. "Commander Wilson's gonna want a statement. Then show him where you found it."

Search boats glided up and down the lake, lights flickering. Waste of their time. Despite all his Bible quoting, Fisherman's destination was twenty thousand leagues beneath the pearly gates.

Five minutes later, a siren wound down, and lights flashing, two ambulances bounced down the rutted utility road. They didn't get far because of the mud. EMTs slogged down the bank with backboards. They strapped Andi and Eli to them and rushed toward the ambulances, where IVs and all kinds of electronic stuff were hooked up. I rained a few ginkgo leaves on Andi as she lay in the ambulance with Fiona at her side. An EMT brushed them onto the floor. Andi's body was pulsing like the minute hand on a watch, and she had a faint rainbow outline. She was in trouble. The Shadows knew that too. They were going nuts, flying into each other and the walls of the ambulance.

Ma'am, I know this ain't a good time, Bennie said, *but I gotta redeem myself or stay lost forever. Mariah says I shouldn't do this, but I'm gonna do it anyways. I need for you to help my mama.* Voice husky with emotion, Bennie revealed where to find her bones. *My mama, she needs to quit hoping and praying I'll come home. She needs to know the truth.*

We'd talked about it months ago. Funny to talk about death and being buried when you're already dead and you've already been buried. But Bennie and I wanted a funeral and real graves, maybe even graves beside each other. We were looking forward to seeing who would show up at our funerals besides relatives. It wasn't exactly prom, but for us, still a major social event.

I touched Andi's shoulder. *Ma'am, you can't go yet. I couldn't spend an eternity knowing it was my fault you died.*

Then Bennie turned to me. "She's got a faint glow, little bit of a flicker, but I don't think she's dead. Let's stay with her and make sure she don't give up."

CHAPTER SEVENTY-FOUR

ANDI

HEAD FILLED WITH VOICES, Andi lay in a hospital room, listening to her own heartbeat.

"What you've survived goes beyond what most people suffer in a lifetime," Fiona told her. "Me? Two days down the toilet. Guitar player never showed up at the recording studio. We had to find a replacement. Once we started recording, my phone was off. Forgot to turn it back on when I left to pick up your birthday cake. Then, idiot that I am, I dropped my phone when I was putting the cake in the car and didn't notice until I ran over it. Had to find a store where I could get a new one."

Amazing Grace, how sweet the sound, that saved a wretch like me. I once was lost but now am found, was blind, but now, I see . . . Bennie's rich alto singing rose.

The machine next to Andi's bed beeped.

A cart or a gurney clattered by.

An elevator dinged. Soft footsteps sounded in the hallway outside.

"You killed that son of a bitch. Now come on back to us." Fiona's voice cracked. "I don't want to lose my favorite drinking partner."

Through many dangers, toils, and snares, we have already come . . .

"Come on, Andi!" Fiona's voice grew louder as it always did when she made her best pitch. "You made it through five hours of surgery. We need to celebrate. Bailey called and said we could have his Moët and Chandon."

That annoying beeping. Why didn't someone turn the damn thing off? And the air reeked of broccoli cooked for too long. A warm hand clasped hers, pressing against the sticky strips glued to her skin. Cold tubing snaked up one arm.

"I need you too," Eli whispered.

'Twas Grace that brought us safe thus far, and Grace will lead us home . . .

Something tightened around her arm, squeezing hard, releasing. Her body floated through whiteness. It would be so peaceful if Fiona stopped crying.

". . . lost too much blood. God, Eli, she could end up brain damaged . . . and she's been out so long."

A deep sigh from him.

She'll make it, Eli, Mariah whispered, but Andi wasn't sure he could hear the girls anymore. The space between life and death had opened when he'd lain in that ditch dying, just long enough for him to get a view of the Otherworld.

"Happy birthday, Andi. Come back to us." Eli began to chant softly. Words as rhythmic as his heartbeat when she'd been huddled against him.

Synapses misfiring like errant tennis balls, she hovered above them, suspended in real time, trying to get back. The whiteness faded to gray, then bloomed to full color. She opened her eyes. Eli sat in a wheelchair and Fiona on her bed. Bennie's singing and Eli's soft chanting wove in and out of synchrony. When one of the Shadows draped an arm around Fiona, gave her a kiss, and did victory laps throughout the room, Andi laughed.

"Will you stop singing? I'm not dead." The voices stopped. Fighting the sedation, she closed her eyes and opened them again. Might as well be a funeral wake, based on their expressions.

You don't like the song, Bennie chimed in. *I can sing "Ave Maria" if you want.*

Andi smiled.

You sing beautifully, Bennie.

"God Almighty, Andi. You made me pray! First time in twenty goddamn years. Thought for sure you weren't coming back."

"How do you feel?" Eli winced as he shifted in his wheelchair, reached for her hand, and kissed it.

"Really tired." Andi tried to rub her eyes with her other hand, but it was in a splint.

The door swung open. A man in green scrubs holding a metal chart came bedside. He looked familiar, but she couldn't place him. "Looks good," he said as he examined her fingers.

It's my daddy. Mariah was sitting on the end of the bed with Bennie. *Hollister asked him to do your surgery. Daddy's the best hand surgeon in the country.*

Andi stared down at the bulky bandage encasing her hand.

Culverton had that veiled professional look. "You'll need to keep your hand elevated and still. On a scale of one to ten, how's the pain?"

"Still pretty numb. Maybe four," she said.

"Good." The doctor nodded and turned to leave but hesitated. He ran his tongue over his teeth and pursed his lips as if wrestling with some emotion. Staring at the foot of her bed, he said, "If you . . . if you . . . see my daughter, tell her I love her. Tell her I'm sorry I couldn't protect her."

Andi swallowed hard. "I will."

Mariah wrapped her arms around her father's waist. *I made a stupid decision, Daddy. I'm sorry. Tell him that. Please, ma'am. He can't feel this. Can he?*

Andi repeated Mariah's words.

Lips pursed, he lowered his head. "Tell Mariah we'll always love her. No matter what." He walked out and the door swung shut behind him. The girl's sobbing filled Andi's head. Bennie put an arm around her. Together, they vanished, leaving behind a single ginkgo leaf. Two other sets of eyes held hers. She supposed by now Eli and Fiona could tell when she was seeing things nobody else could.

Andi glanced from Fiona to Eli. Dark circles, face scratched, fading black eye, Eli looked exhausted. Fiona's fair skin had a blue cast, especially under the eyes. Blond hair hung in tangled clumps. No makeup, a stained sweatshirt. "You guys look like a hot mess," she told them. "Especially you, Eli."

"Speak for yourself, pal," Fiona teased.

Eli laughed, picked a gingko leaf from her sheet, and gave it to her.

"Bennie and Mariah saved our lives, Eli."

He nodded. "So how do you repay a spirit?"

"I don't know. I'll ask my mom. She came to me when I almost drowned."

Grateful she and Eli had survived Fisherman, she was almost afraid to ask. "What about Rachel?"

"They found her." Eli flashed her a smile. "DHEC, of all people, found her. Realtor trying to sell an adjacent property sent DHEC to inspect Fisherman's property. Complained about snakes and rats and an unkempt yard. The DHEC people heard Rachel screaming and called the police. She'll need plastic surgery for the marks he cut into her and some psychiatric help, but she's alive. According to Rachel, Fisherman planned to bury what he didn't use of her under a berm on the golf course that backed up to her house in Charlotte."

"And the missing police officer, Parker," Fiona added. "He was in the trunk of the police car Fisherman was driving, minus his jacket and responder. Agent Lowell is okay too."

The IV bag dripping steadily felt like a nagging reminder of an unsolved problem. "What about Melvin?" Andi asked.

"Confessed to being Fisherman's accomplice. According to Melvin, he had some kind of vision where Jesus told him to come clean, went totally nuts one night and threw toilet paper all over his cell." Eli raised his hands palms up. "And you? You're off the hook. Your prints weren't found on the Glock at your house. ERT used superglue fuming, on the bullets. Forensic people can detect latent fingerprints on smooth surfaces by creating superglue fumes in a special machine that coats the nonporous surface. Fiona's fingerprints were on those bullets. Same serial number as the gun Irv gave her. Police believe Fisherman stole Fiona's gun when he broke in. Handwriting specialist is working on the note he left."

"Why bother checking the handwriting?" Andi asked.

"Tying up loose ends," Eli explained.

Andi glanced over at him. He wasn't wearing his patented veiled look, and she wondered why. "Mariah's mother?"

CHAPTER SEVENTY-FIVE

ANDI

A T GOOD SHEPHERD CHURCH, Eli sat on Andi's left, looking handsome in a black suit, white shirt, Navajo-patterned tie, and cowboy boots. Fiona was on her right, wearing the only dress Andi had ever seen her in, a slinky black thing she referred to as her mortician's dress. Worried about being struck by lightning, Fiona wore rubber-soled Doc Martens.

The Episcopal church had pews of dark wood varnished so many times they were slippery. Sunlight streamed through the stained-glass windows, casting splotchy watercolor patterns across the mourners. Candle wax and floor polish mixed with the smells of perfume, leather, and cigarette smoke.

Andi wondered if the girls would attend their own funeral.

On silent wheels, two matching silver coffins glided up the aisle toward the altar. Their bodies had seen life, death, and the world between. The pallbearers, a mixture of young faces Mariah's age and older men, probably relatives, wore somber expressions. Andi knew what lay inside. Two pitiful piles of bones. A blanket of carnations and sweetheart roses cascaded over each lid. She wondered how Bennie felt about all those flowers. Nothing about the girl said rosebuds and velvet, but death may have made her miss girlish things.

Andi looked down at the stitches in her hand. They ached from time to time, a permanent reminder along with the tattoo on her other hand. She'd been released from the hospital five days earlier. A day after her release, a K-9 unit found Bennie's bones in the crawlspace of an abandoned house not far from their Holiday Inn. The text message from Hollister was short: *Found bones near "Holiday Inn," hand missing.*

Later cadaver dogs found the remains of more missing girls at a construction site nearby. The project had been financially struggling toward completion for several years. Fisherman must have buried them there and figured the bulldozers and landscapers would take care of the rest.

Bennie's mother had visited Faith Culverton in the treatment center. Latoya Johnston was a strong, convincing woman, like her daughter. From what Andi heard, they'd bonded instantly. Faith wanted the girls to be buried together. The mothers planned the memorial and asked for an empty seat on each side of the pulpit. Both families had collected items to place on the chairs. Drumsticks, a band hat, music sheets, Mariah's worn black journal. On Bennie's, a pink baby hat, booties, and prize ribbons from singing contests. The tattered sneakers her mother had added seemed out of place yet appropriate. Bennie had seen a lot more of life and death than most girls her age.

When the tape of ten-year-old Bennie singing "Amazing Grace" began, Andi took a deep, shaky breath and swallowed back tears. Eli placed a hand over hers. She listened to the platitudes spoken by the minister and mentally struck each down.

The girls were not angels, not gifts on loan from God. Their Creator did not have a good reason for taking them too soon. It was not God's will but the twisted choice of a killer. Now, they were two young women caught between worlds, doing their best to find a way home.

The ceremony droned on for an hour as relatives spoke of happy memories from each girl's childhood. But an odd thing happened after the first fifteen minutes. Items began to tumble off the symbolic chairs. First the hats, then the drumsticks, then the music and journal and ribbons.

Thinking they'd knocked them off when they came up, the relatives tried to replace the fallen items. Seconds later, something else would drop.

When Bennie's sneakers toppled end over end down the red carpeted steps, Eli cast a knowing glance at Andi.

A sad smile tugged at his lips. "Somebody's having fun," he whispered.

Chairs finally empty, the girls sat in them.

"Can you see them?" she asked Eli.

He shook his head.

Somewhere they'd found black dresses and hats. Bennie's hat sported one outrageous peacock feather and black netting to her nose. Mariah's hat looked royal, very Kate Middleton. She grinned at Andi. Bennie gave her a thumbs-up. They sat, hands folded on their laps until the congregation sang the final hymn.

Eli, Andi, and Fiona followed the long procession of cars to the cemetery. Their burial rite was short. The girls' mothers embraced, then made their way back to a waiting limo. Grief had a way of making strangers into friends. She wondered how they'd ever lead a normal life again. Tom Culverton lingered over the dark brown hole his daughter had been lowered into. Surely, such a chasm in the heart would never close. "I love you," he whispered to Mariah. "I never told you enough. We were so proud of you." He turned away from the open grave and walked toward Andi, head down.

"Thank you," he said, glancing at Eli. "Both of you. For finding our daughter. Young people are supposed to make mistakes. They shouldn't have to die because of them."

Andi nodded.

Halfway to the car, Tom turned back. "Tell my daughter not to be a stranger," he called.

In streams of rainbow colors, the girl materialized and gave her father a fierce hug. He stood absolutely still for several seconds. Andi hoped that meant Mariah had found a way to let him know how much she loved him.

Wiping tears from his eyes, the doctor turned and trudged toward the limo. There, his wife stood by the open door. He took her hands in his, kissed her, then whispered something in her ear. She looked up at him, confused. Then she smiled, turned to Andi, and nodded.

Andi remained until the last car drove off. She held up a hand to stop the gravediggers' shovels and hurried toward her car. White florist's box in her hand, Andi returned. She opened the box, peeled aside the thin green tissue paper, and removed two wrist corsages. Tied among the roses and baby's breath were the empty bezels, the beads, and two small satin packages containing what was left of the girls' bone pendants.

She tossed the first onto Mariah's grave. "For the senior prom you never had a chance to attend." The bezel hit the lid of the casket with a muffled clink, slid a few inches and stopped.

Andi bent over Bennie's grave and dropped the second corsage. "This is for all the beautiful music you would have made." The corsage landed squarely on top of the casket.

Eli smudged their graves with an abalone shell and sage to purify their journey. Smoke from the sage bundle rose, gathered under the canvas awning, and drifted down upon the dead and the living.

Lifting a handful of ginkgo leaves from the box, Andi let them flutter over the caskets. "Like butterflies," she said. "Too sweet to be captured, their season finished too soon."

She touched the locket around her neck. "Safe journey, girls," she whispered.

A gentle breeze sent two gingko leaves into the air, and they floated and fluttered until they came to rest in Andi's hair. "It's good luck to catch a ginkgo leaf," she told Eli.

He took her hand. "Looks more like they caught you."

ACKNOWLEDGMENTS

I OWE DRINKS TO MANY.

Special mentions first. To Dr. Bonnie Culver who accepted me into the motley crew that became my Wilkes University MFA cohort, thank you. Dr. Nancy McKinley (who read a four-hundred-page manuscript three times) and Lenore Hart (who read multiple versions too) brought this piece to life and the world beyond. My favorite chapter, the first Mariah chapter, was an MFA assignment about incorporating music. And thanks, Nancy, for suggesting I could come up with a better ending than Elvis the alligator. Dr. J. Michael Lennon, you thought the man with the messy yard I wrote about was fiction. Someone very much like him lived next door to me. He became my villain, thanks to that assignment. I leaned heavily on my cohort partners Maureen O'neill Hooker, Sharon Erby, and Andrea Janov for moral support as well as providing a ride to classes when the Pocono roads were icy.

Peter Senftleben, you were the chariot driver my tarot reader alluded to. I credit you with taking me to the finish line. You understood what I was trying to do, and with your patient and skilled direction, the manuscript was sculpted into a better piece. The tarot reader said a male would be my chariot driver. It might've been a joint effort between you and Clay Stafford of Killer Nashville.

David Wilson, you remember only my voice, due to your toxic-metal hip replacement, but we spent hours in *your* car (because I couldn't find my way out of a paper bag) on the way to writing conferences, talking about writing until we were hoarse. We were in critique groups together for years. You have a very special place in my writing heart, so I borrowed your name.

Delaware Valley Sisters in Crime provided a steady flow of information on police procedure and forensics as well as the craft of writing a mystery. All those Saturday mornings, and I came away with good writing friends: K. B. Inglee, Jane Shaw, Gretchen Hall, Kathleen Barrett, Judy Clemens, Diane Kiddy, Nina De Angeli, and Janis Wilson. An early reader, Kathleen Barrett appreciated my goofy sense of humor. Thanks for the feedback. Nancy Daversa, a history buff, connected me with a medium (name withheld at her request) who was conducting spirit releases in her B and B. Oh, the stories she told. Nancy helped when I was trying to figure out how to keep the ghost girls talking after their pendants went to the crime lab. The medium provided the structural supports for my spirit world building.

Pennwriters gave me writing partners and more. I owe everything that's behind the bar to these people. All I know about writing came from attending their conferences and workshops. I crown Paula Matter the Queen of Untangling Plot Snags; she's a genius and a very good friend, always there when I needed her. Brilliant and talented writers Connie Scharon and Vickie Fisher read more than one version, edited, and gave me feedback. When I said, "What do you mean that doesn't work?" they always had an answer. At times they brainstormed with me. Jack Hillman, a playwright at heart, helped with blocking the boat scene at the end. Hats off to Annette Dashofy for offering advice on the business side of things and Susan Meier for her help with pitches, writing synopses, and all things writing related.

Irmo Chief Brian Buck was my consultant for police procedure in South Carolina. I apologize for anything I got wrong, and by the way, I made up places in South Carolina and Pennsylvania that don't exist. I also talked to an anthropologist at Penn Museum and to Kathy Reichs about getting evidence from the carved bone in the pendant. If I got anything wrong, it's my fault and not theirs.

Vicki Croul, my jewelry-loving friend, you were the first to see my moon-face pendant, and when I said, "What if . . ." you said, "Eeew." Later you read it and liked it, which was high praise from someone who taught the classics for decades. I knew there was some magic in this book when I was invisible in that Philly restaurant. Jen Brookover and Delee Laird, you dusted me off and sent me forward whenever I needed it. Amy Santagata, Eve Cornell, and Delilah Jones, you believed in me and gave me good advice about finding a developmental editor. Joy McClure, thanks for your encouragement and support over the years. Patty Wain Smith, my late-night writing buddy and dear friend, thanks for always answering the phone when I was stuck or flummoxed. Dana Ridenour, retired FBI agent, thanks for steering me correctly when it came to the FBI. If I got anything wrong, it's my fault, not yours. Cindy Diffendall, I really wanted to use your name for Lance's mistress, but I couldn't bring myself to portray a character with your name as a bimbo.

Maryann Appel, thanks for your cover and book design. How lucky I am to have choices. The cover is amazing. A special shout out to the invisible saint of line editing, Ellen Leach, my copy editor who taught me a few things along the way. You and Helga should be canonized.

Sue Arroyo, thanks for taking my pitch without an appointment. I was on my way out the door to the Nashville airport after Killer Nashville. Two writing friends—one Northern, one Southern—were in my head telling me if I didn't pitch, they'd kill me. I may be alive today because you listened to my pitch. And thanks for the writing environment you've created at CamCat. I am proud to be one of your authors.

Yes, I've saved the best for last. My CamCat editor, Helga Schier: I gave you a gem in the rough, and you polished it and gave it facets. You plugged every hole and made me reach higher. You were by my side, armed with ideas, phrasing, and plot twists I hadn't thought to use. When I came up with crazy ideas, like cutting out four chapters, you were the voice of reason. Somehow, you are able to enter the voice of the writer and make suggestions based on that. For all the time you spent with Andi, my ghost girls, and Fisherman, thank you. Together, I think we've created a book with laughter and tears and compassion and wisdom.

If I've left anyone out, that means double drinks the next time I see you.

ABOUT THE AUTHOR

BORN IN ALEXANDRIA, VIRGINIA, Terry S. Friedman is a writer and a rockhound. During summers, when she wasn't cracking rocks in the driveway, she was eating strawberries, peaches, plums, and blackberries from the backyard and swearing the birds ate them. On a weekly basis, Terry cycled to the local library and filled her basket with mystery books that kept her reading long past bedtime. Because Terry was plagued by nightmares as a child, her mother suggested she give the dreams happy endings. But some nights it took until morning to do that. One of those nightmares became her first foray into writing a novel.

Terry began her writing career freelancing for a small newspaper outside Philadelphia. Later, she taught English in West Chester, Pennsylvania. She earned an MFA and two thumb surgeries from Wilkes University and also graduated from the FBI Citizens Academy in South Carolina. Twenty-four of her fiction and nonfiction pieces have been published, and she coedited Delaware Valley Mystery Writers' short stories anthology *Death Knell V*. She is a

Pennwriters Board member and a longtime member of Sisters in Crime.

Recently, her debut novel, *Bone Pendant Girls*, was a finalist for Killer Nashville's Claymore Award in the supernatural category. It finished second in the Southeastern Writers Association contest for Best First Novel. Her humor piece finished first in the Southeastern Writers's contest humor category. In addition to writing, Terry creates jewelry from opaque gemstones and shells. Her jewelry site has collections named for characters in her books. Currently, Terry writes suspense and paranormal thrillers from coastal South Carolina. She has traveled the world from Fiji to Delphi and brings to her writing a solid respect for diversity as well as for things that go bump in the night.

If you've enjoyed
Terry S. Friedman's *Bone Pendant Girls*,
consider leaving a review
to help our authors.

And check out
Kate Michaelson's *Hidden Rooms.*

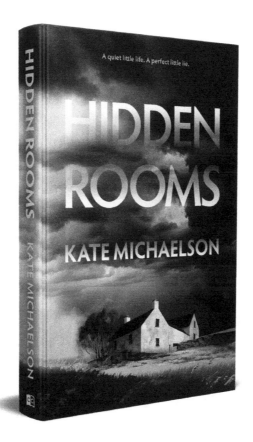

CHAPTER ONE

Late September 2022

I GREW UP INSIDE A lightning bolt, in a family of pure momentum. My siblings and I were young, stupid, and fearless in our white gingerbread house, surrounded by dark earth, green shoots, and wild woods—untamed beasts running loose from morning to night. We snarled and bucked, more a pack than a family.

Born less than a year apart, my brother Ethan and I spent most of our lives scrapping after the same few things, pinching each other where we knew it would hurt the most. But we also protected each other. When Trevor Paltree shoved Ethan off the tall metal slide the first day of preschool, I kicked Trevor's little ass, and I'd do it again.

Only, now, I didn't know what protecting my brother looked like, though I felt fairly certain that kicking his fiancée's ass was not it. Besides, I couldn't even say what exactly Beth was up to, which (admittedly) undermined my argument. Putting my head down and going along with the wedding might feel cowardly, but it also seemed like the least destructive path forward.

So, that's how I found myself pulling up to Ethan and Beth's house to pick up my puce monstrosity of a bridesmaid's dress with Beth's recent words still replaying in my mind. "Riley, you know I'd never do anything to hurt Ethan." The problem was that she also once said with a wink and a smile that what Ethan didn't know *couldn't* hurt him.

I parked in the shade of a low-limbed oak and got out, lifting my hair off my neck to catch the breeze. The autumn sun had built throughout the afternoon into the kind of fleetingly gorgeous day that makes up for Ohio's multitude of weather sins: one last warm postscript to summer. Rain loomed in the low shelf of clouds to the north. I crossed my fingers that it would hold off until I could get home to walk Bruno. Maybe I could even get a run in if my energy held out.

My phone buzzed, and I knew without looking it would be Audra. She called most days and knew that just the previous night, I'd finally worked up the nerve to have a conversation with Ethan about Beth. She would want the details. I was amazed she had waited this long.

"How'd it go with Ethan?" Her melodious voice skipped along briskly. People usually went with what she said simply because they were so swept with how she said it. As her sister, I was an exception.

"Hello to you too." I continued toward the house but slowed my pace. "I'll give you one guess how it went."

"Hello, *dearest* Riley. I guess he got mad."

"Not just mad. He guilt-tripped me. I asked him if he'd noticed anything wrong with Beth and he acted all injured about it. He told me, 'she thinks you're her friend.'" I mimicked Ethan's self-righteous tone. The jab still stung. "I told him I think of her as a friend too, which is how I know she's hiding something." Admittedly, I couldn't untangle what it was. It was something I sensed more than saw—a shift in posture or flicker behind an expression. The past few weeks she'd become more self-contained than ever, which was saying something for her.

"Yeah, but can you really be friends with someone who has no personality? It's like being friends with a mannequin. I don't know how you can tell if she's hiding something when she never shares anything—"

"Look, I can't talk about it now." I lowered my voice as I neared the house. "I'm at their place getting my dress. I'll call you later."

As I climbed the porch steps, the front of their house looked so Instagram-perfect that I wondered whether I'd been seeing problems that weren't there. The afternoon light slanted across pumpkins and yellow chrysanthemums that Beth had arranged just so. Dried bundles of corn rattled in the breeze. Beneath the pale-blue porch swing, Beth had set out a matching ceramic bowl full of kibble for Bibbs, the half-feral cat that had adopted her and Ethan.

The only thing amiss was the open door of the old-fashioned cast iron mailbox nestled amidst the pumpkins and flowers. Beth would kill the mail carrier for ruining the ambiance. I grabbed the few pieces of mail in the box and shut the little door obligingly, like a good future sister-in-law.

Careful not to disturb a precarious wreath of orange berries, I knocked on the screen door and tapped my foot, ready to grab my puffy dress and go. I had been a whirl of motion all day, zipping through work and crossing items off my to-do list. I worked for Wicks, an oversized candle company that sold overpriced candles. Today was my last day in the office before a trip to England to set up the IT network at our new British headquarters.

For months, I'd been fighting some kind of long-term bug my doctors couldn't figure out, but today I felt a glimmer of my former self, twitchy with energy and moving at a clip to get everything done. Deep down, I sensed that rather than a sudden return to health, my energy was more of a fizz of nerves, arising from the uneasy note I'd ended on with Ethan the night before. Our squabble had nagged at me throughout the day, like an ache that couldn't settle in my joints as long as I kept moving.

I rapped on the door once more and when no one answered, I tried the handle. Unlocked. This was not unusual in a town where nobody locked their doors, but Beth wasn't from here. She'd moved to North Haven her senior year of high school, and to people that meant she hadn't lived here long enough to qualify as a local. But, to be fair, that usually took a lifetime.

I plastered a smile on my face and stepped into the house—immaculate as usual and smelling faintly of cinnamon. I couldn't tell if the homey scent came from something baking or wafted from a candle. I liked to tease a copywriter friend from Wicks with terrible ideas for candle taglines. My brain began composing a homespun blurb about the charms of cinnamon. *Nothing welcomes 'em in like cinnamon!*

Appalling. I'd write it down later.

"Beth?" I called out. The only reply came from the ticking of the grandfather clock down the hall. I peeked into the small kitchen, where the pale blue vintage-style fridge rattled and groaned inefficiently in the corner. My mom once described it as looking cute and sucking up energy, much like Beth. I had snorted, mostly relieved my mom had directed her acidity at someone other than me.

I poked my head into each room downstairs: each as spotless and Bethless as the last. Checking my phone, I sighed. Nothing. I replied to her last text with *At the house to get my dress. Where are you?*

It seemed fair to look in the backyard and then leave in good conscience. The moment I stepped into the small kitchen again, I noticed that the door to the backyard stood open a few inches. I pushed it wide open and descended the steps off the back porch.

Deep down, I sensed that rather than a sudden return to health, my

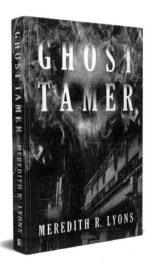
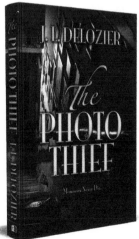

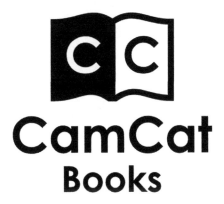

CamCat Books

VISIT US ONLINE FOR MORE BOOKS TO LIVE IN:
CAMCATBOOKS.COM

SIGN UP FOR CAMCAT'S FICTION NEWSLETTER FOR
COVER REVEALS, EBOOK DEALS, AND MORE EXCLUSIVE CONTENT.

CamCatBooks   @CamCatBooks   @CamCat_Books   @CamCatBooks